1)
2015

About the Author

Patrick Ugo Maidoh is a UK trained Investment Manager with many years of experience in the UK Banking sector. He is a mentor and a motivational speaker with a desire to reach the next generation and give them a second stab at life.

He holds an MBA degree from the Business school at the University of East London and is a member of both the Chartered Insurance Institute and the Institute of Financial Service in the UK.

Patrick was born in Nigeria where he spent many years; he would continue to hold deep roots and affection for his birthplace. He is married to Chigozie and they have two wonderful boys, Henry Kosisochukwu and Austin Chukwubuikem. They live in Bricket Wood, St Albans, Hertfordshire in the United Kingdom.

Dedication

This book is dedicated to two sets of people and to my Alma Mater

THE LOVING FATHER

To the loving father who loves his child unconditionally regardless of the child's failures or successes, the father who does not judge or condemn, but rather encourages, edifies and nurtures his wonderful gift of life.

A father who helps his child discover their purpose in life and is keen to help them along the straight and narrow road that leads to eternal life, helps them on the way to fully maximising their potential in life.

A father who says to a child "all is well," In spite and despite what the past situation was, what the current circumstance is and what the future holds.

A father who would gladly give up his own life as atonement for the shortcomings of his child without a second thought.

THE LOST SHEEP

This book is also dedicated to all those people who have been given a second chance on this side of eternity and are making the most of their second chance. Those who are still struggling to grasp and make the most of it, keep the faith – as weeping may endure for the night but joy comes in the morning.

MY ALMA MATER

To my Alma Mater, an institution that gave me a foundation in life, an institution vast in the history of turning boys into men of substance, purpose and integrity as encapsulated in this prayer:

Oh God Our Father, Thou Searcher of Men's hearts.
Help us to draw near to Thee in sincerity and truth.
May our faith be filled with gladness and may our worship of Thee be natural.
Strengthen and increase our admiration for honest dealing and clean thinking and suffer not our hatred of hypocrisy and pretence ever to diminish.
Encourage us in our endeavour to live above the common level of life. Help us choose the harder right instead of the easier wrong and never to be content with a half-truth when the whole can be one.
Endow us with courage that is borne of loyalty to all that is noble and worthy: Loyalty to our parents, loyalty to our class, loyalty to our COLLEGE and loyalty to our country.
Loyalty that scorns compromise with vice and injustice and knows no fear when truth and right are in jeopardy.
Guard us against flippancy and irreverence in the sacred things of life. Grant us new ties of friendship and new opportunities for service. Kindle our hearts in fellowship with those of cheerful countenance and soften our hearts with sympathy for those who sorrow and suffer.
Help us to maintain the honour of our COLLEGE untarnished and undiminished, and to show forth in our lives the ideals of CHRIST THE KING COLLEGE: Bonitas, Disciplina, Scientia, in doing our duties to Thee Oh Lord, to our COLLEGE and to our country.
All these we ask in the name of our great friend and Master, Jesus Christ. Amen!

REV. FR. N.C. TAGBO
Ex-Principal CKC Onitsha

Patrick U. Maidoh

THE PROTAGONIST:
A TALE OF TWO HALVES

AUSTIN MACAULEY
PUBLISHERS LTD

A CIP catalogue record for this title is available from the British Library.

ISBN 9781785545832 (Paperback)
ISBN 9781785545849 (Hardback)

www.austinmacauley.com

First Published (2015)
Austin Macauley Publishers Ltd.
25 Canada Square
Canary Wharf
London
E14 5LQ

Printed and bound in Great Britain

Acknowledgments

This pacey and riveting story would not have been conceived without the following people contributing their time, effort and encouragement.

I would like to say a big thank you to the Raymond Ukadikes of this world, they have inspired me to tell a story and I hope that I have done a good job at it.

This book was prompted by Dr Okey Onuzo, who pointed out the need to leave an enduring legacy for the next generation "Thank you sir".

A special thank you would have to go to my 'spiritual' father, Pastor Agu Irukwu, despite your gruelling schedule, you spent late nights reading this story and giving constructive feedback. You saw the potential in this book from the start and you shared your vision regarding this book. Your feedback inspired chapter 25 of this book.

The foreword written by Professor Sylvester Monye was second to none, it portrayed the deep rooted passion and belief that you have for the next generation and I strongly share that passion with you. Thank you for your time and the potential that you see in The Protagonist – A Tale of Two Halves.

A mention must go to Pastor Chizor Akisanya for your welcomed feedback on this book, I still remember my manuscript being returned and riddled with red marks and underlines. Your constructive feedback inspired chapter 2 of this book.

I would like to acknowledge Dr Matthew Offord, MP for Hendon. Thank you for giving my manuscript a read and the commendation that followed.

This book would definitely not have come to light without the support and backing of my wonderful family – my wife, Chigozie and the boys (Henry and Austin) and my siblings (Albert, Daniel, Hetty, Charles and Michael).

My sincere appreciation to my late father, Justice Augustine Nwanneamaka Maidoh, a tough disciplinarian but a wise man. I wish you were still around to have seen this book published.

To my mother, Chief Rebecca Maidoh, I say thank you for all your effort in my upbringing. I hope that this book makes you proud.

To Uncle Ray Ugboh aka 'Godfather' and Pastor Attah Ogbole, thank you for your contribution.

Thank you to everyone who has helped give life to this book in one way or another, your labour of love can only be rewarded as this book begins to touch millions of lives.
It would be a travesty not to acknowledge my best friend and master, the one who gives seed to the sower, the one that had inspired the story and had given me the ability to express the story. Thank you **God**.

I strongly believe that we cannot afford to lose the next generation, if we lose them then we would have lost everything. Let us join hands together to heal our children for the simple reason – they are the **next generation**.

Commendations

"I truly believe that everyone in life should receive a second chance, and this book is a great advocate of that philosophy. Throughout the novel Patrick demonstrates how with hard work, determination and a little guidance one can turn the darkest of situations into a life full of light and inspiration. In a world where we so often find ourselves confronted with challenges, both big and small, this book will offer a thoughtful and informative read on how to meet these challenges with courage and integrity. I commend Patrick on such a fantastic debut novel and cannot recommend it highly enough."
Dr Matthew Offord MP, Hendon UK

"This is a must read for both the young adult and parents. It opens your eyes to what exists out there and how if not careful can lead to a wasted life. Every parent would need to be extremely watchful. On the other hand, it makes you appreciate the greatness and mercy of a loving God."
Pastor Attah Ogbole. Author of *Apples of Gold*

"Patrick Maidoh's *The Protagonist* is the latest addition to an increasing body of work written by members of Nigeria's post-Biafran War generation, Nigeria's Generation X. And like all of the others, it is a worthy addition."
Dr.Eghosa Imasuen. Author of *The Fine Boys* and *To Saint Patrick*

Gripping…, intriguing…., compelling…, awesome narration, I just could not put this book down once I had picked it up. This book demonstrates the power of salvation and its ability to change lives. Well done Patrick, I am proud to be your sister.
Hetty Ugboh

FOREWORD

The true story behind *The Protagonist - A Tale of Two Halves* is a very compelling and intriguing one. It is a book that tells vividly, the story of how good morals could easily be corrupted; it is a poignant reminder of the need to heal the next generation and the importance of a new beginning. This is a must read, especially for young adults and their parents!

This is one book that is crying out to Nigeria, especially young Nigerians, in secondary schools and universities, to buy it and read, digest it and NEVER FORGET the story it encompasses.

The author has done his country and his God a service in writing this much-needed book. He has provided an insight, a much-lacking one, into the nether world of cultism and cultists. He has provided secondary and university authorities with a road map into the murky alcohol and narcotic-world of cultism.

How critical is the cultism problem in Nigeria? Has the level of the problem been fully appreciated? Nigeria has been in great danger of this problem, much-talked about but less addressed and even lesser understood. But this author has in "The Protagonist" A tale of two halves exposed the magnitude of the problem, the festering sore that has afflicted universities and from there to the ministries, the state and legislatures, and where cultists themselves run the universities ... much like the proverbial mad people running the asylum.

This is a scary book; it is not a gay recital, but a grave and grim one. Were it not a grim recital, I would have concentrated the reader's attention on the spicy ways the book-writing was executed – the story in this book does not move in a straight form but sections would jump out of the woods on you – like a cultist on a killer-mission. The book would keep one's adrenaline running on end; but the masterful way it was written pales before the message that has been so masterfully packaged.

Hey, is there a soul so dead, a parent so unconcerned about the state of Nigerian universities that he would not be scandalized by this? (from a section of the book)

> *"I was in my final year in the department of Accountancy and was keen to graduate on schedule. As I sat in my lecture hall of about one hundred and twenty people, I looked around and could easily count about thirty Marauders in my class. I could also count the numbers of well-known Eiye, Mafioso, Vikings, Buccaneers and Pyrates in the same class and it suddenly dawned on me that more than half of the students in the hall were affiliated to one confraternity or another.*
>
> *We were careful to be cordial to each other during the day and during lectures but outside the lecture hall and especially at night we would split each other's throat in a heartbeat.*
>
> *I was distracted from my thoughts by a note passed to me by Theo. Theo was a guy after my own heart, a very experienced Marauder who would stand by his word and was not pious in any way. He was the head of the*

Council of the wise men and he had the gravitas required to hold the position; I had plenty of time and respect for him.

The note read that Oscar, one of the belligerent Marauders, had been involved in a fight with two Viking Henchmen at the NFA joint; the two Vikings had come out of the fracas worse off and bloodied. I tore up the note as I made eye contact with Chucks 'the deputy seer' at the other end of the lecture hall and I nodded towards him, which was a cue for him to get me a situation report.

I got the report from the Seer within hours, indicating that the Vikings were rallying at a strategic location with the intention of bringing down Oscar.

I knew that Oscar was an experienced Marauder with his own clique within BNM and that he would not go down without a fight. I was not scared of a war with the Vikings as they were a minor group without much 'liver' punch behind them but I was not looking for a senseless war either. I remembered what Charlie Angel' once told me, "for you to fight a justified war, you must first understand the language of peace." We had experienced a rare period of peace within and outside the BNM and I had come to realise that there was growth, peace of mind and progress during that time; I was in no hurry for that to change.

I knew that I had to intervene immediately. I sent a message to Hammer to deploy two armed squads to the location where the Vikings were congregating. Another squad was to go and provide backup to Oscar. However, most important, I sent my hit squad led by the popular 'The Bulldog' to the Vikings' main man with a clear and simple message: "Make a move and we will completely obliterate you guys off the face of the planet." The Vikings knew better than to mess with us and with our movement on that night, they knew that wahala fit dey town. The Vikings backed down quickly and quietly to lick their wounds; my Seer and Voice nevertheless kept watchful eyes on their movement for a couple of days.

Two days after the fracas, I paid Oscar a visit under the cover of night in the company of 'The Bulldog', Bilado and Alahaji. Oscar got the beating and mending of his life for disobeying my direct instruction of avoiding the NFA joint."

Many people would see this book as troubling. That is the way it should be; the book was written to disturb your conscience. May it reach as many hands as possible – may people buy it, give it out as gifts to others – in millions – and may it bring about a national renaissance as Nigeria begins to push cultism out of our schools, offices, political parties and general life.

Professor Sylvester Monye, MFR
President, Africa Institute of Public Policy &
former Special Adviser to
President Good luck Ebele Jonathan on
Performance Monitoring and Evaluation

PROLOGUE

Everyone has a story to tell. I was born Raymond Ukadike; some of my friends call me Remy, others call me Remyleon and this is my story. It describes more real life events than fiction, so sit tight for the ride.

Chapter 1

I woke up with a start. I did not have to turn around to know that my wife of seven years was lying on the other side of the bed fast asleep; I could hear her heavy and deep breathing. I tried to guess what time it was, but had no clue – so I turned to look up towards the clock on the wall. Although I could hear its ticking, I could barely make out the face, much less tell the time.

After about five minutes of lying there motionless, I propped myself up on one elbow and reached for my mobile phone, which was lying on the chest of drawers beside me. As I turned it on, the time flashed up at me: 3:45 am. What in heaven's name was I doing awake at this time of the morning? My alarm would be going off at 7:00 am. *"I have to get back to sleep,"* I said to myself; but all efforts to settle down proved unsuccessful.

An event from the previous day kept replaying in my mind. I had failed an assessment at work, and I hated the idea of failure and having my name put on the company's internal communication page.

"I am better than this," I thought. I wished I hadn't left that mandatory sentence out of the report, but how rigid could my company be? It was unbelievable that one missing sentence had caused me to fail.

"Well, there is no need to cry over spilled milk now. What I cannot change, I have no business grieving about," I told myself. As I lay in bed, my mind wandered to the first time I had ever failed an examination. This was about twenty-nine years ago, when I was ten and being assessed for admission to one of the elite Federal Government Colleges in Nigeria.

"That was painful," I thought. And there, too, I had failed because I could not pronounce the word 'admiration' during my reading assessment. *"Just one word ... one word. What is this jinx with the number one?"*

At the time, the repercussions of failing had not dawned on me for a couple of hours – until I had to explain to my father how and why I had failed to do what my older siblings had achieved without breaking a sweat.

Failure was not acceptable in the Ukadike household; we had it drummed into our heads that people who passed and excelled were human beings just like us and did not have two heads.

I remember standing there shaking like a wet leaf in front of my biological maker, and wondering what fate awaited me now. Would it be just the cane, or was it going to be a tongue lashing? I attempted to push the blame for my failure onto the assessors, because they had not asked me to read words that I was conversant with. Furious but bemused, my father told me to "Go tell that to the Marines."

I would have settled for the cane – but I knew I was not going to get off that easily. I was verbally berated. The summation of that ten-minute encounter with my father was that I was reminded that I was a failure, and the black sheep of the family. I was sent off to the room that I shared with my three brothers, with instructions to start preparing for an assessment for a local secondary school that would take place three months later.

The alarm going off beside me jerked me back from the past. I struggled to get out of bed, to make sure I got into the bathroom before my wife and three sons had to use it. Getting up, preparing myself, and going to work had become a laborious chore for me, and in the last eighteen months I had come to despise what I did for a living.

The last four years had not been good or kind to the financial industry in the UK; banks were now seen as the anti-Christ, the cause of the global financial meltdown. Every media outlet had something negative to say about the financial industry. I had been in the business for eleven years, moving from one position to another, and in all those years, I had never seen it this bad. The public and media perception of us was tainted and we were no longer seen as the heartbeat of the UK economy.

As I set out on my twenty-five minute journey to the office on the motorway, I could not help but remember how I got into the banking sector many years ago. It was a bitterly cold winter that year, 2000; I had finished my postgraduate degree in business administration about four months earlier, and was looking for a permanent placement in any organisation.

At the time I'd been trying out, through an agency, for a major UK Government department, but there was nothing available. I already had a shoebox full of rejection letters from many companies, with reasons ranging from my having no experience to being over-qualified for the advertised position.

On that particular day in November 2000, I was on my way to buy my usual cheap lunch of chicken and chips, when my eyes were drawn to a poster in the window of a high street building society-turned-bank, advertising for cashiers. I decided to try my luck. I walked in and enquired about the position and to my surprise I was invited to return the next day with my CV, for an interview and assessment. Delighted, but oddly suspicious at this sudden stroke of luck, I was unsure how to react – but tomorrow would surely tell.

I had fancied working in a bank ever since the age of eighteen, when I would visit my elder sister at the Nigerian bank where she worked. I would admire the well-dressed, well-suited and well-groomed young bankers, who carried themselves with such panache. I thought about how great I would look in a sharp suit. So that day, I went home to my bedsit, pulled up my CV on my laptop, tidied it up, and rehearsed my responses to some competency-based questions.

The next day could not come quickly enough! It eventually did dawn, and I slipped away during my lunch break to attend the interview. I must confess that the maths assessment was well below my standard, with only basic addition, subtraction, and division.

After the written assessment, which took about fifteen minutes to finish, I was ushered in to see my interviewer, Michael Stevens, who was the branch manager. He took one look at my CV and assessment results and right on the spot, he offered me the job of a banking adviser – one level above a cashier. His parting words to me were that he saw me eventually doing his job, but was not sure how long I would want to remain with the company after I had gathered relevant experience.

But I wasn't looking that far ahead; I was just grateful to get that proverbial "foot in the door"! I was so ecstatic that I forgot to go back to my temping job. Instead, I headed for my usual fun spot, to cool my head with one or two cold pints of beer.

I was jolted back to the present when I realised that I was already in the office parking lot, and a colleague was knocking on my car window.

"Good morning, Rem," said Jay, "I hope you are alright because you've been sitting in your car for some time, staring straight ahead."

"I'm fine, mate," I replied. "I was just lost in my thoughts, and with the auditors coming to the branch soon, I have a lot on my mind."

"Come on Rem, you need to learn how to relax a bit and take it easy, mate. We've had quarterly audits for years and the branch always gets through with flying colours."

Jay was the 35-year-old chief cashier. He was in charge of the operational risk and the counter team in the branch; he reported directly to me and he was one of the most knowledgeable, dedicated and opinionated people I had ever met. I had worked with Jay for the past two years, after I had moved from being an investment adviser into branch management. I had learnt a lot from him, especially about the risk side of the business. Jay had no interest whatsoever in the sales side and he made that abundantly clear.

Being a branch manager had not really been part of my career plan, but being an ambitious young man, I was willing to defer my future goal of becoming a company director. As a branch manager, I had the overall responsibility for the branch and the buck stopped with me when it came to the performance or non-performance of the branch.

The time was now 8:30 am. Jay and I were standing at the front door about to start the procedure of opening the branch, when Jenny turned up. Jenny was a blonde-haired single mother of one; she worked as a part-time cashier and had been with the company since she was 16. She had no ambition to further her career and was content with her current job and looking after her daughter.

Jenny loved a good night out; she organised the branch's social outings and she had a reputation for being the wild one at any social event.

I was responsible for the ten-person team at the Notting Hill Branch, and I also worked with two other business partners who reported to their individual area managers; the three of us worked hand-in-hand to meet the branch's objectives and overall business goals.

My mobile phone rang and as I reached into my breast pocket, I could almost guess who was at the other end of the line. As I saw the name "Gary" flash up on the caller ID, my face dropped and my heart skipped two beats.

Gary Pratt was my retail area manager and my direct boss, and I had become convinced that his name fit him to a tee. He was an ex-rugby player, about six foot five inches tall, with a nose broken on the rugby field. He was direct, straight-talking, and lacking in any human feelings or diplomacy.

He was known as "Gary the brute," In some areas of the business, while in others, he was just called "Gary the prat." The only form of strategy he knew was micro- and consequential management.

I was tempted to ignore the call, but I knew that would be at my own peril. "*No need to postpone doomsday,*" *I thought*. "Hello Gary, how are you this wonderful morning," I said. There was a brief silence and then I heard his deep baritone reply, "What is wonderful about this morning, Remy? Your sales figures were shocking and awful yesterday."

There was a brief silence. While it is normally said that silence is golden, this particular silence was excruciatingly painful. *"Na waooo,"* came the exclamation in my mind; alarm bells were resounding in my head, and I knew that I had to find a "Get Out of Jail Free card" rather sooner than later; if not, I was going to become shish kebab early this morning, and I did not need this right now.

"Sorry, Gary, I can't hear you clearly, you are breaking up, hello, hello, can you hear me; I will have to call you back from inside the branch after we've opened up and had the morning huddle. Can you hear me?" I yelled into the mobile phone before switching it off.

I did not need a seer to tell me why Gary was calling. The branch was having an abysmal week in our sales performance. Our customer service rating was brilliant at 125%, but sales were king and we were languishing at 56%.

The financial industry and the banking sector in particular had been going through very turbulent times, with negative press and publicity. The position of a branch manager had lost the respect, integrity and glory previously associated with it. The value of the position had been diluted to the extent that the title was not worth the business card or the name badge that it was printed on – but the role was more demanding than ever.

Having worked the retail-banking sector for eleven years had not fully prepared me to grasp the demands placed daily on a branch manager.

In this position, I had to manage ten different product lines and handle customers' dissatisfaction. I had to deal with colleagues' motivational issues, conflict amongst staff members, staff shortage, the union, obtain new customer funds in a difficult environment, oversee operational risks, carry the failures and successes of the branch ... the list is endless.

Looking back at the years when banking had been fun and wonderful work, I could not help but smile at how motivated I had been – willing and ready to take on the world, smashing all sales targets, and enjoying attending the recognition events.

What a shame that the banking sector was now a shadow of its glorious years; I had seen it change from focusing on customers to becoming self-serving. The work was no longer about the customers, but more about the profit margins. I detested customers being seen as a product – a credit card, or a bank account – I preferred to see my customers as individuals with different and unique needs. Frankly, I detested what I did for a living and I couldn't wait to get out.

Thinking about things I detested, my mind wandered back to when I was a pugnacious 11-year-old, full of energy, curiosity and adventure. After flunking that test to get into an elite secondary school, I had detested having to settle for a local secondary school called Dominion College. It was a relatively good Catholic secondary school situated at Awka in the

Eastern part of Nigeria but it did not have the status associated with a Federal Government College.

Dominion College was an all-boys secondary school, renowned for producing clergymen, professors, and sound intellectual minds. My father prided himself on being a product of this school, and he could go on and on about the "good old days." Dominion College was halfway between a learning institution and a seminary, and you had to be a practicing Catholic to study or teach in the College, which was headed by a no-nonsense, 6-foot-tall, bald man of the cloth – Father Uka. He had been a Dominion student in the 40s, coincidentally a classmate of my father.

Father Uka had been the principal of the College for twelve years when I arrived; and legend had it that once, when he had taken the cane to a particular student, the book the student had hidden in his shorts to protect his backside had split in two. Legend also had it that Father Uka always carried seven canes of different sizes, all hidden in his cassock. Rumour said that he would continue to be the principal of the school for all his life time.

I would never forget my first day at my new school. I remember embarking on the two-hour journey with my father and the driver, and as we approached the impressive school gate, my initial excitement began to wane and turn into fear and anxiety. I was unsure of what to expect, and the thought of living away from home filled me with trepidation. I glanced at my father for some form of reassurance – but none was forthcoming, and it dawned on me that I was in this alone.

My father and I made our way to Father Uka's office, where the receptionist handed my formal admission letter to my father, who had to sign an undertaking on my behalf. I was immediately handed a letter that confirmed my student number and hostel name. We were escorted to my new hostel, called Bishop Flannigan house, and I was allocated a bed space reserved for new intakes. My father spent about forty-five minutes helping me settle in; he had a word with the hostel prefect and gave him some spending money before asking him to keep an eye out for me.

As my father's blue Peugeot 504 pulled away, I could feel the tears start to roll down my cheeks. I felt so lost and abandoned, my body and mind were numb, and all my faculties of reason deserted me at that moment. I could not see anything positive about my situation, and education was a waste of time as far as I was concerned.

I must have stood there miserably for about ten minutes before I was jolted back to reality by a hand on my shoulder. I looked up and saw the hostel prefect by my side. He led me into his private cubicle, and sent for another student from Class Three called Chuka who would be my guide.

Chuka was to be my buddy, showing me how things worked, the different hostels, and the general layout of the school. He took me on an hour-long tour of the school; midway through, he pointed to a nondescript looking building in the centre of the school and said, "That's the 'white house'." I looked at him with total puzzlement and replied, "What do you mean by the 'white house'?" Chuka laughed and said to me jokingly in Pidgin English, "*You bi real JJC* (Johnny just come), don't you know that that is the most important building in this school? That is the refectory, and the person who controls the food controls the economy. He's got the real power."

The next six years at Dominion College proved how right Chuka was. As we headed back towards Bishop Flannigan house, I kept fighting the feeling of abandonment and rejection within me; I knew I had to stay strong. My father's mantra came flooding back into my head: "They are people like you; they do not have two heads." I have always seen myself as the street-wise and tough one in my family, the 'never-say-die' type, the fighter, and I just could not afford to show weakness, even to myself.

I came from a family of seven – father, mother, four boys and one girl – in which I was the last child but one. My father was a well-known Professor of Law at a Federal University, and my mother was the Principal of the local girls' school.

Coming from such an educated background meant that there were many expectations placed on the children to do well; our paths in life were already mapped out for us. My eldest brother was to become a lawyer like my father, my second brother would become a medical doctor, and my only sister was to become an accountant. I was to be an engineer, and my youngest brother was to be an estate surveyor.

I detested my position in the family. I could not help but feel like a spare wheel, as if I really did not count. I was just there to be sent on errands and bullied by the older ones. I felt unappreciated and unloved, and it seemed that my eldest brother, my only sister and my youngest brother got all the attention; the only way I could get any attention was by falling ill or being naughty.

I was not as academically gifted as my elder siblings, but I was the most sporty and adventurous. I was good at sports and many physical activities; any sport that I took up, I excelled in, winning several trophies and certificates in track and field and football. During my primary school days, I was nicknamed 'the Little Pele' because I was smallish in stature, quick and relatively skilful.

But all my physical talents and skills paled to insignificance when, at the end of the school term, my report card showed a marginal pass. My father could not understand why I seemed determined to waste my life, by not excelling the way my other siblings did. I was banned from playing football until my grades improved, but I kept sneaking out of the house to go play; on the field, I felt so at peace and one with nature that I just did not care what punishment awaited me at home.

The first time I stole out of the house to play football, I received six strokes of the cane and was threatened with twelve strokes the next time it occurred. The tears had barely dried when I hit the playing field again, the next day after school – I just couldn't help myself, it I was like I was possessed.

I received twelve strokes as promised by my father, and was threatened with twenty-four the next time. But that did not deter me, and I was soon back on the field showing off my dribbling skills. When the football game ended, I did not want to go home. I knew what fate awaited me, and the euphoria of the game had worn off. As I dragged myself home, I could see my father's figure from afar – sitting in his favourite chair in the courtyard, with a cane on the floor beside him.

I guess it was time for me to submit to my fate; I'd had the pleasure of the game and now it was time to take the pain. I took my punishment again in good faith, and I was threatened with forty-eight strokes of the cane the next time.

There was a strong temptation to head out to the playing field the next day after school, but the thought of forty-eight strokes of my father's cane was quite daunting. I weighed up my options: sixty minutes of excitement versus forty-eight strokes of the cane.

I was still going through this in my head, standing a few yards from the gate of the playing field, when my friend Nnamdi called out to me. I approached the locked gate with much apprehension, but the sight of the football in Nnamdi's hand had me climbing over the gate against my better judgement. I played that football game as if it was my last day on earth; I did not want it to end, and then have to go back home to face my father and the cane.

As the light faded and the game was finished, I had no excuse to avoid going home. I dragged my feet in the direction of home. The nearer I got to the house, the more I wished the building would recede. My heart was pounding.

I eventually reached the gate, and stood there for about five minutes. I knew that the more time went by, the graver the consequences would be. *"Well,"* I said to myself in Pidgin English, *"all die na die, play the game take the pain."* And with that thought in my head, I walked into the compound like a condemned prisoner.

My father looked at me in disgust before asking me where I had been – not because he wanted that information, as the answer was obvious from my appearance. "I went to play football after I finished studying, with Nnamdi from across the road," I answered.

My father spent five long minutes looking at me and trying to decide what to do next. Then, to my greatest surprise, he stood up, shook his head and left the room, muttering under his breath, "This boy must be possessed." I knew then that I had won a major victory in my life; I had just conquered the cane. But that night, I slept with one eye open, in case my father changed his mind and decided to give out punishment.

Chapter 2

Austen Ukadike stood staring out of the south facing bedroom window that he shared with his wife of many years. There was a worried look on his face as he gazed out of the window without paying much attention to the sound of rain drops on the bedroom roof.

He had just come back after a very long day at the office, all he had wanted to do was to undress and tie his wrapper around his waist and get some supper but his mind was very unsettled.

One particular challenge was weighing on his mind heavily and he was getting frustrated that he was not getting much head way.

"Four out of five cannot be a bad result," murmured Austen, "that is eighty percent and a good return" he tried to console himself.

"If four out of my five children succeed in life and reach their full potential then I have not done badly, I would have passed with flying colours" he said as he continuously paced the room.

He continued to pace from one end of the room to the other while murmuring to himself – "I have not failed, I have not failed, and eighty percent is a good return." Austen had not realised that his wife had entered the bedroom and had been watching him pacing the room for the last three minutes.

"Austen, Austen, Austen odi kwa nma? What is the matter? My mother asked my father as she approached him standing in the middle of the room. "Your supper is on the table and it is getting cold."

"What is the matter, Austen? Please talk to me, is it work related or is there a problem in the village? My mother asked with genuine concern written over her face.

"Justina, it is that your good-for-nothing son, Raymond, I have tried with that boy ooo, but nothing is working, that boy is the devil's incarnate.

Of all my children, he is the one that would disobey me, steal other people's mangoes, insult his elders, tell lies, not do well in examinations and then have total disregard for everything and anything. None of his other siblings would have the guts to disobey me but that little coconut head will do it. Ya bu Nwata a'da atu egwu," my father said.

"I am at my wits end with that boy, what is left for me to do is to disown him and dash him to the government for free," my father concluded.

My mother stood there looking at my father for what seemed like an eternity before she finally opened her mouth to speak. "Austen, is it not strange that when the children are doing well, they are your children but whenever something bad happens they then become mine"?

"Nwata ka Remy bu kwa, he is just 11 years of age and you want to treat him like an adult, you are very quick to use the cane. I hope that you know that the cane is not a panacea for all issues," my mother warned.

"What do you mean that he is just a small boy, at his age my father had died, I had to sell firewood to pay for my school fees, trek four miles each way to get to school and go hungry when my mother could not afford to put food on the table. So being 'nwata' is not an excuse for bad behaviour."

"Austen nwa Ukadike, my mother interjected, I have not come here to argue with you ooo, I have come to inform you that your food is ready and is getting cold. If you do not want to eat it now then we can put it in the fridge for you." My mother said as she turned to leave the room.

My father's next statement stopped her in her tracks. "You and your mother are the ones spoiling that boy, Remy bu nwata, take it easy on him, do you want to kill him, you are going to make him hate you. That is all I keep hearing from you people," my father accused my mother.

My father continued without giving my mother a chance to respond … "I will discipline my son in the way that I see fit and if I have to flog the demons out of him then I will. A child that says that his father would

24

not sleep, then that child would not sleep himself" he concluded authoritatively.

My mother took one long look at the man standing before her and shook her head more out of pity than of disbelief.

"Aaeeeeeee, Austen, Austen are you so blind or stupid that you do not recognise that Remy is just like you in every sense especially in his attitude, take another look in the mirror before you point a finger," with that last statement, my mother stormed out of the bedroom.

Austen stood in the middle of the room before walking towards the window, he could still hear his wife's voice echoing in his ears "Remy is just like you … Remy is just like you," was he living in self-denial or was he just too blind to see how right Justina was. Remy was demonstrating a lot of traits that he himself had shown as a boy.

Losing his father at a very young age was a big blow to him, his siblings and many other half brothers and sisters. He was the first male child of his mother but the second son in the line of twenty three children.

Life was hard and tough without the presence of a father figure; it was even tougher going from a life of adequate provision to a life of near penury. His father's assets including expanse of land were immediately inherited by the 'diokpa' of the Ukadike family leaving Austen and his family to fend for themselves.

Although he was a relatively bright student, he was regularly sent home for not paying his school fees on time. His life changed for the worse when the demons that he had tried to suppress reared its ugly head on one hot afternoon. He had been singled out and flogged by the headmaster before being sent home for not paying his school fees.

His mother was already indebted to many money lenders and could not find the money, so Austen with fire in his eyes and frustration in his veins marched to the house of the 'diokpa' of the Ukadikes family demanding for his inheritance. All hell was let loose and mayhem ensued as Austen attempted to burn his house down.

The repercussion of that event was a very painful experience and he did not want to remember the after effect.

"Raymond cannot fail on my watch; eighty percent is not good enough because I want all my children to be successful. Solomon, Michael, Alice and Fredrick were all doing very well, why not Raymond? Families that achieve this one hundred percent success rate do not have two heads" Austen thought.

He laid on the bed and the last thing he remembered before drifting off into a troubled sleep was the wailing and the anguish of his mother from his many misdemeanours.

It was about 10:30 pm and I was struggling to sleep, as I lay in bed at the other end of the bungalow, I could hear my father's snoring coming from the master's bedroom. I did not want to begin to contemplate what fate would befall me if my father was to discover that I had my report card hidden underneath the mattress that I was laying on. The report card had been there for the last 2 days and it was only a matter of time before my parents would demand to see it.

My report card did not make good reading, I had achieved the 40th position again out of a class of 45, and showing my father this report card would be a death sentence for me.

There had to be a way out of my predicament; it was going to be difficult changing my score, the last time I almost got away with it until my form teacher expressed her disappointment with my performance to my mother in Church.

All hell had broken loose when my mother came back home that evening and mentioned it to my father. I had received double punishment for my poor result and for deception. While my friends were out playing during the holiday, I was made to practice my school work over and over again by my father.

"That man hates me," I thought to myself, "he never likes to see me happy, he prefers me being sad and miserable, I cannot wait to be an adult and leave this house for good, but not before I had shown him pepper," I concluded.

I prayed that tomorrow would never come but when it does come; I prayed even harder that it would give me a new dimension on how to tackle my problem. I slowly fell into a restless sleep dreaming about being chased by a dragon with two heads and spitting out fire, the two heads on the dragon were those of my father and my form teacher.

I was still at sleep but I could hear my name being called repeatedly "Remy, Remy, Remy, daddy is calling you" said my youngest brother Frederick as he shook me awake. I came out of my slumber reluctantly to the known fact that tomorrow had finally come.

"Daddy is calling you oo," he repeated as he stood over me with his hand on my shoulder. I slowly got out of the bed as I could sense from my brother's face that all might not be well. "What have I done again? Ki kam mezi? I asked with the hope that my brother could divulge any information.

"Raymond, Raymond," I heard my father bellowing my name from the parlour, he was the only one that calls me Raymond in the house and I could sense trouble.

"Sir," I replied.

"Bring yourself and your report card here immediately," my father demanded, I could see the pity in my brother's eyes as I left the room to go and face my biological maker.

"Where is your report card"? My father asked authoritatively with his right hand stretched out, "I cannot find it." I replied, "I put it in between the pages of my maths textbook and then into my school bag, and now I cannot find it."

"So are you telling me that your report card suddenly developed wings and flew out of your bag"? My father asked perplexed.

"Sir, I swear, I can't find the report card, I put it carefully into my school bag after I had received it from my teacher and I just cannot find it," I said tearfully.

"Shut up, you silly boy, good for nothing, how dare you swear in this house, let me make myself clear, if you do not produce that report card today I will skin you alive."

I stood there, not knowing whether to leave the parlour or to beg, but what should I be begging for? – I asked myself.

"If you cannot find your report card, at least you should know whether you passed or not"? My mother said as she came into the parlour from the adjoining room,

"Yes I passed," I replied.

"Thank God for that at least, now that we have established that you passed, what was your position in the class"? Came the next question from my mother.

I could see my father from the corner of my right eye slowly lowering the newspaper that he was reading, waiting for an answer from me as he peered at me.

"I passed," I replied desperately trying to avoid the actual question asked, "My friend, that was not the question that you were asked," interjected my father as he leaned forward in a threatening manner.

At this point my mouth went dry and my hands were shaking and I knew that I had to come clean. "I came fortieth but I believe that they made a mistake in my report card," I said.

"Tell that to the Marines," my father responded, and then continued "how many are you in the class"? He asked.

"We are 45 students in the class," I replied slightly timidly,

I could see the disbelief on my father's face as his mouth fell slightly open, "So you mean to tell me that you came fortieth out of 45? – that is failure of the highest proportion," my father declared.

"Bbbbut I passed, sir, I did better than Nnamdi and 4 other people in the class," I reminded my father.

"Ooooo I see, it is now alright for you to compare yourself to Nnamdi and others at the bottom of the class, go and see your other siblings, they are consistently in the top 5 in their classes. Will you get out of my sight before I slap the living daylight out of your eyes ewu," my father dismissed me.

I walked out of the room feeling gutted and deflated, I could hear my father's voice behind me saying "what hope does he have in passing the common entrance examination into the Federal Government Colleges."

I walked out of the house with tears in my eyes and with a heavy heart; I started walking towards the main gate without any destination in mind. I must have walked continuously for over an hour without an idea of where I was heading.

It was only when I got to the west side of town that I did finally stop and I sat down on the kerb with my head in my hands. "Why me, why always me, why can't I be like my other siblings, why am I such a failure, why … why … why … why," I cried out in much desperation.

"Could that man really be my father," I thought, "I need to find a way to ask my mother who my real father is. How can a father take so much pleasure in afflicting pain and anguish on a son, I wish that I hadn't been born into this family," was my last thought before I got up and headed for home determined to prove that man wrong.

Chapter 3

At Dominion College, there was a sequence and timing to the ringing of the great school bell; I must confess that I had never heard such a timed ringing of a bell in my life. The bell was situated close to Father Uka's office, and could be heard in every nook and cranky of the College. It was used as a means of communication, to inform students of events that were happening or about to happen within the school compound.

The bell rang differently for every event. On my first day at school, we heard a fast-paced ringing; Chuka turned to me and said, "It must be 6 pm; time to go and pass our plates." Chuka was already hurrying off in the direction of the hostel as I called out after him, "What do you mean by passing our plates?"

"It means taking your plate to the refectory within fifteen minutes or you lose the opportunity to eat," he yelled back at me. I was not hungry, and food was the last thing on my mind as I hurried after Chuka. We went into the hostel, opened up our lockers, picked up our plastic plates with our initials written underneath them and dashed off to the refectory.

We made it in just in time, seconds before the doors of the refectory closed. There were thirteen tables; one each for the twelve hostels, and one table for all the school prefects. Chuka led the way, pointing towards a particular table with various sizes and colours of plates on it. We put our plates with the others and headed towards the door, which was manned by a hefty-looking door boy whom I guessed must have eaten plenty of food on his watch.

He let us out while preventing the late comers from coming in. I asked Chuka what fate would befall the late comers, and he replied nonchalantly that they would have to go without, assuring me that this would teach them a lesson for next time. We went back to our hostel and waited for the bell to ring again and after fifteen long minutes of waiting, the bell finally sounded, indicating that the apportioning of the food was over. We dashed towards the refectory; boys were sprinting from all directions to get there in time to secure a seat.

As Chuka and I approached our table, everyone was trying to identify and grab their plates. I finally identified mine, picked it up and was bitterly disappointed with what I saw – half a piece of boiled yam and a spoonful of stew. I could not believe my eyes: how could anyone survive on this ration? This was definitely worse than what Oliver Twist experienced.

I stomached my disappointment and found some space on the bench in which to plant my buttocks; I said a silent prayer in my mind and proceeded to taste the yam. I had barely started chewing on an awful mouthful that tasted like rubber when I felt a slap on the back of my head. In shock, I turned to see and hear the senior food prefect bellow at me, "Who asked you to eat that food before general prayer – *Anu ofia* (bush animal)?"

I looked around and all eyes were staring at me from every corner of the refectory; and at that moment, I could not hold back the tears and they came streaming down freely. The pain that I felt was not for the slap, because I had received so many in my young life; it was more about the humiliation on my first day in a new school. I wished that I were far away from this awful refectory and this awful school.

We had thirty minutes to finish our food, before the bell was rung to mark the end of dinner. We all piled out of the refectory and I could see people staring at me with pity. I was in a hurry to get back to my hostel and bury my head in my pillow.

Prep time was from 7:30 pm to 8:30 pm, during which boarding students were expected to be in their respective classrooms studying. My classroom was Class One A, beside the Assembly ground. There were quite a number of us in the room, and we introduced ourselves and settled down at our desks. I opted to read a novel called *Eze Goes to School*, which perfectly depicted my current situation.

At 8:30 pm, the great bell sounded to mark the end of prep time and we quickly filed out of the classroom towards the school chapel for the night prayers, which lasted for about fifteen minutes. We had about forty-five minutes after that to get back to the hostel and ready ourselves for bed. The lights went out at 9:30 pm and not one minute later; strict adherence to the rules was monitored by the hostel prefects, who were overseen by the school senior prefect. God help you if you were caught out of your bed.

I remembered lying in bed that night, attempting to run through all the events that had transpired in a single day. From being dropped off by my father, to the incident in the refectory which I would love to forget forever, to the night prayer to lying in my bed now.

I was in a deep sleep but the noise that woke me could have awoken the dead; it was the sound of metal meeting metal, and I jumped up and was staring into the beam of a torch light. This was the early morning wake-up call. *"What a ridiculous way to wake people up, what happened to the old fashioned way of a gentle tap?" I thought.* This thought was pierced by a voice shouting at me, "Will you move before I move you?"

I did not like the sound of that threat, so I jumped down from the double bunk. The time was 5:00 am on a bitterly cold day during the Harmattan season. I put on my slippers, picked up my bucket, and headed with the others towards the giant water tank. The water prefect was there, with his deputy rationing out the water; your morning ration was dependent on your body size. It took me about ten minutes to get half a bucket of water, which was for brushing my teeth and washing my body.

The water was cold and the air was freezing. I hesitated for a bit, summoned up enough courage, and started having a wash. The water felt like ice on my skin and the cold Harmattan breeze compounded my discomfort.

We had thirty minutes to wash and get dressed; morning devotion started at 5:45 am in the chapel, and lasted about forty-five minutes. It was officiated by the chapel prefect (the sacristan) and his deputies. Morning chores followed soon after; these included sweeping the inside and outside of the hostel, clearing any blocked gutters and cutting the hedges, between 6:00 am and 6:45 am.

From 6:45 am to 7:15 am, we were to get dressed in our school uniform: a clean white shirt, white shorts and white socks with the school crest on display. Our loaves of bread arrived at about 7:30 am, and after breakfast, all beds must be made, with a white bedspread and the colour of each student's hostel at the foot of the bed.

Inspection of all the beds in the hostel took place before 8:00 am, at which time we would hear the sound of the great big bell ... DONG ... DONG ... DONG ... DONG ... DONG ... DONG – time for morning assembly, and you dared not go late, for fear of being turned into a shish kebab.

Morning assembly at Dominion College was an event, and one that would stay in my memory for the rest of my life. I did not know what to expect at first, but it began with all the students queuing up according to their classes. The teachers formed a horizontal line behind the vertical lines of students, to demarcate the upper quadrangle from the lower one. The lower quadrangle was used to hold the late comers.

Two hymns were sung, followed by the school anthem (*Three cheers for Dominion*); then the great bell started to chime at a different pace, to signify that the school's senior prefect was approaching. Senior Eugene was a tall handsome boy, and he was an all-rounder; academically good, brilliant in sports, and a great orator. He approached the Assembly from the top balcony, wearing an impeccably clean white shirt tucked into white trousers with the school's black and white blazer. He climbed down the steps to the platform to address the students. Rumour had it that senior Eugene studied the dictionary as a hobby, and was forever looking for new words with which to serenade our poor souls every morning.

The senior prefect would normally spend about twenty minutes talking about various things, ranging from the importance of having the right attitude to rule breakers; he would not fail to throw in some of his big vocabulary, with words like bamboozle, innuendo, and belligerent. My favourite one was Niminy Piminy; any time he spoke "big English" we cheered. The bigger the English, the louder we cheered. More often than not, he left us all bamboozled at the end, but he was one of the most charismatic senior prefects ever.

After senior Eugene's speech, the great bell began to chime again continuously, announcing the man himself: Father Uka began to walk slowly along the balcony, past the bell ringer and past the imposing pillars, and started to descend the steps. Every step he took was met with a chime of the bell until he got to the platform; and then there was dead silence.

He opened his book, adjusted the microphone and his glasses, and said, "Let us pray, O God, thank you for this day that you have made." Somewhere in the prayer, he uttered, "O God, help us to live and uphold the creed of Dominion College and be *Primus Inter Pares.*" He would always finish his classic prayer with, "O God, help us today to choose the harder right instead of the easier wrong." Father Uka would take a scripture from the Bible and draw out the morals and the message of the scripture; he would then motivate us to be better students. The great bell started to chime the moment his book closed, and he started to climb back up the stairs to his office.

Lessons commenced at 9:15 am sharp and each subject could last for about forty-five to sixty minutes. There were about forty students in my class and we were all expected to study a combination of Sciences, Social Sciences, Arts and Languages. Latin was a compulsory language subject until Class Three and this was not negotiable; in fact, every Friday evening was singing practice, and we all came prepared to sing in Latin from start to finish. One incorrect word in the song got you into hot soup – which could be detention or some strokes of the cane administered by the chapel prefect or choir prefect.

I was in Class Two when I first met Kanayo, a.k.a. "stone face." My life changed from that moment. I was playing football with some classmates in the lower quadrangle, when someone called out my name and asked, "Are you Remy Ukadike?"

"Who wants to know?" I replied. "My name is Kanayo Chikode and we have a mutual friend called Chris Obum," he said.

"O yes, I know Christo, we went to the same primary school, what a small world," I said. Kanayo was stout and built like a village wrestler; I must confess that he was facially challenged and the nickname "stone face" fitted him to a tee. He was also aware that he had a mean-looking face and used it to his advantage by wearing a frown most of the time, thereby putting off senior students from approaching or punishing him.

Kanayo and I hit it off like a house on fire, and he became my new best friend. This happened for various reasons; firstly, we came from the same region in the country. Secondly, we both spoke the hard-core Pidgin English that I had learnt in the streets. Thirdly, we had a mutual friend in Christo, and finally yet importantly, Kanayo was an incredibly funny person and knew how to tell a story with much embellishment.

Kanayo and I could both hold a crowd of people captivated for hours on end, telling stories that were both real occurrences and make believe.

Wherever I was, Kanayo was never far away, and we were known as *"Umu Bendel"* (kids from Bendel state). We were in the same class and sat side by side. Kanayo was good at Maths and Spelling, in which I was rubbish; but I was strong in English Language, Literature and Religious Studies, and we helped each other.

Kanayo was OK at sports, but that was where I excelled. I became a member of the elite junior football team, and also represented Dominion College at junior athletic meets. I accidentally stumbled upon the game of lawn tennis, which was only played by the senior students; I took to the game like a fish to water and was soon giving senior students a run for their money.

Father Uka was an ardent football fan; he had been the principal of Dominion College ten years earlier, when the College had won the World Secondary School Football Competition (WSSFC) in Finland. Father Uka was hell bent on bringing that glory back to Dominion College at any cost.

Being a member of the elite junior football team came with many privileges that were not bestowed on mere mortals. I had my morning chores reassigned to someone else, as my new chore was practising and playing footy. We had our own table in the refectory and the portions were generous; the football team became known as *"Umu Father Uka"* (Father Uka's children).

Whenever we had a big game he was there and woe betide you if you missed a glaring opportunity. Boy, did we know how to tap leather. The school games master was a smallish-looking man nicknamed "Agility" who had once played semi-professional football. He had been personally interviewed and endorsed by Father Uka for the position, and he knew that he had to deliver.

Playing on the school football team swiftly boosted my popularity. Everybody knew me, from the students to the teachers. I was easily one of the most popular junior students, and senior students were eager to court my friendship and company. Life was great; it was very different from my first few days at Dominion College. Kanayo and I were still classmates and the best of friends; I spent more time with him in Azikiwe hostel than in mine. We were always sharing jokes and banter, being boisterous young boys.

I remember meeting Kobi, Jude and Dominic through Kanayo. These boys all lived in the same neighbourhood in Lagos, and were part of the Lagos crew. They were always full of exciting Lagos stories; they talked about parties and travelling abroad during the summer holidays. They had pictures of their trips, and I found them utterly fascinating. An impressionable young boy, I desperately wanted to be like them; all my popularity vanished into thin air when I was in their company.

Kobi and Dominic were brothers and in Class Four and Five respectively, while Jude was in the same class as Dominic. Kanayo and I were only in Class Two, but we were accepted into their fold and with time, we met other "happening" boys.

I vividly remember one particular hot Saturday afternoon, when I went in search of Kanayo after my football game. I couldn't find him in his hostel but his bunkmate told me that he had gone to see the Lagos boys, so I set out in the direction of Ikoku hostel.

As I approached the entrance of the hostel, I expected to hear voices and the usual banter that occurred when Bendel boys and Lagos boys congregated. However, I was surprised that all I saw was a group of boys huddled together under a bunk bed at the far end of the room. I could barely make out Kanayo but as I approached, I realised that all the boys were staring at a magazine with total engrossment.

As Kanayo caught sight of me, he beckoned to me to come closer. I was not sure what to expect but what I saw next affected my young, innocent and fragile mind for a very long time to come. The huddle was around a pornographic magazine with men and women of all shapes and sizes going at it in every way and manner imaginable. Every sense in my body went berserk. I knew that I should not be looking at this magazine but I could not take my eyes off the pages. After about five minutes of staring at the magazine, I realised that parts of my body that I never knew existed had responded accordingly. I was looking like a porcupine in heat.

The only time that I had ever come close to a girl was in primary school, when a friend had dared me to kiss a classmate named Tola. This I did, but then I bolted, with Tola running after me and threatening to report me to the headmistress.

Looking at this pornographic magazine became a daily routine for both Kanayo and me, and the more we looked at it the more our imagination ran riot. We found ourselves discussing *"bolongo"* (sex) all the time, and we started lusting after and having fantasies about our female teachers. These thoughts dogged me everywhere I went, from morning prayers to the Assembly ground, from the hostel to the football field, from waking up to going to sleep.

I woke up one particular morning feeling wet, and I feared that the worst had happened. This could not be happening to me; had I just peed in my pants – impossible! – How would I face my hostel mates? I had to think up a strategy to get out of this embarrassing situation, and as I lay in bed contemplating my next move, I realised that my bed wasn't actually wet – it was just the front of my pyjamas and it was a sticky fluid.

When I told Kanayo about my ordeal, he nearly laughed his head off. "O boy," he said, "you had a wet dream; your mind must have been saturated with evil thoughts the day before."

"*Na waoo*," I replied, "is there any time that I am not thinking about *bolongo* these days?"

Our end-of-term exams were fast approaching and we threw ourselves into our studies. We had eight subjects to prepare for, and two weeks of examinations before our six-week holiday. My first exams at Dominion went well, and then we were all excited to be going on a long summer holiday.

My father's driver picked me up from the hostel. He put my box and bags into the car while I raced off to say goodbye to my best friend. I promised to call Kanayo on his house phone, and hook up with him some time during the holiday.

Chapter 4

After the team briefing that morning, I sat in my office at the bank, trying to make sense of all the data in front of me. I had to get a grasp of all the figures and plan a strategy to improve the branch sales performance, before my impending telephone conversation with Gary. There was so much to be done and so little time. It reminded me of my early years growing up in a strict Catholic environment, both at home and at school.

My family went to every church activity, ranging from Sunday mass to Benediction, from the Stations of the Cross to the Eucharist, from Good Friday to Palm Sunday. We had all been baptised as babies and we had all received our first holy communion. I had my confirmation in the chapel at Dominion College by Bishop Ezeanya, and there was an early indication that I might end up becoming a Reverend Father; but all that quickly evaporated as soon as I discovered girls at an early age.

We lived in a four-bedroom bungalow in the senior lecturers' accommodation. I shared a room with my three brothers while my sister had a room to herself. My parents had the master bedroom, and the fourth bedroom was for the female house help. The drivers lodged in the one-bedroom boys' quarters behind the house, and had separate utilities within the complex.

Ekaete, the house help, was about 16 years of age and was training to be a tailor. She did her chores during the day and went off every evening to take sewing classes. I had never considered her in a sexual way before, but that summer vacation, I began to realise for the first time how physically endowed she was becoming.

I found myself spending more time with Ekaete, and my hormones were raging – should I or should I not? My young mind was obsessed, and I would find myself deliberately brushing past her in the kitchen or falling on her theatrically when laughing at her jokes. I could not take it any longer, so I finally decided to make a proposition to her rather sooner than later.

As fate would have it, my proposition never happened, because she urgently had to travel back to her village because of a bereavement in her family. That was the last time I ever saw or heard from Ekaete; she never came back.

My grandmother on my mother's side was now living with us due to ill health, and needed hospital attention. She was not literate, but was easily one of the funniest women I have ever met. She had looked after me as a baby, and she would tease me about peeing on her night after night as an infant. She was always very protective of me and would step in to prevent any punishment that was coming my way.

She was fun to be around – she would tell so many tales of the good old days. She could easily recount the events of the Nigerian Civil War and how she had had to give up schooling to get married. Mama, as she was fondly called, was a classic. I vividly remember one occasion when I heard my grandmother screaming and raining abuses on someone. I dashed into the living room to see what was happening, and behold – Mama was screaming insults at the television as two wrestlers were slugging it out!

"What did he do to you that you want to beat him to death, hey he wants to kill him oooo, wicked man, devil, God will punish you, and somebody call the police before he kills this man!" As soon as I realised that she was shouting at the television, I nearly laughed my head off before explaining to her that it was just play-acting and not real life. It took her weeks to get her head around the fact that wrestling on television was not for real.

Mama had on one occasion refused to be photographed until she had put on some perfume; it took some convincing to persuade her that wearing perfume does not affect your photograph, as people looking at the photo cannot smell the fragrance! Mama's pastime was drinking tea; she would have numerous hot cups of tea no matter the time or the weather. She'd drink her steaming tea in the scorching heat, sipping it out of her favourite cup, which could easily hold half a litre; we quickly nicknamed her *"Mama na la soso tea."*

Mama's panacea for every aliment was *"Dogonyaro,"* which was a bitter liquid extracted from the bark of a specific tree found mainly in the Northern part of Nigeria.

My summer holidays passed quickly, and I soon had only one week left before school commenced. I was required to write down a list of things I needed for the start of the new school term. My list comprised textbooks and provisions, including a tennis racquet; my father questioned this inclusion.

I was so determined to have my own tennis racquet that I told my father that it was a mandatory piece of equipment for physical and sports education. I told him that there would be repercussions from the games teacher if I did not have one. My father was a smart man and he must have known that I was trying to outsmart him; I believe that he just humoured me.

Going back to Dominion College for the start of a new term was exciting because I was going to be in Class Three, only one year away from becoming a senior student. I was looking forward to seeing Kanayo, a.k.a. 'stone face', because I had plenty of anecdotes and stories to tell him.

The first few days back at school started slowly as expected, but football practice was already in full swing; new entrants were trying out in full force for the football team.

Dominion College was a mixture of boarding and day students, and so we heard many stories about what was happening in town. We did not have the guts to leave the school compound without an exit card – the gate man, nicknamed Book, was a very angry, aggressive and pugnacious man in his late fifties.

Book was so nicknamed because as a young boy, he had refused to go to school to get an education. He was therefore determined in his advanced age to learn how to read. He was always seen attempting to read a newspaper or a storybook, but usually holding the book upside down.

The senior and day students took delight and pleasure in taunting Book at every opportunity, and Book was equally determined not to give in. It was not uncommon to see Book chasing after students with a stone in one hand, yelling insults at them and their parents.

Olisa was a boy in my class who had a reputation for being the chap around town. He had girlfriends, and told us stories of his escapades in town. He boasted about how he would hook up the senior students with girls in town, when they sneaked out of school at night for some fun.

Olisa was quite close to Kanayo and me; he saw us as happening *"Umu Bendel"* who had their groove on. He enjoyed the stories we told with so much embellishment, and he was keen to sort us out with some action soon.

The euphoria had waned around the pornography magazine at this point, and we wanted to experience the real stuff. Olisa was the person to make it happen.

It was on a certain Friday evening after dinner that Kanayo came into my hostel looking excited and worked up. *"O boy, wetin dey happen man,"* I asked in Pidgin English. Kanayo dropped his voice to a whisper and said, "The eagle has landed." Without another word, I knew that tonight was the night that Olisa was going to sort us out with some action.

Dominion College was fenced all around and there was spiked barbed wire running all along the top of the fence to prevent both students and intruders from scaling over it. The College was situated on a twenty-four-acre area of land situated near the bustling town centre of Awka.

The only legitimate way to get out of the school compound was via the school gate, but Book was a major obstacle; however, there was another way out if you knew where to look. This was a weak spot in the fence, created by the senior students who crept out of school at night. The hole was large enough to allow one student through, but it was not noticeable unless you knew exactly where to look, as it was hidden by removable blocks.

The Lagos boys gave us the location of the weak spot after a bribe of bread and sardines. I met Kanayo at our rendezvous spot at about 7 pm, under the cover of darkness. We carefully removed the blocks, exposed the hole in the fence and crept through. I could feel my heart pounding with excitement and fear; but nothing was going to stop this adventure.

On the other side of the fence, we quickly discarded our school daywear and changed into something more suitable for the occasion. We hid our clothes behind some bushes and set out in search of Olisa. He was waiting for us behind an abandoned car near the market square. We set out in search of fun and some action. Our first port of call was Hotel Soloso, known for its highlife music and cheap local brew of sweet palm wine. We settled down and ordered some fried bush meat with chilled palm wine.

The plan was that Olisa would arrange for two local girls to join us at the hotel. We would then get to know them better, have plenty of drinks, and hope the rest would be straightforward. It was crucial that we get back to school before lights out – otherwise, this exciting evening would quickly turn into a disaster.

The clock on the hotel wall was showing 8 pm, yet there was no sign of the local girls, and time was quickly ticking away. We were already high on the local brew and all the hormones in our bodies were on high alert. Olisa kept reassuring us that they were on their way, but he could not tell for sure, as there were no mobile phones in those days.

Disappointment began to set in at 8:30 pm when there was no sign of these phantom girls, and Olisa, sensing our frustration and disappointment, suggested that we shift base to another hot spot called Sakura. Sakura was about a fifteen-minute walk from Hotel

Soloso, but due to time constraints, we opted to use a motorbike, popularly known as "Okada."

Sakura was the joint of prostitutes; whatever size you wanted was available for your picking. When we got to the front entrance of Sakura, Olisa pulled us aside and told us not to pay more than three Naira (about £3) for the service rendered by the girls.

We went in and had barely sat down when we were approached by two women old enough to be our mothers. "Customers how far, *we dey here ooo*," one of them said. Olisa gestured to me to choose the one I wanted. I was already too high on the local brew to consider facial beauty, my member was aching from standing at attention for hours, and the time was fast approaching lights out.

I followed the woman closest to me to her makeshift room, gave her five Naira, and did not bother to ask for change. I confessed to her that I had never had sex before and did not know what to do. *"No worry yourself my broda, I go show you wetin to do,"* she said as she descended on me.

We got straight to our business, which lasted for about four seconds. Those four seconds seemed like heaven had come down on earth, and I fell in love with Agnes for what she had done to me within that time.

I was thirteen when I lost my virginity to Agnes, and I can still remember every second of that four-second encounter. I started visiting her on a regular basis for the next three months; on several occasions, I would give her extra money to cook some food for me. I began to see her as my girlfriend, and she was happy to oblige me even though she knew that she was more than twice my age.

My pocket money was dwindling quickly and I had to look for a way to replenish it, so I sold my wristwatch, which my mother had bought me on one of her trips to London. I got just half the price for it, but I really did not care as long as Agnes was making me happy. I bought her a handbag and sunglasses, and the sex got better and hotter.

I got angry and miserable when I had to wait outside her room or in the bar area while she serviced her other clients, but I had to learn to take it in good faith.

On one particular Saturday evening as I was preparing to visit Agnes, Kanayo came into my hostel with another boy called Chidi, a.k.a. Chisco Mbaga.

Chidi was from Port Harcourt and was repeating Class Four because he had failed the final examination to enter Class Five. He was from a rich polygamous family, and had travelled to London and America on many holidays. He was a "bad boy" and knew most of the fun joints in town.

"O boy are you going to see that old babe tonight? Man, forget that old mama yoyo," Kanayo teased me. "Yes," I replied, *"and she dey cook wait me for her room,"* I informed him. *"Are you sure that woman never put juju for the food that she gives to you to chop, as your brain don scatter finish,"* Kanayo enquired.

"Remy, for your information Chisco get one happening joint for us to fall into tonight, and you know say we need to go there sharp sharp and be back before lights out," Kanayo said.

"Make we dey roll," Kanayo added, and was already heading for the door with Chisco; I did not want to disappoint Agnes tonight but curiosity got the better of me, so I went off with Kanayo and Chisco.

Chisco took us to the opposite side of town, near the motor park and the College of Education, and he introduced us to our latest joint, called "The Lobito."

The Lobito had a large open-air courtyard where the resident band played every night and the huge loud speakers blared out highlife music. The courtyards had various sitting sections, arranged to give a good view of the dancing area. The beer parlour was situated in the inner building and had rooms that housed the girls. The girls would come out in twos or threes and strut their stuff, shaking their backsides provocatively to the beat of the music; they would then approach various sitting sections for business.

A beautiful young light-skinned girl of about twenty-two years of age with a big bosom approached us, and as I caught sight of her face, my heart melted. She had an oval face with a thin scar on her forehead, her smile was infectious, and I wanted her badly. Kanayo was already drooling after Ada and it became a battle between us as to who would spend more time with her. Agnes became a distant memory, as it was all about Ada and the Lobito.

I later learnt that Ada had dropped out of primary school after becoming an orphan, and had moved from one relative to another ever since. She had run away from her big aunt's house at age 16, after she was raped by her aunt's husband. She was living on the streets at the mercy of area boys when she met Rebecca, who had introduced her to prostitution two years before I met her.

Ada's dream was to have a family with many children; she strongly held on to that dream, and believed that her current line of work was just for survival. I was convinced that I was the right person for her, and continuously told her so; she continuously laughed at my naivety.

Ada was a practising Catholic and went to evening mass on Wednesdays and to Sunday service. The weekends were her busiest time of trade, and she was a very popular girl with many customers queuing up for her services. I continued to patronize Ada and other girls in the town's red light spots for many months, until my grades started to slip and I began to get average marks in my two favourite subjects.

All Class Three students were required to sit for the Junior Secondary School Certificate Examination, to determine who was fit and ready to progress to Class Four. Determined to be successful, Kanayo and I channelled our energy towards our studies and visited our fun spot only once or twice a week to release some tension, rather than daily.

The exams came and were tough, lasting for one and a half weeks. I was particularly scared of Maths and Chemistry, while Kanayo was not sure of Physics and

Literature. Results were not due until three weeks later – we would discover our marks during the long holiday.

I did not go home immediately for the long holiday – instead, I hatched a plan with my father's driver Sunny to pick me up from Kanayo's home in Benin City in a couple of days. So the day school closed, I set off with Kanayo by public transport on a journey that lasted for about three hours.

Kanayo lived with his mum and older sister in a rented three-bedroom flat near Airport Road. Mama Kanayo, as she was fondly called, was a widow, as Kanayo's father had passed away four years earlier. I was not a stranger to her, as I had met her on numerous occasions during her visits to Dominion College.

She was a very hard-working person and was self-employed; she ran three butteries (tuck shops) in the three campuses of the University of Benin, and she had been providing for the family before and after the death of her husband.

The few days that I spent with Kanayo were packed with fun, and he introduced me to the girl next door, called Amaka. Amaka was a year younger than I was and she was light-skinned, slim and pretty. We got on so well that we spent hours chatting and laughing. When Kanayo and I were not hanging out with Amaka and the other neighbourhood kids, we were at the tuck shops helping out and stuffing our faces.

Kanayo, at his own discretion, had told Amaka that I spent most of my holidays in the UK and the USA, and that I was a true and proper "aje butter." Kanayo was insistent that I act the part of the privileged son of a renowned legal advocate; Amaka was head over heels in love with me by now.

Thanks to Kanayo's connection and sugar-coated tongue, Amaka and I officially became boyfriend and girlfriend. We would spend hours talking and I was always on hand to serenade her with poetic words from the gospel according to St. Remy.

I did not have to tell her about my family background as Kanayo had already done all the work. Kanayo was brilliant at embellishing the truth, and all I had to do was to concur.

Amaka and I were in love within two days of our meeting, and I would never forget the first night that we kissed under the staircase. It was not the most exciting kiss that I had ever experienced, but since it was coming from Amaka, it was beautiful all the same.

I was not in for some quick action with Amaka, as this was my first true puppy love; I was determined to love her and grow old with her.

Amaka was a virgin and sexually naive; I was much more experienced than she was, but that did not bother me. I knew that it would happen eventually, and I did not want to pressure her so soon.

I needed some relief – *"body no be firewood"* – and because I was staying in Kanayo's house, we could not sneak out looking for fun spots at night-time. It became increasingly frustrating for me but not for Kanayo, and I wondered why, until he revealed all to me one night.

Kanayo showed me how he got his relief through masturbation, and as I watched him do his stuff in the bathroom, I wondered how successful I would be when I had a go. It took me three times as long to finally find some relief, and then I was like a kid with a new toy; it became a regular fall-back option for me for a very long time to come.

There were tears flowing down Amaka's face as I got into the front seat of my father's new official car on my way back to Asaba. I promised her that I would call and write to her regularly and when the opportunity presented itself, I would come and visit her again.

The deal with Sunny 'the driver', in exchange for his coming to pick me up from Benin instead of Awka, was that he could carry passengers with the car on our way back to Asaba, and we would share the proceeds. We made about 80 Naira from the trip and split it between us, with Sunny taking the lion's share.

Sunny was my main man and we were very close. He was teaching me how to drive and would allow me to drive around our quiet neighbourhood in Asaba. We would talk about girls and we often stopped for a drink on our numerous road trips together. Sunny was a slim fellow of about 35 years of age, and had two children from two different women. His pastime was women and alcohol was his "feeding bottle." You would hardly see Sunny eating; rather, you would see him with his regular bottle of Star beer.

My father had warned him on several occasions about his drinking habit, so Sunny no longer drank on duty; instead, he drank twice as much during his free time. He was a trusted and reliable driver, and knew how to handle the steering wheel; he once showed me how to make a car dance and I have seen him drive the car while doing up his shoelaces.

Sunny was my person and I had his back and would always stand up for him at home, especially when he stepped out of line. I always jumped at the opportunity to go on errands with him, because I knew that I would be the one driving the car.

Amaka my sweetheart was constantly on my mind and I would regularly dream of what I wanted to do to her, both in sexual and non-sexual ways. I tried calling her a couple of times but could not get through, so I called Kanayo. Kanayo told me that her phone line was down, and he would arrange for her to come to his house to take my call in about thirty minutes' time.

I finally spoke to Amaka, and found she was scared that I had abandoned her. She told me of how she had my picture under her pillow and how she dreamt of marrying me some day and having my children. She informed me that she had already written and posted a love letter to me, but refused to tell me what she had written.

I was concerned that the letter might fall into the wrong hands; so I solicited Sunny's help. He was to check for any letter addressed to me before he handed the mail from our private post box to my parents.

Amaka's letter arrived a week later and as I opened it, my nostrils were assaulted by a strong sweet smell. I recognised the scent as the one from "Drummer Boy," a brand of air freshener; and as I pulled out the folded pages of paper, a dried-out hibiscus flower fell out. This was my first love letter and it did not disappoint; it was three pages long and contained every human emotion possible on planet Earth. The letter was signed at the bottom of the last page with a kiss.

I slept with this letter under my pillow and perused it regularly. I was yearning for the opportunity to go to Benin to see Amaka again as soon as possible.

Coming from such an educated background meant that my family home was always full of different books, ranging from voluminous academic tomes to every kind of novel. I remember hearing my two elder brothers, who were both at university, talk about a book that they had just finished reading, and I thought it sounded interesting.

Not wanting to feel left out, I picked up this book – and it changed my life. It was a book with a yellow cover called *The Last Testament of Lucky Luciano*. It was the autobiography of a gangster called Charlie "Lucky" Luciano, thus dubbed for his numerous escapes from varied murderous attacks.

Charlie, the son of an immigrant miner, had worked his way up the ladder of the mob to become the *Capo di tutti Capi* – the "boss of all bosses." This was one of the most intriguing stories that my young mind had ever comprehended; it was full of plots and counter-plots and the sex, suspense and violence were explosive.

I could tell the story verbatim from cover to cover, and held my listeners captivated for hours as I narrated how Charlie manoeuvred his way through the ranks with the help of his henchmen. I had read other intriguing books, like *The Godfather* by Mario Puzo and books by James Hadley-Chase, Sidney Sheldon and Harold Robbins, but Charlie's story was the one that made the strongest impact on me. I dreamed of being like him and run my own outfit someday.

I was so carried away by this book that I had it on me 24-7, and would frequently refer to it for any information that I needed. I was gutted the day that the novel had to go back to its rightful owner, and I missed it for weeks.

Books and academic law journals and publications had always been part of my childhood. My father had gone to a UK university to study law in 1954. This had been made possible by winning a regional scholarship and by the efforts of his local community, which had sponsored a couple of their bright sons to study overseas; he had fortunately been one of the chosen recipients.

My father combined his studies with working two full-time jobs. With the monies he saved from his jobs and bursary, he was able to buy a three-bedroom house for about £5,000.

He had liked and enjoyed his time in the UK and was always quick to play down the issue of racism during this period. I think he felt obliged to the country that had given him a solid foundation in his career and a head start in life.

Thus it became a tradition in the Ukadike household that every child should visit the UK at least once to gain that exposure. My elder siblings had all been there, and it was now my turn, but this was conditional on my passing my Junior School Examination.

The wait was excruciating during those summer holidays, and one week seemed like a thousand years; I was particularly scared of Maths and Chemistry.

The results were published on the notice board at Dominion College, and so I had to endure the two-hour drive to my school to see them. As I approached the school entrance, my mind raced back to the times I had spent visiting Agnes, Ada and the other women, when I should have been concentrating on my studies. *"There's no use crying over spilled milk,"* I said to myself, *"you play the game, you take the pain."*

There were many people milling around the notice board and I could hear shouts of joy and voices thanking God, but at the same time, I could see looks of despair and watery eyes. I approached the notice board with my heart beating slowly at first and then harder and harder.

I searched for my name under the letter U and I could not find it. *"Chineke, I am dead,"* I thought to myself. *"This is my London trip out of the window, I must have failed. But it's impossible,"* I thought, as I could not have failed my favourite subject, English Language and Literature. I gripped the hand of Simon, my classmate. "What is happening, I cannot find my name on the board?" I asked him.

At that moment, the typist came out with a supplementary list of names that he had missed out at first. My heart was really pounding against my chest and I thought that I would suffer a heart attack any moment now. I summoned up enough courage to look at the list. YES---YES---YES! I had passed, with one A, five Cs and two passes.

I was ecstatic and shouting at the top of my voice. I calmed down just in time to see Kanayo checking for his name; he had passed as well. We hugged each other and spent a couple of minutes talking about other events. I told him that I would be travelling to London on holiday soon, and he jokingly asked me if I was going to take Ada with me. "O boy, cool down, *no be so*," I responded before departing.

The two-hour drive back home was not as bad as the earlier one, and because I was in a good mood I allowed Sunny to carry passengers on our way back to make some money, which we split.

"I passed my exams!" I shouted as I went into the house. My father was sitting at the dining table and he looked at me over the top of his glasses. He stretched out his hand to see my grades and I saw a frown appear on his face. "So you could only manage one A and you got two passes, too; those people who had eight As, do they have two heads?" he asked. "Don't ever bring this kind of result to this house again, have you heard me?" He then continued, "If you do, I will disown you. You do not concentrate on your studies, always playing football and tennis and wearing stylish shorts," my father concluded.

"Yes, sir," I replied and made my way out of the dining room area; for me the most important thing was that I had passed, but deep down I knew that I could have done better if not for the sweet distractions of Ada and Agnes.

I would be in Class Four on the resumption of school, which would make me a senior student. I could officially wear trousers, and punish any junior student who misbehaved or stepped out of line.

Chapter 5

We left Asaba for Lagos on the 14th of August 1987, on our way to the UK. The plan was to spend the night in Lagos and fly out the next day from Murtala Muhammed International Airport. Lagos was then the capital city of Nigeria and the commercial hub of the Federation. It epitomized the hustle and bustle of a typically over-populated state, and was made infamous by the local boys who invariably tried to rip you off. You needed to have eyes in the back of your head to survive in Lagos.

Lagos State was indeed a unique kettle of fish, and it reminded me of Sicily in Luciano's Testament. The local boys (touts) were a nuisance to society, never missing an opportunity to exploit vulnerable citizens. There was a well-known joke about boys in the area charging a Johnny Just Come from the rural area some money for staring at some high-rise buildings at Obalende.

Lagos was a fast-paced place unlike any other; it promised glory, fame and fortune to the brave-hearted, and yet was unforgiving to many.

My mother, sister and I spent the night at my uncle's house in Surulere, and we planned to leave early to get to the airport because of the chaotic traffic between Surulere and Ikeja.

It was difficult sleeping that night because of the excitement ahead. I tried to imagine what London would look like, wondering if I would get to visit Buckingham Palace and have tea with the Queen. I was keen to see the Marble Arch, Piccadilly Circus, Mayfair and Old Kent Road, places I'd only seen by name on the Monopoly board.

I finally went to sleep at about 2 am and did not have to sleep for long before the break of dawn; I was up like a flash, and was very soon dressed and ready in the living room, waiting to hit the high road.

As we approached the airport, my mind drifted back to my friends in school and at home, who were green with envy about my trip. I felt like the luckiest boy alive. Johnny, the boy from across the road, cheekily nicknamed me "the London Remy"; and my mates accorded me much respect, while giving me a long list of requests to fulfil.

My father had given me a sum of £300 to spend on shopping in the UK, which I had quickly handed over to my mother for safekeeping. The money was to cover my shopping for school and home, and I had already drawn up a long list.

My uncle's driver dropped us off at the airport, and we paid the porters to help carry our luggage into the Departures lounge. I looked around, trying to take in all that was happening around me. Wow, this is great, thank you God! I was used to being the one escorting parents and siblings to the airport, but this was my moment and I was relishing it.

My mum and sister had been to the UK before and they knew what to do and where to go; so I just followed sheepishly until we came to the Departures entrance. I turned around for a brief second and whispered under my breath, "London, here I come!"

We boarded a British Airways Boeing 747, and took our seats. I had never been inside an airplane before and was fascinated with what I could see. My sister informed me that food was normally served on the plane after reaching cruising altitude, and I waited eagerly to see this happen.

As the plane started to taxi onto the runway, we held hands and said a quick prayer for God's mercy during the journey. We prayed that God take control of the airplane, but I still refused to let go of my sister's hand after the prayer, as the plane was taking off; my heart was in my mouth.

It was an exhilarating experience as I felt the plane ascend and then stay in the air. I quickly forgot about my fear of flying and settled down to enjoy the experience. The air hostess eventually served our meal, but I was not impressed with the portion and gladly accepted my sister's as well when she offered it.

The Captain's voice came on the air to announce that we were a few minutes from beginning our descent into London Heathrow, and we quickly fastened our seat belts and waited. The plane touched down and as it hit the tarmac, there was a round of applause from the passengers.

We were about to clear Immigration and as I stood there taking in the whole environment, I realised that I had never seen so many Caucasians in one room at the same time in my life. The Immigration Officer who gave us clearance was a pleasant young man, and he wished us a good holiday and suggested that we visit Madame Tussauds and the Tower of London.

We picked up our baggage from the baggage reclaim and proceeded to clear Customs. As we approached the Arrivals gate, I could feel my heart beating faster with excitement. We made our way towards the taxi ranks pushing our trolley, and proceeded to board a taxi to Dollis Hill in North West London, where my father's house was located.

I was quiet during the drive from the airport as I stared out of the window in amazement. I was trying to take in everything around me at the same time, from the traffic lights to the people walking in the streets. This was so different from where I had just come from, and I could not help but think that this was what Heaven looked like.

My father's house was a three-bedroom terraced property that had been converted into a rooming house. My father's sister efficiently managed the property and the rental income was repatriated to my father periodically.

There was always a spare room available when my family visited, but that meant less rental income for my father, so he was not that keen on regular visits by family.

The room had a double bed, a chair, a television set and a chest of drawers. It was tight for three people, but I did not care – I was in London! Night-time was interesting, as we all had to sleep on the double bed together and as the youngest, I was stuck in the middle.

We stacked our baggage in one corner of the room and started to clean it up. My sister and I did all the hard work while my mother supervised. After the cleaning, my mother and sister decided to take a nap. I was too excited and worked up to want a nap, so I switched on the television and watched Top of the Pops, which was airing on BBC 1.

I remember the BBC showing musicals such as "Dancing on the Ceiling" by Lionel Ritchie, "Thriller" by Michael Jackson, "Headline" by Five, and "I Want to Wake up With You" by Morris Gardner. I also remember watching movies such as *An Officer and a Gentleman*, *Diamonds are Forever* and *The Godfather* on television.

My visit to London was beyond exciting, it was, in fact, a dream come true – I saw my cousins, whose accent I struggled to understand. I visited famous attractions with my uncle such as Big Ben, Downing Street, Madame Tussauds and Trafalgar Square. I learned about the battle of Trafalgar and Nelson's Column. We also visited London Bridge, which has been falling down for ages, Buckingham Palace, Oxford Circle, the Marble Arch and the Tower of London. The list was endless and I wore my uncle out by taking innumerable photos.

I accompanied my mother and sister to the Portobello, Camden and Shepherd's Bush markets. I spent more time at Rontex Fabrics in Willesden Green than at any other place. I remember going into Argos with my mother on a particular day and spotting "the watch" – it was a Casio Helifighter game watch which had a game of a helicopter shooting alien space ships down and it cost £30, a lot of money in 1987. I still had a balance of about £130 left from my allowance and I was determined to get this particular watch, and Argos stores were the only stockist.

I was keen to pay that amount but the real problem was selling this proposition to mother. I had to convince her that spending £30 on one item was worth it, since she was the custodian of my money.

We had four days left in London before we were to fly back to Lagos, and we decided to take a trip around London in one of the open-roof double-decker buses. We started at Marble Arch, through Piccadilly Circus and Charing Cross. The tour lasted for about two hours and was very informative; the tour guide gave us the background and history of London's various landmarks and sites.

We later got on a double-decker bus plying Route 16, from Victoria Bus Station towards Dollis Hill. I had always wanted to know what the top deck of the bus looked like, and here was my opportunity to see and experience it. I eagerly went up the stairs while my mother and sister stayed below. I was not sure where the bus stop for Dollis Hill was, but I was assured that either my sister or mother would notify me when we got there.

It was about sixty minutes into the bus ride that I sensed that something was wrong, as neither my sister nor mother had come up to get me. I quickly went down the stairs to the ground floor of the bus and to my shock and horror, my mother and sister were no longer on the bus. I later learned that they had alighted four stops before and had forgotten that I was still on board.

Panic set in and I was terrified to the core of my being. I was just a fourteen-year-old lad and I was lost in a strange and foreign country where people spoke through their noses. The image of my father's blue Peugeot 504 disappearing from sight after he had dropped me off at Dominion College came flooding back and the feeling of hopelessness enveloped me.

I sat down on a bus seat for a brief moment to gather my thoughts and decide what to do. I stood up and then approached the conductor of the bus, who was of Jamaican origin, and narrated my plight to him; he informed the bus driver, who in turn radioed in to the bus garage.

The Police picked me up ten minutes later and I was driven home based on the address that I gave them. The Police were impressed that I knew my home address by heart, and as we approached the front of my father's house, I could see my mother and sister standing in front looking frantically worried. *"Serves them right,"* I thought; I wished that I could have extended their anxiety for some more hours.

The Police had some words with my mother before departing. I refused to speak to my mother and sister for the rest of the day, feeling betrayed and abandoned. I finally came around after I was told that I could buy my coveted precious watch from Argos at Kilburn High Street the next day.

The London Underground fascinated me. I just could not get my head around how people could go into the tube that was underground and emerge at another end of the city. It was complicated for me as a fourteen-year-old to try to understand the tube map. My mother and sister were good at reading the map, and all I did was follow and hope that they would not lose me again.

My visit to the UK provided many surprises, and there was one kind of culture shock in particular. I was amazed and bewildered to see people getting intimate in the street and on the underground. This kind of behaviour would definitely not happen back home; in fact, it would be considered an abomination and a taboo to make such an open and public display of affection in the streets of Nigeria. I thought that there were certain things that should be reserved for the privacy of a closed door.

I could not help myself and it was not unusual to see me staring at this public display of affection. I could not help but imagine what these couples did behind closed doors.

We spent our last day in London with my aunt. It was a very memorable day, as various relatives and friends came to say good-bye. Plenty of food and drinks and presents and good wishes were exchanged.

I had only seen the UK during the summer, and I had heard stories of the winter and the unpredictable nature of the weather – but I did not care. All I wanted at the end of that holiday was to live in London for good and enjoy the basic social amenities such as the constant water supply, stable electricity and reliable transport system.

The next day, we had to leave for Heathrow Airport to catch our early afternoon flight back to Lagos. As we drove away from the house, I could not help but remember a verse in the Holy Bible that says, "To everything there is a season ... a time to weep, and a time to laugh ..." I guess that for me it would be "a time to come and a time to go back."

We boarded a Lagos-bound British Airways flight and, as the plane took off from the runway, I was overwhelmed with a bitter-sweet emotion. It had been a once-in-a-lifetime opportunity, but it was already over.

After about six hours' flight time, the pilot's voice came over the public address system to notify us that we were circling Lagos airport and about to start our descent. *"Back home," I said* to myself and as I looked out of the window, "O my God," I heard myself exclaim; there was no light in most parts of Lagos.

If I had had the authority to turn the plane around and go right back to London, I would not have hesitated to do so; but I was back to the harsh reality of life in Nigeria and the aggressive mosquitoes in Lagos.

Sunny had arrived from Asaba earlier that day and was waiting for us at the airport. The plan was that he would take us to my uncle's house in Lagos for about half an hour's rest before we started on our three-hour journey back to Asaba.

We began our journey back home at about 8 pm that night. The journey was quite a challenging one, with bad roads riddled with potholes and police checkpoints, but we eventually got home at about 11 pm.

My father was anxiously waiting for us in front of the house and as the car came to a halt, everybody came running out of the house to welcome us back home.

I did not go to bed until midnight as there were many tales to tell; and by then, I could hardly keep my eyes open any longer.

I slept like a baby and dreamt about wearing my new Casio game watch in the neighbourhood, and being the envy of all my peers.

Chapter 6

I was now in Class Four at Dominion College and officially a senior student. All seniors wore light brown trousers and blue checked shirts as their after-school uniform, but we wore white trousers and white shirts with the school crest on display during school hours.

Being in Class Four had great benefits but also had its own challenges; we were bullied by the Class Five and Class Six students, as neither bunch would hesitate to flex their muscles and authority on us constantly. They saw us as an easy target.

I vividly remember my first night back in school after the long holiday. The Class Six students rounded up all the Class Four students at midnight and frog-marched us half-naked around the school. We were made to chant and sing songs that demeaned us, after which we were all given six strokes of the cane and made to understand our position in the hierarchy of the school.

Virtually everybody in school knew me as the London Remy, and I wore my new wristwatch with much pride. I could spend hours playing the helicopter game in the watch with those of my friends who were privileged enough to touch my prized possession. I used every opportunity to tell stories of my trip and show off photos of myself at various famous landmarks. I became arguably one of the most popular boys in the history of the school.

I continued playing for the school's junior football team, but this was proving to be a challenge, as I was fast growing taller than the maximum height for a junior player. I was amazed that the team captain Goddy a.k.a. "Nna," who was easily three years older than I was, had no issues fitting under the maximum height.

Goddy called me aside and informed me that I had to do something about my height; he then let me in on what he and other players did to stunt their growth. I was shocked because he advised me to start carrying bags of cement on my head on a regular basis to stunt my growth, and hunch my shoulders and distort my posture to seem shorter.

I had always wanted to be tall, and this did not fit into my aspirations and dreams; however, what was my alternative? I was not big and strong enough to play in the senior football team. Besides, the competition for a place in the senior team was fierce, and I had heard stories of players deliberately breaking other players' legs on the pitch.

The more I tried to stunt my growth, the taller I grew. This was becoming a dilemma for me and I could no longer play for the junior football team.

Lawn tennis was another option for me, but tennis didn't come anywhere close to football. Football was the primus at Dominion College, and the privileges and fame attached to College football were awesome.

I decided to take my chance and try out for the senior football team. In terms of skills and speed, I held my own; but I was let down by my strength and stamina. I managed to make the waiting list for the third reserve team. I was devastated and I could see all my privileges being withdrawn – and then disaster struck.

A rumour had been making the rounds that Father Uka was leaving Dominion College. I had dismissed it as total rubbish, as Dominion College was Father Uka and Father Uka was Dominion College. If you were to cut Father Uka with a knife, he would bleed the colours of the College. He was expected to be the Principal for life.

At 1 pm on the 4th of March 1987, the great bell started to ring frantically to signal the importance and urgency of the situation. Students poured out from all corners of the school onto the Assembly ground. We all gathered with great trepidation; anxiety and uncertainty hung in the air.

Father Uka was nowhere to be seen, but one of his deputies called Mr Uba, a thick-set man with afro hair sitting on an oversized head, stood on the platform to break the news of Father Uka's departure. He did not offer any reason for such an unceremonious exit.

That day was like a day of national mourning, and we felt as if we had lost an icon and an enigma. Father Uka's classic assembly rhetoric came flooding back and I had to wonder who would step into his big shoes.

Father Uka was summarily replaced by the most nondescript-looking man, nicknamed ECC. He was so nicknamed because of his car registration number, which began with these letters.

ECC was a short man with a big head and was a pale version of the almighty Father Uka. He was an experienced principal in his own right and believed in the old-style educational method; he was not a sports lover and did not give two hoots about any sports accolade.

He came in and made many sweeping changes. He withdrew all the benefits accorded to footballers and banned football practices that would clash with normal school-time activities. He reshuffled the teaching staff, and gradually got rid of the Father Uka loyalists. He reduced the total number of school prefects and seemed to be hell bent on dismantling the history upon which the College had been built.

He wanted to do things the ECC way, and instil his ethos in the College; he suspended teachers and students who stepped out of line. Teachers and students were petrified and ECC reigned supreme. Although he was half the size of Father Uka, the man was surely punching above his height.

ECC banned all forms of inter-school social activity, and this irked the senior students as they missed socialising with the neighbouring girls' college. The ban caused great dismay among the senior students but they were not sure how to react.

ECC was a one-man army and did not need any backup. He was anywhere and everywhere imaginable; he sometimes dressed up in the school colours and mingled among students at night. He had spies among the students and teachers and seemed to know about any planned event or uprising before it happened.

He introduced a black book in every classroom; this book was submitted directly to him every Friday by the class prefect, with the names of all the bad boys and truants in the class. These truants were disciplined and then given a portion of grass in the College lawns to trim with a cutlass; your name appearing in the black book was like a death sentence.

Kanayo was the class prefect and he made sure that my name never featured in the black book; however, he did threaten me once with this, when I refused to lend him some money to buy bean cake and bread.

For the next six months, there was a lot of dissatisfaction amongst teachers and students. The Catholic Church, with which Dominion College was affiliated, was becoming worried, but the Board of Trustees were always quick to step in to protect the new Principal.

Academically, Dominion College was still holding its own compared to other schools in the state, but socially it was dead. ECC did not believe in that aspect of development – he believed that school was for learning and not socialising.

But the aura surrounding ECC was shattered in public on one hot dry afternoon, when we heard a woman shouting at the top of her voice and raining insults and abuses on someone. We dashed out of our classes to find out what the commotion was all about, only to see ECC on the floor with a heavily-built woman sitting on top of him and raining blows and insults down on him.

The woman turned out to be his wife, and she had brought a domestic quarrel to his place of work. We learnt that ECC had not given Mrs ECC money for housekeeping for the last two months, as teachers' salaries were in arrears.

ECC was unfortunate that his wife caught up with him during school hours and in public. She did not intend to let him get away from his responsibilities this time; he had been as slippery as an eel for the last month.

This was a show of shame; students formed a circle around the pair, cheering on Mrs ECC as she dealt with the dreaded Principal. After several minutes of using ECC as a punching bag, she finally got off her husband and stormed off towards the staff quarters, hurling insults at him as she left.

For the first time in six months, my heart went out to ECC, and I tried to imagine the degree of pain and hurt that he was going through at that moment. I looked into his eyes as he sat on the ground, and I saw a defeated man who had just lost his dignity, manhood and integrity in front of the whole world. One part of me wanted to reach out and help him up, but another part of me felt that he deserved what he got.

ECC quietly got up, dusted off his French suit, and walked straight towards his office without looking around. There was a grave-like silence all around, and we all stared at ECC as he climbed the stairs leading to his office and disappeared into it. The teachers who had witnessed the humiliation of ECC quickly dispersed us, but some students were still milling around wanting to witness the conclusion of this event.

The great bell rang to signal the end of the school day, and we headed to our respective hostels and stayed there until further notice. At about 7 pm the bell for the refectory rang and students set out towards the building, but you could see pockets of students discussing the afternoon's events.

There were various rumours going around. One was that Mrs ECC had a mental issue and went mad during a particular period in the year; others said that she was a witch and used "remote control" on ECC. They said that she had tried to kill him on various occasions as an offering to her fellow witches in the coven, but ECC had refused to die, so she was now taking her frustration out on him.

We did not see ECC for the next three school days, and as usual, the rumour-mongering started again. Some said that his wife had finally killed him and that his cadaver had been offered to witches; others said that he was now infected by his wife's madness and was residing in an asylum. The two Deputy Principals took charge and the school returned to its usual routine. However, we were all eagerly awaiting the return and emergence of ECC.

"Cometh the hour, cometh the man," ECC showed up on Monday morning at the Assembly ground and it was business as usual. No questions asked and no answers volunteered, but it was apparent from ECC's demeanour that his pride had been severely dented.

As the days turned into weeks, students, especially the seniors, began to taunt the once-feared ECC mercilessly. During Assembly, it now became commonplace to hear one shout out, "ECC is a lazy man" or *"I go soon call madam oo."*

ECC took all this taunting on the chin, but the more he tried to go back to his old regime of hard discipline, the more he was taunted.

Ehime, a.k.a. *"khaki no be leather,"* was one of the Lagos crew, and he taunted ECC relentlessly; the more he was flogged and punished, the more he taunted the poor man. ECC was careful not to expel Ehime, as his father was one of the leading legal authorities in Nigeria and ECC did not want any lawsuit on his hands.

Ehime spent more time in ECC's office than in the classroom. He was happy to tell anyone who cared to listen that his main purpose in life was to frustrate the man. On one occasion, when Ehime was being dragged to ECC's office by another teacher for truancy, on spotting them approaching, ECC came out of his office and shouted, "Ehime, what did I do to you in this school? Every bad thing is in your hands, when the junior students complain, it is about you, the teachers complain, it is about you. I will run away from this school because of you oooo."

ECC must have gone to church to give thanks when Ehime finally left Dominion College to finish his last year in Lagos; but there were many more miscreants ready to fill Ehime's shoes, and ECC continued to battle these students.

Aromi, a.k.a. "Orjomila," was a known bad boy inside and outside school; he was a day student and the known leader of a gang that specialised in picking pockets. The reason he was in school was to learn to count his loot and to have a cover. Both teachers and students feared him. He was known to beat up teachers outside the school premises, and so they were afraid to go home if they had crossed Aromi's path on the school campus.

ECC decided to expel Aromi after he insulted and threatened a female teacher. ECC barked out his offence, and gave the boy his marching orders.

Aromi looked at the short man in front of him and gave ECC a hot slap on the cheek before pushing him down. He ran down the stairs towards the school fence and effortlessly jumped over it. We never saw Aromi again in school, but later heard that the police had killed him during an armed robbery operation that went bad.

Meanwhile, as all these events transpired, I carried on my correspondence with Amaka; but with me writing the bulk of the letters, because we both knew the risk of her letters being intercepted by the school authority. Initially I was determined to be faithful to Amaka, but after four weeks, I could not bear the sexual yearning. As they say in Pidgin English, *"body no be firewood."*

So Kanayo and I continued to visit our fun spot, and we discovered new joints and new girls with whom to sow our wild oats. Ada by this time had moved to Lagos in search of new pastures, and she was now only a distant memory as new girls entertained us.

Kanayo, Chisco and I became inseparable. Although I was still known as the London Remy, as a group, we became known as the three musketeers. We knew all the weak spots in the school fence and most of the bubbling fun spots in town. We had each other's backs covered and were ready to jump into a fight to protect each other.

We started smoking and drinking during our regular visits to town; our favourite brand of cigarette was Target as it was the cheapest available.

Getting out of school at night was becoming increasingly difficult, as roll calls and checks would be carried out at random times. Woe betide you if you were not present during the roll calls. Because we were friendly with most of the prefects, we were able to get away with missing some of the roll calls; however, when these were done under the supervision of a prep teacher, escape was impossible.

We had arranged to meet up one night and head to our new fun spot in town. As I would be delayed by a rehearsal for a new play in the drama society, I suggested that the other two go ahead of me; I would catch up with them later.

I finished my drama rehearsal at about 7:30 pm, but the whole atmosphere felt strange. The school was swarming with movement, there were prefects patrolling the premises, and quite an unusual number of teachers. A major roll call was taking place, so I decided to hang around; but it was not possible for me to stand in for both Kanayo and Chisco.

The next day, I was expecting Kanayo and Chisco to give me an earful for not showing up in town the previous night. I was keen to warn them that they had missed the roll call, and that they might be in big trouble. However, I could not find either of them where we normally met before Assembly. As I made my way towards the Assembly ground, there was still no sign of my pals. And then behold, ECC stepped out of his office with Kanayo and Chisco behind him, both looking unkempt and with bloodshot eyes.

I did not need a seer to tell me that this was bad: on returning from their outing, my friends had crawled through the hole in the fence, right into the waiting hands of ECC and two other teachers.

Kanayo and Chisco received twelve strokes of the cane each, and were expelled from Dominion College. Through all the punishment they endured, they refused to rat on me or on any other student.

I watched from the background as Mama Kanayo, accompanied by her brother, came to pick up her son and his belongings from the school; I could clearly see the look of disappointment and despair on her face.

Chisco was hauled off to a local school in Port Harcourt under the watchful eyes of his parents; that was the last time I heard of him. Kanayo, through his uncle's connections, got into a relatively good local school in Benin City.

My social life at Dominion College came to a standstill with the departure of my friends, especially Kanayo. I became the last man standing and an easy target for the other senior students, especially those in Class Five. I tried to align myself with the Lagos crew but it was not the same without Kanayo and Chisco.

My street reputation had taken a battering, as rumours were flying around that I had a hand in Kanayo and Chisco's expulsion. The rumour mill was churning out questions: why was I not with them when they were apprehended? Did I rat them out to the authorities?

Some people even believed that I might have some kind of Bendel "juju" or "voodoo" that warned me of events ahead of time.

To me all these insinuations were a lot of rubbish – I was just lucky to have escaped that evening, while Kanayo and Chisco were just plain unlucky.

With all the rumours making the rounds, I became increasingly isolated until I met Okey a.k.a. "Bongo" towards the end of the third term of Class Four. He had transferred from another school into Dominion College, and he lived in Awka. I gave Okey the nickname Bongo because his bell-bottom trousers swept the ground as he walked along.

Bongo's eldest brother was in the local university and was the "Don" of the deadliest confraternity, the "Black Night Marauders." Everyone in the town of Akwa had heard of "Don Loco" and his exploits. He had single-handedly waged war on three other secret cults and won; the story had it that he disappeared when his back touched the wall during any confrontation.

Bongo would spend hours telling me about the exploits of his brother and his main lieutenants, who had nicknames such as OBT (obtaining by trick), Captain Slaughter, Smallie, Ra Tata, Steel, etc. All these stories were so fascinating; they reminded me of Charlie Lucky Luciano. By this time, I had already made up my mind about what confraternity I would affiliate myself with when I gained admission into the university.

Bongo was also at the receiving end of some harsh punishment from the senior students, whose relatives had had some bad experiences with Don Loco and his crew.

So Bongo and I decided to fight back – and the Dominion College Mafia (DCM) was born on the 22nd of October 1988.

Chapter 7

For DCM to have the bite, reputation and sense of invincibility we needed, Bongo and I knew that we needed more bodies and like-minded people to join us. We agreed that seven was the maximum number of members that we needed; we wanted to recruit from the bunch of disgruntled students who had no love for ECC, some teachers, and some belligerent senior students.

Within two weeks of forming DCM, we were officially seven in number: Olisa my old mate, BBC (Born before Christ), Johnny a.k.a. "the good," Juggernaut, Big Joe, Bongo and I. We took an oath of secrecy and allegiance on the Holy Bible in the middle of the night, and our motto was, "All for one and one for all."

Our *modus operandi* was to choose a target, which could be anything or anybody, strike swiftly, and leave a calling card, just to add a cloud of invincibility and mystery.

Our first target was a human by the name of Jude Arinze, and he was the senior food prefect in Class Six. Jude was rude, harsh and obnoxious, and he took pleasure in abasing other students, because he knew that he had control over the food. The best thing about this target was that he was the younger brother of a former food prefect – the very same one who had slapped me on my first day at Dominion College. Who said that revenge was not sweetest when served very cold?

We were to trail our target for one weekend, find out the pattern of his movements, and then hit him swiftly and disappear. BBC and Bongo were to trail him and report to the rest of us; based on the report, we could map out our strategy to carry out the hit.

We learned that Jude normally had a wash in the shower rooms around 7:15 pm, just before prep time. We therefore targeted him early one Sunday evening. Three gang members went to take him out, two acted as spotters on guard, and the remaining two blended in with ongoing activities in the vicinity.

Jude didn't know what had hit him as he struck the shower room floor; he was beaten black and blue, and then lashed with a cane until he lay motionless. We wrote the initials DCM with Jude's blood on the shower room wall and dispersed silently under the cover of the night.

There was chaos and fear on Monday morning as people heard what had happened to Jude. A student had found him as he crawled out of the shower room covered in blood, and the alarm was raised. He had been rushed to the school infirmary and then to the hospital the same night.

Rumours began to fly around the school that external mercenaries had hit Jude. Some said that it was his fellow classmates that had set him up, others said that it was the deputy food prefect who wanted to assume his position.

Few people were sympathetic to Jude's situation, but understandably, the other prefects had to show solidarity towards their wounded colleague.

The following Monday's assembly was different; all the teachers and school prefects stood surrounding the upper and lower quadrangles. The question on everybody's lips was, "Who are these DCM people?"

ECC came into the assembly ground looking expressionless, and as I stood there observing the whole atmosphere, I could not help but try to glean what was going through ECC's big head.

"Who are these DCM people? I want answers now," he barked. "We are not going to have any classes today until we get to the bottom of this senseless and evil attack on a good and conscientious student." ECC continued, "We are going to deploy both spiritual and physical resources to get to the bottom of this malicious act."

I could feel a smile gently playing on my lips as I listened to the ranting of this toothless bulldog that had no clue what had happened. I looked across to where Bongo was standing and gave him a knowing wink. The so-called investigation and interrogation lasted the whole day and nothing came of it.

The general message was that we should all keep our eyes open and be vigilant; we were encouraged to report any suspicious movement or activities on the school premises. It took about four days for things to settle down, and Jude came back to school after two weeks off, looking subdued. He gave up his position as the senior food prefect and became a day student.

We planned our next attack, and this time we were going after the big fish himself – well, not him personally, but his prized possession. ECC's white Peugeot 404 was our next target. We vandalised the car under the cover of the night, slashed all four tyres and wrote the initials DCM on the windshield.

ECC was furious and distraught; he could not fathom where this attack was coming from, and decided to buy a dog and employ a security guard for his house.

The DCM held Dominion College in its sway; it raided the school poultry, the canteen, the Chemistry and Physics labs, the kitchen, the chapel. A number of teachers also suffered at the hands of the DCM hit squad.

Bongo and I became inseparable; we were both in Class Five now and we were already making plans for life outside secondary school. We both knew which confraternity we were going to enlist in at university. I occasionally went to Bongo's house on weekends, and this was how I met the great Don Loco.

"Don Loco" came into the living room where I was hanging out with Bongo, and we both extended our greetings to him. Bongo introduced me to his brother, he extended his hand for a handshake, and I grabbed his outstretched hand with both of mine in total admiration.

"O boy how you dey, my brother dey talk about you well well," Don Loco said to me in Pidgin English. "*I dey fine bros,*" I replied. "Make sure you guys study hard and don't join bad company ooo." He did not wait for a reply before heading for the exit.

I stood there in awe of the legendary Don Loco. If he had asked me for my kidney, I would have offered it up to him willingly. Bongo later informed me that Don Loco and some of his henchmen were in the boys' quarters chilling out.

We lay in wait at a window that gave a good view of the entrance to the boys' quarters, and after a forty-five-minute wait, we saw Don Loco and three others come out of the building. Bongo pointed out Smallie, Ra Tata and Captain Slaughter to me.

Of the four, Captain Slaughter was the most menacing-looking. He was about six foot two inches tall with a scar running from his cheek to his mouth, and he walked with a limp. He had this dead and ghostly look about him, and his eyes were red.

Smallie on the other hand was smallish and very chatty; staring from the window, I could see him talking and gesticulating. Rumour had it that he was the cause of most of the problems on campus; he had the heart of a lion, and his favourite mantra was, "a match stick is small but you cannot light it and put it in your pocket."

Ra Tata was a nondescript-looking fellow of average height and build. He was a good boy gone bad; he had been first-class material in his first year at university, until he veered off track. His nickname came from his love for handling guns: he was a trigger-happy fellow and could handle any weapon with ease.

Bongo was now one of my two closest pals, since Kanayo and Chisco had been expelled; the other was Big Joe. Big Joe, as he was fondly called, was big, tall and handsome, towering over us all. And he knew how to dance – in fact, he was born to dance.

Big Joe was born Joseph Halim in Brooklyn, USA. He was the youngest of three boys. His father had been an ambassador to the USA and Big Joe had spent his early life going from one private school to another. His father had eventually become fed up with his truancy and repatriated him to Nigeria to continue his education, aiming to give him a reality check and plenty of discipline.

Everybody wanted Big Joe at their party, because he was the life and soul of every gathering. He had presence, and once he started to dance, everybody became mesmerised. Big Joe taught me many moves such as the camel walk, the shuffle, the running man, and the crazy legs.

When songs like 'Every little step' by Bobby Brown, 'Dial my heart' by The Boys, 'Sensitivity' by Ralph Tresvant, 'Jump' by Kris Cross and raps by Warren G,

Dr Dre and Digital Underground were playing at a party, people forgot about the music and concentrated on Big Joe and me.

He was always full of stories about life in the USA, and had never entirely forgiven his father for sending him back to Nigeria and messing up his life. Big Joe was also a master at fables and embellishment. I remember him recounting an incident that happened in a top New York hotel. He said that he had walked up to the reception desk to make an enquiry when his wallet fell to the floor. As he bent down to pick it up, someone else had already picked it up for him; and guess who it was? It was Eddie Murphy.

Big Joe had money to burn: he got money off his divorced father, he got money off his mother, and he got money off his eldest brother who was a US Marine.

Big Joe, Bongo and I had little time for school food – we always ate at restaurants outside the school premises. Our favourite joint was called AZ restaurant. Madam AZ offered all types of African dishes, her portions were generous, and as we were her regular customers, she would give us extra food free of charge.

Madam AZ had a beautiful daughter, who took a huge fancy to Big Joe and his many stories. Her crush on Big Joe got us more free food when she was serving. On one occasion, I heard Big Joe telling her that he could organise an American visa for her and take her on holiday with him.

One early morning in the year of 1989, Big Joe and I were on our way back from a party at the Palace hotel.

As we approached the College from the East side of the walled fence, we were accosted by a group of locals, known as 'the neighbourhood vigilante'. Their job was to keep the neighbourhood safe from hoodlums and local boys, and they were armed with locally made guns, machetes, hand axes and charms.

The 'happening boys' at Dominion College had a good working relationship with this group, as we normally sorted them out with drinks and money. I personally knew the leader of the group, known as Baba Shoky, an ex-army Corporal.

However, the group that accosted us that day were different from the ones we knew and had in our pockets. I told them that I knew their leader, and that Baba Shoky was my Oga. Mentioning Baba Shoky's name was a big mistake as apparently there had been a nasty power struggle between the different groups. Baba Shoky was currently in the hospital, suffering from bullet wounds and lacerations.

Big Joe and I suffered the beating of our young lives from this group; slaps and blows rained down on us from all angles. After what seemed like an eternity, the beating stopped and we were made to lie with our faces pushed into the dusty road before we were interrogated by them.

When they finally realised that we were students of the College, they released us, but we were given a stern warning never to cross their path again. In addition, the money in our pockets was taken from us.

Our challenge now was getting back into the school compound without drawing attention to ourselves. We looked like people who had been in the boxing ring with Mike Tyson; secondly, we were not dressed in our daywear, but rather in dusty party wear; thirdly, Assembly was about to commence and the school compound would be crawling with prefects and teachers.

It was even more risky to walk about the streets looking the way we did. A teacher or parent passing by could easily spot us. We decided to take shelter in a half-constructed building not far from the College, but a mad man who had taken possession of the place had us moving again.

We decided to brave it and enter the College compound by jumping over the fence on the South side. We successfully cleared the tricky fence after many attempts, no thanks to Big Joe; we made our way towards our secret hideout, where we collected our daywear, hurriedly changed into it, and headed towards the dorms.

We knew that there was no way we could walk into the classroom in our daywear and looking this rough, so we decided to hide behind Azikiwe hostel until break time, which was at about 1 pm.

It was about 11:15 am when we heard a loud voice behind us asking, *"This boys wetin una dey do for here?"* We turned around in horror to see Book the gate man coming for us, and we took off running for our dear lives – right into the waiting hands of the senior school disciplinarian.

We tried to explain ourselves to him, but he was not buying any of our explanations. We were marched straight to the office of Mr Uba, who was in charge of the school because ECC was on annual leave.

Mr Uba looked at us in total disbelief when we told him that we had been attacked by unidentified people while we slept in our beds, and that was why we had overslept. He ordered that we fetch our machete, go down to the lower field and start cutting a portion of the grass under the supervision of the disciplinarian, until we could recollect what had happened to us.

We spent the whole afternoon in the lower field cutting grass until the great bell rang to mark the end of school. We were summoned to Mr Uba's office again, but we still stuck to our incredible story of what happened. Mr Uba spent a few minutes in silence before suspending us from school until we brought our parents to meet with him for a discussion.

We were asked to go to our hostels and pack some belongings before going home. Suspension was not a good outcome, but it was better than being expelled; and we knew that if we had told Mr Uba what had really happened, that would have been our fate.

Big Joe had no choice but to go and get his guardian, as his father, who was well known to the school authorities, was currently in the USA.

I could not go home to tell my very busy father that I had been suspended from school. If I had, it would have been a first occurrence in the family history, never to be forgiven. So I left the school compound and went to Olisa's family house in town. I knew that I could not stay there for long and needed to come up with a plan quickly.

The great master plan eventually came from Nonso during our brain-storming session. Nonso was Olisa's cousin. He asked me if Mr Uba knew my father in person; when I answered no, he suggested that I rent a father for the day. *"What a genius,"* I thought, *"Now where do we find an adult that would be willing to pose as my father?"*

We decided to approach Olisa's uncle, who was an Okada rider (bike man) with seven children and always broke. He agreed to go with me to school to pose as my father, so long as I settled him very well. I gave him some family details and we did some role-playing to see how real and convincing he would look in front of Mr Uba.

As we entered Mr Uba's office the next day at 2 pm, he got up to shake my rented 'father's' hand, and introduced himself as the Deputy Principal. He then proceeded to tell my 'father' what had happened and why I had been suspended, adding that all he wanted was the truth from me as to what had actually happened on that fateful day.

I maintained my unbelievable story about what had happened, but before I could finish my story, my rented 'father' jumped up from his chair and gave me a resounding slap across the face. This action took me by surprise and the shock nearly knocked me off my feet;

but I exaggerated the whole scene even further, and threw myself across Mr Uba's table screaming for help.

My rented 'father' was now shouting insults at me and swearing that he would disown me that very day. I could see disbelief written over Mr Uba's face as he watched the extreme reaction of my 'father'. Mr Uba quickly stepped in to pacify him. "Sir, you know that boys will always be boys and they are very boisterous; I will allow him back into school, and I will personally keep an eye on him," he suggested.

"Thank you," my 'father' said to Mr Uba, and then he turned to me and said, "This is your last chance, and the next time I hear any negative report about you, I will skin you alive."

"Yes, sir," I replied as I stepped out of Mr Uba's office; after about five minutes, my rented 'father' joined me. I did not utter one word to him until we got to Olisa's house, where I exploded, "*Why you go slap me like that, that was not part of our role play ooo?*" I added angrily, "In fact for that slap, I will reduce the amount that I was going to pay you, I get to go buy Panadol for the headache from the slap."

"*We get to make am look real if not the teacher fit pick sey na wayo, but you must give me my money complete,*" replied Olisa's uncle. I paid up in full, packed my bags, and headed back to the College.

Big Joe was back as well, and we both kept a low profile for about two weeks before things went back to normal.

It was time for the DCM to choose another target and, without further contemplation, we chose Simon Okafor, the senior school disciplinarian, a.k.a. 'Shot put'. This target was a tricky one, because Simon was built like an ox and was known to have been attacked by four people only to leave his would-be attackers very much the worse for wear.

There was no way we could take on Simon physically and win; rather, we decided to attack him in a different way. We waited until lights out before approaching the Class Six classrooms, where we located Simon's desk, which contained all his textbooks and term papers.

Big Joe and I quietly carried the desk out of the classroom, while Juggernaut kept watch. We then headed towards the lower field, where Johnny, BBC and Bongo were waiting with buckets of water. We proceeded to fill the desk with three buckets of water, before carving the initials DCM on the wooden surface.

Simon's desk was discovered at noon the next day, his textbooks and notes all ruined. It was a bad blow to Simon, as he really needed this material for his final senior secondary examinations.

At about 2 pm that afternoon, the great bell started ringing to gather all the students together. ECC was furious as he narrated the situation. He called Simon up to the platform for everybody to see how much he had been affected by the prank. Simon looked like a goat that had been eviscerated, like a bulldog that had had all its teeth pulled out. Yet I felt no compassion for him.

The College had to purchase second-hand textbooks for Simon, and notes from different subjects were photocopied in time for him to start preparing for his final exams.

DCM now had to suspend all attacks as the exams were fast approaching and passing them was important. I had to get through these exams to proceed to Class Six.

We had one week of exams and then it was holiday time –we were all looking forward to coming back to College as Class Six seniors.

Chapter 8

I had known Victoria since she was 8 years old; she was the shy girl next door, the younger sister of my pal Toma. Over the years, I had seen her grow from a shy little girl to a confident blossoming flower. She was now 13 years old and was developing some feminine curves and attributes.

My long-distance relationship with Amaka was beginning to fizzle out, especially with Kanayo not being in the mix any more. I had spoken to Kanayo on a few occasions and he was now doing well at his new school. I had considered passing through Benin on my way to Awka to see Kanayo and hook up with Amaka, but the opportunity had never materialised.

One fateful Saturday evening, I was on the tennis court playing a competitive tennis set, when Victoria came over to the tennis court to watch me demolish my opponent. She sat down on the lawn close to the tennis court and watched the game; I could feel her penetrating eyes on me and I could not help doing some showboating.

After the set was over, I went over to where she was sitting; she looked extremely pretty. Tall for her age and dark-skinned, she had the most mesmerising eyes that I had ever seen. I could not believe that this was little Victoria.

"Was that performance for my benefit?" she asked. "Of course not, I play like that all the time," I replied. "You were not playing like that when I was watching you two days ago from afar," she replied. I enquired jokingly, "Victoria, are you now spying on me, or are you a stalker?"

She looked at me with those lovely eyes and I was sucked into them, and for a couple of minutes the whole world stood still. Her smile was captivating and transported me to a place from which I never wanted to come back. I was dumbfounded and could no longer help but to comment on her beautiful and innocent smile.

"I have got something for you," she said as she got up and handed me a sealed envelope. "What is this?" I asked. "You will find out in good time. But I have to go home now to help out with the evening meal – see you soon," she said as she set off on her way.

I stood there for about five minutes with the sealed envelope in my hand, not sure whether to open it now or later. I decided to open the letter in the privacy of my bedroom, and I could not believe my eyes as I read its contents; the more I read, the more I felt cool.

Victoria had written the most beautiful love letter to me, describing how she had always had a crush on me, lying awake in her bed at night thinking about me. She wanted me to be her first and her last lover; she wanted to be the mother of my children, and would love me until her last day.

Waoo, this letter had just knocked me for six, and I sat there motionless. After a couple of minutes, I could easily foresee the challenges ahead. Firstly – Victoria was my pal's younger sister and he was very protective of her; secondly – Toma and I shared most of our escapades with girls; and thirdly – Victoria was the only girl in a family of six.

I tried to avoid Victoria for as long as I could, and I even stopped going to their house to see Toma. Toma was unsure what was happening and he thought that he had offended me in some way. We still met up on the tennis court or the football field, but I always declined an invitation back to his place.

It was inevitable that Victoria and I would cross paths sooner or later, and it happened one Sunday evening as I was walking home after the evening mass at the local Catholic Church. Victoria was on her way back from her tutorial classes and we ran into each other at the gate.

There was no place to hide and as I stood face to face with her, she looked at me with a cheeky smile on her face and said, "I have not seen you for some time; did my open confession scare you off?" I replied, "Are you kidding me, I have been waiting for the right time to talk to you."

"Ok, you see me now, start talking," she said with her hands on her hips. I had outgrown my shyness many moons ago, but I could feel myself blushing; I knew that I had to give her an answer right there.

"Victoria, you are my friend's younger sister and you are like my own sister; how is this going to work?" I asked her. "No one needs to know but the two of us," she replied. I looked at the dark-skinned, beautiful and confident girl standing in front of me with her hands on her hips, and all of a sudden, "little Victoria" just disappeared into thin air and I longed to hold her in my arms right there.

My secret relationship with Victoria was born on that evening; I was almost four years older than she was and definitely more sexually experienced than she was. She was, unsurprisingly, a virgin, and drew most of her romantic experiences from the novels that she read, such as Mills and Boon.

Victoria looked up to me as I was her first true love, and she would want to do things to please me. I did not want to take advantage of her. She knew that I had been sexually active and begged me not to cheat on her; she wanted to lose her virginity to me. I promised to stay faithful to her and I meant it, because I only had eyes for her.

I had the bedroom to myself now, as my elder siblings were away at university and my younger brother had now temporarily occupied my sister's bedroom. There was also a backup room in the boys' quarters for any quick action– the same room that Toma and I had often used for our many escapades.

I met up with Victoria at our usual rendezvous spot under the mango tree, and I led her through the back bush path behind my house to the boys' quarters, and into the room. This was the day that the fairy-tale would become reality; she was looking beautiful in her blouse and shorts.

There was passion in the air and we could not keep our hands off each other. She was following my lead as the more experienced maestro, and I was leading the orchestra brilliantly. We were both naked and caught up in sweet sensation when all of a sudden she pushed me aside and jumped up from the bed.

I was shocked and taken aback. "What is the matter?" I muttered, "Are you OK?" She looked at me with fear in her beautiful eyes and said. "Remy, I am not ready – *I am scared.*"

I looked at her in total amazement and disbelief. This was not what I had bargained for; I was upset, but worse still, I was in clear discomfort with my member at full alert and ready to do battle.

"Remy – I am frightened," she said again with tears beginning to flow down her cheeks. I felt compassion for her, and I was no longer worried about my sexual desire. I took her in my arms and held her close, until she stopped crying and fell asleep. As I lay there, my mind was beginning to work overtime. I felt somewhat trapped; I adored Victoria, but I could not help but wonder if all this aggro was worth it.

Victoria and I kept seeing each other secretly, but we were very careful around Toma, as we did not want to arouse any suspicion. The stolen moments we spent together were priceless, and I looked forward to them; but every time it came to sex, she would quickly become frigid and it was becoming frustrating.

One cool Saturday evening, I was hanging out with Toma and Ejiro at Mama Tess's local beer parlour. We had already spent about thirty minutes drinking the local brew of sweet palm wine and eating some fried bush meat, when Tess walked in.

Tess was the eldest daughter of Mama Tess; she was about twenty years old, and had just gained admission into one of the Federal Polytechnics. She was not the most beautiful girl around but she was very attractive, with curves in all the right places.

Tess's father had remarried after his divorce from her mother. He had no contact with Tess and her siblings, so Mama Tess was the sole breadwinner, and had to run a beer parlour to supplement her day job as a nurse.

Tess had realised at a relatively young age that she had something that men wanted; and she was quick to exploit all her attributes towards helping her family financially.

"Tessy babe," hailed Ejiro, "How far now, you are looking really sweet today and your jeans *na one in town ooo*," he flattered her.

"Thank you, Ejiro, how are you, Toma, how your people?" Tess asked. "They are fine," Toma replied. "Have you met my guy Remy before?"

"No," replied Tess, "You guys refused to introduce me to the fine bobo," she said teasingly.

"Hello," I said and extended my hand for a handshake. We shook hands and everyone sat down to have a good long chat. I could not help but notice how attractive Tess was; and she was very touchy feely towards me, and I was not complaining.

I found myself spending more time at Mama Tess's, and Tess was always very delightful and hospitable. We could spend several hours discussing our lives and current events. Tess was becoming very comfortable with me, and she would open up to me about the many men she had dated for money. I was not there to judge her.

One evening at about 7 pm, barely two weeks after I had first met Tess, we were sitting in her mother's joint as usual talking about various events when I noticed that Tess was staring at my lips. I stopped talking and felt a bit uncomfortable, so I asked her why she was staring at my lips.

"You have the most amazing and kissable lips that I have ever seen," she said. "I feel like kissing you right now." Without warning, she leaned forward and kissed me fully on the lips. That was the "very kiss" – I was catapulted from Asaba to London, and I did not even need a visa to travel.

This was the beginning of a steamy and passionate romance with Tess; and whenever we got physically intimate, it was fireworks all the way. She taught me things that I had never known existed, both inside and outside the bedroom; I was living the life.

At this time, Victoria was beginning to notice the changes in me, as I was no longer interested in initiating any intimate contact with her. I was always ready to come up with excuses to dash off to see my hot and luscious Tess.

I was in a quagmire, caught between the young, beautiful and naive Victoria and the luscious, passionate, wild and interesting Tess – each in her own way wanting to please me. This was a position that many young men would have loved to be in, but it was fast becoming a dilemma for me.

I decided to confide in Tess, who was very objective about my dilemma. I knew that I had to do the right thing and end it with Victoria, because I was not ready to give up the mind-blowing romance that I was having with Tess.

I was meaning to tell Victoria about putting a break to our relationship, but she mistakenly heard Toma at home discussing my affair with Tess with a mutual friend.

In all my years of knowing Victoria, I had never seen her angry; she was very good at keeping her emotions in check but that day, all hell broke loose. As I came back from football practice, she accosted me with venom in her eyes and demanded an explanation.

I tried to explain to her that I loved her too much to want to put her in this situation, but she was having none of that. "Is it because of the sex?" she enquired. "So Tess is blowing your mind with wild sex; I am ready to give up my virginity to you. Please do not leave me," she sobbed.

I looked at her and I could not even begin to comprehend what emotional tumult she was going through right now. "Victoria," I said, and tried to reach out for her; but she recoiled from me and turned her back. As she walked away from where I stood, I could hear her speaking through her sobs. "You belong to me, Remy, and I am going to fight for my knight in shining armour."

"O boy," I said to myself, *"Not this Mills and Boon garbage again, I am not a knight and secondly, I do not go around in shining armour."*

I must confess that I did not like how this situation had played out; I would rather have gone about it in a more diplomatic and tactful way. But it had happened, and I now needed to pick up the pieces.

For a couple of days, Victoria kept out of sight. I casually asked Toma about his sister and he just murmured something about her having a little girl's crush on the musical group called The New Edition. If only he knew that it was more than a crush on a band.

I had less than two weeks of my school holidays left and I was gradually getting ready for the start of Class Six. One day, after going out on an errand with Sunny, I was driving back with him in the passenger's seat when I caught sight of Victoria having words with Tess in front of the senior lecturer's quarters.

"*What is going on?*" I asked myself as I drove past them towards home. My mind kept racing back to what kind of conversation could transpire between my two love interests.

As I approached Mama Tess's beer parlour later that evening, I could see Tess sitting in front of the building and gazing into the distance. "Hello beautiful," I said, wrapping my arms around her, "What have you been up to today?" I asked innocently.

"Do you really want to know what I have been up to?" she sneered, "Well, I have been spending some quality time with your little girlfriend," she said sarcastically. "You're kidding me," I said, feigning ignorance, "What did she want with you?" I asked with a quizzical look on my face.

"Well, Remy, let me put it this way, you need to go and sort out any unfinished business with her ooo, because I don't want any small pickin to come and insult me oooo," Tess replied. "Tess babe, cool down, I will sort it out sharp," I assured her.

"So what did she want?" I persisted. Tess answered, "Well let me put it this way, she loves you and wanted to know if I was just using you for a fling."

"So what did you say to her?" I asked suspiciously. "Well, I told her that I was just having my wicked way with you and after I had finished with you, she could have you back – that is, if there is any part of you left to salvage," Tess said with a cheeky grin before jumping on me laughing.

I got home that evening to the sad news of the passing away of my maternal grandfather. This was the second time in my young life that I had had to deal with death. The first time was when a classmate of mine called Courage had died from a complication of sickle cell anaemia at age thirteen, in Class Three. It was always sad to lose someone that you know well; Courage used to sit to my right while Kanayo sat on my left.

My grandfather had been a local headmaster, and had fourteen children with three wives. He also had countless grandchildren. The last time I saw him was in the hospital, where he was suffering from swollen feet caused by water retention in his kidneys.

He had been a very prominent member of his local community, one of the first people to build a two-storey building made of mud. He was a strict disciplinarian and you dared not cross his path. He was not a very friendly man, and I had never looked forward to visiting him as a child because he was no fun.

The burial was to take place in about two months' time, to allow most of his children and grandchildren to gather for the ceremony.

I went back to school four days later, not having dealt with the Victoria issue. I was hoping that it would resolve itself, with Victoria moving on and forgetting about me.

Chapter 9

Going back to school for my final year at Dominion College was exciting and a relief at the same time – exciting in the sense that it was my final year in college, and a relief because I was away from the grieving atmosphere at home and the complications of my love triangle.

I became the school sports prefect, and my duties included making sure that as many students as possible participated in as many sports activities as were available. Dominion College was not known for participating in more than a handful of sporting activities. I was determined to introduce new activities to the college and make sure that the existing ones received adequate attention.

Our biggest challenge was not human resources, but financial resources. ECC was not interested in channelling funds towards sports, although he was quick to bask in the glory of any sporting achievement by the students.

The football teams had started playing with their bare feet, and the number of practice footballs had dwindled. We were now resorting to patching up punctured footballs; this would have been unheard of during Father Uka's era.

One game that I wanted to re-introduce was basketball. The original court was overgrown with grass, and was currently used as a rubbish dump. My plan was to have the rubbish cleared and the court weeded before reinstalling the hoops.

The Lagos crew were ecstatic about this plan, and were happy to contribute the basketballs and help in the refurbishment of the court. It took forever to get the approval from ECC but it came, with the help of the games master.

We swung into action and within a fortnight, we had a near-decent basketball court; the Lagos boys were actively involved in the game, and became the kings of the court.

Meanwhile, the lawn tennis court had potholes, the net was riddled with holes and a game of tennis could take forever, as it was commonplace to witness arguments during a game as to whether the ball had passed over or under the net.

The funds for refurbishing the tennis court and replacing the net were not forthcoming, so we had to improvise. We used ropes to knit together the numerous holes in the net, and we filled the potholes in the court with a mixture of sand and cement. We managed to restore all the lines with the free paint that we got from the paint market.

The tennis court still had some irregular patches, but it was far better than its previous state and we were happy enough with the outcome.

Being a senior student was fun, as you were no longer at the receiving end of things. You had a school son or sons who did all your chores for you, such as washing your clothes, passing your plate, making your bed, and fetching your water. In return, you looked out for their welfare by protecting them from the other seniors and harsh punishment.

I did not have one particular school son since I usually hijacked any junior student available to run errands for me, until I met Bede. Bede was in Class Two and had run a few errands for me. I could not help but notice that he always had a smile on his face, and that his bubbly disposition was infectious.

I was taken aback on one particular hot Saturday afternoon when I noticed a human figure lying face down in the lower quadrangle under the blistering sun. He was sweating profusely, and crying his eyes out. I approached him to make sure that my eyes were not deceiving me – and behold, it was Bede. I had never seen this usually cheerful boy crying.

He told me that a Class Five student was punishing him. I was livid with rage when he told me the nature of his supposed offence. Ugo had asked him to run an errand for him; he had politely informed Ugo that he was on his way to run an errand for me, and for this had been punished. I asked him to get up and go have a wash, and report to my cubicle.

By the time Bede came to my cubicle, Ugo was lying face down under my bed after suffering some harsh drilling from Bongo and me. He was charged on two counts: one, for punishing Bede in the manner that he had done, and two, for having the effrontery to disdain my authority.

I took Bede under my wing and gave him my full protection from other senior students. They never bothered him again, because they knew that they would have to contend with me.

As the games prefect, I was not on the same pedestal or echelon as the school senior prefect and some other major prefects, but my influence was far-reaching and nothing happened in the school without my knowledge; Bongo was my ever-trusted lieutenant.

When some of the school prefects planned a raid on all the Class Four and Five boarding house students at midnight, I was one of the main architects. I was seen as an inspirational figure, and would always stand my ground no matter the consequences. I had always had a gift with words and oratory, and I had no problem convincing and influencing people to follow my line of reasoning.

Albert, who was the school's senior disciplinarian, approached me on one particular evening after games for a very important meeting with some other prefects. I had heard some rumours flying around about a certain prefect, but I had not given much thought to them.

As I entered Albert's cubicle, there was an air of tension, seriousness and anger in the room. I looked around; I knew everybody in the room except for a handsome junior student who was standing at one end of the small room.

"What is going on here?" I asked suspiciously. "Come in and close the door," said Albert. There were two other prefects in the room. Romanus was the senior sanitarian, while Ebele was the deputy senior prefect.

"Stephen *bu homo*," Albert said in Igbo language. The directness of the statement hit me like a sledgehammer; but I was careful to respond. "That is a rumour that has been circulating for quite some time," I said. "This is not a rumour, this is true, he is a homosexual and I can prove it," Albert said definitely.

"So how can you prove it?" I asked him with interest. "He has taken a fancy to my school son over there, and he has propositioned him. Stephen wants him to come to his cubicle tomorrow night during prep time," Albert replied. "Then go to the school authority with this evidence; this is a Catholic school and it is instant expulsion for Stephen if he is found guilty," I said, already knowing the answer to my suggestion.

"No way would we take this to the school authority. Stephen would easily sweet talk his way out of it and we do not have solid evidence yet. It is Stephen's word against Kene's," Albert said angrily.

I had no personal beef with Stephen; however, a number of senior students disliked him. He was the deputy senior refectorian in charge of food. As I had learned many years ago, the person who controlled the food controlled the economy within Dominion College. I had never liked refectorians in general, after my first encounter with one on my first day in the school.

By all indications, Stephen was pious: he was first in line for prayers and had been known to withhold food from students who missed prayers.

"Why am I being involved in this?" I asked. "We need your support and your input as to how to bring this Stephen boy down once and for all," Albert replied. I took time to weigh the situation in my head, and came up with two solutions.

The first solution was to get DCM involved, and take him out cleanly with no questions asked. However, the challenge was that I could not afford to expose the group in relation to this particular issue; I quickly discounted this solution in my head.

I asked Kene to leave the room while we deliberated. "I am going to tell you my mind. If you are happy with it then I am in, if not then I am out," I said. "We need concrete evidence to bring down Stephen, but we need to use Kene as the bait."

"There is no way I am going to allow Kene anywhere close to that monster," Albert shouted. I looked him straight in the face and said, "You have no evidence against him, period." Romanus then interrupted saying, "Let us finish hearing what Remy is proposing."

"We have to catch him with his pants down in a compromising position, and then we move in and take care of the rest," I said with all seriousness.

It was about 8 pm the next day when we lay in wait by the side of the building, as Kene went into Stephen's cubicle. We stood there waiting for the signal from Kene; and when the signal finally came at about 8:20 pm, we kicked the door of the cubicle down without any hesitation.

Behold, standing there was Stephen, naked but for his underpants, with Kene sitting on the bed just in his underpants as well. There was no peradventure in this; as we had our hard evidence. We pounced on Stephen and the beating started from the cubicle into the quadrangle. As we dragged him towards the staff quarters, Stephen was pleading and making offers to us ranging from food to money, all to no avail.

We knocked on ECC's door and as he appeared at the door, we handed over Stephen to him and left without a word said. That was the last time we ever saw Stephen at Dominion College. ECC never asked any questions and no explanation was given.

The news of Stephen's departure spread like wildfire and rumours started flying around the school that a teacher called Mr Nworah had inducted Stephen into homosexuality; some ignorant ones said that it ran in his family lineage.

No one knew what made Stephen become a homosexual, but in our young and naive minds it was an unacceptable taboo. To date, no one knows the whereabouts of Stephen Madu, but I was sure beyond any doubt that he was not the only homosexual in Dominion College.

Chapter 10

Time had passed quickly, and we had one month left before our final Senior Secondary School Examination. This was a big deal for all the Class Six students. We had all handed over our prefect roles to the Class Five students and were concentrating on the forthcoming examination.

We sat various mock exams in preparation for the final examination and when it came, it lasted for twelve days and it was intense. After the last paper, there was a huge fanfare and celebration to mark the end of secondary school.

I left Dominion College for the last time in the year 1990 and went back to Asaba for two weeks' rest, before beginning my preparation for the University Entrance Examination, known as JAMB (Joint Admission Matriculation Board).

The JAMB comprised four modules depending on what university course you wanted to study. I was looking to get into university to study Accountancy and was focusing on Maths, English, Economics and Literature.

I joined a tutorial class to help me prepare for the competitive examination that was due in about four months' time. I was determined to get into university on my first attempt, as I knew the repercussions of staying in the same house with my father for another year to re-sit this exam. I was not keen on contemplating this fate.

Toma's father had moved to Benin to take up a position at the University of Benin, and his family had relocated there. Victoria had sent me a letter via Sunny to inform me about the move, confessing that I would always have a special place in her heart even though I had hurt her. She was going to send me her new home address and school address as soon as she had settled down.

Tess was currently in her first year at the Polytechnic and was preparing to take the JAMB examination the same year to get into university.

It was during a tutorial class in Economics that I saw Ifey for the first time. She stepped into the lecture room, and immediately owned the room. Even the Economics teacher had to stammer twice, could not keep his eyes off her, and kept referring to the new girl in class.

She was pretty, light-skinned, and dressed in an ostentatious manner; everything about her oozed class and panache. I knew from the moment I set eyes on her that she was going to be a much-welcomed distraction.

Most of the people attending the tutorial were falling over each other for her attention, but I deliberately ignored her. I had learnt from experience that when you ignore a pretty girl and go against the grain, you arouse her curiosity.

I discovered that Ifey and I were taking the same modules, and I made sure that I came across as an intelligent chap in the classroom. I was quick to answer questions and deliberately read ahead of the syllabus to impress her.

I started to notice that Ifey was drawing closer to me; she began by reserving a seat for me close to her, suggesting that we do extra studies together. She started joining me at the canteen for drinks, and our conversations were becoming longer and personal.

I had also seen her hanging out with another chap in our tutorial class called Valentine. Valentine was a good dresser, like me and he had a reputation as a ladies' man, like me; but I was not going to lose this battle.

I had a joker up my sleeve and I was now ready to show my hand. I arranged for Sunny to come and pick me up after tutorial classes; he parked the car close to the school bar, gave me the car keys and disappeared into the bar for a drink.

I had been driving secretly for the last two years and I was now proficient. Gone were the days when I had to put a pillow underneath my bum to elevate me to see the road. I was now seventeen and almost six feet tall.

As I drove the grey-coloured Peugeot 505 belonging to my mother to the bus stop where Ifey was waiting, I stopped and offered her a ride home, where she lived with her sister. She jumped into the front seat of the air-conditioned car and we drove away. As I drove past Valentine queuing to get on the bus, I deliberately slowed down to catch a glimpse of the defeat on his face as I drove off into the sunset.

I took Ifey to her sister's flat and she introduced me to her sister. I stayed for a couple of minutes chatting with them before setting out to pick up Sunny at the bar. Ifey and I became an item from that day; and Valentine later became a good pal as well.

Sex with Ifey was amazing, especially after studying. This routine went on until a few days before the exam, when Ifey had to travel back to Lagos to sit for her examination. It was hard letting her go, but she left her contact address and promised to come back.

The JAMB examination was challenging and I knew that Maths could be a sticky point for me; I decided to make up for a possibly poor score in Maths with a very high score in English and Literature.

The JAMB results were not due for another two months; in the interim, my Senior Secondary School Examination results were released and posted to me by Dominion College. My results were good; I had performed well above average, making 2 As, 4 Cs and one pass in Igbo language. This result was good enough for me but not for my father, as my older siblings had performed exceptionally well during their time.

It was torture waiting for the JAMB results; it seemed like an eternity, but I had Tess to keep me company. She was at home for the break and also awaiting her results.

The results finally came out after that long wait, and I had scored 235 points out of 400; this was not a bad result, as it was a pass. However, for the course that I was planning to study, it was not adequate. The cut-off mark for Accountancy at most Federal Universities was a minimum of 260 points.

I had to wait to see if my second- and third-choice universities would take me and if they did not consider me then I was stuffed – it would mean waiting for another year to retake the JAMB. My father was not pleased and he took me to town at every opportunity he had.

My father was a well-known and respected Law Professor and he knew many people in various tertiary institutions; but he was very adamant that he was not going to use any personal influence to get me into a Federal University.

I had to travel regularly to my second- and third-choice universities to see if I could facilitate a quick response. I waited for quite a while before I finally gained admission into my third-choice university, which was a relatively good state university. It was top in the country in Law and Accountancy, but had a frightening reputation as a haven for cultism.

I had one week left to get ready for university and lectures were due to start very soon. I did not have much time on my hands, as there had been a major delay in receiving my admission confirmation. I bought the basic necessities to start with; my father had already arranged to open a bank account for me.

I had a list of books and study materials to buy, so I travelled with Sunny to Onitsha main market to get some of the books. Buying anything from Onitsha was a daunting task; this was the commercial heartbeat of the Eastern part of Nigeria. You could find anything you desired in Onitsha; if you wanted your own brand of soap, you needed only to ask and you would find it at your disposal. I was able to find most of my textbooks at one of the market's major stockists but I was going to procure the rest of my study materials from the university bookshop.

I remember my first day at university as if it was yesterday; I set off from home on the two-hour journey with Sunny. As we approached the massive and impressive university gate, I could not help but feel liberated.

I had already paid for my student accommodation in the boys' hostel and I was looking forward to finding my room and settling in. We drove towards the boys' hostel and parked in front of the gate. I jumped out of the car very excited, and headed with Sunny towards the hostel.

I found out where my room was located, and we headed towards the room. As I entered it, I was hit by a big wave of disappointment; the room that I was standing in was slightly smaller than my prefect's cubicle at Dominion College. I tried to mask my disappointment, but the more I looked around the room with the hope that it would suddenly start to expand, the more apparent my disappointment became.

"Hey, are you the new guy Remy? My name is James and I'm your roommate," said a voice. I turned to look at the speaker. James was about five foot seven inches tall and was light-skinned; he was thick-lipped with an oval-shaped face.

"Yes," I replied, trying harder to hide my disappointment. "This is your bed," James said, patting the top bunk. The room had originally been designed to house two people, but it currently held two double bunks and there were two wardrobes at the far end of the room.

"How many people reside in this room?" I asked, hoping to be proved wrong. "Well, officially two but unofficially four," was the response I got from James.

Sunny helped me for a few minutes as I unpacked, but he had to make a move to commence his two-hour journey back to Asaba. I spent the next two hours unpacking and settling in with the help of James and Wilson, another roommate, who was a third-year Law student with a birthmark on his forehead.

I also met Austin, who occupied the bottom bunk and was built like a bull; he was dark in complexion and was into bodybuilding, keeping his precious dumbbells underneath his bed. Austin was a second-year Political Science student.

James and Wilson went out of their way to take me around the male students' halls of residence; they showed me the toilets, canteen, barber's shop, and cafés. They pointed out where the girls' halls of residence were located and I could see a beehive of activity at the front gate. There were cars of different makes and models parked there with music blaring from high bass speakers.

They took me to Café A, where we had dinner. I opted for the safe choice of rice with stew and dodo, while Wilson and James went for the heavy-duty pounded yam and melon soup. After the meal, James and Wilson expected the new guy (me) to pick up the bill, which I did without a fuss. As we walked back towards the room, both James and Wilson stopped often to introduce me to their friends and neighbours.

Sleep did not come easily that night, and I lay in bed at about 11 pm listening to Austin's deep breathing beneath me. I could not help but cast my mind back over life in general; here I was, an eighteen-year-old boy, alone and far away from home but ready to take on the new challenges ahead.

I could clearly hear my father's voice admonishing me before I set out on my university journey. I could hear him saying, *"The road ahead is tough and you now have the freedom to do whatever you want to do – but remember who you are and the family name you bear, remember that the choices that you make from now on will define your future."*

"Remember that I am not sending you to university to become a member of a secret cult or confraternity. Don't even attempt to

associate with people who are members of the palm wine drinkers' *club, just face your education and God,"* my father had said. *"If* *I hear that you have joined the wrong group and have been* *apprehended by the Police, I will summarily disown you and dash* *you to the government,"* he had finally concluded.

I had stood there listening to my father finish his speech, wishing he knew what was going through my mind. I had always been rebellious, ever since I could remember, and I knew that I was going to be a number one candidate for membership in a secret cult.

Sleep finally came with the sweet and exciting thought of Tess; she had not been successful in getting a place in university, but she was adamant that she would keep trying until success came.

I was awoken by Austin's alarm going off; I looked at the wall clock and the time was 7:30 am. It was Monday morning and my first lecture was to start at 9 am sharp. I jumped out of bed and headed to the shower room. On my way, I saw a number of students carrying buckets. *"That is strange," I said* to myself. I got into the shower cubicle, took off my towel, and turned on the shower regulator; and to my shock and horror, there was no water coming out. Now I understood why people were carrying buckets: the showers had not worked in the last twelve months.

I somehow made it in time for my first lecture, and as I approached the lecture hall, I could not believe my eyes. The hall was packed full and overflowing; there were people standing outside the hall and trying to get a glimpse of the writing board and the lecturer through the window. People were trying to take notes while standing on top of tables and chairs.

I managed to squeeze through one of the doors, but it was like a jungle in the room. The room was stuffy and the air was polluted with various body odours. "*How are undergraduates supposed to learn under these conditions?*" I thought. "*I should have scored a higher mark in the JAMB and gone to a better university,*" I berated myself.

I was in the Faculty of Social Sciences and we were due to move to our permanent lecture theatre, so we had to endure three more weeks of stuffy lecture conditions. The move to our new 200-seater lecture theatre was a dream come true, and we could now sit comfortably and listen attentively.

It was during one of my elective courses that I had my first encounter with Osato, a.k.a. "Makosa," a.k.a. "Portoholo"; he reminded me ever so much of Kanayo and Bongo rolled into one, and my gut feeling warned me that he was a necessary evil that I had to know and endure.

Osato walked into the lecture hall through the back entrance about fifteen minutes late, and the lecturer decided to make an example of him. "Hey young man, are you a member of this class?" he asked. "Yes sir," replied Osato. "So why are you late to my class?" enquired the lecturer. "I lost my way," replied Osato. The lecturer looked at Osato for a few seconds, and Osato looked back at him with a frown on his face in a confrontational manner. "Don't ever turn up late to any of my classes again and that goes for all of you in this hall," the lecturer said and continued with his teaching.

I looked over to where Osato was sitting and we made eye contact. His eyes were as cold as the eyes of a Jaguar and they looked straight through me, and this sent a shiver up my spine. After the lecture had ended, we all started filing out of the lecture hall and as I walked towards the canteen, I could see Osato coming up beside me from the corner of my right eye.

"O boy, how you dey, my name is Osato and my friends call me Makosa but my enemies call me Portoholo." We shook hands and I introduced myself, "My name is Remy and I guess both my friends and enemies call me Remy," I said with a cheeky grin.

Osato and I became friends and we started hanging out and sitting together during classes. Osato was a guy of medium build with a slightly oversized head; he was rather hyperactive and boisterous. He had the potential to be a sadist and the tendency to be a misogynist. He was also living in the students' hall of residence, and his block was behind mine, so there was no getting away from "Makosa."

Then there was Cyril. The name Cyril, a.k.a. "Don CY" conjured fear in the hearts of lesser mortals on campus. He was a thickset guy with well-built muscles and he had a gap between his front teeth. He was supposed to have graduated two years ago from the Law Faculty, but he had been rusticated for secret cult activities. It was rumoured that the Police had caught him with a human skull during a confraternity initiation.

He had been arrested by the Police and kept in detention for three months, after which he had been arraigned before the University Senate and rusticated for two years.

On his return to the university, Don CY had to sign an undertaking of good behaviour and non-involvement in any nefarious activity on campus. His reputation had preceded him. Students were falling over each other to have him on their side, and it was common to see people queuing up to buy him food and drinks in return for his protection. Don CY was the former Capo of the Mafioso family, and he still held much sway and influence on campus.

I remember buying him food and drinks a few times, and he would always thank me and ask after my roommate James. I heard that in his heyday as the Capo, you dared not enter the shower room when he was having his shower, and he had two bodyguards with him at all times.

I was in awe of Don CY, fascinated by the respect and homage paid to him; but I had already made up my mind that I was destined to join the Black Night Marauders. I knew that they were active on campus, but I did not know how to make contact.

I ran into Dan, who had been two years my senior at Dominion College, one Tuesday afternoon after lectures when I was on my way to the café. He was so glad to see me that he invited me back to his room off campus. He lived in a boys' quarters about fifteen minutes from campus, and his room was nicely furnished with a television, a fridge and a good sound system. He warmed up some food cooked by his babe, while we talked about the good old days and secondary school. Dan cautioned me about the perils of belonging to any gang on campus and warned me to steer clear of the confraternities.

I visited Dan regularly, and he would check up on me on campus. He introduced me to some of his mates and a couple of them had cars on campus. Wow, having a car on campus was the ultimate big boys' fantasy. Most of the babes on and off campus wanted a guy with wheels, and they were willing to fall over each other in order to get the guy, no matter how ugly looking he was.

After a couple of weeks, Dan asked me if I would meet him at a joint on campus called "The Scene." He said that he wanted to introduce me to some of the "fine boys" on campus; I was curious what this fine boy move was all about.

I walked into "The Scene" and sitting at a table in the far right corner were Dan and two other guys. As I approached the table, Dan turned around and beckoned to me to come over quickly.

"This is the freshman that I was telling you guys about," said Dan to the two other guys, "O boy how now," replied one of the guys, called Osita, in a baritone voice. Osita was a mixed-race dude with a ponytail, and had most of the girls on campus eating out of his palm; he owned a grey Honda Accord and was the guy around campus, a true ladies' man.

I shook his hand and sat down with them at the table, and after about ten minutes of chitchat, Osita said to me, "Dan will bring you to our party tonight." With that, he got up with the other guy, who was very aloof, and left.

"You did not tell me that a serious jam was happening tonight," I enquired from Dan. *"Abi, you no wan make I flex with you big guys?"* I asked.

"No no no, I was going to tell you yesterday but I forgot. I will come and get you at about 8 pm tonight. And don't tell anybody ooo, this na exclusive party," Dan warned.

I wanted to know what the dress code was and Dan told me that I should wear dark-coloured jeans and a dark-coloured shirt with comfortable shoes.

I met Dan at the campus bus stop and we both boarded a bike or "Okada" as they were popularly called on campus. Dan told the bike man to take us to the West side of campus; I was surprised at the direction in which we were heading, because I was expecting the party to be off campus.

Dan and I got off the bike after about fifteen minutes; Dan paid the bike man and we continued our journey on foot for another five minutes. As we came to a crossroads, Dan decided that he wanted to take a wee and left me standing there. He went into some bushes and I heard him whistling in a strange manner; then all of a sudden, I saw two heavily built six-footers jump out of the opposite bushes. They were pointing a flashlight and a locally-made pistol at me.

"Wetin you dey do for here?" one of the guys barked. "I was going to a party and must have missed my way," I replied, trembling like a wet leaf. "You have come to a party, what kind of party dem they do inside bush?" he enquired of me, and before I could reply, I found myself flat on my back, floored by a thunderous slap. As I hit the ground, I felt my body stiffen from a combination of fear, panic and pain.

I was hauled up by the scruff of my neck and dragged off, deep into the bushes. I was kicked and punched all the way, until we got to a holding ground. There they made me sit down with my head in between my knees, with about fifteen other "baggers" as we were being called.

We all sat there for about ten minutes before we were ordered to stand up and take off our clothes. Stripping down to our underpants, we handed over our clothes for safekeeping. We were then marched even deeper into the bushes for about five minutes until we came to another clearing, where we were made to stand in a circle with our eyes closed. I could hear people screaming and pleading for mercy, as the sound of a cane lashing flesh filled the night.

After about twenty minutes of flogging, we were made to stand up with one leg raised, in the posture of a praying mantis. Every time someone dropped a leg, the unfortunate soul got more flogging. After about ten minutes of punishment, they told us to sit down again with our faces between our knees.

"Baggers arise, and open your eyes," bellowed a deep voice, and as we rose up still standing in a circle, I could barely make out the image of a smallish guy standing in the centre of the circle; then a flashlight was held up for him to read out names from a list in his hand.

He was a very handsome chap, fair in complexion and wearing glasses; he looked like the kind of guy most girls would want to take home to meet their mother. He held the list in one hand and in the other, a pistol. "Baggers, welcome to your worst nightmare, this is the Mafioso party," he said. He was high up in the Mafioso family, and was in charge of this "pre-initiation" ceremony.

Based on the list, we were divided into groups of three, and each group was taken aside and the beating or "mending" began again. We were punched, flogged and beaten until we were all rolling on the ground; and the more we begged for mercy, the more beating we received. This lasted for fifteen minutes at a time, and we were given rest for a couple of minutes before the beating started again.

After this they lined us up in twos in front of two coconut trees and we were asked to climb the trees as quickly as we could and pluck imaginary coconuts. When my turn came, I started to climb the tree but I could hear some of the henchmen of the Mafioso clan laughing at me and pointing at my underpants. However, at this point, I did not care that my scrotum was hanging out of a hole in my underpants.

This first pre-initiation round was about four hours of intense drilling; we were later reunited with our clothes and shoes. The henchmen led us out of the bushes towards the halls of residence under the cover of night. I never laid eyes on Dan throughout the night and was unsure how to react when I saw him again.

I sneaked into my room without putting on the light. I could hear Austin and Wilson snoring, but I could not see James in the room as my eyes got use to the darkness. I quickly got my towel and bucket, and went to have a wash. My back felt raw from all the flogging and mending, and I could feel the swellings all over my flesh.

Pouring water on my body first brought some major discomfort, as the cold fluid flowed down the swellings and filled the lacerations; but after a while, it began to bring some welcomed relief. I finished and went back to the room and got into my bed, struggling to find a comfortable sleeping position. I finally had to lie on my belly.

I lay there with a host of thoughts and questions running through my mind. The most important question that I had to answer was: did I really want to become a member of the Mafioso clan, or should I opt out now and wait for an opening for the Black Night Marauders? I fell into a restless sleep.

I opened my eyes with difficulty the next day, still hearing the resounding slaps and beating ringing in my ears. *"Thank God that it's Sunday morning,"* I said to myself; it felt like I had been in the boxing ring with

Mike Tyson. I fell back into bed and sank into a deep sleep again.

I was awakened at 3 pm that afternoon by the sweet smell of tomatoes been grilled by my next-door neighbour, and I realised how hungry I was. I jumped out of the bed and found that James was getting ready to go into town.

"O boy, you have been sleeping like a pregnant woman since morning, that party you went to last night must have been one in town," James remarked. "My guy, the party was *bam man*, with plenty of pure babes and nice 'sushises'," I replied.

"How come I did not hear about this party on campus?" James enquired. *"O boy, you yab, why you no tell me, I for fall out with you men, big time,"* he concluded. By now, I was eager to get away and find some food. As I sat down in Café A with a big portion of pounded yam and vegetable soup in front of me, I kept having flashbacks to the previous night. We had been informed that the next 'party' was in two weeks' time, and that we had two more to attend.

My father's advice came flooding back to me and I quickly pushed it aside. I finished my meal and headed for Osato's room. As I passed the students' buttery situated at the centre of the halls of residence, I could see some kind of commotion going on inside the buttery; a crowd was gathering around. All of a sudden, Don CY came bursting out of the room, with a smallish chap in pursuit. As Don CY got to the front of Hall B, he shouted a command and from nowhere, three mean-looking men dressed in black and wearing green berets appeared.

They formed a backup line behind Don CY, and one of the men had his hand inside a backpack. The smallish guy approached them with his hand in his pocket; he swiftly pulled out a dark-coloured beret and put it on. This was a standoff between one member of the Black Night Marauders and four members of the Mafioso clan.

The smallish guy, whom I later got to know as "The Bulldog," pointed to Don CY and his guys and said, "Mess with the best, you die like the rest." He was full of so much confidence that it was unbelievable.

People started to disperse when they heard whistles coming from the security men, and the Man O War comrades coming in to quell the disturbance.

I found Osato outside his room, and as usual he had first-hand info about what had gone down. He told me that the buttery had been busy with people queuing to be served, when Don CY had demanded to be served first. People in the queue had been happy to oblige, but not the smallish guy, who had come to visit a friend.

I learnt that insults had been traded between Don CY and The Bulldog and that Don CY, underestimating the size of the opposition, had slapped The Bulldog. The Bulldog had responded with two slaps and smashed a bottle on the head of Don CY. Every person in the buttery had fled thinking that The Bulldog was a dead man, but they were proved wrong, as The Bulldog was a young, fearless foot-soldier of the BNM.

At that moment, I knew that I was not going back for my initiation into the Mafioso clan: if one member of the BNM could fearlessly face four members of the Mafioso in a standoff, then there must be something special and unique about the BNM. I had always been told that if you had to eat a frog, you should eat the biggest and the juiciest one, and that was what I intended to do.

Chapter 11

I avoided Dan like the plague for the next week, while attempting to find a middle-man to get me into the BNM confraternity. I tried to locate the smallish chap called "The Bulldog," but all to no avail; he seemed to have disappeared into thin air.

As I was walking with Osato towards the campus library one Monday evening, I noticed that he was limping slightly and there was a slight bruise around his right eye. I asked how he had sustained the injury, and he quickly brushed it aside with an unconvincing story about how he had fallen down a staircase.

Osato seemed restless as we sat beside each other in the library, studying for our fast-approaching first semester examinations. I reached out and tapped his back to get his attention, and he wriggled away in pain from my touch – but not before I had felt the swelling on his back.

Osato finally confided to me that he had gone for the first round of an initiation ceremony for the BNM confraternity the previous night, and he felt like a walking corpse. I eagerly asked him to connect me to the linkman he had used and he promised to do that, but not before seeking approval from the linkman.

I had to wait for four days before Osato came back with a reply. He had set up a meeting the next day between the linkman and me at the NFA (No Future Ambition) joint behind the Law Faculty.

The next afternoon after the day's second lecture, I made my way towards the famous NFA joint for my meeting. As I approached the spot, I could see Osato sitting with a guy who looked as if he had stepped right out of my worst nightmare.

He was facially challenged, dark in complexion with two missing front teeth. He was a Waferian (from a town called Warri), badly dressed, and his choice of colours reminded me of a clown.

He had a bottle of Guinness in one hand and a Benson and Hedges smoke in the other. Osato introduced him to me by his nickname, "Gandoki the great warrior." Gandoki was a very popular and notorious member of BNM, and was dreaded by most students on campus. The university authorities also had him on their radar, and he was well-known at the local Police station where he was a regular customer.

Gandoki stared at me for a brief moment before asking, *"Na you be the guy wey wan become fine boy abi?"* "Yes," I replied, and waited for the next question to follow; but it did not come for a few minutes. Finally, he said, "You no go buy me something to wash my mouth with."

I quickly ordered two more bottles of Guinness Stout and some more cigarettes for him. He did not bother to thank me, but leaned over and whispered something into Osato's ear; Osato got up and beckoned for me to follow him.

"O boy, Gandoki say you look like heavy aje butter (a softie) and you fit be *Kelebe yanyan* (a Police informant)," Osato told me as we walked towards the lecture halls. "That is total gibberish, you know me better than that," I replied.

"Well, he said that he will get back to me about your matter soon," Osato replied as we entered the lecture hall for another round of afternoon classes.

I did not hear from Gandoki before our first semester examinations started; because of the volatility around that period of the year, armed security agents and the Police were on campus a week before exams to help quell any riot or disturbance.

There was a history of disturbance on campus towards the exam period, instigated by secret cult members eager for the institution to shut down.

Exams came and they weren't so bad; in fact, I was expecting a couple of good grades in my major modules. I was looking forward to the results coming out at the start of the second semester.

One Wednesday afternoon, two days before I was to go home for the semester break, I ran into Gandoki and two other guys. They were standing outside the girls' halls of residence, and as I approached, I could see

Gandoki whispering something into the ear of one of the guys.

I walked past them, unsure whether I should wave; I decided to be courteous and wave. I got no response from them, but no sooner had I walked past them than they started following close behind me. I did not know whether to increase my pace or run. I began to walk faster, hoping to get into the male halls of residence where activities were happening and my roommate Austin would be around.

Austin was an intimidating-looking guy that you did not want to mess about with; unfortunately, I was cornered before I could make it into the room. Gandoki stood in front of me with these two guys in a horseshoe formation; the one called "Sunshine" was an albino and was carrying a backpack with no smile on his face. His eyes were red and bloodshot from smoking "Igbo" (Marijuana) and when he spoke, I could see the discolouration of his front tooth.

"My guy said that you owe him some money and you got to pay up now now," said Sunshine, referring to Gandoki. "What money?" I enquired, "I do not owe him any money and I will not be intimidated by you because I know my rights," I said with a combination of anger and fear.

"*Ehen, you dey speak big big English and law for us,*" he sneered. I could see the other guy reaching into the backpack and I knew this meant trouble. I also knew that as a fast sprinter, if I were to make a dash for it, they would never catch up with me.

I took my chance and made a dash for my room, in the knowledge that Austin would be there studying. I knew that these guys would not want to mess with him. They gave chase and as I approached my room, I called out Austin's name at the top of my voice – but to my great disappointment, he was not in the room.

"*I am dead*," I thought, and decided within a split-second to make a dash for Austin's friend's and reading partner's room. As I entered the room, Austin with his bulging biceps was standing there with his friend Eric.

I had barely started to explain the situation to Austin when Gandoki and his crew appeared on the scene. Austin instinctively stepped in front of me to protect me. He was greeted with a thunderous slap from Gandoki, and before I knew what was happening, he was flat on his back on the ground and Sunshine had a foot on Austin's chest.

I could see the fear in Austin's eyes, and I heard him cry out to Gandoki, "I did not do anything, it was not me."

"*It was not me, wetin make you put your big chest for road?*" enquired Gandoki, looking down at Austin lying on the ground.

A small crowd had started to gather around us now, and Gandoki pointed at me and said, "Expect the unexpected," and with that, he left with his crew. Austin slowly got up from the ground, dusted off his clothes, and left the scene without saying one word, heading back to the room. When I got there, I found him crying as he told both Wilson and James what had just happened.

I could not believe that the heavily-built man whom I had hoped would protect me was such a spineless and cowardly human being. What hope did I have now? James suggested that I go home as I had finished my exams, but I really did not want to leave so early because this was the most fun time of year on campus. Exams had finished and there were various parties on and off campus, and I did not want to miss them.

I went to see Osato and told him about what had transpired earlier; he suggested that I go talk to Don CY, and ask him for advice and some cover before I went home. I found Don CY nursing a bottle of beer in the buttery, hailed him and ordered another bottle for him, and explained my situation to him. He told me not to worry about it, but to give him some money to settle the people. As I handed some money to him, I could not help but feel humiliated. I was nearly nineteen years old, an adult, and I was been held to ransom by another human being who was no better than me. This was unbelievable and I would never let it happen to me again, as long as I had breath in me.

The next two days were fun, filled with parties; it was at one of these parties that I met Prince. Prince was a second-year Political Science student and lived in Asaba not far from my home, and we had some mutual friends. He lived off campus and was enjoying the freedom and the babes. He told me that babes felt more comfortable coming to a guy's place off campus, rather than visiting the small, dingy and claustrophobic student accommodation on campus.

Prince seemed to be a very popular guy around the university, and at the party people were queuing up to hang out with him. He had this easy-going and relaxed air about him. He introduced me to a couple of babes he knew and encouraged me to have plenty of fun at the party.

I left campus the next day for a three-week break. I had the time during my journey home to reflect on my first semester. It had been a bittersweet experience for me, and whenever my mind wandered to my encounter with Gandoki and his crew I shuddered.

Coming home was always nice but this time around, it felt empty. My eldest brother was now practising Law in Warri, while my second brother had just finished his PLAB and was practising medicine in the UK. My sister had married long ago and had moved away to live in Lagos, and my younger brother was away at secondary school.

So the holiday became about relaxing and meeting up with friends, and I was allowed to use the spare car at home to run errands for the house and myself. My usage of the car was highly regulated by my parents, and the car had to be back home by 6:30 pm sharp.

It was about 3 pm on a Saturday afternoon when I pulled up in front of Prince's house, which was close to the Pointer newspaper house. I enquired after Prince but was told that he was with some friends at Mama

Ngozi's beer parlour, and I was pointed in the right direction.

I walked into the beer parlour and saw Prince sitting at one end of the room with three other guys; as I approached the table, Prince looked up and beckoned me to join them. We exchanged pleasantries and he introduced the other guys to me. He ordered me a bottle of beer with some pepper soup; he said he was expecting his cousin Pascal to join us soon.

We had spent about twenty minutes talking about university, politics and babes when Prince looked over my shoulder towards the entrance and a broad smile appeared on his face. "Pascal, my brother, where have you been?" I heard him say to somebody behind me.

"My brother *I dey*," was the reply that came from a soft but confident-sounding voice; and as I turned around to see who was behind me, I nearly passed out. Standing before me was "The Bulldog," the very guy who had confronted Don CY and his crew in front of the buttery. I got up and shook his hand as Prince introduced us; we ordered more drinks and meat, and the conversation rapidly moved from one topic to another.

It was getting late and fast approaching my curfew, so I had to leave; I promised to meet up with them again the next day at the same place. I could not believe my luck as I drove back home that evening. *"This must definitely be some kind of heavenly orchestration,"* I thought, and I was bent on capitalising on it.

Over the next few weeks I spent a lot of time socialising with Prince and Pascal, and during one of our many meetings, I pulled Pascal aside and narrated the ordeal that I had experienced with Gandoki and his crew; I told him how much I wanted to belong to the BNM.

Pascal had warmed up to me by then, and promised to take me under his wing and guide me through the process of becoming a member of the BNM; but he warned that it would require some financial commitment on my part. I told him that I was up for it and wanted to delve deeper into what had happened between him and Don CY.

"No mind that yeye boy, ewan try Iroko tree, I for show am American wonder," Pascal said in Pidgin English. "As a strong man, you fear nobody because you hold your side," he continued in a braggadocio manner, "I was ready to fall all of them with my 9 mm," he added as he gesticulated with his fingers.

"Remy, my guy, I am a very notorious and well known BNM guy; if they try themselves and mess with the best, they go die like the rest," he said. "So for your own security, Remy, if you see me on campus, don't associate with me ooo, if not you go blow your cover when you never even join the level," Pascal warned.

I took the advice that The Bulldog gave to me and stored it away to be used in the future. I was hanging out more and more often with Prince and Pascal in Asaba, but every time I enquired from Prince if he was a member of the BNM, he laughed and replied that he was a lover, not a fighter, and was more interested in the babes than in chasing other guys around campus with a gun.

Chapter 12

I arrived back on campus for the start of the second semester and went right to my Faculty to check my results. I was amazed to learn that I had done far better than I expected, with three As, four Bs and one C. I was delighted and went in search of Osato.

Osato was sitting in the NFA joint, smoking a cigarette and looking pensive. I joined him and lit up my own brand of St. Morris. "I failed two of my modules," Osato said to me sorrowfully. I tried to console him. "It is just two modules, don't worry, you will do well in the re-sit my brother," I assured him. By the time we had finished our lights, Osato had cheered up a bit and we headed for the bike garage on campus, which was always a beehive of activity.

Lectures soon began in earnest and because we had a lot to cover, the classes were fast-paced. We had between three and four lectures a day; sometimes they ran on into the late evening, and before we knew it, the semester was half-gone.

It was a welcome relief when I learnt about a big birthday party happening one Saturday, off campus at the Nova Hotel. It was the talk of the campus and was being organised by a babe called Eve. She was one of the numerous girlfriends of a state-based politician. The invites went like hot cakes and through Wilson, we got one; we could not wait for Saturday to come, and when it finally did, we hit the road to Nova Hotel.

There were many makes and models of cars in the parking, from the small Mitsubishi Colts to the big 4 by 4 Pathfinders. The music of Shabba Ranks was blaring from giant loudspeakers, the grand hall was packed full of beautiful babes dressed to kill, and the guys were looking their best and ready to impress.

The music was superb and the drinks were flowing as they had flowed at the wedding in Canaan; there were copious amounts of food to go around. The party continued into the early hours of the morning and at about 2 am, we heard screaming from outside the hotel premises with bottles being smashed and girls crying.

Apparently, Eve's party was under the protection of the BNM, and was restricted to invitees. A top member of the Trojan Horse confraternity and his crew had turned up at the party uninvited, upset that his girlfriend had attended the party without his consent. He wanted to flush her out, but the BNM were not having it, and the party descended into chaos.

Bottles and fists were flying and blood was flowing. The Trojan Horse boys came out of the confrontation far worse off – they had never stood a chance, easily outclassed by the ruggedness of the BNM. The battered Trojan Horse boys had their pockets emptied and were made to sit in humiliation by the roadside until daybreak.

Eve's party had to come to a stop at about 3 am because of all the commotion outside, but we had to stay inside the hotel premises until it was safe for us to get a bike and return to the halls of residence.

Going to church the next day was not an option; I slept all through the morning and into the afternoon, and got up at about 6 pm only to get some food.

By the next day, we were back in the swing of things, from one lecture to another, from one assessment to another, and from one project to another.

We were approaching mid-semester and with it came a long-awaited event: the most anticipated, biggest show on campus, the beauty pageant to find the most beautiful girl on campus. The pageant was due to take place in two weeks' time, and the buzz and hype were palpable: there were posters and billboards everywhere, mobile announcements were made all over, and I was looking forward to the show.

The artists on this year's billing were going to be fantastic. They included the young and upcoming comedian called Ali Baba; the Rub-a-dub master called Blackie, and Alex Zitto and Daniel Wilson, who were two of Nigeria's top musicians at the time. Our very own campus band, Shabba Ranks, was also billed to perform.

Guys were making plans on which of their babes to take to the show, while babes were looking for guys who had deep pockets and were not afraid to spend. Young lovers were also looking forward to the events as another opportunity to have a great time together.

The organisers knew that for the show to be successful and hitch-free, they had to get the main confraternities on their side. Therefore, they "settled" the people at the top echelons of these confraternities financially, and gave free entrance to some of their members.

There were six major confraternities on campus: we had the notorious BNM, the Pyrates, the Buccaneers, the BB (Black Berets), the Mafioso and the Eiye. There were other smaller crews still searching for credence, such as the Trojan Horse, the Skull and the Vikings. The palm wine drinkers' club was more of a social outfit than a confraternity.

The "families" with the strongest influence and greatest nexus were the BNM, the Pyrates and the Buccaneers, and these three families' secret cults were different in style and approach.

The BNM, a.k.a. "the Marauders," were the notorious bad boys on campus, ready for a fight anywhere, anytime and anyhow you wanted it. It was rumoured that they used human blood and coffins during their initiation ceremony; their regalia had the insignia of a human skull and bones.

The Pyrates, a.k.a. "the Sea Dogs," on the other hand, were of a gentler nature; they were from affluent homes and saw themselves as the big boys on campus. Some of them had cars; they picked their fights carefully; and they had a history dating back to the old medieval days when there were real Pirates on the high seas, hence the name Sea Dogs.

The Buccaneers, a.k.a. "Aloras," were the party boys. Always looking for a good time, they threw most of the big parties off campus, and they had the flashiest cars and bikes. They went out with the finest babes on campus, travelled abroad, and were regarded as snobs; the BNM hated them with a passion, more out of spite than for anything they did.

The organisers of the show also had to engage the Man O War (MOW) comrades who were also a force to be reckoned with; their job was security-based. They staffed the gates to the pavilion, checking tickets and maintaining order; but they knew their limitations when it came to the BNM.

The show was meant to start at 9 pm, but by 7 pm the campus was already buzzing. Guys and babes were hanging around and holding hands, music was blaring from huge speakers in front of the open-air pavilion, cars blaring music were parked around the venue by the "big boys," and the whole atmosphere was electrifying. The MOW in battle fatigues took command of the gates by 8 pm, looking menacing with their bloodshot eyes.

I was let down by Harriett, whom I was going to take to the show. She was a fine babe in my class and I had been propositioning her for some time; but she came down with the flu and had to leave campus. I queued up alone to buy my ticket, and I made my way towards the front of the pavilion to get a good spot. I was excited and could not wait for the show to kick off.

The back end of the venue was a volatile area and not for the faint-hearted, because that was where all the members of various confraternities converged. They had their territories in different areas along the backstretch and more often than not, mayhem began there.

The show did not start until 10:30 pm. But when it began, it was great. I had never laughed that hard. Ali Baba regaled the crowd with his rib-cracking jokes and jibes – it was just brilliant. Blackie and the other musicians put on a great performance too, and it was all going wonderfully well until the contestants came out for a Q & A session.

The booing and jeers began when one of the contestants made a blunder when answering a question, saying, "I will sing a sing for you" – and this particular contestant was a third-year English student. It got worse when another contestant mispronounced the word bizarre as "bizaray" – the booing got louder and louder. We were finally finished off by another contestant who said, "There would be chaos in the nation," and pronounced chaos as "cha wos" – at this point there was no redemption for some of the contestants.

The show eventually finished at 2:30 am. Overall, it was a great night and I enjoyed myself, even without a date. I headed back to my room, not wanting to be caught up in the after-show atmosphere, because that was another volatile time where fights and cult rivalry escalated. I knew that I could not afford to be caught up in any tussle as I was still a 'Bagger'

As I made my way towards the halls of residence, I could see lovers holding hands and whispering sweet words to one another; and I thought to myself that maybe I might have had a chance with Harriett this morning. I went to bed wondering about my chances.

The morning brought a realisation that a number of rooms, both in the male and female halls of residence, had been burgled during the show yesterday, but this came as no surprise since the campus had been crawling with a multitude of people.

All the rooms on my block had been burgled, except my own; I could not understand why, but I put it down to luck.

I had caught sight of The Bulldog on one or two occasions on campus, and he would give me a knowing wink and walk on. However, today I received a note from Prince, with whom I often hung out off campus, and the note read, "Game on, tomorrow @ 8pm, at the reservoir, wear dark coloured clothes, bring 100 Naira and bring yourself."

The reservoir was located in a secluded area on the East side of campus. It had a thick forest behind it, and as I approached the structure at the appointed time, a figure stepped out from the bushes behind me and pointed a gun to my head, saying, "Identify yourself." my mouth became dry and my knees started knocking together in fear of the cold steel pointing at my head.

"My ... my my name is Remy," I said, and the voice barked for me to turn around, and I was staring into the cold eyes of a masked gunman.

"What are you doing here?" he asked. "I ... I ... I ... I am mee mee meeting a friend," I stammered. "What is the name of this person that you are meeting?" the masked gunman asked. "His name is Pascal," I replied, almost peeing on myself. I had not finished saying the name of Pascal when I was floored by a punch in my stomach, *"You stupid mumu, na so you go go call person name give school authority and Kelebe (Police)."*

"I am sorry, sir," I said as I struggled to get up to my feet. At that moment The Bulldog stepped out of the shadow laughing. *"Oboy we just dey check your liver, just to make sure you gather enough courage my guy,"* he said as he patted me on the back. *"This na my main man Rago,"* he continued as he introduced me to my assaulter.

Rago offered his hand for a handshake, which I dared not refuse. *"We go take care of you my broda,"* he said.

The Bulldog collected the money from me, as he had to pay for my registration fee and also grease some palms of the top BNM guys to accept me, as I had already missed the first round of the initiation process.

As we walked along, we approached a footpath that would take us into the neck of the forest; we started hearing some whistling, and another masked gunman stepped out of the shadow. He greeted The Bulldog and Rago, and greeted me with a slap on the back of the head.

We continued through the thick forest for another fifteen minutes, meeting different masked men at regular intervals along the path. We finally got to a clearing where I was stripped down to my boxer shorts and made to lie down with other unfortunate souls.

The Mafioso initiation that I had attended was child's play compared to the one of the BNM. This was intense and frenetic, with little time for rest. The beating and mending were impossibly prolonged. I was singled out personally for special treatment, meaning that I got double beating and mending because I had missed the first round of initiation.

This round of initiation ended at about 2 am, and we were informed that the next and final one would be in two weeks' time. We were handed back to our sponsors and escorted to the exit.

I made my way back to my room feeling badly bruised and nearly eviscerated, wondering what fate would befall me at the final stage. My back felt raw and tender, and I had to make sure that none of my roommates found out I was injured.

I carefully avoided taking off my shirt in the room when there were people around; I chose to get dressed in the shower room after washing, before returning to the room.

The final stage of my initiation was bloody; the number of new recruits had dwindled drastically, from fifty to fewer than half the number. The beating and mending went on from 9 pm until 11:30 pm. We were given little rest and we could hear singing and dancing and the beating of drums; as I lay there face down waiting and praying for the final round to finish, I could sense someone standing in front of me.

"Raise your head up with your eyes closed," said a familiar voice that I could not place. I did as I was told, and a flashlight was pointed into my face. "Remy, what are you doing here?" asked the very familiar voice. "I lost my way, sir and ended up here," I answered. "You lost your way and ended up here of all places?" the voice enquired, to which I replied, "Yes, sir."

"Open your eyes," said the voice. I opened my eyes and stared into the face in front of me, with the help of the flashlight. I almost fainted; squatting in front of me was my roommate James, with a grin on his face.

"Na here your papa send you com go school," he enquired. "No, sir," I answered. "So you thought you could do this in secret without me knowing, you small boy," James said as he patted my sore shoulder and left me lying there. The singing and dancing continued well into the small hours, and the drumbeats were so captivating and moving that I forgot all about my pain and suffering.

I was finally initiated, alongside Prince and Osato, into the BNM confraternity in June 1991. It was a welcome relief that at last it had ended, and I could now start the process of my physical healing. At the same time, it was exciting to become a member of the brotherhood.

James pulled me aside after the initiation, congratulated me as a brother, and said something that stuck with me for a very long time. "*Now that you don become one of us, this is where your wahala and trouble starts.*" He continued, "You will be wanted by the school authority, by the Police, and hunted by other confraternities; my advice to you is to keep a low profile and don't mingle with the well-known and notorious BNM guys."

"The classic mistake that most new Marauders make is that they want to prove themselves too soon and too quickly, they want to show themselves approved as hard men, they then tend to cry louder than the bereaved. Just be yourself!" with those words of advice we headed back to campus.

Campus life continued as usual, and I got to meet many other BNM members. We had a special way of greeting each other and I learnt to spot a fellow brother from certain words and movements that he made. I was astonished to discover that BNM had been founded in the early seventies and that it had a binding constitution and was strongly organised and structured.

Chapter 13

My telephone conference that day at the bank, with my area manager Gary, was one of the most painful ordeals that I had ever endured. There were twelve of us branch managers on the call, and he drilled down into every aspect of our branches' performance, very critical of all our proposed strategies to uplift sales.

I left the telephone conference feeling eviscerated and de-motivated, but I knew that I had to put on a brave face for my colleagues and customers and push on with the day's activities.

As I settled down at my desk, the year 1972 caught my attention on the computer screen. *"That was the era that BNM was founded,"* I thought to myself as I drifted back into the past.

The BNM was founded by five impressionable young men in response to the oppression of the masses in Africa. Its original objective was to be a force in the emancipation of the oppressed, and be the voice of the voiceless. What is attainable now at various Universities was very different from the original concept.

Within the tertiary institutions, the BNM structure was well defined, with the number one man known as the Alfa. The Alfa was the father of the clan and occupied the highest echelon of authority. His word was law and he was the *Capo di tutti Capi*, the "boss of all bosses," revered by the clan, but feared by many.

The Alfa was the heart and soul of each local clan of the BNM and he was guarded like a precious jewel. If the Alfa were to suffer a hit or an attack, then BNM was finished – it was like cutting the head off a viper.

To become an Alfa, you must show your prowess not necessarily on the battlefield, but more in the area of mental sagacity and the ability to think on your feet. Once the Alfa had spoken, no one could counteract his command other than himself.

The Omega was the Alfa's second in command, the mother-figure of the clan, who took charge when the Alfa was not around. He was also the oracle of the clan and communicated with the gods on its behalf. He was the lead musician and could serenade clan meetings with melodious songs for hours on end. He had the Alfa's right ear, and he alone had the authority from the gods to brew the magic potion called "Goskolos."

The Executioner had the Alfa's left ear; he was the war general, in charge of all the clan's arsenal. He carried out orders from the Alfa to the letter and reported directly to him. The Executioner meted out punishment to erring clan members and was normally in charge of the initiation rites; he was built to be mean and brutal.

There was also the Council of wise men; there were five of them, the most experienced hands in the clan and well-respected.

The tax collector was the bookkeeper of the clan, and kept the financial records of what went in and out. There were other minor Executives within the clan, like the Voice, who was responsible for the dissemination of information and messages.

The Seer did all the legwork and the spying; he was responsible for the extraction of information within our campus and on other sister campuses as well.

I was content to be a fee-paying member of the BNM, having fun knowing that the clan had my back in times of trouble. I kept a very low profile and avoided the NFA joints on and off campus; I hardly went to the beer parlours and spots where BNM members would normally converge.

The semester went by so quickly, and the examinations were just two weeks away. There were very few social activities going on and students were beginning to burn the midnight oil.

These exams were tougher than the previous ones, but I believed that I had put in a decent effort for each module. The only reservation I had was about one of my core Economics modules, taught by Mr Emahie, a no-nonsense lecturer and a devoted member of the Jehovah's Witness. He did not suffer fools gladly and would never allow any female student into his office unaccompanied, lest they tempt him with their evil ways.

He would never accept any gift from a student, in case there was an ulterior motive behind it. He never celebrated Christmas or birthdays. In short, he was the most boring and nondescript human being that I had ever met.

To get an E grade in his module, you must have attended at least eighty percent of his lectures and done all the required assignments and assessments. He personally supervised his own examination, and was famous for ripping up the answer sheets of students who were caught conferring.

With my exams now finished, I had decided to go and visit a good friend of mine at Onitsha. We had attended Dominion College together, but he had left before completing his final secondary school examinations. Onitsha was about two and a half hours from my university by road and about twenty minutes from Asaba, so I decided to visit him first before heading home.

My friend, Emmanuel, was from an affluent family. He was the youngest child and only son, with four older sisters, and was the apple of his parents' eyes. Manuel, as he was fondly called, was very modest and unassuming and that was what endeared him to me right from when we first met. He was always eager to hear my many stories which were full of embellishments.

I arrived at the Upper Iweka motor park in Onitsha, and jumped on an Okada (motorbike) that took me straight to one of the posh parts of the Government Reservation Area (GRA). Manuel was waiting for me in front of his parents' home; we went in through the massive and impressive-looking gate straight to the boys' quarters, where my friend had his room.

I had been to his house on several occasions during our secondary school days, and in fact I was known to his sisters and his parents. "Remy, my guy, it is happening tonight, there is a big groove in town and it is being held by a guy from Yankee (America). He attended Dominion College for a few years before going back to America," Manuel told me.

"We must fall out to the groove big time, any dress code because I gotta hold my side big time," I said with some major attitude and swagger. "Dress code has to be razor sharp but my wardrobe is full of clothes, help yourself," Manuel said.

We had something to eat and relaxed, watching an Eddie Murphy movie with chilled bottles of beer. We started getting ready for the party at about 9 pm and finally drove out of the compound in Manuel's black Mercedes E Class, which was a present from his mum.

The party was jamming by the time we arrived and the hall was packed full with fine-looking babes and guys; the music was a mixture of new and old school. Manuel introduced me to some of his friends, including the Yankee guy.

We got some drinks and stood in a corner from where we could observe events in the room – and that was when I caught sight of Isabella. She was not the most beautiful babe I had ever seen, but she was fine and attractive with the body of a goddess, and boy, *could she dance*.

I was about six feet tall and a relatively handsome dude, and into bodybuilding. I fancied my chances with her, and I started to dance towards her. Beginning with my Jeffery Daniel dance moves, I then got into my Bobby Brown and MC Hammer moves. I was only a few steps away from her when another guy suddenly cut in front of me and began dancing with her.

I continued dancing on my own, until it started to feel awkward and embarrassing. I was thinking of an exit strategy to get off the dance floor and at that moment, she excused herself and headed for the door. I followed her, hoping that she was not about to leave.

She was standing in the courtyard taking in some fresh air when I approached her. "You are such a wonderful dancer," I said to her with all sincerity.

"Thank you," she replied. "I was hoping that you would graciously accord me one dance tonight," I said hopefully.

"Why should I?" she asked with her hands on her hips, looking at me in a teasing stance. I knew this game – I had played it so many times in my young life. "Well, maybe you might learn how to dance properly from me," I said cheekily.

"Wooow, you better put your money where your mouth is," she said as she dragged me into the hall and back on the dance floor. We danced and danced and danced to the music of Bobby Brown, Shabba Ranks and many other artists, and thanks to my old friend Big Joe, I did not disappoint. After forty minutes of physical exertion, we went out together to get some fresh air.

"I must give it to you *sha*, you can dance, but I danced you under the table," she said, with a smile playing on her attractive face. "I beg to disagree, you were the one struggling for breath at the end of day," I challenged her.

We stood there talking, moving from dancing to music and then to education. She told me that she had recently been accepted into university, but she was still expecting her admission letter. I asked her which one, and the next few words that came out of her mouth sent chills down my spine.

"You are kidding me, that is where I am doing my degree," I said in disbelief. "What is taking you all the way there?" She told me that her JAMB scores weren't high enough to make the Federal Universities, but that she had secured a place in the Political Science department at my University.

I must have died and gone to heaven as I stood there mesmerised and dumbfounded. I finally found my voice and asked her when she was planning to resume her studies, and learned that she was anticipating joining once she had received her admission letter.

We stood there talking for what seemed like eternity, and we were finally brought back to earth by Manuel joining us. I introduced Isabella to Manuel and it turned out that Manuel knew her older brother. It was fast approaching midnight and Isabella had to go home. I did not want her to go; I wanted to spend every last minute possible with her.

"How are you getting home?" I asked. "I live just down the road," she replied and started to walk towards the gate. I caught up with her and insisted on walking her home, as it was dark; we talked as we strolled down the road, until we came to an imposing mansion.

"This is where I live," she said, "I have to go in now before my father sends out a search party," she warned me, half joking.

We said good night and I watched her enter through the massive gate. I had a spring in my step as I walked back to the party; I felt as if I had won the lottery.

The party was still jamming when I got back and alcohol was flowing like water. I found Manuel busy chatting up a big-busted babe on the dance floor, but I was no longer interested in any other babe at the party. Isabella was all I could think about right now, and I knew that I was falling in love with her and could not wait to see her again on campus.

We left the party at about 2 am and headed for Manuel's house. Parking the car in front of the gate, we staggered in through the side gate and up to his room. We lay in bed talking about the party and how much it had been until we both fell asleep mid-sentence.

I left Onitsha for Asaba two days later. Isabella was constantly on my mind and could not wait to see her again. The next two weeks were going to be the longest of my life. To keep myself occupied, I hung out with Prince and Tess.

Two weeks finally passed by and I had never been so keen to get back to university, for two reasons: I had secured a flat outside campus with James and another chap called Sly, and was eager to go and settle down; and more importantly, I could not wait to see Isabella again.

My new abode was a newly built block of flats off Poultry road, about fifteen minutes' walk from campus. Having a flat off campus was more expensive than staying in the university halls of residence, and I remember paying 2,500 Naira in 1992 for the privilege of living off campus for the year. My father had not originally been in support of this move, but I was able to convince him of the merits of living off campus.

My room was slightly bigger than my previous room at the boys' halls of residence, and it had an en-suite. I wanted my room to look better than Dan's, so I had arranged to take a spare carpet, a television, a sound box and a fridge from home.

James and Sly were sharing the room opposite mine, and we all had a common kitchen. There were six blocks in the compound, each made up of four-bedroom flats. Three of the blocks were for women.

I settled down in my new flat and was waiting for lectures to commence in about two days' time. One evening before the start of term, I decided to go into town to see Prince. I boarded an Okada and headed towards the town centre; and as the Okada went past two girls walking down Poultry road, I heard somebody call out my name. I turned to look back and at that moment, my Okada rider lost control and headed straight into the nearby bush.

I came out of the bush feeling ruffled and embarrassed. I started to dust myself off, and there was Isabella standing in front of me and looking concerned. "Remy, are you are OK? Are you hurt?" she asked, looking as charming as she had the first time I set my eyes on her. "Not at all," I replied, trying to regain my composure and machismo.

At this time, I had completely forgotten about the bike and the bike man and my attention was focused on Isabella. She introduced her companion. Esther was a second-year Law student, showing her friend around the vicinity. "Why are you in this vicinity?" I asked ignorantly. "I live in one of the newly built self-contained hostels down the road," she replied, and pointed in the direction of her hostel. "What a coincidence, Isabella! I live off this road too," I said, pointing to my block of flats.

Over the coming months, Isabella and I became inseparable. We spent every spare moment in each other's company, and I had no intention to rush her. I enjoyed courting her and delighting her with love songs, jokes and presents. We fell deeply in love and could not bear to be away from each other.

I remember the day I almost lost my life because of Isabella, one night when I had gone to see her. Her room was situated on the fifth floor of a five-storey building. We loved standing in the balcony and looking up into the sky, charting our future together. As we stood there in each other's arms, she decided to do a new dance move for me, so I moved back to watch her. I had my back resting against the balcony railings while watching her do her move – and then I suddenly felt the railing give way behind me.

I could feel myself starting to fall backwards, and did not see Isabella reach forward to grab me by my shirt and pull me back from the edge of the balcony. I stood there dumbfounded and shocked, realising that she had probably saved my life. She came into my arms and whispered into my ear, "I love you so much and I am not ready to lose you." I could hear a voice in my head saying, *"You wan go kill yourself because of babe,"* but I quickly dismissed the lone and errant voice.

We refused to let each other go that night, and we spent hours together in wild ecstasy, although she was very naive in the act of love making. This did not matter to me, and I soon discovered the reason – she was a virgin and had been embarrassed to tell me, wanting to avoid scaring me away, as she was aware of my numerous conquests with the opposite sex.

Our relationship was like a house on fire. She virtually moved in with me, and only went back to her room when her parents came visiting. Lectures continued as usual; I did not need to take any elective modules in my second year, and concentrated on my main Accounting and Economics modules.

All this while, I was very careful not to let Isabella know that I was a member of the BNM. I tried not to be seen with Osato regularly. Osato was now well known by most students as an active member of the BNM, and I made sure to avoid hanging around notorious people or in joints where confraternity men converged.

I took care to pay my dues, called "school fees," to the tax collector on time and I stayed away from all the NFA joints on campus, because that was where all the troubles and fights started and mere mortals did not hang out in those joints.

The Voice started crying out in and outside campus about an intended gathering of the Marauders in two days' time. The news of the meeting spread within the confraternity; the location was never made known until the day itself.

The day came and I told Isabella that I had a group tutorial in town and that I would be back late. James and I headed for the rendezvous spot, where we met up with Osato and other members of the BNM. The Seer directed us along a bush path; we had another twenty minute trek through the bush until we came to our destination. The meeting spot was a piece of farmland deep in the bushes, surrounded by tall Iroko trees; we identified ourselves with our bush names and then stood in a circle. The air was saturated with the smell of "Igbo" (Marijuana).

The Executioner and his deputies were there to maintain order and deliver appropriate punishment as required. He had a horsewhip in one hand and in the other hand, he held a gun, eager to bring down any miscreant within the circle for some thrashing. The

Omega was in the middle of the circle, leading the singing and dancing, and after fifteen minutes of soul-lifting singing, the Alfa suddenly appeared and there was dead silence.

You dared not talk or move when the Alfa was in the gathering and inside the circle, until he spoke. This age old tradition was there to show the importance of the Alfa and the reverence shown to him as the leader of the clan. "I hail you great Marauders," shouted the Alfa. "We hail you our Alfa," we responded. The Alfa went through housekeeping issues and other matters, and after thirty minutes, he came to the issue of offenders.

Some BNM members had been caught extorting money from "baggers" (civilians), others had threatened babes and asked for protection money, and still others had not paid their dues. The Alfa pronounced judgement according to the offense, ranging from flogging to mending (group beating).

The Alfa was a smallish-looking chap who walked with a limp, sustained during an attack on him two years ago. He was currently in his final year in the department of Microbiology. He was a no-nonsense chap and had vast experience in the affairs of the BNM. He had once been a member of the Council of wise men, and he knew the constitution well. Rumour had it that after the hit on him by the Black Beret confraternity, he had instigated and led the bloodiest war between the BNM and the Black Berets where four members of the Black Berets lost their lives.

The Alfa was known to be single-minded and was ready to crush any opposition to the supreme rule of the BNM, inside and outside the campus.

The gathering of Marauders ended before twelve midnight, and the Seer and his deputies led us out of the bush. As a matter of governance and rule, we could not leave the meeting using the same path by which we'd arrived, and there must be at least five exit routes.

I must confess that I was slightly disappointed with the structure and proceedings of this gathering of the Marauders. I had not expected people to be beaten and flogged as a form of punishment after going through all that pain during initiation. As it was my first meeting, I did not know what to expect, but I felt that the whole gathering and treatment of people lacked a bit of class.

Isabella was the love of my life and we had a very passionate relationship. She was the oldest daughter of an illiterate entrepreneur who sold spare vehicle parts all over the country and was the sole distributor of a certain brand of tyre in the whole of West Africa. He was a high chief, not just in her village but in five other villages as well, and was well-respected and widely revered.

Isabella had four siblings and she was the apple of her father's eye, as much as of mine. She was always well-dressed and had an angelic face to match the body of a goddess – a proper "aje butter" to the core. It was so obvious that Isabella had lived a sheltered life – she did not know how to make a sentence in Pidgin English, and she was very naive in matters of the world; but she had a kind heart.

This girl was my true gem. She was not just compassionate, but she was real. What tripped me the most about her was her almost unbelievably modest attitude and behaviour.

My first semester examinations were swiftly approaching, and lectures were happening at a faster pace and stretching on for longer, sometimes well into the night. I was in a group of classmates who read and brainstormed together.

I vividly remember one particular night when at about 9:30 pm, I had gone to the campus with Isabella to read for the forthcoming exams, and we heard gunshots coming from a classroom further down the block. There was suddenly an air of panic and commotion everywhere, and people were falling over each other to get out of the classroom; some were jumping through the windows while others were attempting to create an imaginary door through the wall.

Isabella had gone pale and was shivering with fear as she attempted to get up from her seat. I held on to her hand to reassure her, and then whispered into her ear to sit down. I had learnt from reading Mafia books and watching movies that you do not run aimlessly during a commotion or stampede, as you might be running right into the source of danger.

The room was empty before I got up and crept to the door, where I peeped out and caught sight of a group of guys wearing green berets standing over a body lying on the ground. Now that I knew where the danger was, I took Isabella's hand and led her through the window and behind the flowerbeds, until we came out close to the boys' halls of residence. I knew this area very well, having lived on campus for a year. I would have liked to cut through the bushes and look for a shortcut to Poultry Road, but for the safety of Isabella behind me, that was not an option.

I knew so many people living in the halls of residence and I knew that this was the safest place to be right now, because most of the Man O War comrades stayed on campus. I settled Isabella down in Wilson's room and made myself comfortable in the chair opposite her.

We left the campus for Poultry Road the next morning, and after Isabella was safely in her room, I went in search of Osato, who lived five minutes away. I learned from him that the previous night's fracas had been between the Mafioso and the Eiye. The Mafioso hit men had gone to carry out a hit on the "Eagle" of the Eiye confraternity, but had missed him and ended up taking down one of the foot-soldiers. This attack had been triggered by a recent feud between this two gangs as the Eiye had failed to show the required respect to the Mafioso clan.

The Eiye confraternity were not as strong as the Mafioso, but they could prove to be a hard nut to crack if they were rubbed the wrong way. The Mafioso having pulled this audacious act of going for their "Eagle" meant that it was going to be a fierce war. The Eiye would be looking to retaliate, and they would certainly be gunning for one of the top Dons within the Mafioso clan.

As we sat in the room discussing the event, Dave and Fred came into the room together. Both members of the BNM, they shared the room with Osato. We greeted each other in the unique way of the brotherhood and Dave, who had spoken to the Voice of the BNM earlier on, confirmed that there was an urgent gathering in two hours' time at one of our many locations, called "down the valley."

We arrived at the gathering place; the Alfa and Omega were standing in the middle of the circle. "I hail you great Marauders, *this na very sharp and snappy meeting, you must have all heard wetin happen for campus last night?*" he asked. Not waiting for an answer, he continued, "This is not our fight, however *I no wan hear sey na mistaken identity, sey they go fall one of us becos if e happen, na yawa.*"

"So all men hold your side, watch your back, walk in groups and keep your eyes open." The Alfa turned to the Executioner and ordered, "Make sure say all our weapons dey ready to be deployed one hand and no slacking." "Yes, my Alfa, no shaking," bellowed the Executioner.

The gathering was over quickly and we all used different routes to exit the valley and re-enter civilisation. The atmosphere on campus the next day was tense, and members of the other confraternities were on high alert – but nothing happened.

Things remained quiet for the next couple of days and the campus returned to normal. Examinations were due to start in seven days' time, lectures were being rounded up, and people were working late and hard, when the Eiye confraternity struck.

They carried out two simultaneous hits, on campus and off campus. The one on campus was like a scene right out of a gangster movie. It was broad daylight; a pickup van drove into campus in a menacing manner, and when it reached the Law Faculty, a group of masked men wearing blue berets jumped down, armed to the teeth.

A rapid series of gunshots followed as they headed to the Law Faculty. It was pure pandemonium on campus, as everybody around scurried for cover and their dear lives. University security was not equipped to handle this deadly situation and the Man O War comrades had taken to their heels with everybody else.

By the end of the day, the Mafioso clan had suffered three casualties on and off campus, including a hit on their Enforcer (their third in command). It was now going to be an outright war; the Mafioso started mobilising for retaliation.

The university was closed down immediately and all students were sent home until further notice. A crack squad from the Nigerian Police Force called "MOPOL," a.k.a. "kill and go," were deployed on and off campus and given orders to shoot on sight. No student was going to wait around or attempt to mess with the MOPOL, and the university town was quickly transformed into a ghost town as all students vacated it.

Isabella and I hitched a ride in Ben's car to Asaba, and from there jumped into a taxi straight to Onitsha, where Isabella lived. I went to spend a couple of days with Manuel, and saw Isabella every day until I finally left for home.

Chapter 14

We went back to university after six long and painful weeks at home, and we were all made to sign an undertaking of good behaviour and pay some money for the damage done to the Law Faculty.

The examinations started two days later and they were very intense and fast-paced, with two modules a day. Lectures resumed immediately after exams, as there was a lot of lost time to cover.

Results were released about two weeks later, and I did not perform as well as I had in my first year. In fact, I failed one of my main modules, which meant that I had to carry it over into my third year. Gradually life returned to normal, and the parties resumed both on and off campus. Isabella and I were like a married couple; we were always around each other and she was virtually living with me.

Osato, David and Fred had formed a strong nexus and they ruled the area. James and I tried to distance ourselves from them during the day, but we hung out with them sometimes at night-time.

I met Charlie a.k.a. "Charlie Angel" on one such night. He was in his third year of Biochemistry and was an experienced member of the BNM. He was the most peculiar person that I had ever met. "Charlie Angel" was not an angel by any stretch of the imagination. He was dark in complexion, relatively handsome and had chubby cheeks; but he had the most devilish eyes that I had ever seen. He had eyes like a cat when he laughed; his laugh was like thunder striking and the pupils in his eyes shrank and contracted like those of a cat.

Charlie Angel's grandfather was a well-known witch doctor, and it was rumoured that he would take young Charlie to his witch doctor's meetings, which was where he learnt how to play the drums. No one I knew handled the drums like Charlie Angel; his drumming was soul-lifting and riveting.

Charlie Angel was a very mysterious individual; often he would suddenly appear from nowhere, and you never knew when he left. I was very keen to learn more about him, but he was very guarded about what he divulged to people. After a couple of weeks he became more comfortable with me and gradually opened up.

From Charlie Angel, I learnt a lot about the history of the BNM. He taught me about unpredictability, which was the best asset for a member of the "brotherhood" according to him; that way, people did not know when he arrived and left. He told me that he never took the same route to campus twice in a row, and never sat with his back to a door. He also talked about certain herbs in the bushes with which he could communicate, and how he could read the signs of time. He was not concerned that some people thought that he was strange and weird.

I learnt some valuable lessons from Charlie Angel, but I was not ready to go into the deeper realms of occultism that he wanted to introduce to me. Isabella could not stand him and wanted me to cut all ties with him; she felt that he was the anti-Christ. Therefore, I kept the two away from each other.

The Mafioso clan were probably biding their time before carrying out a strike on the Eiye; but the Eiye were no fools or novices in the art of warfare. They were on high alert, always in groups of six or more at any time of day, and sleeping in the same room in groups at night.

The Buccaneers were the party boys and they were holding a super bike party at Nortell Plaza. This party was strictly by invitation, and most of the big boys with super bikes on and off campus would be attending. Babes were falling over each other to be invited, as it was the Ivy League of all parties.

A few key BNM members were invited as a token of goodwill and to avoid any "bad belly" from them. I got to attend this groove through Isabella's connections, as her cousin was one of the Buccaneer biker boys and was an easy-going guy – or so I thought.

The party was the bomb. There were copious amounts of drinks and food, the music was great, the DJ was well renowned in the area and he knew how to drop a beat. The babes were looking sweet and sexy and were dressed to kill and the guys were wearing designer apparel from head to toe.

Some of the dudes were hanging out with their babes around their bikes, some were on the dance floor; the whole atmosphere and setting was like a scene out of a Hollywood movie.

The party was one of the best that I had ever attended and it went on into the early hours of the morning. We got a ride home at about 4 am from Isabella's cousin Tobe.

There were many shows happening on and off campus, and the most anticipated one, due to happen in the next four days, was the great Afro beat king Fela Anikulapo-Kuti's performance in town. We all loved Fela in Nigeria as he sang against injustice, corruption in the government and the oppression of the masses; in fact, he was a crusader for a better Nigeria and Africa in general.

The university authorities refused to allow the show to take place on campus, because they were scared that Fela's music could incite students to rebellion, as they could not censor him. The Christian community put the school authorities under enormous pressure, because the lyrics of Fela's music could be sometimes vulgar. The gyrating dance moves of his dancers were not just vulgar but could be deemed distasteful to the Godly.

We loved Fela all the same and the show was scheduled to be held off campus – until, to our huge disappointment, the show was cancelled at the last minute, because Fela was deemed too much of a risk to be let loose in a university town filled with impressionable youngsters.

It was a major let-down and the organisers tried to bring in some other musician to replace Fela, but the event was already doomed and the show was a big flop.

The campus was always a beehive of activity; male students were constantly scoping out babes in famous joints on campus, such as the NFA joint, the bus and bike stops, the school butteries and the admin block.

The front of the admin block was always rowdy, especially when freshmen were coming to gain admission into the university. Students and admin staff brokered many deals there; it was a known fact that some students offered bogus admission papers for sale to people desperate to gain admission.

The campus also offered you the opportunity to see the latest fashions in town – babes wanted to look good for the guys and the guys wanted to impress the babes. Fashion had gone crazy in 1992; some of the babes were now wearing see-through tops, fishnet stockings and micro-mini skirts and some of the guys would turn up wearing workmen's overalls with huge work boots.

There were also rumours flying around about female students sleeping with lecturers for good grades. It was well known on campus that some unscrupulous lecturers were exchanging good grades for sex and cash. I had also heard about some decent girls who had rebuffed certain lecturers' sexual advances, only to fail those modules with no right to appeal.

The BNM had also held three gatherings during the semester, and the punishment for non-attendance was a five-minute "mending" by a three-man squad. The alternative was six lashes with a horsewhip; there was no exception to this rule.

Examination time was fast approaching and lectures were winding down. Students were busy catching up on any lectures they had missed, and extra lessons were being organised by groups of bright students to help out fellow classmates.

The examinations were tough and the invigilation was even tougher. I was tested on eight modules within the span of a week and a half. I heaved a huge sigh of relief as I finished my last paper, and against my better judgement, Osato and I made our way towards the NFA joint to cool down with a cold bottle of beer and a fag.

As we sat there, discussing the last paper, a group of campus "Deeper Life" members approached us and began to preach to us about finding salvation and accepting Christ as our Lord and Saviour. I could see Osato starting to get angry at this intrusion. "*Who tell una say Christ no be* my Lord and Saviour?" he enquired from the group.

"If he was, you would not be sitting here drinking alcohol and smoking cigarettes," a girl in the group replied. I knew Osato had just been rubbed the wrong way, so I stepped in and diplomatically got them to move on by accepting a leaflet from them.

As the group left us to find someone else to bother, I could not help but ponder how much my life had changed. I had gone from attending church every Sunday and Wednesday at Dominion College to not attending church at all. I had not attended church in the last fourteen months, except at Christmas on the insistence of my father.

We finished our drinks and our cigarettes and I headed to my flat. Osato wanted to hang around campus to see a babe that he was "toasting." I jumped onto an Okada and was heading for the school gate when I heard some kind of commotion going on in the Faculty of Social Sciences; but I was keen to get back to my room and just chill out with Isabella.

I was half asleep when Osato came knocking on my door three hours later. Isabella was studying for her last examination and was visibly upset about the disturbance. She opened the door and called my attention to Osato's presence, and I went outside with him because he wanted to speak with me privately. He told me that the Mafioso had carried out a hit on the 'Falcon' of the Eiye confraternity. The Falcon was the third in the hierarchy of the Eiye.

Three Mafioso hit men wearing green berets had opened fire on the Falcon and two of his henchmen as they came out of the exam hall; the news going around was that the "Falcon" was dead and the Eiye were crying for blood.

The university authorities acted decisively and swiftly, and heavily armed police officers were drafted into the campus to allow the final exams to be completed. Curfews were imposed inside and outside the campus, and the police were patrolling the town.

The university was shut down immediately after the final exams, and we were all asked to vacate the campus as well as the university town, for our own safety. Isabella's father sent a driver and a police escort to pick her up and I hitched a ride back to Asaba.

I stayed at home for a couple of days, hanging out with Prince and other members of the BNM. I also attended the regional gathering of the BNM in Asaba, but I missed Isabella so much that I had to make up an excuse at home to travel to Onitsha to be close to her. Head over heels in love, I could not imagine life without her. We were soul mates and very passionate about each other; we had even discussed the number of children that we would have after getting married.

I spent about a week with my friend Manuel, and hung out with Isabella every day. During one of our evenings together, we ran into her cousin Tobe at a dried meat "suya" joint. He was pleased to see his cousin but was rather cold towards me, which I attributed to the fact that he did not know me well. I headed back home to Asaba a couple of days later.

Then on a Sunday afternoon, I got a disturbing phone call that left me distraught for many years to come. It came from Isabella; she was weeping over the phone as she narrated her ordeal at the hands of her father.

She told me that her cousin Tobe had asked her for a substantial amount of money and she had declined, as he still owed her a previous loan. In retaliation, he had gone and told her father that she was living with a boy who was a secret cult member.

"Remy, I did not believe what my cousin accused you of because I know that you are not a member of secret cult. I verbally attacked him and vehemently defended your reputation," Isabella told me.

At this point her father had physically assaulted her and declared that her fate would not include education anymore; rather, she would be married off to the first suitor who asked for her hand. It was heart-wrenching, soul-destroying, to hear the love of my life say these words. I vowed to rip Tobe's heart out with my bare hands.

I had never felt this confused and helpless in all my life, as if a vital organ had been torn out of me and I was going to die at any moment.

Isabella was under lock and key and was not allowed outside the house, except to go to church on Sundays. She was a prisoner and her parents monitored her closely.

There was no way for me to see her in person, but I managed to speak to her once – she told me that a suitor had come for her hand, and she was going to be forced into marrying a pot-bellied man.

She had nobody to turn to for help and her mother was petrified of her husband. I went to seek legal advice on her behalf, but was told that it was a waste of time and energy; her case would not stand up in a customary court as she was still under her parents' control. I confided in and sought advice from friends in my own age group and adults, desperately looking for a solution.

The response was almost unanimous: I was advised to walk away and not mess with a family affair. I remember vividly what an elder said to me regarding the issue, "Do you think that you have her best interests at heart more than the people who gave birth to her?" he asked.

"This cannot be right," I thought, that a young girl of nineteen should be forced into an arranged marriage. I encouraged Isabella over the telephone to seek help from her church priest; but she was very sceptical about that as her father was a major donor to the church, and they would not want to meddle in his personal affairs. After a couple of weeks spent searching for a solution, I was at my wits' end. But I knew deep down in my heart that I could not afford to let down the girl I loved so dearly. I would never be able to live with myself if I could not protect my precious gem; so I came to one desperate but unfortunate solution, and that was to elope with her.

We hatched the plot together over the telephone, and with the help of her younger sister. She escaped from home two days later. Isabella arrived at my home in Asaba that evening, and I remember the pain that I felt on seeing her.

She had lost her long and beautiful hair from the physical assault by her father; she was now sporting a very short hairstyle that gave her an Angelique Kidjo look. We spent the night in Asaba before departing for Benin City the next day. I knew many BNM members there, and I chose to stay with James, who was my flat mate and like a brother to me.

James's brother was based in the USA, and James had the key to his house. He was happy to accommodate Isabella and me for as long as we wanted to stay.

We settled down quickly, as the house was well furnished. James made sure that there was enough food to last for months and we were content because we had each other. We kept a very low profile and only went out under the cover of darkness, to a few select places.

We did not know how this episode was going to end; but we were willing to hold on for as long as it took. It was now about three weeks since we had eloped – and we were running out of money. The strain of being in this situation and being away from the life to which she was accustomed was beginning to tell on Isabella, but I constantly tried to keep her upbeat.

I got information from various sources that Isabella's parents had now been able to trace my parents to Asaba, and they were threatening to institute a court case against me for the kidnapping and forceful imprisonment of their daughter. My father, as a renowned legal luminary, was gracious enough to point out the fact that their daughter had left home of her own free will.

My parents were keen to locate me in order to bring this so-called madness of mine to a quick end, before things got out of hand. They sent out a message through my younger brother, who knew some of my close friends; but to no avail.

The university term had now resumed but lectures had not commenced, and James had to go back to complete his registration. He would be gone for two days and I was keen to hear what was happening on campus upon his return.

James came back with only one piece of good news, but a lot of bad news. The good news was that lectures had not started; but the bad news made my heart sink. Isabella's parents had now notified the police in the university town, and the police were looking to drum up a charge of abduction against me. Her parents had formally withdrawn her as a student of the university and had cleared out her room; and they now had an idea of our location.

I felt as if I had been physically eviscerated and could sense the net beginning to tighten around us. How long could we stay in hiding, now that our money was fast dwindling and the police wanted us?

What were the options available to us now? I thought about getting her pregnant and demanding to marry her; but I knew that this would ruin her bright future and mine as well. I even considered the Mark Anthony and Cleopatra ending, but quickly dismissed that option as stupid.

We both sat down and concluded that while we still had the advantage, we needed to leverage it, rather than be left in a position of weakness. We decided that she had to go back home.

She needed a mediator to help ease her way, and we concluded that she had to go to her parish priest, present herself, and ask him to help broker her return home. It would be soul-destroying to see her go but I knew that it was the best for her future.

I watched Isabella get into the taxi that would take her on the two-hour journey to Onitsha and I could not help but wonder if this was the last time that I would ever see her. I knew she was scared, but putting on a brave face. I kissed her and reassured her that everything was going to work out for the best; and as I watched the car pull away from the taxi park, I found myself saying a silent prayer under my breath. I felt the same emptiness and abandonment that I had felt when my father's blue Peugeot 504 had pulled away on my first day at Dominion College.

I went back to James's brother's empty house and lay in bed. I could still smell Isabella's perfume on the pillows and bed sheets, and the spirit of depression descended and took hold of my soul. I must have lain there for many hours, because I woke up to James coming into the house the next morning to check up on me. He could see that I was in bad shape.

James and I left Benin City to go back to our university flat and loneliness continued to dog me for many months to come. I promptly began attending lectures, having already missed a few days. I jumped straight into the thick of things and I had no time for any social events. I went from the lecture hall straight to my bedroom for the next four weeks. Not eating properly, I lost weight drastically.

By the end of the fourth week, James and Sly were very concerned about my health and made every attempt possible to get me back to my usual bubbly self – but all to no avail. To fill the void, I started hanging out regularly with Osato, Fred and David and smoking Igbo with them on a regular basis. Marijuana was a temporary high that took away the void and the pain of losing Isabella.

The more I wanted this temporary high to be permanent the more I smoked Igbo. After several weeks of smoking Marijuana with Osato and his crew on a regular basis, I decided that Marijuana alone could not sustain the high that I was craving.

My new high came one night when Osato and David let me in on their money-making venture. It was called "obtaining," but my conscience called it armed robbery. It was about taking a bike man to a secluded location, where we would dispossess him of his daily takings; we were armed with knives, hand axes and a replica pistol.

The first time I joined in this act of robbery, I could fleetingly hear my father's voice telling me to always uphold the family name. I quickly brushed this voice aside, as always.

We made some money from this nocturnal venture and spent it on beer and more Marijuana. This carried on for a couple of weeks; and that was where I got the nickname of "Remyleon," given to me by David. He said that although I had the most innocent and "aje butter" looking face, I was ruthless when it came to knocking bike men out with a single blow.

"Remyleon" was a cross between Remy and a chameleon, and I revelled in this nickname. Most bike men stopped operating around our vicinity, so we had to go further afield to carry out our lucrative venture.

But it soon, of course, came to a point where this venture coupled with Igbo smoking was no longer enough to fill the void left by Isabella's departure; and my conscience was becoming a heavier burden to carry by the day.

So I dropped out of the whole venture and turned to sex as a new high. James and I became a formidable force to reckon with. No one could take Isabella's place in my heart – but many girls took her place in my bed. Patricia, Angela, Stella, Ancey, Amaka, Philomena, Jane, Joy a.k.a. "lover," Agatha, Chioma, Nkechi, Stella, Barbara, and so many more that I cannot even remember their names.

James gave me a new nickname, "the bolongo master," while I called him the "guru of bolongo." Life was unrestrained and I was fast becoming a renowned sexual predator. It was ironic that whatever path or route one chose to tread in life, there would always be someone available to assist and encourage one on that path.

We now had a new Alfa in the BNM confraternity, as the previous one had been rusticated for two years for examination malpractice and assaulting a lecturer. The new Alfa was a bull-necked, belligerent chap and not one to make compromises. He believed in the old philosophy of the BNM: one member of the BNM was worth ten Mafioso, Buccaneers and Eiye put together. Feared and revered within and outside the BNM confraternity, he was not keen on taking prisoners. He was very insular in his ways and his commands were sacrosanct.

We were always on the verge of fighting many wars; the Alfa surrounded himself with like-minded people and there was a lot of war-mongering going on. The benevolent and level-headed members of the BNM were all side-lined.

The new Executioner was another belligerent guy who took delight in taunting and oppressing members of other confraternities, especially the Buccaneers and the Black Berets. He regarded the Buccaneers as more of a social club than a secret cult. The Black Berets were a breakaway faction from the BNM that had originated from the East; he hated them with a passion, and was known to obtain money from them at every opportunity.

There were two factions developing within the BNM: the bull-necked Marauders, and the level-headed ones who wanted to graduate from university. The

Executioner was of the opinion that a strong Marauder must wear his colours with pride and in public, and be ready to fall out at any time.

This new regime continued for the next four months until the inevitable occurred. The Buccaneers and Black Berets teamed up and came after us big time; for the first time in almost three years, a major war was declared, and we were called upon to fight this war on two fronts.

The Buccaneers came at us with firepower that we did not know they had. Though surprised, we retaliated with twice their effort, and went for their heart: we took the war to them and destroyed their cars and bikes. We even took the war to their zonal coordinator, who lived in the next town; he fled for his life.

I was part of the squad that rolled after the Black Berets; we went looking for their "Big Chair," but missed him by a whisker. In anger, we destroyed all his personal possessions. The war was fought mainly in town; but when we realised that both the Buccaneers and the BBs had fled to the campus, we sent masked BNM squads to campus at night.

The squads moved frenetically, combing through the campus, and at the end of the night the Buccaneers and the BBs had suffered five casualties in total; and we were not finished.

The university was closed down immediately and all the students were asked to vacate the premises. Security operatives from the state CID flooded into town, picking up suspected cultists. They picked up the Executioner and some well-known BNM members.

Chapter 15

Following the university closure, I headed once again for Onitsha to see my good friend Manuel, and to find out if there was any news about Isabella. Manuel's younger sister Ijeoma knew Isabella socially, so she was my link into Isabella's life.

I saw Isabella again for the first time after about six months, when she came to Manuel's house with Ijeoma. She melted into my arms and I was healed of all my emptiness and loneliness; she was looking well and her hair had started to grow back.

"I am so blessed to be able to see and hold you in my arms again," I whispered into her ear, "we have a lot of catching up to do, sweetheart." She began her story from when the taxi had driven out of the park and headed for Onitsha; she had arrived in the afternoon, gone straight to the office of the Bishop of the diocese, and submitted herself to his mercy.

The Bishop had summoned her parents to his office that same day, and they had sat down to address the issue at hand. Isabella's father had a very high regard for the clergyman, and he agreed to bury the hatchet and take her back. He rescinded on his initial stance but in return, Isabella was to cut any ties with me and move to another university closer to home. She was also to carry out the sacrament of confession and book a mass of penance in church.

I was not perturbed that she'd had to choose her future over me; in fact, I was glad that she had her life back and was now studying computer science at a Federal University and doing well. We saw each other regularly for the next couple of weeks, as we had a lot of catching up to do; she gave me her new address.

My university remained closed for many months, not just because of the confraternity issues but because the National Union of Lecturers had gone on strike again.

Lectures began immediately on the reopening of college and were now moving at a fast pace, as we had already lost about four months of the academic calendar and the final year students were at risk of missing out on the National Youth Service.

The CID officers had released the Executioner of the BNM after letting him cool off in detention for about three months; but he was due to face the university senate in two days' time alongside eighteen other offenders, for secret cultism and bringing disrepute to the university.

The BNM had gone further underground as we became the major target of the CID and the university authorities. The local CID now had their operatives posing as undergraduates, and most BNM gatherings were suspended until further notice.

The University Senate was a panel of five distinguished Professors with unblemished academic and personal records, whose main function was to look into and take important decisions affecting the university. They served as the judicial arm of the university and had the authority to rusticate or expel any erring undergraduate student or lecturer.

The Exccutioner's fate after standing before the Senate was a two-year rustication from the university, with immediate effect. This was a big blow to the bull-necked section of the BNM; but some other members were not sad to see the back of this belligerent miscreant. The Executioner was the backbone of the Alfa, and the latter was becoming increasingly isolated, especially with the selection of a new Executioner.

The new Executioner was chosen by consulting the five wise men of the BNM, and the man of choice was a level-headed, gregarious, experienced but sturdy guy, nicknamed 'Hammer'. Hammer was a muscular six-footer, the son of an ex-army captain, and he had in-depth knowledge of various weapons and arsenal; he had in the past helped to procure and service all of our heavy-duty weapons.

The Alfa's position became untenable when he unwittingly raped the cousin of a Marauder. Under normal circumstances, nobody would have had the effrontery to challenge the Alfa, as he was the supreme leader and authority. The Council of wise men would always be wary of exercising their constitutional rights against the Alfa.

But the rape of a BNM member's relative was a step too far, and this act was deemed to be an insult and a smear upon the office of the Alfa. The national body of the BNM put the Council of wise men under immense pressure, but the latter still did not have the courage to challenge an Alfa.

The national body had no option but to evoke one of the by-laws, and by the power vested in them as custodians of the BNM, they excommunicated the Alfa. Excommunication was no easy or straightforward process; the Alfa had to go through all the rites he had been through on the day of his initiation, including the beating and mending, after which his symbol of the brotherhood was broken; from then onwards he was an ordinary civilian, and could not come to any gathering of the Marauders.

The Council of wise men were relieved of their positions, as they had failed to take decisive action against the now-excommunicated Alfa. A caretaker government was appointed to manage affairs until a new Alfa and Council of wise men could be appointed.

Many of the rebels within the BNM were enraged by the interference of the national body in our local affairs; but we were subject and accountable to the national body, as stated in the BNM constitution.

Under the watchful eye of the national body, the new caretaker government stayed in place for the next three weeks. They helped with the careful selection of the new Council of wise men and oversaw their immediate swearing-in.

It was now the responsibility of the new Council of wise men to find another Alfa. They had a few days to do this, and their decision would be final. The search for a new Alfa involved a process of elimination, and the various candidates were finally trimmed down to just two finalists. Although we all knew that the selection was down to two candidates but we did not know who they were at this stage.

The Voice started crying out about a very important, mandatory BNM meeting one night at 10 pm, up the mountain on the West side of campus.

I had made up my mind not to attend the gathering that night and take the punishment that would follow, as I was still settling into my new place. I had moved out of my old flat after James and Sly graduated, and was now staying with Marcus and Patrick in a three-bedroom apartment, within a well-secured compound strategically located in the heart of the university town – a dream apartment for the start of my final year at university. The landlord was an ex-army officer based in Lagos.

From my new apartment, it normally took about fifteen minutes on a bike to get to campus, but only five minutes in Marcus's car.

I had also arranged for a new babe called Lillian to spend the night; I had been "toasting" her for the last three weeks and was not prepared to lose this opportunity with her. I had already ordered some fried rice and chicken with drinks from Tommy's kitchen, and I had a Michael Bolton CD in the player ready to belt out the tune "Soul Provider." And as for me, man, I was already in the zone.

It was about 8 pm that evening when Osato came bursting into my flat, dressed in black from head to toe. "Remyleon, we got to fall out sharp sharp," he said. "I am not stepping out of this house my guy, I get better sushi 'babe' that I am expecting," I replied, rubbing my hands together with glee.

"Forget babe my guy, *they don talk say na big wahala for people that don't turn up*," Osato warned. "Your flat mates are around, let them entertain the babe until you get back, just for two hours," he insisted.

I rethought the implications of not attending the gathering and decided to show my face there for a couple of hours before sneaking back for my rendezvous with Lillian.

We made our way through the thick bushes towards the proposed site, and as we passed the guards on duty we gave them the customary brotherhood greeting. There were extra guards positioned at strategic points along the way, armed to the teeth, doped out of their heads, and ready for any action.

"Wetin, dey happen tonight?" I asked one of the guards. *"Na today we dey get our new Alfa,"* he replied as he waved his pistol in the air. I moved on quickly; I wasn't quite ready to be the victim of an accidental discharge from a dope-head.

As the Council of wise men stood in the centre of the circle along with the Omega and the Executioner, the atmosphere was tense and there was an air of expectation all around. One of the wise men whispered into the ear of the Omega, and handed him the ceremonial staff of office.

The Omega broke into a spiritual song that eulogised the god of the BNM. He sang for about ten minutes and then suddenly stopped, shouting out in a loud voice: "By the power conferred on me by the supreme Council of the wise men and by the oracle, I now declare ----- (very long pause) Marauder with bush name 'Fine boy' as the new Alfa of the Black Night Marauders. I hail you my new Alfa, supreme leader of the BNM."

The silence hanging in the air was intense; the Omega cleared his throat twice, and took a deep breath and a step forward before bellowing in a louder voice, "I pronounce Marauder with bush name 'Fine boy' a.k.a. Remyleon as the new Alfa of the Black Night Marauders, I hail you my Alfa."

I stood dumbfounded and rooted to the spot for what seemed like an eternity, with my mouth wide open. Had I heard my Omega correctly? Before I realised what was happening, I was bundled towards another section of the bush. I received five minutes of mending before I was deemed worthy to go into the circle to complete the final rites and take my staff of office.

After the rite was completed, the insignia of office was handed to me and as I held it, all the Marauders shouted out together, "We hail you our Alfa." As I stood there, I could feel this strange force envelope me, and I knew from that moment that my life could never be the same again. I became the supreme leader of the BNM on the 1st of January 1996.

I took control of the gathering as I had seen previous Alfas do, and my message was simple. It was about the unification of the brotherhood, the coming together of all factions to form a tight nexus. I highlighted the fact that in the brotherhood there was no discrimination, no partiality, as we stood together as one. I also made it abundantly clear that I was not going to tolerate any form of thuggery and anti-social behaviour, as we had to clean up our image.

As the Alfa, I was now the heart and soul of the BNM in the university, and I knew that I had become the most powerful confraternity lord in the university. I was not too deluded to be aware that I would also be the most wanted guy in the university. I remembered the warning James had given me long ago and I was determined to keep a low profile and continue life as normal.

I chose my own two bodyguards, who were always armed and never too far away from me. I did not want bodyguards who were known to the whole university as cult members; I wanted clean guys, to avoid drawing unnecessary attention to myself. My bodyguards were specially trained by Hammer, and they knew how to mix in with the crowd when on campus with me. I knew that they were around me on campus but they never made contact.

I was very careful to surround myself with civilians; especially the babes. All Marauders were banned from paying homage to me on campus or coming to my flat. I made it very clear that I was not looking for new friends, as I wanted to keep a low profile. The BNM issued me with two 9 mm Berretta handguns, which fired six and nine rounds of live ammunition. I was required to carry at least one steel with me at all times. Although I had never used a handgun in my life before, my Executioner was there to teach me.

I had a vision for a better BNM. I wanted more of our members to graduate, rather than be expelled. There was no sense in fighting meaningless wars when we should be enjoying university life. I wanted a BNM that would fight against oppression, and not be the oppressor. It was going to require a complete overhaul of the members' current mind-set and this was not going to be easy, but I was willing and ready to give it my best shot.

Aiming to be a different kind of Alfa, able to influence my brothers within the BNM, I started reading leadership and motivational books for my own development and self-fulfilment. From reading these books, I realised that we could still maintain our core values, remain deadly and fearsome, but also do things differently.

I banned all Marauders from hanging out at the NFA joints on campus. I believed that when we came to school for lectures, we should attend those lectures and not the NFA joints. The NFA joints were the main hotspot for trouble and fallouts between confraternities.

It was unacceptable to be involved in any form of "obtaining" and theft, and this was punishable by serious mending depending on the degree of the offense. Rape was an abominable act and would result in instant mending and excommunication.

I was determined to restore respect and sanity to the BNM, but I was fully aware that we were not a social club but a secret cult, and had a certain core ethos driving us. There were certain things that I could not amend or attempt to eradicate.

Victor was the Omega of the BNM and I met with him under the cover of darkness three weeks after becoming the Alfa. We shook hands and did the usual situation report; he was keen to tell me about a group of disgruntled Marauders who felt that we were now becoming a social club.

Victor was the oracle of the confraternity and was responsible for all consultation with the gods on behalf of the BNM; he also brought us words from the gods.

Victor was adamant on taking me to visit our designated witch doctor, called Baba *"dem no dey catch air."* He was renowned in the state as a strong medicine man, able to invoke rain, thunder and sunshine at his will. He had once put a tortoise into a bottle.

"My Alfa, *you no fit carry ordinary body for this runs, I get to carry you go see Baba, make e cook you well well,"* my Omega insisted. I had seen black magic work before,

207

but my religious upbringing had always deterred me from that option. I was of the opinion that it would only work for those who believed in it.

"Why don't you do it on my behalf?" I suggested, as I was not keen to visit any juju man. "You already do it for the whole clan," I concluded. "My Alfa, don't forget that you are the father, the heart and soul of BNM, we can't chance any scratch on you," he reminded me and he reiterated that he had already booked an appointment with Baba for tomorrow.

I knew that my Omega was forcing my hand and I did not like it; but I also knew that my office carried a huge responsibility.

The next day, I went with Victor to see the juju man and I was visibly nervous as we knelt before Baba. He looked at me and I stared back at him; he then turned to Omega, whom he knew very well, and asked him, *'Na your new oga be this,"* to which Victor replied, *"Yes Baba, we wan cook am well well."*

He asked us to put our consultation fee in the bowl beside him. He then took the chicken we had brought along and started chanting incantations repeatedly; he asked me to strip to my boxer shorts and kneel in front of his oracle. The incantations went on for about five minutes, after which he killed the chicken and used its blood to draw some strange symbols on my body.

He mixed the blood of the chicken with some native chalk and made some more strange marks on my forehead. Then, dipping a small broom into a different mixture, he used it to circle my head, and said some more incantations as he walked around the shrine.

The juju man asked me to go and take a bath in an inner shrine, which had what looked like a pool. I noticed that the water in the pool was milky and I could not see the bottom. As I hesitantly stepped into the pool and sat down, I could feel a strange force descend on me, and I felt empowered, albeit in a strange way.

After about three minutes of bathing in the pool, I got out and dried myself using a towel that I had brought along with me. I hurriedly changed into my clothes as the juju man handed me a cowry tied to a string. He asked me to put it on, which I did; he then pointed to some native chalk at the far end of the shrine, and asked me to go and get it. As I turned around and made my way towards the chalk, I heard the loading of a gun behind me and instinctively turned around, just in time to see the juju man fire the gun at me.

I thought that I was dead and had gone to hell; but there I was, standing with my hands held up to my face. He fired again at a closer range – and again, I could not feel or see any bullet penetrate my body. As I looked on in disbelief, I did not see the juju man's son come up behind me and strike me on the back with a sharp machete. The machete hit me squarely on the right shoulder – and bounced back off it. I felt no pain; in fact, I felt nothing. I heard the juju man then call out in a strange voice as he looked at his oracle.

"You *don fortify well well*," he said to me as he shook my hand. I thanked him and as I turned to leave, he called out to me, *"Make sure you dey wear your cowry and no ride horse* (sleeping with a woman) for seven days."

It took Victor and me about an hour to return to the university town and on our way back to the university, Victor kindly volunteered some jaw-dropping information. He told me that the milky-coloured pool in the shrine housed a big Python that came out once every fortnight.

This information sent shivers down my spine, and I could feel and see goose-bumps starting to appear. I made my way back to my flat and, as I lay in bed reflecting on the day's events, I could not help but feel disappointed with myself. Right from a young age, I had been taught at home and in Sunday school that my body was the temple of the Lord. I could not help but feel that I had just violated it, given it over to the dark side completely, with this particular event.

My social life returned to normal and there were many shows and events on and off campus. I kept away from as many of these events as possible and only attended the odd one or two when cajoled by a new babe.

Since becoming the Alfa, I was very cautious about the way my fellow Marauders treated me in public. I regularly reiterated the fact that I did not expect them to pay homage to me in a public place where everybody was watching; I also banned Marauders from smoking Igbo in public.

I must confess that my life changed completely since becoming the Alfa. I now had to carry a gun on me at all times, and had two bodyguards around me by virtue of my position. Marauders were falling over each other to be in my good books, and my bills at restaurants were paid for before I had the chance to eat the food.

I was now arguably the most powerful man on and off campus; the *Capo di tutti Capi* of the university community, I had the power to do and undo. I had the power to have the Vice Chancellor of the university kidnapped if I wanted to.

The BNM had three official suicide squads that were available and overseen by the Executioner. These squads were made up of daredevils willing and capable of carrying out the most daring and dangerous missions. They were a merciless bunch of Marauders who would carry out any instructions given to them to the letter.

In addition to these official squads, I set up my own squad of five that reported directly to me; and they were as, if not more, ruthless than the official suicide squads. My personal crack squad included the likes of The Bulldog, Bilado, Ike "the killer," Alahaji, "Onye Hausa," and Otoro. I also had some substitutes that I could utilise for other missions.

The reason for having my own hit squad was that I needed a few people I could trust with my life, people with no affiliation to any section of the BNM, who were ready to move at the drop of a hat.

I needed a group of dedicated Marauders who would help enforce my new vision for the BNM, do things like making sure that Marauders were attending lectures; they were my eyes and ears for what was happening on and off campus.

All Marauders were now aware that when my hit squad paid you a visit, it was not for tea and biscuits.

Chapter 16

I was in my final year in the department of Accountancy and was keen to graduate on schedule. As I sat in my lecture hall among about one hundred and twenty people, I looked around and could easily count about thirty Marauders in my class. I could also count the number of well-known Eiye, Mafioso, Vikings, Buccaneers, and Pyrates in the same class; and it dawned on me that more than half of the students in the hall were affiliated to one confraternity or another.

We were careful to be cordial to each other during the day and during lectures, but outside the lecture halls and especially at night, we would slit each other's throats in a heartbeat.

I was distracted from my thoughts by a note passed to me by Theo. Theo was a guy after my own heart, a very experienced Marauder who would stand by his word and was not pious in any way. He was the head of the Council of the wise men, and he had the gravitas required to hold that position; I had plenty of time and respect for him.

The note read that Oscar, one of the belligerent Marauders, had been involved in a fight with two Viking henchmen at the NFA joint; the two Vikings had come out of the fracas worse off and bloodied. I tore up the note as I made eye contact with Chucks the deputy Seer at the other end of the lecture hall; I nodded towards him, which was a cue for him to get me a situation report.

I got the report from the Seer within hours, indicating that the Vikings were rallying at a strategic location, with the intention of bringing Oscar down.

I knew that Oscar was an experienced Marauder with his own clique within the BNM, and that he would not go down without a fight. I was not scared of a war with the Vikings, as they were a minor group without much "liver" punch behind them; but I was not looking for a senseless war either.

I remembered what "Charlie Angel" had once told me: "For you to fight a justified war, you must first understand the language of peace." We had experienced a rare period of peace within and outside the BNM, and I had come to realise that there was growth, peace of mind and progress during that time; I was in no hurry for that to change.

I knew that I had to intervene immediately. I sent a message to Hammer to deploy two armed squads to the location where the Vikings were congregating. Another squad was to go and provide backup to Oscar.

However, most importantly, I sent my hit squad, led by The Bulldog, to the Vikings' main man with a clear and simple message: "Make a move and we will completely obliterate you guys from the face of the planet."

The Vikings knew better than to mess with us and with our movement on that night, they knew that *wahala fit dey town*. They backed down quickly and quietly went off to lick their wounds; my Seer and Voice nevertheless kept a watchful eye on their movements for a couple of days.

Two days after the fracas, I paid Oscar a visit under the cover of night in the company of The Bulldog, Bilado and Alahaji. Oscar got the beating and mending of his life for disobeying my direct instructions to avoid the NFA joint.

I had gone to visit Isabella a couple of times at the University of Nigeria Nsukka, one of the premier universities in Nigeria, where she was now studying. It was a five-hour journey by road, but I did not mind as I was so much in love.

I was planning to go to Nsukka in two days' time, which happened to be the 13th of February in the year 1996, to see my jewel, when Osato sent a coded message to me announcing a surprise visit. I sensed that he was warning me. When Osato came bursting into my flat at about 7 pm with Isabella behind him, my frown quickly turned into joy as I immediately kissed her and lifted her off her feet.

What a pleasant surprise! She had come all the way from Nsukka for Valentine's Day and had gone to my old flat looking for me. She had luckily run into Osato, who still lived on Poultry Road.

We were loved up for the next five days, and Isabella and I were inseparable. We went for romantic walks in the evening, had candle-light dinners at the Plaza, and went to most of the shows on and off campus held to mark Valentine's Day.

Isabella was quick to observe that people were most eager to pay for our food and drinks whenever we went out; but I dismissed it as just a mere coincidence. The four nights that she spent with me were the most memorable and passionate nights I'd had in a very long time.

I felt that loneliness start to grow in my heart again as she stepped into the taxi that would take her on the long journey back to Nsukka. My mind flashed back to when she'd had to leave me for Onitsha some years ago. She waved to me as the car pulled away and I promised to see her during the semester break.

As I climbed on an Okada back to my flat, I felt that the time was now ripe to take my revenge on Isabella's Buccaneer cousin. The porridge was long cold – revenge should be sweeter now; but I did not want to make it look like a direct hit from the BNM.

So I sent my personal hit squad on this mission. The task was simple – it was for them to send Tobe to hospital for a few weeks, but to do this fully masked and flying the colours of the Black Beret confraternity.

The mission was carried out swiftly and successfully as planned, and we sat back and watched the Buccaneers and the Black Berets get into two days of serious fighting before they reached a truce. The Black Berets were forced to pay for Tobe's hospital treatment; and to this day, the Buccaneers still hold the Black Berets responsible for the hit on Tobe.

I had no sympathy for the Black Berets – it would serve them right for teaming up with the Buccaneers against the BNM many semesters ago.

I then redirected my attention to the affairs of the BNM, as we were fast approaching the period of initiation. I gave the go-ahead to Hammer to open up the canvassing period to all Marauders who had prospects in mind.

To be considered for the first stage of initiation, the prospect, called "a bagger," must have a sponsor from within the BNM and must have paid a 300 Naira registration fee. It was a known fact that Marauders could charge a bagger twice that amount; but woe betide any Marauder who tried to short-change the Clan.

After two weeks of canvassing, we had received two hundred and fifty applications. I was dumbfounded at the high number of interested prospects, as Hammer briefed me; during my time, we had been about fifty candidates, half of whom had dropped out after the intense drilling.

Hammer was in charge of the initial initiation process, with the assistance of the Omega and Council of wise men. I did not get involved until the final stage, where I performed the official letting of blood and laying of hands. I gave Hammer instructions to reduce the number of candidates by half, as the BNM was not known for numbers but rather for its heart, tenacity and ruggedness. I would rather have ten solid men than have thirty lily-livered boys.

After the first round of initiation, Hammer reported a reduction of candidates by fifty; but we had received an additional thirty new applications. We were making good money from applications, as the fees were non-refundable; but we had a dilemma.

I sent in my hit squad to support Hammer at the next stage, during which the drilling, beating and mending were intensified; yet only ten people dropped out.

I sat with Hammer, Theo and Victor trying to find a way out of this quandary. I could not help but feel sorry for parents who worked hard and sacrificed a lot to send their children to university to study, when in return, these children were only hell bent on joining a secret cult. "*What is wrong with the children of today?*" I thought to myself.

I was prepared to accept no more than fifty people on the final initiation day, which was at the beginning of the second semester; so we had to address this challenge urgently. The third round of pre-initiation drills was to take place "down the valley" and I showed up unannounced, fully masked, with my loaded 9 mm Beretta tucked into my trousers.

I was the first Alfa ever to show up at a pre-initiation drill; but I was keen to get the numbers down. I turned away all "baggers" that arrived late; and any

Marauder with outstanding dues to the brotherhood lost their chance of putting forward a prospect. The heat had been turned up to boiling point, and it was now a case of the survival of the fittest.

After the end of the third round of drilling, we came down to a respectable number of seventy-five; additional applications were still pouring in, which were declined. We now had our sights set on the final stage.

At 6 pm on a certain evening, I had just finished my last lecture for the day and was leaving the hall from the upper exit, when I caught sight of Tima sitting on the staircase and waiting to go in for her lecture. She was a beauty to behold; she reminded me of Victoria. Tall for a girl, she had "aje butter" looks.

I approached her and introduced myself, and she told me her name just as she got up to leave. I watched her enter the hall for the second-year Accountancy lecture and decided to hang around for the next hour. I discharged the bodyguard hanging around, but before he left, he made sure that I had my Beretta fully loaded on me.

After what seemed like an eternity, Tima finally came out with a male classmate. She seemed to have grown even more beautiful during her lecture and I was infatuated. But she was not interested in holding a conversation with me, and kept answering me in monosyllables. Well, I was quite persistent and was able to find out where she lived, which was coincidentally on Poultry Road.

Over the following weeks I saw Tima regularly in the Accountancy department. She became freer with me, and we started chatting and became friends. She was aware that I had a soft spot for her, but she was looking to take her time and not jump into any relationship.

I remember going to pay Tima a visit one night, at the flat she shared with her cousin Eva. Eva's boyfriend was a well-known Mafioso called Solomon, and he was trying to hook Tima up with his friend, so my showing up on the scene was not welcomed.

I had spent about thirty minutes at Tima's flat when Eva came in with Solomon. Tima introduced me to Solomon, who nodded his head and barely acknowledged me. I smiled and kept my cool, and continued my conversation with Tima. About ten minutes later, Solomon's friend came knocking and was let in. He took one look at me and I could see the anger brewing on his face. I quietly felt for my Beretta and was reassured as I felt the butt of the weapon.

The atmosphere was getting too tense for my liking, so I opted to step out for some fresh air with Tima. We spent another ten minutes talking outside the flat, before I decided to go meet some of my civilian classmates. I got an Okada straight to the town centre, and stopped over at the egg joint called "Eggies."

With my face hidden under a face cap, I went in quickly to get the house special of bread, egg and corned beef. The joint was bustling with activity, and the song "power show" by Fela Kuti was blaring from the speakers. Surveying the place, I could make out the pockets of people in various corners, including a couple of well-known Marauders; I nodded in acknowledgement. I picked up my order and gave the cashier money, which was refused as someone had already paid.

I murmured thanks to the cashier and wished that I could sometimes pay for my own food without being beaten to the draw. Later, having decided to walk the rest of the distance to my classmates' house, I turned the corner into their street and had barely taken five steps when three guys jumped out of the bushes all dressed in black and wearing black balaclavas.

I stood still with my heart pounding and my hand immediately going towards my steel. I was very careful not to assume that they were Marauders because they were wearing black face caps. "Identify yourselves sharp sharp or dead body go follow," I called out. *"Na our Alfa be that ooo,"* I heard as they all jumped back into the bushes and ran for cover in different directions.

It then dawned on me that these guys must be recalcitrant Marauders who were "obtaining" money and goods from people.

The next day I sent out urgent instructions for my Seer and Voice to identify the guys behind the previous night's stunt; and before nightfall I was given three names. I had my hit squad pick them up one after the other, and take them into the thick bushes. After about forty-five minutes of intense mending and drilling, they confessed that they were indeed the people who had accosted me the night before.

I was going to set a harsh example with them as a lesson to others, by excommunicating them. However, on second thought I changed my mind, when I realised that two of the Marauders were new to the confraternity and needed more orientation rather than excommunication; but the older Marauder got additional mending for two more consecutive days.

The news spread that I was on the warpath against any act of obtaining or oppression of civilians, and the recalcitrant Marauders became extremely careful in their nefarious acts.

Soon we got news that there had been a bloody fall-out between the Marauders and the Mafioso at another university, which was about two hours' drive from us. The situation report was that one Marauder had been badly injured and two Mafioso were dead, one of them a top general and ex-Don called Lopez.

Lopez had an equally deadly twin brother called Lorenzo, who had been with Lopez when he fell in the hail of bullets from the Marauders. Their university was forced to close down immediately for an indefinite period, but Lorenzo was out for blood. Reports said that he and a group of Mafioso had rolled into town and were congregating around their stronghold. I knew that we could not take any chances with their arrival in town.

I ordered my Voice to cry out to all Marauders to head for "down the valley," In groups. Hammer was under strict instructions to take two crack suicide squads and go into the Mafioso stronghold area, while my hit squad covered the entrance to and exits from "down the valley." I led the squad that held the area surrounding the town centre and the motor park, in case additional Mafioso reinforcements came into town.

The Mafioso knew that we were extra-ready for any falling-out, and their number two man approached Hammer for a dialogue; this was rebuffed by Hammer, as we did not negotiate with terrorists. He was told that if their people were happy to take on an issue external to our university, then we were game. Hammer told him how keen we were to try out our newly acquired sub-machine guns.

The Mafioso were quick to concede that this was not their fight and to move their external brothers to another university. We held our position for two extra nights until we were sure that all the intruders had left town.

The story of our pre-emptive action spread like wildfire to other universities and institutions, and my university became a point of reference. The national and regional bodies of the BNM were quick to latch on to this event and promote the way we had handled the confrontation with the Mafioso.

The Alfa of one of the Federal Universities, about sixty five miles to the North, was having his final initiation ceremony. He wanted some reinforcements from us in form of human resources and artillery, and he sent an emissary with this request.

The final authorisation would come from me after the vetting by my Executioner. Hammer was happy to release some human resources but was not keen to release any of our firepower, for obvious reasons.

The Voice brought a message that the emissary from the other university would like a meeting with me, so we set one up for 8 pm at Victor's house. I arrived at about 8:10 pm, because people had to wait for the Alfa and not the other way round.

As I stepped into the room and saw the emissary, my jaw dropped and almost hit the floor. Standing before me was a face and figure that I would never forget. It was my good old friend Bongo. We threw caution to the winds and hugged each other; it was as if my long-lost brother had come home.

We forgot about the matter at hand and started to catch up on old times, right from when we finished at Dominion College and went our separate ways. I asked Bongo where he was staying and invited him to my place.

After forty minutes of catching up with Bongo, I excused myself and stepped out with Hammer to the backyard. Hammer was not keen to release any of our ammunition to an external clan. I understood his reasons and accepted them; however, because of my personal friendship with Bongo, I authorised Hammer to release two of the locally-made hand guns called "Awka," to be taken there and brought back by our own Marauders.

Bongo was delighted with the compromise and stayed the night at my flat. I showed him around the university town and he received the Marauders' hospitality. He continued to tell me about his life journey after secondary school, and I asked after the other members of the DCM, such as Juggernaut and Johnny the Good. I was keen to know where his brother the legendary Don Loco was, and how he was doing.

Bongo left the next day and I promised to pay him a visit soon. I also promised to send some Marauders with the goods he'd requested a day prior to the big event, but I had to decline the invitation to attend myself, as I would be tied up.

Victor accompanied by seven Marauders carried the goods to the final destination, and represented me at the ceremony.

Life on and off campus continued as normal and Tima was still playing hard to get. She was sceptical about having a relationship in school, as she was from a Muslim family and having a relationship or sex outside marriage was unacceptable.

I really liked her and was willing to play the waiting game with her while I sampled other babes. Isabella was still my sweetheart, but the distance was becoming challenging, so I kept myself occupied as best as I could.

The first semester examination was fast approaching. On a Monday evening, I had just finished my last lecture and was heading home on an Okada, as I did not like to hang around campus longer than necessary.

I noticed that my Voice was on a bike behind me, tailing the Okada and trying to get my attention. I asked my rider to turn into an off-road surrounded by bushes and I got off the Okada. I was wondering what the urgent message was, and when my Voice delivered the news, I was shocked and stood there in disbelief.

He told me that a Marauder called Maurice had gone to a church on campus the previous Sunday and had publicly renounced the confraternity. I was more disappointed than mad, because Maurice was one of the more level-headed Marauders that I knew.

Under the BNM laws, the punishment for a defector and turncoat was death; it was unheard of for a Marauder to renounce the brotherhood so publicly, and worse, in church.

My disappointment was so potent because I had had plans to make Maurice a member of the Council of wise men; to be hit with this news was a shock. I asked my Voice to get the Council of wise men to convene and deliberate on this issue immediately, and I wanted their verdict by the next day at the latest.

The verdict promptly reached me for my ratification, and unsurprisingly it was to be a hit on Maurice. All that was needed was my final approval. I was used to reacting on the spot – as an Alfa I had to be swift and decisive – but with this one, I wanted to think about it overnight.

I consulted Victor and he was in support of the verdict of the Council of wise men; he felt that we needed to make an example of Maurice, as a deterrent to others.

I did not sleep well that night; I lay pondering the verdict. I liked Maurice; he had been a faithful Marauder ever since I had known him, and he was a final-year Law student. *"Why would I want to waste such a promising life?"* I thought, and yet I did not want to send out the wrong message to other Marauders.

When I woke the next morning, I knew what I had to do. I summoned Maurice to meet me at a secluded spot, wanting to ask him the all-important question: WHY? When Maurice saw me, he broke down and fell on his knees weeping. He told me that he had given his life to Christ and had now received redemption through His blood, the forgiveness of sins, according to the riches of His grace.

"I do not understand why you had to do it publicly, please explain that to me. Because that really made us look bad," I challenged him. "My Alfa," Maurice started to address me, but I cut him short. "Don't call me that. You have lost the right and privilege to do so," I said acidly.

"I did not do it publicly to make the BNM look bad or to spite you, my leader, but the Bible declares that if I do not confess Him as my Lord and Saviour publicly, then He would deny me in front of the angels in heaven," Maurice said, shaking in front of me.

"I think we must have been reading different Bibles, because the last time I checked, it did not say 'renounce the BNM publicly to get your salvation'; in fact, I think you have used this whole 'born again' bullshit to gain leverage for you to graduate," I bellowed at him.

"Whatever you decide to do to me my leader, I will take it in good faith. God is my protector and shepherd and in Him I have my rest," he concluded.

I walked away from that meeting having made up my mind about how to proceed. I sent my final decision to the Executioner and to the Council of wise men, which was that Maurice was to be excommunicated. No Marauder was to be in contact with him on or off campus; he was to be a civilian indefinitely.

The Council of wise men and Victor were not happy about my final decision, but they were not brave enough to undermine it. Looking back now, my decision was largely influenced by my religious background, and I was not willing to take a life that now belonged to God.

The Voice and his deputies disseminated the news of Maurice's excommunication and a gathering was fixed for that evening at "down the valley".

The meeting was quick and to the point; the issue of Maurice was mentioned very briefly, but the main topic was our final initiation and our much-anticipated boogie night the next semester. Exams were now only three weeks away and I reiterated the need for Marauders in their final year to graduate, and for others to focus on getting good grades.

Chapter 17

Returning to Asaba after my first semester examination was a welcome relief, because at home, I would not have to be the "Alfa." I could just be plain Remy. However, I found to my dismay that that was not the case, as all Marauders from other universities who were living in Asaba had now started to defer to me.

Two and a half weeks into the five-week break, a group of local Marauders approached Prince, The Bulldog and myself as we were hanging out at our usual joint, and informed us that there had been a fracas between some Marauders and some local Vikings that evening. Therefore, they wanted us to watch our backs for the next couple of days.

I had wanted peace when I came home from university, and here was trouble beginning to brew again. I was tempted to jump into a car and head for Onitsha to stay with Manuel until things calmed down; but that did not seem like a very good option as I could not envisage myself, an Alfa, taking the easy and cowardly way out.

I sent a message to the local head of the Vikings, called Andy, to hold his boys back. I knew Andy, as we attended the same gym and had shared drinks a couple of times. He assured me that he would call his boys to order.

I kept away from public places and popular joints for a couple of nights and, as things started to settle down, news reached me that Peter was in the emergency wing of the general hospital. He had suffered a hit by a group of Vikings, including Smash, Pope, Gerald and Emeka. I was reliably informed that Andy had given the order for the hit and was even present during the hit.

I was enraged as I stood by Peter's bedside. He had been ambushed on his way home at about 10 pm and his scalp had been opened up with a machete; in fact, he was lucky to be alive. His head was stitched and bandaged up and he looked rather like an Egyptian mummy.

Peter's mum and siblings were weeping uncontrollably; my heart went out to his mother, as Peter was her first and only son and she had lost her husband recently in a car accident. I immediately deployed Prince and The Bulldog to take turns watching over Peter in the hospital.

I vowed then and there to settle the score. I had no plans to go after the Vikings' foot-soldiers as they were just small boys. Rather, I was going to go after Andy. I was determined to hit him where it hurt the most and after that, we were going to expunge the name of the Vikings from Asaba.

The drawback was that we did not have weapons. Even my service Berettas were with my Executioner, who was their custodian, and he lived far away in Lagos.

The BNM at the local College of Education had only one locally made handgun, which was out of service. After a couple of days of hunting around for suitable weapons without success, I decided to make the two-hour journey to the university at Awka. I knew the Alfa at the university personally; in fact, he had left my current university for Awka in his second year, and he was also a good pal of Bongo and Don Loco.

I arrived at Awka and went straight to the most famous hang out of Marauders off-campus, called the 'The Gas Station', where I made contact. The news spread like wildfire that an Alfa was in town. Twenty minutes after my arrival, the Gas Station was a beehive of movement; and within a couple of minutes, the local Alfa called Cosmos, a.k.a. "Watata," stepped in.

We greeted each other warmly. He introduced me to his Omega and Executioner, food and drinks were ordered, and I told them about the purpose of my visit. Cosmos had no problem releasing guns to me; but they currently had an ongoing feud with the Black Berets and needed their entire arsenal. However, since I had personally made the journey to ask for help, he was happy to release a locally-made double-barrelled hand gun for three weeks.

I stayed with Cosmos that night and the next day the gun was packaged for me with some "groundnuts" – cartridges. He escorted me to the park and I jumped into a taxi heading for Asaba with the gun taped around my thigh. I had never in all my life felt so uncomfortable – carrying a gun on my person and travelling such a long distance. My mind was all over the place, but I could not back down now, I was too far gone.

The car had barely travelled for forty-five minutes when we encountered the first Police checkpoint. As they pulled the driver over, I could feel my stomach churning. My heart was palpitating at a hundred beats per second, a cold sweat started to form on my forehead, and my hands were shaking.

The police officer asked the driver to get out of the car to settle them. As the driver got out, another police officer approached the car and looked in. He moved his gaze from one passenger to the other and as his gaze stopped on me, I almost peed on myself.

The officer moved out of the way to allow the driver to get back into the driving seat, and only when the taxi pulled away from the checkpoint did I heave a big sigh of relief. We encountered two more police checkpoints; money swiftly changed hands and we were on our way. Each time we were stopped I felt as if I was sitting on hot coals.

I finally reached Asaba towards the late afternoon and made my way home. It was a welcome relief to be back. I had lied to my parents, telling them that I was travelling to my university to check if my first semester results were out. As I sat down and pondered the journey, it gave me goose-bumps.

The police officers at any of the checkpoints could easily have searched me. The gun could have been discovered, and there would have been no guarantee that they would not have executed me and then labelled me as an armed robber.

Cosmos had given me three weeks to return the gun, so we had to move fast. I asked for an intelligence report on Andy and his crew, and was informed that they had been strutting around Asaba as if they owned the place. Further intelligence revealed that Andy had a babe whom he visited regularly at the College of Education hostel; we decided that was where the hit was going to happen.

We put our strategy in place and got our eyes and ears within the college to find us two exit routes for after the hit. We set the day of the hit to coincide with a show in the college, to help mask the noise of gunshots and make it easier to blend into the crowd.

I wanted to pull the trigger myself when I came face to face with Andy; but Prince and The Bulldog would not let me. Indeed, as the Alfa of the BNM, I should not be carrying out hits – my place was to give the command.

I gave the command and it was all systems go. I gave specific instructions to the two hit men that I wanted Andy floored, but under no circumstance should they hurt his babe; she was not a party to our beef.

Andy must have been the luckiest man alive; he was blocked by the two masked men in his babe's room with his shirt off and lying on her bed. He had no hope in hell of surviving – but the hit man pulled the trigger not once or twice but several times, and got no response from the "Awka" handgun. The firing pin had jammed. Andy was dragged out of the room and was beaten mercilessly and stabbed before a passer-by raised the alarm. We used our exit route through the bushes and the back roads, and made our way to a safe house nearby where we cooled down for some time.

The rest of the Vikings fled when they heard that their "Oga" had fallen the previous night and was in intensive care in hospital. The Bulldog was keen to go and finish the job at the hospital; but I felt that was too dangerous.

Coincidentally, Andy was in the same hospital as Peter, but in a different ward. One week after the hit, I paid him a visit on my way out after visiting Peter. I could see the fear in his eyes as I stared at him. I asked him sarcastically what had happened to him and he replied, *"No be your people wan kill me but my head too strong for them."* I laughed and responded, "Good for you; just to let you know, I am going after the rest of your crew, especially the one that swung the machete." With that, I walked out of the ward.

A new intelligence report came that the Viking who had swung the machete was Pope, and that they had all fled. Pope and Smash had fled back to the university at Awka, and that news delighted me. I had two weeks left before my university resumed and I had to return the gun to Cosmos.

For my return journey to Awka, I wrapped the malfunctioning gun in a carrier bag, and buried it at the bottom of half a sack of millet. I got into Awka and made contact with Cosmos and the other Marauders. He was very upset that the gun had not worked and ordered that his Executioner be given a five-minute drilling for not maintaining a BNM weapon to the required standard.

Intelligence came back to us that afternoon that Pope and Smash were presently at a lecture, due to end in thirty minutes. I knew that this was my chance to get the elusive duo.

I did not know them by sight and nor did they know me; so I used a Marauder who lived in Asaba to point them out to me. I was given another loaded handgun, which I tucked into my waistband and headed for the school centre. After about twenty minutes, the two guys came out with other students and headed for the NFA joint.

The Marauder had pointed out Pope and Smash to me and I approached them. There were school security officers around, but I did not give a damn as I came face to face with the guy who had swung the machete. The blow to the face dropped Pope to the ground and before Smash could react to the surprise attack, I had flattened him with a kick to the mid-rib.

I was like a possessed lion as I laid into both of them in broad daylight, with blows, kicks and head butts. Blood was flowing out of their noses and mouths; they were both dazed from shock and from the beating that was being meted out to them. From the corner of my right eye, I could see the security officers moving towards the scene. At that moment, I pulled out my gun and released a shot into the air and the whole school went berserk.

Everybody ran for cover, including the security officers. Some Marauders were there to give me cover as I made my way away from the scene with them.

The Vikings in the university were mad and aggrieved that a stranger had had the audacity to humiliate their men in public, and they were calling for blood. The Vikings started to reinforce themselves for war and at about 7 pm they came out in full force.

They headed towards the gas station where I was sitting with thirty other Marauders, drinking and waiting for them to make their first move. As they approached, the Omega and Executioner, with two-crack squads of Marauders, met them in front of the Station.

The war general of the Vikings wanted to know why the Marauders were protecting a stranger who had badly beaten up two of their members; they wanted blood for blood.

"That man na our man," replied the Executioner of the university of Awka; he was well known for his ruthlessness and hatred for other confraternities, and he was an avid warmonger. "We are ready to close the school down right now with blood flow if you guys *no*

fade sharp sharp," the Executioner warned. "After all, *this na external wahala and not our own wahala,*" he concluded, with his hand resting on the butt of his gun.

The Vikings' war general stepped back to consult with his lieutenants. They soon realised they were outnumbered and outmuscled, and were not as battle-savvy as the BNM. They finally backed off, but not before sending a warning to me that if they ran into me on or off campus I would be a dead man.

I remained under the protection of the BNM at Awka, and still held on to my locally-made gun; I also had two fully armed bodyguards assigned to me for the duration of my stay.

I left Awka the next day as I had to go home to prepare for my next semester. My two bodyguards escorted me to the car park, and made sure that I was seated and that the taxi had left the car park before they departed.

The news of my adventure and sheer bravado had reached Asaba even before I did, and messages of good will and praise were pouring in from the local Marauders. I paid Peter a visit the next day at his house, as he had been discharged two days earlier; he was full of praise for me and did not hesitate to pronounce me the boldest Alfa he had ever met.

It was good to hear all these accolades from my fellow Marauders, but on further reflection as I lay in my bed that night, I could not help but realise how foolish and myopic I had been in my reasoning and actions the last couple of weeks.

In every action that I had taken, I had put my own life at risk – at every stage, without thinking about the consequences. I was not keen for the Council of wise men and the Executives of the BNM at my university to find out that I had put myself in harm's way for a war that had nothing to do with me and was outside my jurisdiction.

Chapter 18

Activity on campus was slow to kick off, as students returned in patches. I agreed with the Council of wise men that this was the best period to finalise our initiation of new Marauders. We set a tentative date for about two weeks later and sent the Voice out to disseminate this news. We wanted all Marauders to have their candidates ready to move at the drop of a hat.

Victor had a few days to complete his spiritual duties and any sessions required with the oracle before the final date, and we were looking forward to a positive result from his consultations with the 'gods'. He came back after one of his many visits with some disturbing news. Baba had foreseen problems on the day of the initiation and he urgently wanted me to pay him a visit. I was not keen on another encounter with the witch doctor after my last one, but Victor insisted that I go, for the success of the grand finale.

I arrived at the shrine with Victor and we were welcomed by Baba; we paid the mandatory fees and handed over a bottle of gin for the gods. Baba started his incantations, which lasted about five minutes, using cowries and beads. He then looked up at me with a frown on his face.

"*I dey see big big wahala for inside your camp on that day, this wahala fit scatter the whole thing and Police fit show but I go try blow the trouble far away but the rest dey your hand my pickin,*" he concluded.

"Baba, *how e take dey my hand?*" I enquired. "*You go see am on that day but my advice for you be say, make you stay strong for any decision wey you take and no look back oooo for the decision, all go go well,*" he assured me.

I left Baba's place with Victor even more confused than when I had arrived there. I turned to Victor and could tell that he was as bothered as I was. "My Omega, why is it that all witch doctors tend to paint one gloomy picture after another?" I asked.

"My Alfa, I wish I had the answer to that question but Baba has always come through for us, so we've got to be more careful and vigilant."

I summoned the Seer and Voice as soon as we got back to the university. I gave the Seer two days to look for two new initiation sites, each with two hidden entrances and five secure exits. The new locations were to be known only to myself, Victor, Hammer and his deputy.

The Voice and his deputies were to spread the news that the initiation ceremony would take place in two weeks' time and the venue would be announced on the day. He was also to disseminate a warning that any candidate who missed the final initiation would have to wait for another year and go through the whole process again.

It was in everyone's best interest to be in school for the next two weeks. I asked Hammer to furnish me with the complete list of qualified prospects for the initiation; he submitted about seventy names and I was not best pleased that we could not get it down to fifty.

Later that evening, I sent a message to Victor and Hammer to meet me at a designated place in three days' time, as we were going to inspect two new potential sites with the Seer and his deputies.

The Seer sent word to me within forty eight hours to confirm that two new sites had been found and were ready for inspection.

On the day of the site inspection, we arrived under the cover of darkness with our torches at the ready. The sites were in opposite directions: one was about a twenty-minute trek from "down the valley," tucked deep inside the forest with its own twin entrances and multiple exits.

The Seer and his deputies showed us the layout, where the outpost and guards would be, the holding ground for the prospects, and the main initiation ground; there was also enough room for feasting and merriment. Hammer was impressed and started mapping out his own plans for security and safety at both sites.

I told the group that the actual site would be chosen on the day of the ceremony, due to security reasons. We left the forest that night feeling happy and confident about both sites. I went back with Victor to his place and asked Hammer to join us. I wanted to pick their brains regarding which location best suited us for the ceremony.

Hammer preferred the site closer to "down the valley," while Victor was keen on the one at the opposite end of town. They both agreed that both sites were secure and fit for the purpose.

I instructed Hammer to have his guys and all our arsenal ready and well serviced by tomorrow. I could see the look of surprise on both their faces. "My Alfa, I am not stepping on your tongue *ooo*, but initiation is about twelve days away," Hammer said.

"That is all the more reason we need to be ready to go by tomorrow," I replied, "Let us not leave any arrangement that needs to be done now till later," I concluded. I turned to Victor and said to him, *"Abeg* collect money from the tax collector and get the food and special brew ready for this Saturday, and make sure that all the regalia are ready."

My Omega and Executioner were baffled beyond words and after a few seconds of staring at me, Victor summoned enough courage to ask, "My Alfa, *I no march your tongue ooo*, you are our supreme leader but what is going on?"

I looked Victor dead in the eyes with a cheeky grin and a sly smile on my lips and said, "Did I not tell you, this Saturday is going to be our initiation ceremony and every aspect has to be spot on, mate? We have three days left and plenty of work to do and I believe that I can count on both of you to be discreet in your conduct regarding this matter," I said. "You guys, including Theo, are the people that I can put my hundred percent trust in, so don't let me down," I concluded.

"My Alfa don speak," they both echoed with the look of confusion and surprise still showing on their faces. This was what I was looking to achieve – that element of surprise, where everyone is taken unawares, thereby reducing any chances of any security lapses.

My game plan was to have a meeting with the wise men by midnight on Friday, and then have my Executive Council meet during the small hours on Saturday; I would have the Voice spread the news beginning Saturday morning.

I knew that the element of surprise was the strongest weapon I had. Baba's words were constantly ringing in my ears, and I was looking to play my cards very close to my chest for as long as possible. No one knew the final venue of the initiation, because I had not even made up my mind about it.

All the Marauders and their prospects were to assemble at the crossroads behind "down the valley" and from there we would move to the designated initiation site, which could be either a twenty-minute or a one-hour trek.

My meeting with the wise men and my Executive Council went as I expected, as they had no choice but to support and back me in this audacious plan.

It was 7 pm on that fateful warm Saturday evening in 1996 and it was all systems go. Hammer and all his deputies were already at the crossroads, armed to the teeth. They were showing all the Marauders and their prospects to various holding points, while waiting for the next move.

I arrived at the assembly place at about 7:20 pm under the cover of night, a 9 mm Berretta tucked into my belt and another strapped to my lower leg. I had two fully armed bodyguards, one in ahead of and another behind me.

As I approached the assembly point, everybody jumped to attention, waiting for the next move. I could sense the tension in the air and feel the cowry around my right ankle. I asked Hammer about the well-being of the prospects and as I was having a conversation with him, I suddenly felt myself pulled into a trance and saw Baba; I clearly heard him saying, "Move."

I came out of the trance within seconds and shouted out an order for Hammer and his deputies to enforce. We were all moving to the site about one hour's trek away. Rago, Abbas and some of the older Marauders were not happy about this sudden decision, but they knew better than to challenge me publicly.

The journey to the other side of the jungle took us longer than expected, as we were moving prospects, drums, food and also drinks in big jerry cans. The prospects did all the carrying of the heavy items as we soldiered along.

I had sent Victor ahead earlier with a couple of armed Marauders and some drummers, to clear the path and to get everything ready for our arrival.

As we approached the site at about 9:30 pm from the East side, we could hear the sound of "Egkede," the talking drum, and singing coming from the site. "*Well done Victor*," I thought to myself. Hammer and his deputies moved into position and took charge of the initiation ground; he put all the prospects in a holding spot away from the real men.

The time was 10:15 pm and the actual initiation ceremony had just started. Every Marauder was kitted in black and wearing the regalia with the insignia of a skull and bones. Victor was in black with yellow-coloured regalia and as the oracle of the clan, he had the insignia of a flaming pot. He took control of the circle of Marauders and began his consultation and songs. The combination of the songs and the drumming from very skilful Marauders was out of this world; it always had the magical ability to transport you to a different sphere of the underworld.

As the Alfa, I did not need to come into the circle until about thirty minutes before midnight. I was expected to start the "laying of hand" of new prospects at that precise time. Dressed in black, I had maroon coloured regalia with the insignia of a lion.

While I waited for the important moment to arrive, I held court with the wise men, deciding on the bush names with which to baptise our new prospects. It was not a very onerous task, as a long list of names had already been prepared beforehand.

Hammer and his deputies had the hardest task of all; they had to maintain decorum amongst Marauders who were already high on strong drinks and Marijuana, and they had to look after the prospects and co-ordinate their drilling.

Marauders were marched in groups at regular intervals into the holding spot and asked to "mend" the prospects relentlessly until they begged for death to come. The drilling of the prospects continued, while the oracle serenaded the other Marauders with his soul-lifting melodies.

At about 11:25 pm, the volume of the singing and chorus started to reach the highest pitch, signalling the time for the Alfa to emerge and take over the circle, and start the laying of hands.

As I stepped into the circle, my entrance was greeted with loud hails from all the Marauders, followed by three gunshots. Victor took the cue to step aside, as the circle and arena now belonged to me and to me alone.

The laying of hands and full initiation of the prospects took about twenty-five minutes, and as the time approached midnight, the whole initiation ground went into a frenzy of celebration as we all became one family.

Midnight was heralded with the loudest jubilation and celebration yet, with more gunshots ringing out. The celebration continued into the early hours of the morning, with plenty of food and "Goskolo" to go around.

The initiation ceremony officially ended at 4:30 am and it was now the responsibility of the Executioner and the Seer to lead us all to safety, using the various exit paths identified earlier.

We got to the high road at about 5:30 am as dawn was breaking, and we dispersed into various smaller groups. The Marauders who lived close by had the responsibility of housing as many of their brothers as possible, especially the newest Marauders.

There were motorbikes on standby waiting to take my bodyguards and me into town, but I insisted on waiting until every Marauder had found a designated shelter before leaving. It was 7:15 am on that fateful Sunday morning that I finally hit my bed in exhaustion.

I awoke reluctantly to a persistent knocking on my door. I could feel my head banging as I reached for my wristwatch, barely make out the time through my bloodshot eyes. After a few seconds of trying to focus, I was finally able to make it out to be about 6:15 pm in the evening.

Wooow, I had been knocked out for over eleven hours. I got out of bed reluctantly and staggered towards the door. "Yes, who is that?" I asked in a deep hoarse voice. "It is me, Victor," replied the voice on the other side of the door.

For Victor to have come to my flat, coupled with the urgency and persistency of his knocking, meant that something of importance needed my attention. I unlocked the door to let him in and as he took a seat, I tried but failed to glean from his body language what the issue could possibly be.

"O boy, what is up, I hope none of our guys have been picked up by 'Babylon' Police," I enquired. "No my Alfa," he replied, "the initiation was very successful and from the situation report everybody that attended the ceremony got home safely, except ... Madu."

"What do you mean by 'except Madu', I did not see Madu at the site last night," I quizzed Victor. "We did not see him at the site because he never made it there," Victor replied.

"I think that I must have had too much to drink last night, because I still cannot make sense of what you are telling me," I replied in slight irritation. "My Alfa, Madu was discovered in the early hours of this morning by some hunters returning from an expedition. He had been attacked with a machete, shot with a locally-made gun, and left for dead." Victor continued, "He is currently in the hospital and is in bad shape."

I sat there listening to Victor, nonplussed. "In what part of the forest did they find Madu?" I asked, but Victor had no clue. "Get the Seer to do a detailed situation report for me in the next twenty four hours, get the Voice and his deputies to start combing the community for information. Send some guys to the hospital to see to his welfare, but before they go, let them carry out their due diligence and make sure that 'Babylon' Police are not waiting at the hospital. In fact, use our guy in the Student Union as part of the delegation to the hospital," I ordered.

"And tell the tax collector to be ready to release some money towards his hospital bill; and I want to be kept abreast on a daily basis of the situation," I added. "Yes, my Alfa," Victor said and departed in a haste to get my orders carried out.

It took over a week to get a clearer picture of what had happened to Madu on that fateful night of the initiation. Madu had arrived very late to the rally point, and since he had missed the last guard to direct him, he had decided to head towards "down the valley."

About fifteen minutes into his trek, five masked and heavily armed members of the Mafioso confraternity wearing green berets had jumped him. He was dealt with in accordance with the law of the jungle, and left for dead; but the gang of Mafioso had also made off with Madu's rucksack.

The rucksack contained twenty four live rounds for a 9 mm Beretta, two locally-made handguns and eight cartridges, along with three hand axes and a bullet-proof vest. All these items were part of the armoury belonging to the clan, and Madu had been transporting them to the initiation ground.

I was not upset that Hammer had given Madu some of our arsenal to carry, as it was normal practice to split our goods among trusted and experienced Marauders, both to help with the load of transportation and to avoid having all our eggs in one basket. I was more upset by the fact that an experienced Marauder like

Madu had not been armed when going into the forest, knowing that the backpack was full of ammunition – what an irony.

I immediately summoned a meeting of the five wise men, and asked Victor and Hammer to join in the meeting as representatives of the Executive Council. The meeting lasted for over two hours, and we deliberated on what course of action to take. Some wise men saw this as an insulting and spiteful attack on the BNM, while others saw the situation as a foolish mistake by Madu.

The final decision would always be mine to take. As I sat there soaking up all the information and listening to various arguments for or against the need to strike fear into the Mafioso, I could not help but ask one simple and naive question.

"Did they know that he was a Marauder?" I asked. "My Alfa, they know well well, Madu is a popular figure on campus and he was flying his colour when they accosted him, and he confirmed to me that he told them," replied Hammer. I nodded my head as I absorbed this information. I also remembered what "Charlie Angel" had told me a long time ago about the act of war. He always said, "To fight a justified war, you need to experience and understand the language of peace."

"OK, guys, this is the way I am going to approach this situation," I said thoughtfully. "I have no doubt that this would appear to be a slap in the face, but if the tables were turned and one of their guys walked into our gathering, I have no doubt that they would suffer a worse fate. Let us be glad that Madu is still alive because the guy *mis-waka* well and he paid for it. So we would look after our man, but I want all our goods back from them."

"My Alfa, I no match your tongue oo but we do not negotiate with other confraternities and I do not think it is a good idea to start now," pointed out one of the wise men.

I looked him dead in the eyes and said, "We are not negotiating with them, we are giving them an ultimatum." I then turned to Theo. "I want you to take two guys from the suicide squad when you set up your meeting with their henchmen, and give them forty-eight hours to return all our goods without fail."

"My Alfa don speak," Theo responded. The meeting ended and we agreed to reconvene at the same time in five days' time. We wanted to give Theo and his crew enough time to complete their task.

The next day during an evening lecture, Theo confirmed to me that he had set up a meeting that night with three Mafioso henchmen, including one of their ex-Dons. I reiterated to Theo that his job was not to negotiate but to give an ultimatum.

As I sat in the lecture theatre trying to concentrate on the class going on, my thoughts could not help but wander to the proposed meeting with the Mafioso. Had I taken the right decision sending Theo on this errand, or was this move a sign of weakness on my part? Theo was one of the very few people I could trust to undertake this task and have the dexterity to manage any unexpected upheaval.

The lecture finally ended at about 6 pm and it was arguably the longest two hours that I had ever spent in one place. As we filed out of the hall, I caught up with Osato and asked him to discharge my bodyguards, who were waiting for me under the mango tree, as I wanted to be on my own. I made my way towards the bus stop, unable to shake off that uneasy feeling that was beginning to engulf me regarding the proposed meeting with the Mafioso.

I suddenly found myself making a detour before the bus stop and heading towards the boys' hostels. I went straight to Hall 7, Block A, Room 7, and knocked on the door seven times. "Identify yourself," came the recognisable voice from behind the door. "Na me Remy," I replied.

The door opened slightly and cautiously and I could see eyes peering at me through the slightly opened door before it was quickly flung open to admit me. All the occupants of the room stood to attention as I entered the room. "My Alfa," they all greeted. "I hail ooo, my fellow Marauders. I need you guys to run an errand for me this evening sharp sharp," I said.

Theo's meeting with the Mafioso guys was to take place at around 9 pm in front of Q Scene restaurant, and I wanted my "back up" squad to provide extra out-of-sight cover for Theo and the other Marauders on the mission. No one, including Theo, was to know that they were there; their task was strictly limited to giving back up in the event of any unanticipated ambush.

I wanted a situation report back from them before 11 pm without fail, at the corner of Madam Allen's beer parlour where they were to meet me.

I left the boys' hostel at about 7:15 pm and jumped on an Okada heading towards town. I dropped off at Eggies and ordered some bread, eggs and corned beef before strolling back to my flat. It was about 9:30 pm when I finished my dinner and settled down to watch a movie on the television, but my mind kept drifting to how the meeting with the Mafioso was going.

I got to the corner of Madam Allen's beer parlour at about 11:05 pm, just in time to see the figure of a guy standing in the shadow of the big mango tree. I whistled a signal as I walked into Madam Allen's shop and heard a whistle in reply. I bought a pack of cigarettes from the shop and went out again. The figure followed me and when we got to a darker spot, we stopped.

"How far?" I asked. "*No wahala*, my Alfa, Theo is bam and no shaking, he don make contact with those baggers," he responded. "Well done," I said before handing him the pack of cigarettes and walking across the road to catch a motorbike back to my flat.

Theo gave me a situation report about the meeting the next day during another lecture; he told me that they were keen to return our goods to us, but they first needed to table our request to their current Don and other henchmen. Theo confirmed to me that he had reiterated that they had a deadline of forty-eight hours, and he would be looking to collect the goods from them in person and within the university premises, as this was deemed safer ground for both parties.

Theo explained that he wanted the collection on campus because the Mafioso could easily set him up by anonymously tipping off the Police about what was about to go down, so that he and other Marauders could be picked up after the collection with incriminating evidence.

I thought that this was brilliant thinking from Theo, but again I was not utterly surprised as he was an experienced Marauder and had been around in the circuit for some years.

Life and activity on campus were in full swing, with lectures taking up the bulk of our time, and the two days went by quickly.

Chapter 19

There were eight of us in the small room and the atmosphere was tense. Theo had just finished repeating for the umpteenth time what had transpired at the meeting with the Mafioso. They were only able to account for and return four cartridges, six live rounds for the Beretta and one locally-made gun, and they were not ready to take responsibility for the missing items.

"This is an insult," bellowed Hammer, "those small boys no get fear for body, we will wipe them off the face of this earth, one hand," he concluded.

As I sat in the midst of the Council of wise men, Victor and Hammer, I could not stop hearing Charlie Angel's words to me about knowing the language of peace before war. The majority in the room were clamouring for war and I could not blame them.

Reasoning within myself, I wondered if losing a tiny fraction of our armoury was enough justification to declare war on the Mafioso, but the matter was more about our pride and being at the top echelon than about the actual loss of our goods.

As I sat there observing the theatre of war-mongering unfold, I knew that I had to make a decision quickly. I turned to the wise men, I wanted to know their minds; they voted for war. I tried to glean how Victor would vote, but I was not successful as he had a blank expression on his face.

Finally, Victor looked at me and said, "My Alfa, I vote for war; it is about time to teach those smelly Maffy guys a lesson."

The final decision was in my hands. I had the sole power to declare or not to declare a war against the Mafioso. As I stood up to my full height of 6 feet 1 inch, I spoke succinctly: "By the power conferred on me as the Alfa of the Black Night Marauders, I declare war on the Mafioso."

There were loud cheers and chanting around the room. I raised up my hand to silence the room, adding, "But we are going to fight this war my way, and in a different way."

I continued, "I want little or no casualties of war on our side, so Hammer, get all the official suicide squads ready to roll sharp sharp; you and your deputies will lead from the front," I instructed.

"My Alfa don talk, no shaking at all, all Mafioso don die," Hammer bellowed with great gusto and excitement.

I turned to Victor. "Get my Voice to spread news to all Marauders on and off campus to hold their side and always walk in twos; I want all Marauders that are not involved in this mission to converge at 'down the valley' this evening without fail."

"We go sleep inside jungle for as long as it takes to fight this war, and we will move from 'down the valley' every night to wipe out this Mafioso guys. I want to prevent any casualty on our side," I reiterated.

"When do we move?" Victor asked me. "Tonight; I don't think that they would be expecting us to move at all or this quickly," I replied.

I turned to Theo. "We go map out our final movement and the strongholds to hit, after Hammer has liaised with the Seer this afternoon. We want detailed intelligence that would lead to maximum casualties on their side," I concluded.

"Hammer, I want 'down the valley' fully fortified every night that we roll out on a hit," I instructed, "Make sure we have guards at every path and outpost leading into the jungle."

"My Alfa, we go get plenty supply of water, snacks, torches and batteries, to last for about four days," said Victor.

"No worries Victor, get all the gear you need to cater for the Marauders who would be in the jungle under your care, because I'll be rolling with my own squad tonight," I informed him without batting an eyelid.

"My Alfa, I hail you ooo, na you be our supreme leader and father but our Alfa does not go to war, he sends his lieutenants to war on his behalf," Theo reminded me and there was total agreement in the room from everyone.

I smiled, took a deep breath and replied, "I am not one of those generals that would send his troops to war and sit at home eating cake. I will roll side by side with my people and my decision is final, this is our war and we fight together," I concluded.

"My Alfa don talk and na final talk but my Alfa you go wear bulletproof vest as you dey roll sha," Hammer informed me.

"No problem," I replied. The meeting was ended and we were all expected to reconvene at 7 pm with all other Marauders at "down the valley."

It was about 7:15 pm when we all gathered in the jungle. Looking around, I could smell anger, blood and plenty of Marijuana in the air. I stepped into the circle, and there was dead silence while I stood there for a few seconds. I was dressed all in black, one Beretta tucked into my black jungle boots and the other in my right hand. A rucksack on my back contained a bulletproof vest, an ample supply of ammunition, and a hand axe.

I spent a few minutes narrating the course of events from when Madu was hit to our present gathering, and ended my speech by announcing that as of this night, we were at war with the Mafioso. Overwhelming cheers greeted my pronouncement. I told them that tonight, only the hit squads and some handpicked experienced Marauders would roll, but there would be opportunities for other Marauders to get involved as the conflict progressed.

Hammer and the Seer joined me in the circle to take us through our strategy for the night. Moving with five hit squads, we were looking to hit five key Mafioso locations, three residential locations, and two of their joints.

I was going to roll with my own suicide squad which included Bilado, Otoro, and The Bulldog. We were heading to their current Don's flat, which was off Supermarket Lane. Our intelligence showed that he shared the flat with his girlfriend, and was sure to have at least two lieutenants with him.

On that fateful cool night in July 1996, we rolled out in full force and painted the university community red with the blood of the Mafioso.

There were major casualties on their side, and their joints were ransacked and goods set alight. The current Don of the Mafioso, called "Don Dee," escaped with bullet wounds through the ceiling of the flat. One of his henchmen was admitted to the hospital critically injured.

I had given stern and inviolable instructions that no civilian, especially girls, were to be casualties of this war. We were going after the culprits and the culprits alone; it was going to be two eyes for one.

We battered the Mafioso so badly on the first night that they could not regroup, due to the confusion caused by the surprise and targeted attacks. The second night saw us invading nearby villages where we believed that some of them would have fled. A hit squad went after a well-known Mafioso lecturer in the Political Science department. He wasn't killed, but was badly beaten and told to send a message to his mentees that the heat was about to get fiercer. The Mafioso were finally able to regroup the following day and after two nights of a heavy assault from us, they rallied some of their henchmen and external mercenaries from neighbouring institutions; but they could not find any easy target on our side.

On the third night, we rolled out with more squads; many Marauders itching to prove themselves on the battleground were happy to get involved. We encountered some pockets of resistance from the Mafioso around the market square area as we headed for another of their strongholds.

Gunshots echoed from both sides; there were sounds of locally-made guns and automatics. We easily overpowered them with the use of our newly acquired 'bad boy' sub-machine gun. We pushed them back until they finally fled; then taking over their stronghold, we set fire to all their property.

While all the shooting was going on, the police station that was a stone's throw from the scene went into complete darkness, as they quickly turned off their lights in case any stray bullets hit them. I believed that the police were shocked at the level of artillery that was being used that night.

A truce was reached on the fourth day of the conflict, after Theo and some dare-devil Marauders went to campus to meet up with the Mafioso lecturer and some Mafioso henchmen.

We wanted all our goods back, and we now also wanted payment for Madu's hospital treatment. We were not ready to budge on this, and we got it.

The victory was sweet – although we had to endure the backlash from the Police force, who picked up well-known Marauders (the usual suspects). We gave instructions to our "O C Legal" lawyer, and within three days they were released and the case dropped for "lack of evidence."

Activity on campus slowly returned to normal, and lectures were again in full swing. The news of our victory spread like wildfire around the university community and the other confraternities dreaded us even more. Civilians wanted to belong to the mighty BNM, and babes wanted to be identified with the real men.

Some Marauders took full advantage of our strong brand to achieve many female conquests; they even offered protection to a female confraternity called "The Puppies." The Puppies were mainly girls from the cities of Warri and Sapele; they often went out with Marauders, and the fellow girls on campus dreaded them.

I knew about the shenanigans of the Puppies and the Marauders who aided and supported them, but I was of the opinion that this was part of the spoils of war and victory. Nevertheless, I made it categorically clear that we would never go to war on their behalf, and if they stepped out of line with any of the other confraternities, then it was on their head alone.

Tima was still playing hard to get; she must have been the first girl to make me chase after her for over six months. She was not nasty about it – she just explained that she wanted to focus on her studies and not on guys.

I had a bevy of girls gracing my bed, but there was still that void created by Isabella's absence; and that could have been filled only by Tima.

As the second semester gradually drew to its halfway mark, my dissertation work was beginning to take shape; it involved a lot of research and travel to source relevant materials.

Victor was at the helm of the affairs of the BNM when I was away from campus for a couple of days, and I had given him the go-ahead to start preparing for our much-anticipated end of season party, called the "Brotherhood Boogie" or BB for short.

Our BB was scheduled to take place towards the end of the semester and I wanted it to be the best ever seen in the history of the BNM and the university. Our plan was to hire an entire hotel and its grounds, and to bring in two of the best disc jockeys in town to rock the venue. I wanted to have various types of food, "local" and "English," with two kebab men grilling beef all night. Copious amounts of alcohol would flow freely; but most importantly, there would be a lorry load of babes.

The event was going to involve a lot of money. As we did not have vast amounts in our coffers, we decided to tax all Marauders an additional fee for the BB. They were keen to pay in anticipation of a good night with plenty of "honies" (babes).

I was determined to achieve all that we had promised the Marauders with regard to the BB, and so was directly involved in most aspects of the planning; but the execution of the plan I left to Victor and his committee.

For the next two weeks I poured myself into my research work. I did not have to worry about the examinations yet, because they had been postponed for final-year Accounting students carrying out dissertation work.

We were going to have our final degree examination in about four months' time, and defend our dissertation in front of a panel of lecturers.

I wanted to turn in a good piece of work, as I knew that this would stand me in good stead when I proceeded to pursue my post-graduate education in the United Kingdom.

Chapter 20

The final half of the semester began with a bang. There were so many things to be done; I had to make final changes to my dissertation, and have it typed up, proofread, approved by my supervisor, bound, and submitted before the deadline.

I also had to give the final seal of approval for the fast-approaching BB; Victor had worked so hard to achieve almost all that we had discussed. He'd made sure that we got real value for our money, including very good discounts from the hotel.

Victor had a sugar-coated tongue and even got the hotel management to throw in six chalets free, while we paid for the rest.

We could not afford to leave less than a certain minimum amount in our coffers, because if not, we would struggle with the main activity earmarked for the end of the semester.

This main activity was my handover ceremony, where my Executive council and I would pass on the staff of office to the next Alfa and his team. It was normally an ostentatious celebration in the belly of the jungle, with copious amounts of food and "Goskolos."

I was earnestly looking forward to the handover ceremony, because I had been carrying the weight of being the Alfa of the most deadly and controversial confraternity for about nine months – not an easy load or responsibility to shoulder.

The Council of wise men would deliberate on the choice of the next Alfa following the nomination of two or three candidates, and present their final decision to me for ratification. As the current Alfa, I had the authority to reject their final choice with good reason, pick a suitable Marauder as Alfa, and have him ratified by my Executive Council.

The situation of having a different Alfa ratified by the Executive Council would rarely occur, because the current Alfa would normally present his candidate to the wise men. This candidate would more often than not become the next Alfa.

Sebastian, my Seer, was one Marauder whom I had observed closely and with great interest. He was a third-year law student, experienced yet reserved and not flippant; he was dedicated to the BNM and carried out his duties as the Seer with efficacy.

He was one of the most indefatigable Marauders that I had ever met and from our numerous conversations, I could tell that he was passionate yet objective. He could reason with both his heart and head; he was not just driven and tenacious but also a visionary.

I could easily see the future of the BNM safe in his hands.

I was not unaware that a popular contender for the position of Alfa was a chap called Ken, a.k.a. "Tornado." Tornado was a very experienced Marauder, he had been a well-known face on campus for the last six years and we still did not know what course or year he was in.

Very popular within the confraternity circle, he was extremely passionate about the BNM, wearing his passion on his sleeve. Unlike Sebastian, he was popular, gregarious and full of himself, and was not one to shy away from any confrontation; he could easily start a brawl in an empty room all by himself.

To me, he was all heart but no brain and did not have the gravitas to be a visionary leader; having him as the Alfa would mean that many senseless wars would be fought without any development within the BNM. I was aware that we needed people like Tornado as the muscle, the bruiser and powerhouse of the BNM, but not as the Alfa.

As I grappled with the choice of the new Alfa, my mind could not help but drift to the fast-approaching BB, scheduled to take place in a fortnight; I was becoming ambivalent about attending.

I had kept my cover as the Alfa of the BNM secret for so long that most civilians just knew me as "Remy the ladies' man," because I tended to find myself in the company of ladies most of the time. I still avoided the BNM hot spots and joints in town and would only hang out with people who had already been my friends before I had become the Alfa.

I loved partying and having a good time, but unfortunately this was one party that could easily blow my cover as the Alfa of the BNM. There was going to be a mammoth crowd of people; hundreds of invitation cards distributed to babes had already run out, and there was still demand for more.

This was anticipated to be the groove of the year and all the babes on the social circuit were clamouring to be there. I heard that some babes who fell well below the required social echelon were now deliberately sleeping with Marauders to get an invite.

Over one hundred Marauders got two invites each, one for their babe and the second for another female friend. Prince, who was gregarious and part of the organising committee, knew many hot babes and was tasked with distributing an additional fifty invites. We were also expecting about twenty to thirty different Alfas and Marauders from other towns.

This was not going to be a mere party; it was going to be a jamboree and carnival rolled into one. We were looking to cater for about four hundred people.

Security was also vital to this event; we needed to protect our guests, and most importantly ourselves. Hammer and his committee had used an insider to settle the local Police force, so we would have free passage and no roadblocks.

Hammer was looking at the necessary modalities of having armed Marauders at our departure and arrival points; he was also tasked with making sure that we all arrived safely at our destination and were protected at the venue.

I had a meeting with Hammer, Victor and Theo and we agreed that security was paramount for the BB on Saturday and after; other confraternities, especially the Mafioso, could see this as an opportunity to carry out an unexpected attack, and so we could not afford to let our guard down.

I had given Hammer and his team the go-ahead to do whatever it took to get security tight and right, even if it involved importing mercenaries from other institutions.

Hammer was going to arrange for two cars and armed Marauders to ferry my guests and me to the venue of the BB.

After further deliberation, we agreed to call a bush meeting at "down the valley" to update all Marauders on the progress so far, give them their departure times and drum into them what was required of them.

The bush meeting that Saturday lasted for about two hours. I told them about our meeting point, and I gave them a very brief insight on our security arrangements and the dress code.

I was quick to discuss the behaviour of Marauders before and during the party. It would be gross misconduct to fight during the party or to intimidate any of our guests, especially the babes. There was to be no smoking of Igbo on the hotel premises – there would be on-the-spot "drilling" for any Marauder who fell afoul of any of these rules.

I got Hammer and Victor to go through any other matters and before I closed the meeting, I highlighted to my fellow Marauders my need for personal security as the Alfa. "My Marauders, please do not be unaware that some of the babes coming would be babes of Mafioso, Pyrates, Buccaneers and other 'yeye confras', so do not expose me unnecessarily," I said.

"I have the option of not turning up, but I get to come groove with my brothers now, *so I go dey with some babes for a coded spot, so abeg*, don't come and start shaking my hand with two hands or hailing me as your Alfa," I warned. I concluded by telling them that we were going to have great fun, and that the DJs would be spinning all night long.

Marauders were strange and peculiar people – their passion for warfare was rivalled only by their passion for a good party, and I felt obligated to give them a very good time, after the gruelling war with the Mafioso. In addition, I was determined to make sure that this BB would be talked about for many years to come.

Our Brotherhood Boogie took place on a Saturday night in the year 1996 and it was the bomb – well-organised and perfectly executed from start to finish.

Security from Hammer and his team was spot on, from our point of departure to the return of all Marauders and guests. The music was right on the money as the two DJs were in top form; and there was plenty to eat and drink.

I arrived at the party with my guests at about 10 pm, after making sure that the last coach carrying Marauders had left the departure point. The atmosphere at the venue was like a carnival and I felt a great sense of accomplishment.

I checked into my reserved chalet with Pauline, who was my escort for the evening; Isabella had not been able to make it down for the party as she was writing her examinations. Pauline and I showered and changed into our party clothes.

I was looking like a million bucks in my tight cream Hugo Boss jeans, and an Oxford white cotton shirt with black embroidery around the buttons, which hugged my well-built muscular chest and biceps. I had my famous brown and black waistcoat on as well. Pauline was wearing the shortest black mini-skirt ever made and was oozing sensuality; she had the prettiest set of legs on a human being and she knew it.

We partied for hours to the addictive beats of both DJs, and I regularly acknowledged Marauders with a wink or a nod. I decided to go out into the courtyard with Pauline for some fresh air, and it was like a carnival outside. Marauders were having fun, some were playing a game of snooker, some were singing our bush songs, some were queuing for beef kebab "suya," and some were dancing as the music blared from the external speakers.

I approached the queue waiting for some kebab from the side, and I almost dropped my bottle of beer; standing in the queue were Tima and her friends. I nodded and smiled in her direction and walked on, with Pauline in tow.

I could see the shock on her face and that of her friends when they realised that I was a member of the irrepressible and indomitable BNM; but I received an even bigger shock when I suddenly found myself up in the air, being carried shoulder-high by some die-hard and belligerent Marauders.

They carried me around the venue, singing my praises and dancing; there were fireworks going off and I could hear Marauders screaming and shouting, "Our Alfa, *you too dey oo, you too bam oo, all the babes dey agree your own.*"

I knew that the longer I stayed up in the air the longer I was exposing myself to the world, and it was a welcome relief when I saw Hammer and his team fight their way through the mass of bodies and wrestle me down from the shoulders of Ofili, a.k.a. "Chuchu."

I composed myself after about two minutes and looked around for Pauline, who was in the safe company of one of my security people. I could see the look of admiration and renewed respect in her eyes as she hugged me and held on to me.

I took her back to the dance floor and we started dancing again. As we danced, I made eye contact with my flatmate Patrick, who was now a Marauder; he approached me and I whispered into his ear. I told Pauline that I had to go use the toilet, and that Patrick would dance with her and look after her while I was gone.

I had business to address; it took Hammer and his team less than five minutes to find and drag Ofili and his other two accomplices, nicknamed Ayaya and Expo, to where I was standing in a dark corner with a squad of five Marauders.

"Were you guys at the last bush meeting that we held last week at 'down the Valley?" I asked innocently. "Yes my Alfa, *we dey there*," replied Ofili and Ayaya.

"So Expo, *you no dey come bush meeting again as par why now*?" I asked, again waiting for a response. "My Alfa, *I travel go see my Mama wey dey sick for hospital*," he replied with a trembling voice.

"*Ok ooo, you fit come groove but you no fit come meeting, Ok ooo*," I responded, "So excluding Expo *wey no come meeting, wetin we discuss for the meeting about my security?*" I directed my question to Ofili and Ayaya.

"My Alfa, you talk say make Marauders no shake your hand with two hands or hail you publicly but My Alfa, you no talk say make we no carry you up and dance," Ofili replied. "My Alfa, *you too bam and that is why we sey make we recognise you*," he concluded.

I stood there for a few seconds looking at the incorrigible bunch of Marauders in front of me; I shook my head in disbelief. "*How una take dey pass exam sef when common and simple instruction you cannot follow? Well, na gross misconduct for una and Expo na double mending for you as you no come meeting,*" I concluded.

I turned to Hammer and gave him the order to arrange a ten-minute mending for the three Marauders; but Ofili and Expo were to get an additional five

272

minutes each, for being the ringleader and for not attending the meeting respectively.

I walked away from the scene back to the dance hall, where Pauline was waiting with Patrick. As I approached the pair, I realised that they had stopped dancing and were now standing side by side. It dawned on me that they had stopped dancing as soon as the DJ had started playing some slow romantic jams, as Patrick was petrified to do a slow dance with the Alfa's babe.

I reclaimed Pauline and nodded to Patrick, who disappeared from that area of the dance floor. She held on to me tightly as we danced to the earth-moving song of Michael Bolton. I could feel the warmth of her body against mine as she whispered into my ear, "I missed you and that was the longest toilet break ever in the history of toilet breaks; were you having a baby in the toilet?" she asked teasingly.

I laughed as I spun her around and we danced into the early hours of the morning. We finally retired to the chalet at about 4 am, but not before I had called Victor and Hammer aside to give specific instructions that all our guests must be the first to board the coaches, and must arrive safely back at the designated point.

Our BB was the talk of the whole university and far beyond for many weeks. Babes that had missed out on it were kicking themselves and Marauders were hot cakes both on campus and in other universities.

The only BB that could arguably rival ours in living memory would be the one held by my good old friend Cosmos "Watata" at Awka. They had the water drained out of the Olympic size swimming pool at Joneb Hotel, and they partied inside and around it. It was a novel and exciting way to party, and the only negative about their BB was that the babes were not as hot and beautiful as ours were; and I knew this because I was there.

I got situation reports from my Voice and Seer on a regular basis and their reports indicated that we had just successfully pulled off the greatest BB in the history of the region.

As I stood listening to the words of praise coming from the report of my Seer, I could not help but feel a slight sense of apprehension. It would have been foolish to not realise that my status as the Alfa of the most dreaded confraternity on campus had been exposed; but to what extent, I did not know.

I asked my Seer to carry out another situation investigation to determine the extent of my exposure, especially among the female population. The only positive side of this situation was that I had less than three months left before my final examinations and the defence of my dissertation, before graduating.

All I had to do was keep a very low profile, focusing only on my studies and dissertation for the remaining few months, and I should be fine.

My Seer brought back the situation report that I had been expecting. The gist amongst the female population was that there was this handsome "aje butter" dude, that butter would not melt in his mouth, and he was the boss of the dreaded BNM confraternity. He continued that they did not know the person, but they had heard people call him Remyleon. "My Alfa, *dem just dey trip for you big time*," he concluded.

I could feel my head expanding, knowing that I was the man of the moment; but all the cautious bones in my body were sending signals that this was the time to keep low and go underground. I had less than three months left until graduation and about five weeks before I handed over the reins to a new Alfa.

Chapter 21

The following few weeks were hectic as I threw myself into my final term work, preparing for the final examinations and the defence of my dissertation in front of a panel of senior lecturers.

I also had the challenge of nominating a candidate for the new Alfa position; this was one task that was causing me sleepless nights. The more I thought about it, the more I was convinced that Tornado was the wrong person for the role.

I had grown close to Sebastian, my Seer, and I felt that he was a stronger candidate for the position; however, I still had slight reservations about his people management skills and his ability to carry Marauders along with his plans. Maybe I was looking at the wrong people; I might need to extend my search beyond my Executives.

Rumours were flying around that Tornado was already drumming up support within the Council of wise men and a section of Marauders. I heard that he was already promising positions to certain Marauders in his new cabinet, and rumour said that money was now changing hands.

Victor and Hammer were again tasked with making all the preparations for the handover ceremony to take place in two and a half weeks' time. I still had not submitted my candidate for the Alfa position.

I finally made up my mind after a week of interacting with the grass-root Marauders and picking their brains. I wanted to submit my nomination to the Council of wise men in person, for obvious reasons. My meeting with them was scheduled in nine days' time, because I was too busy with lectures and mock examinations to set any earlier date.

My supervisor had now signed off on my dissertation and I was ready for the defence; my mock examination had gone relatively well, and I knew the areas that I needed to work on. I could not afford to have an extra semester in this jungle, because I had seen past Alfas and Marauders suffer the consequences of not graduating as planned: they had become objects of ridicule for fellow Marauders with a grudge.

I really did not want to be added to that list, so I made sure that I attended all tutorials, settled the lecturers who had to be settled, and studied extra hard for my carry-over module.

Busy with academic work, I hardly spent any time in my flat; but I had been informed by my flatmates that Tima had been combing the whole campus looking for me after the weekend of the BB and was extremely keen to talk to me, but our paths had not crossed yet.

I wondered why she was so keen to see me, as I had given up all hope of going out with her, especially now that she knew my status within the dreaded BNM. I decided to avoid her at all costs, as I really did not want any "goody two shoes" preaching repentance to me.

It was about 10 pm one Thursday night; I had just returned to my flat from a long and cumbersome group tutorial. I alighted from the Okada and started to walk towards my building, when I saw a figure step out from the shadows as I approached the gate.

My natural reaction was to reach for the gun tucked into my waistband; it was already half drawn as Tima stepped out from the shadows into the bright security light. "What are you doing out here alone in the dark at this time of the night?" I enquired. "I have been waiting for you since 8 pm, as you seem to be avoiding me," she replied.

"Tima, I have been so busy with my 'acada' work and I have not even had the chance to take a break yet. But you worry me now, because you should not be out here on your own at this time; times are dangerous off campus," I said with genuine concern in my voice.

I led her into my flat. We sat for a few seconds on the settee staring at each other, and then I asked her why she had been looking for me. "I hope no one is threatening you and you are not in any kind of trouble," I enquired.

"Yes, I am in very grave trouble, but my trouble is you," she said with a helpless look on her face. "I struggled to say no to your advances in the past, and

278

now after seeing you at that party, I cannot get you out of my mind, *I dey trip for you big time.*"

There have been very few times in my life that I have been speechless, and this was one of them. I stared at her for some seconds that felt like eternity; and I could not help but realise that I was staring at one of the most beautiful girls I had ever met.

I knew that I had to choose my response carefully, as I cleared my throat to speak. "Tima, you know that I have fancied you from the first moment I laid my eyes on you; but what has changed since the last time you said no?" I asked, a bit baffled.

"Remy, I have always had feelings for you, but I was fighting them, and I also thought that you were going to get hurt by Solomon and his crew. So I wanted to distance myself from you to protect you," she replied. "Little did I know that I was trying to protect someone that did not need protecting," she concluded.

As the Alfa of the BNM, I had learnt within a short space of time to think on my feet and see the bigger picture; and this picture, though tempting, had all the hallmarks of anguish and disaster at the end.

"Tima, do you realise that I have less than three months left before I leave the university for good? How would you cope in my absence, especially when the word gets out that you are my babe?" I asked. "I do not want to put you in that dangerous situation and then walk away after graduation," I said. "I bet that you have not thought about the scenario of other confraternities targeting you deliberately in order to get to me or draw me out. I am sorry, dear, but I care about you enough not to want to put you in harm's way," I concluded.

"Remy, I love you so much and I am not willing to let go again," she said as she began to well up and cry. "I can't help myself."

I could not bear to see tears fall from those lovely eyes onto those beautifully structured cheeks. I pulled her into my arms and we held each other for a very long time. Kissing her was like being in paradise; her lips were so tempting and as soft as freshly baked bread, her tongue was as light as a feather and her touch was as smooth and tender as silk.

"I can't afford for anything to happen to you my dear, so we have to keep this on the down low, very coded," I whispered into her ear. "OK, sweetheart," she said as she hugged me tightly. It was past midnight as I looked at my watch, knowing that I had a 10 am lecture that morning. "Come to bed," I said, as I pulled her to her feet and led her into my bedroom. As we stepped into my tastefully furnished room, she turned to look at me in the dim lighting and said, in a very low voice, "No hanky panky tonight, I am not that kind of girl."

My blood was boiling hot with passion and I only had one thing on my mind. *"Which kind ogbanje babe be this one again?"* I thought to myself as I forced an innocent smile.

"Remy, we have plenty of time ahead of us, so let's not rush, let it be special," she said in a soft and romantic voice. I could hear her voice, but could hardly understand what she was saying because I was having great difficulty controlling the big boss downstairs.

"Tima, you know that I would not dream of taking advantage of you and I would always be a gentleman," I assured her. She fell asleep as we lay in each other's arms and after a while, it dawned on me that this was the first time in a very long time that I had shared a bed with a female without sex taking place. I ran my fingers over the curves of her body and smiled to myself, before I slowly drifted off to sleep.

I woke up with a start, with the feeling of someone staring at me; my heart skipped a beat when I saw the figure of a human being sitting at the edge of my bed. I was already reaching for my Beretta under the mattress before I realised that it was Tima.

"What time is it?" I asked, having lost all sense of time. "It is 8:30 am," she said and continued, "You look so handsome and innocent when you are asleep, like a baby in a foetal position."

"I have a very important lecture at 10 am and I need to hit the bathroom now," I said as I jumped off the bed and patted her head.

"Help yourself to whatever you want to eat, the kitchen is off the hallway," I said as I left the room. "I will make you breakfast," I heard her shout after me as I entered the bathroom. I was not keen on any babe cooking for me except for Isabella; I had heard many stories of babes putting love potions into the food of their lovers, accidentally killing them or making them lose their senses.

I came out of the bathroom fifteen minutes later, but Tima was still in the kitchen. Dressing up, I kept wondering how to make an excuse to avoid eating the food that she was preparing.

It was 9 am and I decided to use running late as an excuse. She came into the room with a plate of steaming boiled yam covered with egg stew; I looked at my watch as she set the plate on the table. "You are not leaving this room until you have eaten your food, and I will join you in eating in case you think that I have put some juju in it."

"Don't be silly, that thought never crossed my mind," I lied. "I am just running late and if I don't make a move on, I won't get a good seat in the lecture hall; you know how it is now," I said, gesticulating.

"My dear Remy, how do you think I'll feel if you don't taste the food that I put so much time into preparing for you?" she asked.

"Ok – ok, you win, but I only have five minutes to eat." I sat down quickly on the chair with Tima sitting on my lap, and we ate together. I kissed her goodbye and as I left the flat, I knocked on Patrick's door and told him to keep an eye out for her in case she needed anything.

Koko, my bodyguard for the day, was already waiting outside my gate with two Okadas. I nodded to him and jumped on one of the bikes and we headed straight towards campus.

My 10 am lecture was a struggle; it was boring and long-winded, coupled with the fact that I was lacking adequate sleep. I was beginning to lose the will to live, only twenty minutes into the ninety-minute lecture.

This was one of my mandatory modules and an obese middle-aged accountant called Mr Etalor taught it. Rumour had it that he had slept with half of the babes in the department, and still counting. I just wanted to pass his module, so I decided to work hard at it and use any connections that I could get through some of the babes in my department.

It was a welcome relief when the lecture finally ended and I had the chance to catch up with Theo. I told him to meet me at Victor's flat at 9 pm, in the company of Hammer. "My Alfa, I hope that all is well and no yawa," Theo asked with concern on his face. "No yawa my guy, just want to pick your brains before my meeting with you and your 'wise men' in two days' time," I replied.

I left campus and went back to my flat, to find Tima gone and a note on my bed, with petals of flowers arranged in the shape of a heart around the letter. I smiled as I picked it up, noting that it was sealed with a kiss. I was tempted to open the letter, but I decided to save it for later after my 9 pm meeting.

I arrived at Victor's flat at 9:05 pm that evening and the trio were already waiting for me. They all stood up as I walked into the flat. "I hail you my Alfa," they echoed in unison and I replied, "I hail my Marauders."

"My guys, this meeting will only take as much time as it needs to take; we are about to have this discussion because I trust and respect you all. We have being through thick and thin together; whatever we discuss here is highly confidential and must not leave this room."

I told them about my relentless search for a new and suitable candidate for Alfa; I told them that I had finally found a worthy candidate; and I told them who my candidate would be.

I wanted their feedback on my proposed candidate. As chairperson of the Council of wise men, Theo was careful to be unbiased and objective with his feedback. We sat weighing the pros and cons of my nominee, and the general feedback about him was extremely positive from all three.

The meeting ended after about forty-five minutes, but we stayed on in Victor's flat, downing a mixture of "Goskolos" and Guinness Stout. We continued to talk about babes and other confraternities, the wars that we had fought, and the near-misses that we'd had individually and as a confraternity.

I left Victor's flat at fifteen minutes past midnight, feeling relieved but also the worse for wear as I was very high on alcohol. I did not bother to get undressed as I hit my bed; Tima's letter still lay on the mattress.

Chapter 22

I left Tima watching a movie in my room as I stepped out to attend the meeting with the Council of wise men; it was scheduled to take place at 8 pm in Theo's house, off the highway behind Girls' Hostel 1004. I looked at my watch as I jumped on a motorbike; it was about 7:35 pm and I anticipated getting to Theo's within twenty minutes.

As the bike sped away from my gate, I suddenly realised that I did not have a gun on me; I had forgotten to retrieve my Berretta from its new hiding place in the ceiling because Tima was in the room.

I was tempted to turn the bike around, but on second thought, I changed my mind. After all, it was Theo's house and I was going to be in the company of brothers and fellow Marauders, who had seen it all for many years.

As my bike turned into Theo's lane, I caught sight of Rago. I asked the bike man to slow down as we got close to Rago. "My Alfa, I hail oo," he said as he stood still, "I hail you back Rago, *wetin carry you come here?*" I asked.

"We have come to give una back up and security for the meeting," he replied. "What do you mean by 'we'?" I asked inquisitively. "Me and my crew," he replied. I smiled and nodded my head in appreciation. *"Ok, no yawa,"* I said and moved on.

Theo met me at the front entrance of his flat and we shook hands in our usual way. I looked to the left hand side of the yard and saw Ohis, Abass and Walter sitting under the mango tree; they all stood up to shout out greetings to me. I responded and waved to them, and I then turned to Theo. "When did you guys become celebrities that the suicide squad is providing cover for you now?" I asked jokingly.

"My Alfa, don't mind them, I think they are here more to drink and chill out with their babes in the other flat than to provide security," Theo said as he ushered me into his room. The four other wise men stood up and greeted me in unison; I acknowledged them all and shook their hands in turn before sitting down to start the meeting.

Theo was the chairperson of the Council and the authority in the room. He was the one running the show, and I was there not in the capacity of the Alfa but as an observer. Theo decided, with the agreement of the other wise men, to put the issue of the Alfa candidacy as the second item on the agenda. When we got to that item, I told them who my candidate was and they put his name into the pool with two other names.

As I sat there in the meeting, I had a strong feeling that Sebastian, who was my candidate, stood a good chance, and I was going to make sure that I influenced the decision using all the means available to me as the Alfa.

I began to list the many merits of having Sebastian as the new Alfa of the BNM, and I could see the men in the room concurring with me. I was interrupted by a loud knock on the door, and I looked over to Theo, puzzled.

I could see the annoyance and frustration written all over Theo's face as he approached the door. "Who be that?" he bellowed. *"Theo na me,"* came the recognisable voice from the other side of the door. I watched Theo open the door and saw him back-track slowly into the room; and then I saw the gun pointing at his forehead as he continued to slowly retreat into the room.

My lower jaw almost dropped to the floor when I saw the face behind the gun. Standing in front of Theo and still pointing the gun was Victor, my Omega and trusted right hand man. Victor turned to me with the gun now pointing at my chest, as I stood up; I looked into his blood-red eyes and saw Rago, Ohis, Walter and Abass standing behind him.

Theo was quickly disarmed and held at gunpoint by Rago, while Ohis and Abass grabbed me; as they bundled me out of the room, I could hear Victor shouting behind me, "By the power vested in me as the Omega, I hereby suspend you as the Alfa of the BNM."

I was taken to the mango tree where two other Marauders were waiting; I looked around in the dim light and recognised them as Ernest and Udoka. The six Marauders with Victor surrounded me.

I could hear Theo calling Victor and the other conspirators "Judas" and I could hear the sound of Theo and the other wise men being beaten up at the other end of the yard by a different set of Marauders.

I was still shocked and petrified as I stood face to face with Victor. I knew that these people were fully armed, dangerous and high on Marijuana; they were trigger-happy, but I had decided that I was not going to go down as anything less than the Alfa of the BNM.

"Victor, you do not have the authority to suspend an Alfa. You know the constitution very well and only a majority vote by the wise men can suspend an Alfa," I said as I stood my ground. I was beaten and drilled for the next twenty minutes, before being dragged along the muddy ground to where Victor was standing. I was asked to kneel in front of Victor and acknowledge him as the new Alfa.

"So this is what it is all about. You wanted to be the Alfa all along," I said. "I am the Alfa of the BNM, ordained by the oracle and acknowledged by all Marauders," I said defiantly and stood my ground; but not for long. I was soon sent flying back by kicks and blows as they rained onto me. I could feel my lips start to swell, and blood began to trickle down the side of my face from a torn eyebrow.

The beating continued for what seemed an eternity and as I lay on the ground exhausted, I could barely hear the conversation between Victor, Rago and Abass. "*Who go kill am,*" I heard Victor ask, "*No yawa I go pull the trigger,*" agreed Abass, "but get him to renounce Alfa, *because we no fit 'murd' an Alfa,*" Abass said.

"No worry, by the time we finish with him, e go renounce Alfa," Victor assured them. As I lay in the dirt, my childhood flashed in front of my eyes. I could see the younger Remy lying on the football pitch after a tackle, I could see the faces of my siblings, and I could even hear my father's voice in the distance saying, "If you continue on this path, you will amount to nothing." *"Maybe he was right," I thought* to myself as I lay in the dirt... this was the end of the road, the end of Remy Ukadike.

I was hauled up to my feet and a gun was shoved into my mouth. "You get two seconds to renounce Alfa or I go blow ya head one hand," bellowed Abass. I closed my eyes and said a silent prayer, and waited for death.

The final shot did not come. Rather, the gun was removed from my mouth and Theo, who was looking much the worse for wear, was shoved in front of me to convince me to renounce my position as Alfa. As Theo stood in front of me, he motioned with his eyes that there was a gap in the circle. I nodded my understanding and with the last energy remaining in me, I charged forward.

A body builder and sprinter rolled into one, I knew that if I could get a head start, I would be difficult to catch. I charged through the gap in the circle, knocking down the nearest dissident, with Theo behind me. The element of surprise shocked Victor and his co-conspirators as Theo and I stormed into the thick bushes nearby.

I could hear and feel my heart pounding against my rib cage and I could hear Theo panting behind me as we tore through the thick bushes; then came the gunshots and shouting behind me. I continued to tear through the bushes of thorns and elephant grass, and as I ran, I prayed that I wouldn't fall into one of the many abandoned wells dug by farmers and riddled with snakes. I could no longer hear Theo behind me and I hoped that a bullet had not struck him.

I had run for what seemed like forever and I knew that Victor and his crew would be combing the area for me. I could barely make out lights from cars driving past, and I guessed that the highway was not far away; however, I knew that Victor and his crew might be lying in ambush on the highway.

I looked to my left and could barely make out the four-storey building of Twin-cam hostel. I decided to make my way towards the hostel, but as I approached the fence, I heard gunshots coming from the hostel grounds. I could hear screams and babes crying.

Voices from within the premises were shouting, "Where is Remy? We are looking for Remy. We are going to burn down this building, where is that bastard, bring him out."

I decided that my best option was to stay put in the bushes. I had lost all track of time because Ohis had taken my watch off me. Sinking to the ground with my head between my knees, I wept, the tears flowing more out of anger and humiliation than anything else.

"I am the Alfa of the BNM," I said to myself as I got up, dusted myself off, and made my way towards the road connecting the highway to the town. It was quiet and the street lights shone brightly; I kept to the shadows as I walked along cautiously. I had barely walked for ten minutes when I spotted a crowd of people coming in my direction; I quickly ducked behind an old kerosene tank and waited anxiously.

As the mob got closer and closer, I could make out the figures of Hammer, Bilado and The Bulldog, but I remained hidden in the shadows because I did not know whom to trust. It was when I caught sight of Binga in the crowd that I tentatively walked out into the centre of the road.

I was standing about ten metres from the crowd with my face swollen, my shirt torn and my pride battered and bruised. I was overcome with so much emotion that I sank to my knees and in a tired voice shouted, "I hail you Marauders." The response of "I hail you, my Alfa," was deafening.

The sight of their Alfa in such a state sent the crowd into a furore. I did not have to tell them what had transpired, as Binga, who was a member of the Council of wise men, had managed to escape during the fracas and had already told them.

Binga was smallish in stature and had managed to squeeze through the small window in the toilet to escape and go in search of Hammer and the other Executive members.

Hammer offered his vest to me, and then wrapped the two bullet belts across his chest; he had the AK 47 resting on his right shoulder. Bilado passed me a loaded gun and they all waited for my command.

As I held the gun in my right hand, I could feel the unction and real power returning. "Let me be clear," I shouted, "I want Victor, Abass, Walter, Ohis, Rago, Ernest, Udoka and other rebels, dead or alive; in fact I would prefer them dead rather than alive," I concluded.

The time was twelve minutes past midnight when we rolled out looking for the rebels. As we combed the streets, the crowd got larger. We headed for Victor's flat, but he had already fled with the rebels; we ransacked his room and set fire to all his personal possessions outside.

An intelligence report came via the Seer that the rebels had been sighted leaving my flat, and heading for Abass's crib at the outskirts of the university town – it was about twenty minutes away by car. We needed a car or a bus urgently, but first I had to go to my flat.

I was not sure of what to expect as I walked in, but taking one look at Patrick's countenance, I knew that I had to expect the worst.

"Where is Tima?" I asked. "She has gone back to her flat," he replied, and narrated how the rebels had come looking for me after 1 escaped into the bushes. They had stormed the flat, heavily armed and shouting that I was the Alfa of the BNM and must be eliminated.

They had kicked my bedroom door down and found Tima. Rago and Walter were going to rape her, but as Victor intervened, they'd decided to shoot her in the leg. But as Ohis took aim to pull the trigger, Patrick had thrown himself in front of her begging for mercy.

They could not shoot Patrick, as he was a fellow Marauder; so they decided to vandalise my room instead. They smashed my television and sound system, ripped up all my designer clothes and carpet, and defecated on my bed.

I walked into my room; my blood was boiling and I was seeing red, enraged at the lack of respect shown by the people I had called brothers. I retrieved my Beretta from its hiding place in the ceiling, checked that it was fully loaded, and handed back Bilado's gun to him. Now it was time for rebel cleansing.

There were about forty Marauders with me, and I split them into groups of five to comb every nook and cranny of the town. I went with Hammer, Bilado, The Bulldog, Binga, Ike "The Killer," Otoro and Sebastian as a team, in search for a mode of transport.

At about 2 am, we stood in the shadows along Market road, where we waited for about 10 minutes before the headlights of a car approached us from the opposite direction. As the Peugeot 505 approached us and was about five metres away, Hammer, who was masked, stepped out into the road with his AK 47 pointing at the car; Bilado and Otoro stepped in from the sides, and the other Marauders who were hiding in the shadows further down covered the car from the back.

It was like a scene out of a blockbuster gangster movie; the driver stopped the car and put his hands up. He was shaking like a wet leaf as Bilado pulled him out of the car with a gun to his head. I stepped out of the shadows and came face to face with Jim, a guy around campus and a ladies' man. He was not affiliated to any confraternity, but he liked to hang out with the Mafioso and Buccaneers, either gambling or partying.

"Do you know me?" I asked him. "No-o-o s—ir," he replied, quaking in his boots. "Call me your saviour tonight, because my boys would have blown your head off," I said. "We need your car sharp sharp," I barked authoritatively.

Jim made to hand over the car keys to me. "No, you will drive us, in case your car has a de-mobilizer," I said suspiciously.

I got into the front seat with Hammer while four Marauders climbed into the back seat; the remaining two sat inside the boot of the car. Jim turned the car around and we headed for Abass's crib.

Jim killed the car lights as we approached the unpainted building; the rest of us jumped out. Hammer took the car keys from Jim and we made our way towards the building. Three Marauders covered the back exit, and the rest of us went for the front entrance.

Burglary rails with a padlock protected the entrance. I took one swing at the padlock with a hand-held axe, and it split and fell to the ground. We quickly proceeded into the house and behold, Ohis was coming out of the toilet. He froze for a split-second before making a dash for the nearby room, but Bilado was right behind him.

We could hear Ohis shouting for help as he attempted to shut the door, and we could hear the frantic movements of people in the room; we knew that these rebels were armed and dangerous and we could not afford to take any chances.

Abass's voice was audible inside the room as Ohis and Bilado continued to struggle at the door; all of a sudden there was a big explosion and the door fell open. We could hear screams from inside the room and bodies were scurrying to escape through the broken ceiling.

Ohis was crawling on the floor, his shirt soaked in the blood pouring from his abdomen where pellets from the sawed off gun had hit him. I walked into the room, took one look at him and felt no iota of compassion.

"Let's go," I bellowed, "Our job here is done since the other cowards have fled; let his lily-livered crew treat him." We stormed out of the compound in case the police were on their way. Jumping into Jim's car, we took a different route back to town.

Daybreak was fast approaching and the adrenalin was still pumping. We discharged Jim and his car, and continued to comb the town for Victor. It was about 5:30 in the morning and light was gradually penetrating the darkness when I got wind that Udoka had been

295

sighted leaving his girlfriend's house and heading for home.

Apparently, he was unaware that the coup that he was a party to had failed and the rebellion had been crushed.

We rolled towards his crib, and laid an ambush for him in the bushes. Udoka appeared within five minutes, whistling as he walked towards his bedsit at Kent Villa.

I stepped out of my hiding place and came face to face with the dumbfounded and terrified rebel. Udoka turned to run, but found himself staring into the faces of Bilado and Hammer and the rest of my squad. He made a dash for the nearby fence on the right, but was soon cornered.

Trapped like a caged animal, Udoka cowered against the wall with his face in his hands. I stepped forward, rage burning in me. "I initiated you into the BNM and you had the effrontery to plan a coup against me; I saw you throw a punch at me," I said with venom.

I raised my loaded gun as Udoka sank to his knees. I could hear two voices in my head. The first was soft and gentle, yet firm. "Don't do it, don't soil your hands with his blood, you cannot give back life when you take it. Remy, this act would haunt you for the rest of your life, please do not pull the trigger," It advised.

But this was sharply countered by another voice egging me on. "Blast the bloody traitor, how could he mess with the Alfa of the BNM, the small boy had the cheek. Don't slack with this one oo, show an example with this coward, blast his head off one time now," said the aggressive and brash voice.

I was in an emotional quandary; my head was full of voices and as I grappled with them, my blood was boiling, my ego bruised, and my heart filled with rage and anger. I took one look at the petrified figure in front of me as I squeezed the trigger.

I felt the gun jump in my right hand as it exploded with deadly rage and intent...

Chapter 23

I left the branch at about 5:35 pm, feeling a bit happier. Our sales performance for the day was a lot better; my staff had been able to flog a couple of credit cards, bank accounts, and home insurance to a number of customers.

This would give me a temporary respite from my area manager, "The PRAT," for this week. I headed towards the motorway that would lead me home. As I drove my BMW past the glass house that was now my local church, memories came flooding back.

I was married in that building seven years ago. It was a beautiful sunny day in August 2005 and the church ceremony was wonderful, followed by an awesome reception party at a banqueting suite in Finchley Central. We had our families present, some of whom had flown in from Nigeria the previous week to attend the wedding, the food was great, the atmosphere on the day was electric, and we did not want the celebration to end.

People had always told me that marriage was a never-ending challenge, and I came to realise that this was very true. The pre-marital counselling classes were not enough to prepare me for the new challenges that kept rearing their ugly heads.

Every time I thought that I had cracked one challenging test and moved up a level, another one kicked me in the guts, showing me that I was still at the kindergarten level.

I took advice from various sources and read books about how to improve your marriage; they were quite enlightening, but they did not stop the challenges from coming. Older couples advised me that marriage got better with age, but I saw older couples getting divorced as well.

A pastor in my church would often say, during his numerous sermons on the nature of marriage, that a good marriage involves having two good managers managing each other's differences effectively. He was of the opinion that if couples could manage their differences better, then the rate of divorces based on irreconcilable differences would decrease dramatically.

I believed that the expectations placed on marriage could be somewhat over-powering. It seemed like insanity to take two people from two very different cultures and backgrounds, two people with different outlooks on life and different philosophies, and bring them together and expect them to become one and live in unity.

The chances of that happening, especially in the early years, were very low; hence the need to continue to working on and managing the various differences that cropped up, as effectively as possible.

This pastor, a charismatic leader both in the UK and in Nigeria, had once said that couples when courting should be talking about what they did not have in common, and address these things, rather than solely enjoying what they had in common. Based on his vast experience in counselling married couples, he had noticed that married couples tended to discover over the years that they had fewer things in common and more differences.

I drove past Staples Corner as I connected to the M1, and more memories came to me. My aunty lived about ten minutes from there, and it was at her place that I had first resided fifteen years ago on my arrival in the UK to study.

I arrived in the UK at dawn on the 24th of March 1998, to commence a postgraduate degree at a London university. The last time that I had been in the UK was about thirteen years ago as a young teenager, but now I was returning, after various attempts, as a young man.

Before leaving Nigeria, my older brother had advised me to buy a travel card on my arrival at Heathrow Airport, saying that it would enable me travel all around London for the day. I left the shores of my homeland on the night of the 23rd and as the plane touched down at Heathrow, I felt an overwhelming sense of a new beginning in my life.

When I cleared Immigration, I got directions to the ticket counter, paid for a one-day travel card, jumped into the back of a black cab, and gave the address of my aunt's house to the Jamaican driver.

I fell asleep within five minutes of settling into the back seat of the cab, and I was awoken forty-five minutes later by the driver's voice. I got out of the cab, went towards the driver's side of the car, and gave him my travel card.

The Jamaican driver looked at it and then at my face with a puzzled look, that turned suddenly to irritation. *"What aguan man, what are you give me card for mon?"* he said furiously in Jamaican Patua. "I– I– I was told that I could travel anywhere in London with this travel card," I replied in shock.

"Blood cloth mon, give me mi pounds before my dread na fi bust mon," he threatened. "Did you just come off the boat mon?" he asked. I stood there dumbfounded by the driver's reaction and rejection of my travel card. The irate driver was about to get out of his car when my aunt came out of her house.

She shouted in excitement on seeing me, and gave me a big hug. I explained the situation and she burst out laughing, and paid the driver my fare of thirty pounds.

This was a different London from the one I had visited many years ago; it had turned into an unforgiving and cold city, almost as brash as Lagos. I had to sleep under an electric blanket that night, because it was bitterly cold in my aunt's guest room; the room was probably the size of our store-room back in Nigeria. I reminisced about my journey so far; this was a new beginning for me, and I was going to take full advantage of the opportunity.

I fell asleep with a smile on my face as I wondered what my postgraduate course had to offer me in the UK.

When the next morning came, I got ready and got directions from my aunt's husband on how to get to the university. I carefully avoided all black cabs and took the underground to East London to begin my registration.

The MBA class of 1998 had about 25 students from various parts of the world. There were students from China, Greece, Malaysia, Brazil, Spain, India, Georgia, Vietnam, Ghana, South Africa and Nigeria – a multitude of cultures and languages.

There were two other Nigerians in my class; I was happy to recognise one of them as an old primary school classmate called Ojo, and we hit it off immediately and became buddies. The lecturers were great, and took extra time to speak and explain things to us; they were aware that we struggled to understand their accent and the speed at which they spoke. My MBA class was fun, as we had to attend lectures only three days a week, and carry out some group research work once a week. The rest of the days were for hanging out and partying within reason.

Working with a computer for my research work was a brand new challenge for me; we were given ample demonstrations by the Librarian's assistant, to get many of us from the developing countries comfortable with this device of the new age. I had heard of the computer before, and had actually taken an elective in computer science at my university in Nigeria, but I had never set my eyes on one, let alone used one.

I had never known of the existence of email as a form of communication, and it was mind-boggling to see how effective it was. The university library was stocked with various books, journals, newspapers and ample computer systems, unlike my previous university in Nigeria, where there weren't enough books to go around and we'd had to resort to hiding the books we needed in strategic areas of the library.

The university had a cafeteria on the ground floor, and a pool table in the lounge. Ojo and I tried to spend as little time as possible in the building, as there was plenty of fun outside. Ojo was the son of a Monarch in Nigeria and from a very wealthy family; he had a fully furnished flat and a Honda Prelude at his disposal. He did not have to work and had a lot of family support around him in the UK.

Ojo, right from primary school, had always been a humble and good-hearted individual; he never seemed to let his pedigree and family's wealth go to his head and was comfortable hanging out with all kinds of people irrespective of their background.

I noticed that he would never deliberately flaunt his family's wealth or connections – rather, he would try to keep these things hidden from those who were unaware of his background. Ojo had a very cheeky and humorous streak in him, and would always make people around him laugh. Altogether, he was a very nice young man and knew how to have fun.

I moved out of my aunt's place after three weeks and took up residence in a room in my father's house. It was a decently sized bedroom but I had to share the kitchen and bathroom with another ground-floor tenant called Parvez, who was from Poland. I made my room as comfortable as possible with the little furniture that was available.

I had to start looking for a part-time job fast. My tuition fees had already been paid by my father, and I was receiving a weekly allowance of £30 for food and travel until I was settled. Then it was up to me to fend for myself, so I needed a job sooner than later.

I went to the nearest job centre at Kilburn, and started applying for a part-time job for three days a week; within a week, I had two job offers to choose from. One was a cleaning job at a famous hotel on Marylebone Street, while the other was a street-sweeping job.

I was desperate to start working and to start earning some pounds, but I was not very desperate to engage in street sweeping, as I felt that it was a demeaning job to do for a postgraduate student.

I started my new cleaning job at the hotel through a cleaning agency called Casnap, a family-owned business that had contracts to clean various top hotels in the city. The cleaning was carried out through the night, from 9 pm to 5 am, with a one-hour break in between.

As a student, I was allowed to work for a limited number of hours a week during school term, and unlimited hours during the school break. It was a very hard job cleaning, vacuuming carpets and polishing doorknobs, but I worked diligently and within five weeks, I was made a supervisor of a team.

Being a supervisor meant responsibility for a team of five and an increase in the pay from £3.25p to £3.55p an hour. Looking back now the pay increase was laughable, but I was keen to build up savings and the more I worked, the more my savings grew. I could still spend a few pounds on having a good time with my boys.

I was enjoying my course work and was quite popular amongst the students at the postgraduate business school. I was elected as the representative for the MBA class of 1998, and it was role that I revelled in.

One of the earliest and slightly trivial issues that I had to deal with as a class representative was the matter of addressing lecturers. Some students, especially the ones from Africa, were finding it uncomfortable to address the tutors by their first name; they preferred to call them "Sir" or put a "Mister" before their names, but the English lecturers were having none of that, insisting that we address them by their first names.

It was culturally challenging for young African students to address their lecturers by their first names, and it took almost five months and some persuasion to get the desired results.

Thursday nights were happy hours down at the Student Union pub; drinks were half-price and the music was a mixture of Garage and Disco. The pub was about ten minutes from Ojo's crib and we became regulars.

I met Olga on one of those Thursday nights. She was a big-bosomed Russian and we hit it off immediately; she could easily match the boys pint for pint and she loved her vodka. She was from the old Soviet Union and her father was a top diplomat based in Moscow.

Our relationship was purely sex and alcohol-fuelled, and life was never dull with her. We went out clubbing either as a couple or as a group with Ojo, Shola, Rusalan and Fred. We stormed clubs like Slap Harries, Number 10, Tiger Tiger, Break for the Border, the Electric Ballroom and Corks Wine Bar. You could also find us at Nigerian joints like Obalende Suya, Buka and 805.

Corks Wine Bar was one of my favourite hangouts. The music was mostly R&B, the crowd was mainly from the West Indies and the babes were hot, sexy and knew how to wind. I was having fun to the maximum. However, I knew that I had to work hard in school and I never missed a lecture. It was common for us to go straight to a lecture from a club. I always had a spare toothbrush in my pocket, and a change of clothes at Ojo's flat.

After two and a half months of working for Casnap, I was beginning to feel the strain of working through the night for a management that did not care about its employees' general welfare. I knew that I had to start looking for a new job immediately. I went back to the job centre and I started asking around, especially in the Nigerian community.

One of my older brother's colleagues advised me to try care work. He told me that it paid better than the cleaning job, but I would have to go for some training. He gave me a contact name and telephone number and encouraged me to pursue it. As I had no choice and the thought of a better-paying job attracted me, I made contact with the care agency, and was asked to come in for a face-to-face meeting with the agency's owner and manager.

The agency owner was a friendly and pretty woman from the Eastern part of Nigeria. She was happy to give me a chance to work without experience. However, she was going to provide me with full training in the general care of the elderly. She was also willing to start me off on an hourly wage of £5.45p and to increase it to £6 an hour after I had acquired more experience.

I liked the sound of what I was hearing and I was happy to sign up with her for a training fee of £45, which included a uniform. I did half a day's training and was then posted to shadow another care worker called Carmen, an experienced hand from Kenya. I learnt many practical things from her in the next few days, and I became confident in the role of caring for the elderly and vulnerable.

The pay was relatively good and I became a regular at many care homes. Shifts were coming faster than I could keep up with, so I had to decline some of them. I was making money and saving quite a lot of it tax-free because of my status as a student.

I could afford to buy whatever I wanted, within reason. I bought a bigger second-hand television and a laptop for schoolwork; and my wardrobe did not suffer either. I started sending money back to Nigeria, because of the good exchange rate.

"Remyleon!," I heard someone shouting out my name as I walked along the busy Tottenham Court Road to catch Bus 275 to East London for my early afternoon lecture. I turned around to come face to face with Clifton, an old-school Marauder from the Mid-West region whom I had met a couple of times back when I was the Alfa of my university.

"O boy, strong man, you dey this country?" he enquired as he gave me a strong brotherhood handshake and hug. "Yes my guy," I replied as we stood on the crowded road in London. *"O boy, wetin you dey do for this country?"* I enquired from him.

"I came here two years ago as a refugee and I don arrange one babe from France," he said. "O boy, you be hard man oo but I am heading for lectures and I need to catch the next bus, give me your mobile number and I go hail you later on today," I said.

We exchanged mobile numbers, and I dashed off to catch my bus to East London. I settled into my seat on the bus that would take me on an hour's ride to the university, depending on the traffic. As I sat on the bus, my mind went back to those dark days back in the university in Nigeria, and I could feel a heap of goose bumps start to appear on my arms as memories came flooding back.

Chapter 24

As the gun jumped and exploded in my right hand, I saw Udoka's helpless body jerk in shock and go still for a few seconds. I thought that I had ended his life, until I saw Udoka start to move slowly and gradually sit up with his face in his hands.

I must have been a terrible shot, or God had sent an angel to move my hand; the fact was that I had missed Udoka at point blank range. I stood there staring at the hapless figure in front of me in absolute amazement and embarrassment, with the burning fury still inside me. I took a step forward and took aim again.

I felt an arm grab me from behind and I heard Hammer's voice whisper into my right ear, "My Alfa, he is still our brother, *we no fit kill the dead body wey we go follow bury,*" he appealed to me. I took some time to digest what he had said and after a few seconds of deliberation, I turned and walked away, while barking out an order to the squad to deal with him as they pleased.

As I walked away, I could hear Udoka screaming out in pain as Hammer and his crew laid into him with hand axes and rods. I walked towards the access road, fuming, and I could feel the demons raging inside me as I waited by the roadside. I was joined ten minutes later by Hammer and the others, and they confirmed that Udoka had been sorted out and they had dispatched him to the hospital.

I could not have cared less if Udoka was dead or maimed, as he was just a small fish in the grand scheme of events. I was desperate to get my hands on the kingpins, especially Victor and Abass. It was fast approaching 7 am, the university town was waking up, and with movement all around now, it was becoming increasingly difficult to carry heavy weapons in the daylight.

As we were about to disperse temporarily for the morning and reconvene later in the day, an intelligence report came from Okogie, one of the deputy Seers, that Rago had been sighted entering into "High Mighty," the well-known Marijuana joint, to get his regular fix.

Hammer hid the heavy weapons we were carrying in the bushes, and we rolled out with the lighter handguns and axes.

We arrived at High Mighty on four motorbikes; we all jumped off before they stopped. Bilado, Otoro and Ike covered the windows and all exit points, while The Bulldog, Hammer and I took position at the entrance and demanded that Rago come out before we tore the building down.

Akpola, a.k.a. "smoke no be air," the owner and so-called chief priest of High Mighty, knew many

Marauders and other confraternity men in the town. He knew that Rago was a kingpin within the BNM, and for his people to come looking for him in such a daring way meant that he had to stand aside and stay clear.

After about ten minutes of standoff, Rago finally emerged smiling, with a joint of Igbo between his lips and his hands raised high. Hammer patted him down for any weapons and found a hand-held axe, which he quickly confiscated.

"You finally got me men," he said in his usual braggadocio and "I own the world" attitude. I stepped up to him and with all the anger and venom burning inside me, I took him down with one solid blow to the side of his face.

As he struggled to get to his feet, I stepped closer to him and said in a very angry voice, "Left to me, I would pull the trigger right now but for the sake of fairness, you will answer to your charges in the jungle in front of other Marauders."

He looked at me with his bloodshot eyes and said, "Remy, you better kill me here, because *I no go follow una go kpeme for inside jungle.*" I raised my gun and put it to his temple, and said, "Happy to oblige."

I could see and hear Hammer hold his breath from the corner of my eye; and within that split-second, Rago made a grab for my gun. As I struggled to hold on to the gun with my right hand, I unleashed some blows on his face with my weaker left hand; but Rago would not let go. I could not afford to let Rago disarm me, he was a deadly and unpredictable psychopath.

We struggled for the gun for a couple of seconds until I managed to free it briefly from his grip, and without a second thought, I fired a shot into his left palm. I saw him clutch the hand in pain, with a startled look on his face. I dragged him by the scruff of his neck with his bleeding hand towards the access road, where Hammer and crew had stopped a commercial bus back from its school run.

I had once been told that if you stayed in hell long enough, you would eventually meet the devil, and now I was actually dining with him.

We bundled Rago into the bus and headed towards a nearby place in the bush, which we used for occasional meetings. I sent word out for all the wise men and Executives to join me within twenty minutes.

I sat on a piece of log while Rago stood in front of me, surrounded by about fifteen to twenty Marauders, with his left hand wrapped in a strip of cloth to stem the flow of blood. He looked scared and drained as I tabled the charges against him. I gave him a few minutes to defend himself, and all he could mutter was, "Brother shooting brother," as he raised his left hand.

This was my court and I did not care if I was both judge and jury. Without further hesitation, I pronounced sentence on the traitor. Rago was dragged, screaming and shouting, further into the thicker section of the bushes for my sentence to be carried out by a five-man squad of rugged Marauders. Rago was sentenced to twenty minutes of serious beating, and one hundred and twenty lashes of the "koboko" (horsewhip).

It took about fifty minutes to administer the sentence, after which Rago was physically carried back into the circle. As he lay on the ground, I walked up to him and pronounced: "By the power vested in me as the Alfa of the BNM, I hereby excommunicate you permanently."

I turned to Hammer and said, *"Make una carry am go hospital* as a last gesture of goodwill." I left the bush more determined than ever to bring all the rebels to account for their deeds; I put a price on their heads. We hunted the dissidents day and night for the next two days. We narrowly missed Abass on two occasions, but we were getting closer and closer.

I had spies everywhere and my ears were close to the ground; an intelligence report came back that Victor had fled town the previous night disguised as a woman, and was now under the protection of the Regional BNM.

The regional body had summoned me, but I chose to ignore the summons by making myself scarce and elusive while I hunted my targets. My flat was now deserted and very few people knew where I was staying.

Abass was now a trapped animal and the net was closing in on him; he had nowhere to hide, all the exit points including the motor parks were all covered, and it was just a matter of time before he would be caught. Then he did the unthinkable.

The Police and other confraternities were at sea about what was happening in town. They knew that a major conflict was happening with the BNM and another group, but did not know which other group until Abass voluntarily handed himself over to the Police.

Inside intelligence came to me that Abass had given the Police a list of the key people involved in the current mayhem in the university community, and my name was at the top of the list followed by Theo and six others. He had told the Police that I was the kingpin and the Oga of the BNM and if they could get hold of me, then all the mayhem would be over quickly.

The mention of Theo's name made me wonder where he was. On that eventful night when we both escaped together and ran through the bushes, Theo had fallen into an incomplete well and broken his right ankle. Some hunters had rescued him the following morning.

He was currently in hospital, with his foot encased in a plaster cast. I sent some minders to keep watch over him and I made sure that all his medical bills were to be paid for by the BNM.

We got another intelligence report from an insider in the Student Union that the Police were planning to arrest and handcuff Theo in his hospital bed; so I gave orders for Theo to be moved. We hid him with a discreet local herbalist.

My final year examination was due to start in seven days' time, and I was very unsettled but determined not to spend an extra semester in the university; so I went underground. I dug deep and focused on my studies.

It was sad but apparent that Theo was going to miss some if not all of his exams, but he was upbeat about

315

the situation and was glad that he was still alive. He reminded me, the last time I visited him, that we could both have died on that fateful night of mayhem and betrayal.

I sat there looking at Theo, and it dawned on me strongly that lying in front of me was a man of great courage and character, who was willing to give up his own life to protect me. I was determined to make sure that he was well looked after.

Unlike Theo, I was still indignant at what had transpired that night, and I was going to get my pound of flesh no matter how long it took.

Victor and the others were still highly wanted men and they had no hope in hell of sitting their exams, as the order was to take them down on sight.

The pressure from the regional body intensified, as they too were under pressure from the national body based in Lagos to bring this unprecedented situation under control. The regional body did not want this to fester any longer, so the regional Alfa and his Executives paid us a visit.

Only a handful of extremely trusted people knew where I was staying; it took half a day for them to make contact with me through Hammer. I decided to see them out of respect, but I was still determined to hunt down the traitors.

After the forty-five minute meeting with the regional Alfa for whom I had much respect, I got the impression that they were very keen to douse the fire that was raging out of control. He made me realise that Victor and the other rebels were like my recalcitrant children, and as a father to all Marauders in the university, I had to balance justice with mercy, and I had to come out of my highly charged and volatile frame of mind.

We set a date for all parties involved to meet, at the regional assembly. Many experienced Marauders were against our going there to settle this dispute, because once we walked into the regional assembly, we would no longer have our autonomy as a clan. The regional authority overrode and superseded us completely. However, if we stayed on our turf, we could afford to stick two fingers up at the region.

I made my final decision after a discussion with an insider who belonged to the inner caucus of the regional Executive. He told me that the region supported me 100 per cent, as they had no love for traitors, however they had to show neutrality in their stand; especially with the shooting of a Marauder by a Marauder.

"My Alfa, *we no fit go* regional assembly empty handed, we need to hold our side and have our defence ready," Hammer warned, *"We don't know who we go trust oo, e fit no turn out the way we expect,"* he concluded.

I shared Hammer's sentiment but it was impossible to carry arms into the regional assembly, as everybody who was admitted was thoroughly searched – there was no way of slipping past the security.

As I racked my brain trying to come up with a solution, it suddenly dawned on me that if we could not take weapons in on the day of the meeting, maybe there was a chance we could get them in a day earlier. Now if there was anyone who knew the regional assembly ground, it had to be Binga.

Binga personally knew the caretaker of the regional venue, and he was aware that the caretaker loved his "Ogogoro," the local gin, very well. Therefore, the plan was for Binga, Otoro and The Bulldog to travel to the regional venue. While Binga lured the caretaker away to a nearby beer parlour, Otoro and The Bulldog would scale the fence and bury our arms in strategic places within the compound.

Hammer was to determine how many guns and rounds of ammunition would be required in case we needed to shoot our way out of the assembly. The trio were scheduled to leave the next day, as the meeting was in two days' time.

Ten of us left the university and headed for the regional assembly at about noon on Friday. We needed to catch up with the trio who had left the day before, to get a situation report and map out further plans if needed.

We arrived in Benin City at about 1:30 pm and headed straight to our rendezvous point with Binga and the others, who confirmed that their mission had been successful. We had three 9 mm Berettas and a sawed-off shot-gun buried at strategic locations within the assembly grounds. It was all systems go.

I stormed the regional assembly at 3 pm with Bilado, Binga, Otoro, The Bulldog, Ike "the killer" and Koko, all of them ready for action and high on excessive Marijuana and alcohol. The assembly was to start at 3:15

pm, giving us enough time to identify key spots and allocate resources; each man knew who was handling what and at what signal.

I sat facing Victor for the first time after that fateful night; he could not look me in the eye, and had his face turned towards the floor. He had lost a lot of weight and was looking emaciated and troubled; I guess he had picked the wrong war to fight.

After the usual consultation of the oracle and the traditional opening procedure, Victor and the few crew members who had not deserted him were summoned into the circle, to face the regional body and give their own account of what had transpired.

Victor spoke for about ten minutes and ended his speech with a plea for mercy and intervention by the regional body.

I was asked to respond and stood up to overwhelming shouts of "Alfa" from around the room. I cleared my throat and started to speak. I had a gift with words and I knew how to put my point across and evoke emotion.

I lambasted Victor and his crew as I laid my charges against them; I turned the tables and put the regional body under pressure to hand Victor back to the clan to be dealt with as he deserved. This was an unprecedented case, and it took many hours of deliberation by the regional body and other experienced Marauders.

After much deliberation, the regional body found Victor guilty on four counts of gross misconduct. His punishment was twenty minutes of drilling and mending for each count, plus two hundred lashes of the "Koboko" horsewhip.

The regional body was in a dilemma with regard to me. They wanted me to give up the Marauder who had pulled the trigger at Ohis, but I vehemently refused to rat on any Marauder. I told them that I had led the squad, and that it was irrelevant who had pulled the trigger. I was willing to take the responsibility for shooting Ohis in an act of self-defence.

The punishment for shooting a fellow brother was excommunication from the BNM for an indefinite period. I knew that I had to protect Bilado, so I stood my ground. The regional body could not suspend me, because that would have caused chaos and uncertainty in the clan and they knew that I had not physically pulled the trigger.

The regional body decided to give me a five-minute drilling to loosen my tongue; but Marauders from my clan went berserk and pandemonium ensued. It was unheard of to drill a serving Alfa, and Marauders from my clan would rather die than let this happen.

Hammer and the others were waiting for my signal before they moved into action. I could see them taking position close to the marked spots. The commotion suddenly ceased just the way it had started when a voice shouted out, *"Na me shoot Ohis."* We all turned towards the voice as Bilado stepped forward.

"Na me shoot Ohis but na in self-defence;" I heard the cracking of a gun, so I pulled my trigger first." Bilado addressed the assembly. "My Alfa did not give me any

instruction to shoot and I take full responsibility for my action," he concluded.

I tried to catch Bilado's eye in an attempt to get him to recant his admission; but he was staring straight at the regional Alfa, and was unwavering in his admission.

The whole atmosphere was charged; it was now a shouting arena, with some of the assembly calling for Bilado's head and others crying out in support of Bilado since it was an act of self-defence. The regional Executives and wise men had to go into another sitting to deliberate on this recent development, and after a further twenty minutes, they came back with a verdict.

Bilado was to be excommunicated for six months; he had escaped a permanent excommunication because it was presumed he had acted in self-defence. He was also to receive twenty minutes of drilling and one hundred lashes of the horsewhip before leaving the fold.

We left the regional assembly without having needed to implement our planned strategy. I made my stand clear; Victor would still have to answer to the clan and receive due justice, but it would no longer be as severe as we had planned.

We returned to the university at about 11:30 pm, and I jumped on a motorbike to my secret hideout. I had just five days left before my final examinations were to commence and I needed to focus on my studies.

I still had intelligence reporting to me, looking out for wanted rebels; and I had various squads on standby, ready to move at the drop of a hat. I still wanted Abass and a few other dissidents to be brought to account for their involvement in the attempted coup. Abass was to be treated as the rat that he was; but he was currently under Police protection.

A squad was on the ready, waiting for Abass to come out of Police protection, with clear instructions to bring him down.

My final year examinations began as scheduled and I was as prepared as I could be, considering the circumstances. I had five modules to pass along with the defence of my dissertation, which had to be done before I could be signed out of the department as fully meeting all the degree requirements.

My first paper was my favourite module and I came out all smiles. I had written my heart out, the ink in my pen had almost run out, and I was confident of making a very good grade.

A week later, I had just finished my fourth paper and was coming out of the exam hall when intelligence came to me through my Voice that the police had broken into my flat in town looking for me. They had my flat under surveillance, but they still could not put a face to the name "Remyleon."

Many people did not know my real name, and only knew me under the pseudonym of Remyleon; this was the challenge the police were facing. They did not really know who they were after; they could not go to my department to execute an arrest warrant, because they had only a pseudonym.

The police had broken into my flat after casing it for the last three days, hoping that my flatmates or I would return there to prepare for our examinations; but we had all gone underground. Out of frustration, they had now decided to gain forceful entry and search for evidence to unmask the identity of Remyleon.

I had one final examination module to write in two days' time before the defence of my dissertation; and then I would be out of town for good.

The night before my very last examination was beautiful, with the stars on display in the sky, and the wind gently caressing my skin. I decided to venture into town after my final revision, and jumped on a motorbike and headed towards Tima's place.

I had seen Tima only once since that eventful night. I had thought it best to keep physically away from her for her own security until the "Casala" (mayhem) died down, but I'd had eyes and ears watching out and listening for her, and had sent messages to her frequently.

Theo's former house was on the way to Tima's flat, and on an impulse, I decide to stop there. I was hoping that his girl Nene would be able to tell me about Theo's movements and whereabouts. I discharged the motorbike man and as I stood there for a brief second, the events of that night came flooding back to me. *"This was where it all began,"* I thought to myself as I knocked on Nene's door.

Nene was not at home, but her younger sister Uju was in. I stayed chatting with her for a couple of minutes, hoping that Nene would come back soon; she was the love of his life and would know Theo's whereabouts.

I looked at my watch; it was now 8 pm, and Nene was not yet back. Having left a message for her, I stepped outside and started on the path to the high road. I had barely walked for two minutes when two men stepped out of the bushes and accosted me. I knew within an instant that these were policemen.

"Theo," the one with the gun barked out at me as he pointed his flashlight and gun at me. My heart was racing and my stomach was churning. *"Abeg oo, I am-mmm not-tt Theo,"* I stuttered nervously. "So who are you, where are you coming from and what are you doing here?" the other police officer barked.

"Officer, I am a student and my name is Ugochukwu. I came to visit my classmate to borrow her lecture books," I replied in a scared and innocent voice.

"So, you do not know Theo," the one with the gun enquired. *"I know no who bi Theo ooo,* I swear," I responded. *"So how you take know sey we be officers,* if you no be secret cult member," the other officer asked.

"Meeee, secret cult, God forbid bad thing, *na book my papa send me come read oo, why I call you officer be sey na only police dey hold gun to maintain law and order,"* I said naively.

They looked at me and could not find any guile in the innocent and naive looking face in front of them. "Ok, *make you dey run dey go and no dey waka waka for night anyhow, bad boys full this una school, no go die because of woman oo,"* the officer with the gun warned me.

"Yes, sir," I shouted as I walked away hastily, with my heart still pounding and my legs barely able to carry me. I jumped on the next Okada and headed straight to my hideout. I could not believe that I had been so close to being nabbed by the police. They'd been busy looking for Theo when the biggest fish had just slipped through their net in front of their noses.

Chapter 25

The man sitting in the room was feeling the heat and he was sweating profusely, he was not sweating because of the temperature in room, far from it, as the room was air-conditioned. He was sweating because he had just had a very unpleasant and uncomfortable conversation with his boss the division police office (DPO).

The summation of the 10 minutes conversation with his boss was an ultimatum to arrest and take the wanted Remyleon and his Hench men into custody or his job would be on the line. This was his 20th year in the Nigerian police force and it had been a hard slug to get to his current position, he had spent 6 years static as a desk sergeant due to the bureaucracy within the hierarchy of the police force.

Luck had finally come his way two years ago in 1994 when his kinsman was made the commissioner of police, this had eventually opened a few doors for him in his career and he had been promoted to his current position as an assistant superintendent of police (ASP).

Now ASP Okoli was living the life, his standard of living was not dependent on his improved yet irregular salary. He was making good money from returns delivered by all the police officers under his charge, his entitlement was 40 percent of the stipulated daily returns. Another 40 percent was sent to the 'Oga at the top' while the foot men were left to share the balance.

He was also making good money from the arrest and the detention of people, he could easily make an average of 300,000 Naira in a good month. He was now in the process of roofing his own family property that he had started 12 years ago and had been stuck at the foundation stage.

His six children from his two wives were now having a decent and uninterrupted education and his first daughter was about to get into the university but definitely not this 'yeye' school that was riddled with cultism and moral decency.

He was not prepared to lose his position over the unrest in the university community because of those 'yeye' secret cult boys. "Na Ogun go punish any person wey wan put sand for my garri," he said aloud in Pidgin English as he got up from his chair.

He had to do something quickly; there was an urgent need to change strategy. He approached the door to his office, opened it and stood in the doorway, "I am the law in this town and no bandit and his crew will rule my town," he said aloud as he turned to his secretary in the next room.

"Get me sergeant Oko and ask him to bring his squad to my office for briefing immediately," ASP Okoli said to his secretary before walking towards the toilet to ease himself.

As the squad of five stood before him 30 minutes later that afternoon, the atmosphere in the room was tense and the room had a smell of sweaty bodies. The air conditioning system was no longer working thanks to the interrupted power supply by NEPA.

"So do you mean to tell me that you do not know where Remyleon, Theo and co are? And you call yourselves members of the police force; please tell me where the force in you is?" The ASP demanded angrily.

"We don't even know Remyleon's real name, boys this is not good enough," the ASP said.

Sergeant Oko hated being addressed as boy but had to stomach the tirade coming from his Oga, "Oga, Sir," he began, "those evil boys have all gone underground oooo, and they have virtually disappeared into thin air."

"What do you mean disappeared into thin air, shame no dey catch you to talk that kind nonsense for here," the ASP challenged his officer.

"So tell me; what was the use of having that young chap called Abass in our custody if we cannot capitalise on the information that he has given to us." He continued, "So what have you and your boys done so far?"

"Sir, we are casing most of the safe houses that we know, we have surveillances in place at their girlfriends' houses, and we are also on the lookout within the university campus. We have three of our men about to infiltrate the Black Night Marauders confraternity and we also have Remyleon and Theo's houses under watch. We are waiting patiently sir," Oko responded to his Oga.

He continued, "All of our surveillances have not yielded any fruit so far but we are confident that one of them go mis-waka enter our trap. Our surveillance for Theo's area last night no yield any better fruit at all, we accosted one male student for the area that night but he came to borrow textbook from his girlfriend, so we let him go, sir."

"Oga, those boys don dey use juju wey dey make person disappear oooo but we go show them sey juju pass juju," he concluded.

"Sergeant Oko, we are changing tactics as from today, I want you boys to unmask the true identity of this boy called Remyleon by tomorrow afternoon unfailingly, bust into his room and any other room that need to be busted into, with that information we would then know the devil that we are dealing with," the ASP instructed.

"But sir, we do not have the proper search warrant to bust into their rooms ooo, I hear say this Remyleon papa na lawyer wey know book well well," said the Sergeant.

"Oko, you no well, search warrant for where, for his country, for this town, abeg bust all the rooms sharp sharp and bring me result. We go deal with Oga lawyer later."

The ASP continued, "I want that boy, have you heard me, I want that boy in custody before the end of this week. I don't care if we have to storm his lecture hall, but I want that boy and when I get my hands on him eeeee, I will hang him upside down and show him what we do to pickin wey no dey hear word."

"Yes, sir, but Oga na me go first catch am, the beat wey I go beat that boy eeee, if e see em papa e go call am mama," confessed the sergeant.

"Ok boys get a move on, all dismissed," said the ASP.

As the police men filed out of the office, the ASP called out to his sergeant, "Oko, don't let me down oooo."

Sergeant Oko turned around and saluted his Oga and bellowed, "All correct, sir, no shaking," and with that he walked out of the room.

It was about 2:30 pm that afternoon after the briefing with the ASP when he led a five man squad on a mission with the sole aim of unmasking the elusive Remyleon. His previous strategy of casing the various safe houses had proved unsuccessful, he had also put a surveillance team in place to cover Remyleon and Theo's flats but there was no sign of the bandits or their flatmates.

He was getting too old to be chasing all these small, small boys around town that believe that they have seen life. "They feel because they are in the university then they can speak big big English and misbehaviour, the only thing that would save this Remyleon is if I don't get my hands on him."

He preferred going after illiterate bus drivers and market traders as they were easy to intimidate with arrest, there was no big big English with them unlike these university students that want to prove that they know their rights.

If Remyleon was an illiterate person, all the police needed to do was to go and arrest his parents then the wayward son would be forced to hand himself in.

The black police van arrived in front of a fenced building and three of the police officers had already jumped down before the van came to a stop. They let themselves in via the side gate and marched briskly to flat two as already described by Abass.

The flat looked deserted from the outside; two of the policemen went behind the flat to cover the back exit while the others approached the front entrance that was protected by burglary railings.

It took the policemen about 15 minutes to forcefully gain access into the flat, they headed straight for the room opposite the living room based on Abass's description and within seconds the door was smashed in.

"Shooooooooo," came the exclamation from corporal Obi, the room was empty except for a piece of paper glued to the wall on the right hand side.

Corporal Obi looked around the room in total disbelief before approaching the paper glued to the wall,

"Oga Sergeant, I no sabi wetin dem write for this paper oooo," he said to Sergeant Oko behind him.

"So you no sabi read," said Oko as he pushed him aside. "Too late to catch me," read out the sergeant as he tore the paper off the wall in anger. "Aaeeeeeee, when hand touch this boy eeeeh, e go go Jerusalem come back for my hand," he muttered in rage.

As the policemen hurriedly left the flat and walked towards their vehicle, Oko was deep in thought, he knew what reaction he was going to get from his boss for another failure. Out of desperation, he walked across the road to the Okada man that had just stopped.

"My friend," he barked, "who get this house," he said pointing to the flat behind.

"Na retired Captain Abi, wey dey live for Lagos but the caretaker na madam Cecilia wey get that beer parlour for Poultry road."

"Oya, come take us go there now now now," Sergeant Oko commanded the Okada man.

The policemen arrived at Madam Cecilia's beer parlour within 30 minutes, but had to wait for another 45 minutes for her to return from an errand.

"Madam, well done, abeg we need your help ooo, we heard that you are the caretaker of that blue block of flats for high road."

"Yes oooo, na my cousin get the property," she replied looking to be helpful to the policemen.

"What are the names of the students that rented flat two?" Sergeant Oko asked.

"Emmmmmm, I no fit remember their names again unless I check the rental agreement document," she volunteered.

Sergeant Oko and his men escorted Madam Cecilia to her residence and waited in the courtyard while she went into the house to obtain the rental agreement document.

She came out of her front door holding some papers in her right hand, as she handed the documents to sergeant Oko, she asked innocently "wetin those innocent boys do una sef?"

"Inno what, those criminals … Madam we suppose arrest you join sef for harbouring bandits and criminal elements for your compound," the sergeant threatened.

"Abeg ooooooo, no vex ooooo, I no know sey dem be bad boys ooo," Madam Cecilia appealed.

"OK, we no go arrest you but you go find us money for petrol and beer so that we go kill the matter for here," said the sergeant.

"Ah ah, which kind wahala bi dis one now, I come show una documents, now you want to collect money from me. Ha aaaaa daris God ooooo," she remonstrated.

It was about 6:45 pm when they got back to the police station with two names: Austin Okocha and Rashidi Yekini and with 5,000 Naira of Madam Cecilia's money in their pocket. This was a wonderful outcome and it was time to approach the university authority with an arrest warrant but first Oga ASP must authorise them to proceed.

The sergeant stood in front of the ASP's office for a few seconds preparing himself for the praise that he was going to receive from his boss for cracking the identity of Remyleon before knocking on the door.

He waited for a response before walking in with full confidence into the office.

"Oga, sir, we don crack the case big time," he said before handing the documents to the ASP, "due to my sharp reasoning and investigative prowess, I and my men have finally unravelled the myth behind that yeye boy," he assured the ASP.

There was a broad smile on the ASP's face as he skimmed through the pages of the documents but the smile on his face did not last for long as he repeated the names in the documents.

"Austin Okocha, Rashidi Yekini … Austin Okocha, Rashidi Yekini, haaaaaa sergeant Oko, these names do not sound right oooo, are these not the names of Nigerian footballers? When did Okocha and Yekini start to attend this university?" he asked his sergeant angrily.

"Sir," started the sergeant only to be shouted down by his superior officer.

"Which kind of mumu you bi sef, these are fake names on the documents, chia chia chia, see wetin small boys take una they do?"

Oko stood there speechless and in total humiliation, his mind was almost blank except for the desire to kill Remyleon.

"Now take your silly ass and this useless paper away from my sight and make sure I get a better result before tomorrow afternoon, if not, no road patrol for you and your boys again," the ASP threatened.

"Na wa ooo, this case don tire me, back to square one," Oko thought as he left the ASP's office, where would he begin from now. He went back into the general office and sat down heavily behind his desk. The information that Abass had provided was a pseudonym, they knew that Remyleon was in his final year in the accountancy department, they had busted his flat yet they were far away from unmasking this fugitive.

There was no way of going to the university authority without a real name, maybe he should intensify his effort on the four other names on the list. "If I can't unmask his boy then I will intensify my effort in pursuing his henchmen, that may lead me to unmasking that boy," he concluded in his head as he put his head down on the desk out of fatigue.

The clock in the police station was showing 9:55 pm on that fateful Thursday night when Udoka walked into the police station bearing various physical scars but most importantly with information that changed the whole investigation.

"His name is Raymond Ukadike and he is the Alfa of the Black Night Marauders," he told the police officers under interrogation.

Chapter 26

My last exam was an afternoon paper; by 9 am that morning, my Seer had reported that our insider in the Student Union had confirmed that both Theo and I had being declared as wanted by the State Police Command. Our case had now being passed on to the State Police Division in charge of robbery and firearms.

We were both wanted on three counts: first, for the possession of illegal firearms, second, for attempted murder, and third, for secret cultism.

I asked my Seer and Voice to deploy available human resources at strategic positions on campus, and be on the lookout for police officers. When you became a member of a gang or secret cult, you could smell a cop a mile away and more often than not, their shoes and the way they walked gave them away.

I was on edge before the exam started, and I sat very close to the window for a quick getaway if needed. It was a two-hour exam and not one of my favourite modules. I felt a huge sense of relief as I handed in my answer booklet. I was heading for the exit when a fellow classmate called Bernadette hurriedly walked in, gripped me by the arm, and led me towards another exit. I was baffled but I followed her without questioning her.

"I was in the Head of Department's office when three plain-clothes Police officers came asking for permission from Mr Oghene to arrest one Raymond Ukadike," she said in a panicky voice. "He refused to give them permission because you were writing your final year exam, so you better take off now now," she advised.

I thanked her and headed for the surrounding bushes. I knew the area very well and easily navigated to the boys' hostel. I hung around the hostel until darkness fell before making my way to my hideout.

I had now finished all my exams but defending my dissertation was going to be a challenge, because my department had now become involved and I would have to get Police clearance before being allowed to partake in any departmental activity.

The dissertation defence was not due to take place until all departmental examinations had been completed, which gave me one week's breathing space to come up with a way to solve my problem.

I definitely could not get my father or my eldest brother, who were both in the legal profession, involved; so I decided to seek my own independent legal advice from the regional "OC legal." I left this consultation more depressed than when I had gone in.

The summary of my meeting was that by law, I should hand myself in to the police with legal representation present. However, his advice to me as a fellow Marauder was that I should deal with the police from outside custody, because once you are in, the police hold all the cards.

Handing myself over was not an option, as we all knew the treatment you got in police custody. My best bet was to try to make this problem go away using spiritual help.

I got in touch with two Marauders called Peter and Paul, who were twins and as diabolical as one could be. It was rumoured that they could disappear into thin air when there was danger. The twins were nicknamed "Afro juju" and made no secret of the fact that they were deep into juju and voodoo.

They came to see me at Hammer's crib, and spent about ten minutes consulting with their oracle before taking 30 Naira from me to go and get some materials from the local market for the ritual that they needed to carry out on me.

I released the money without a second thought and stayed at Hammer's crib playing cards while waiting for them. They came back with a piece of red cloth, a live cockerel, some alligator pepper, the shell of a tortoise, some cowries and native chalk. With these materials, they started their ritual with an incantation to their spiritual gods.

After twenty minutes, the ritual finally ended. They offered me the piece of red cloth and asked me to tie it around my loins, while having a bath in water mixed with the blood of the cockerel. They made tiny incisions on my head, rubbed in a dark substance, and asked me to recite a certain mantra while kneeling down holding the shell of the tortoise.

They finally gave me a syrup bottle full of a powdery substance, and instructed me to put some of the substance on my palms at midnight and blow the powder into the wind while facing the direction of the police station. I had to carry out this ritual for the next five days and my problem with the Police would be blown away before the end of the fifth day.

I carried out their instructions religiously for the next five days, but the only report that I heard was of the police intensifying their efforts in the search for me. They had busted into various safe houses in the company of Abass "the rat." My name was pasted on the university registrar's notice board as required by the police and the university.

The ritual was not working, but the twins were quite keen to try something else that involved using the book of Moses in the Bible. I was to carry out this ritual naked in the forest at midnight. Even though I was no longer a fervent churchgoer and was desperate to have my problem sorted out, I did not intend to disdain the Holy Bible any time soon.

Any ritual they were planning involving the Bible had to be done without me: I was not about to budge from this stand, so Peter and Paul decided to travel to see their witch doctor to find another solution.

I was running out of time and as I lay in bed staring into space, the name "Charlie Angel" popped into my head. Angel had an extra semester and was in the process of finishing his last exam paper; I jumped out of bed and went in search of him.

I found Charlie Angel after thirty minutes of searching. He was already aware of my predicament, and he advised that we visit his grandfather, who was the chief priest of all the witch doctors in his village. We agreed to leave the day after his last paper.

We arrived at Obomkpa village late in the evening three days later; I spent an uneasy night at Charlie's home which he shared with his aged mum and two cats. There was an eerie feel to the house which I could not shake off, and I could not wait for morning to come. Going to sleep was the biggest challenge for me and I spent most of the night awake.

I jumped out of bed at first light; I awakened the snoring Charlie and we started getting ready for the journey ahead.

His grandfather's shrine was about twenty minutes by motorbike and a further ten minutes on foot; the shrine was a decrepit building situated in an isolated area of the evil forest called "Ofia Ogbome," In the local language.

We entered the shrine backwards and barefooted. The chief priest himself greeted us; he was a very old man with a long white beard. He was dressed in a combination of white and red regalia, holding a staff in his right hand and a bell in the left.

The sight of the man gave me the shivers; my heart was beating fast as I tried to hold my guts together. I reminded myself that I was desperate for a quick solution to my predicament and I had nothing to lose by being here.

I paid for the initial consultation, which took about twenty minutes, after which the chief priest gave me his prognosis. He needed to perform a ritual that required one female goat, kola nuts, red cloth, alligator pepper and the feather of a bald-headed white owl.

He gave me the option of sourcing these items myself or him providing them at a cost. I did not have the time to go looking for a bald-headed white owl, so I chose the second option. He asked us to come back in the evening to complete the ritual.

The wait until evening seemed like an eternity. Charlie and I killed time by eating bush meat and drinking palm wine at the local beer parlour, while we talked about various issues ranging from Marauders to babes.

We got to the shrine at about 5 pm. I could see a big metal pot suspended in mid-air in front of the open door. There were various kinds of leaves boiling in the pot and steam was rising; yet there was no fire underneath the pot.

The chief priest told Charlie to wait while he took me into an inner chamber full of the bones of animals, earthen objects, and carvings. He told me to kneel down, and he started to sing and dance around me in circles. After about ten minutes, he told me to stand in front of the main oracle, which had animal blood splattered over it.

He offered the oracle some kola nuts, alligator pepper and native chalk before beginning his consultation. About five minutes later, he stopped suddenly and said: "There is no music that could be played that a witch cannot dance to; tell the oracle your trouble and see it vanish," he commanded.

I narrated my situation in front of the oracle, and then the priest gave me a piece of white native chalk to hold in my left hand as we left the chamber. *"I go cook you well well with that pot for outside; when I cook you finish, Police no go see you or mention your name again. All the wahala go disappear pata pata,"* the chief priest assured me.

We left the shrine at about 8 pm, after I had bathed with the substance from the boiling pot and rubbed the native chalk over my body. The chief priest gave me two syrup bottles full of white chalk and another full of the liquid from the mysterious pot, instructing me to use them while taking my bath and to recite a mantra.

I left Charlie Angel behind and headed back to university, full of hope and anticipating a positive outcome. I arrived at my university under the cover of darkness and went straight to see my Seer for a situation report.

Nothing had changed since I had left: Theo was still underground and Victor had abandoned school and missed all his exams. I was still wanted by the university authorities and the State Police Command; and Tima was worried sick, as she had not heard from me in two days.

My department had begun the defence of our dissertations the previous day, and this was due to continue for the next fourteen days. If you had not finished your defence before the compilation of the list of successful graduating students, only the Vice Chancellor could intervene and give you an extension.

The Vice Chancellor was as tough as they come. He was sagacious and quick-minded, one of the few remaining old-school academicians; he had a sterling reputation for putting hard work and dedication before mediocrity. Rumour had it that he had been one of the early members of the Pyrate confraternity, and that he was very good friends with the Nobel Laureate Professor Wole Soyinka.

There was no way on this earth that he would be willing to grant me an extension, knowing that I was the suspected kingpin of the BNM. There was no love lost between the Pyrate confraternity and the BNM; as Marauders, we just hated all other confraternities.

I carried out the ritual religiously for the next seven days with much trepidation, but with the hope that all these troubles would blow away and life would return to normal.

It seemed to be working, from the situation reports that I received from the insider within the Student Union; Abass had been released from detention, but had to report daily to the police station. Theo was now out of hiding, and was reporting to the police station with his lawyer; my name was no longer on the university registrar's list and the Police had gone quiet.

All these had to be good signs that the ritual was working and that the problem was blowing away. I became more confident and went into campus to register for the defence of my dissertation, but was informed that I still needed police clearance first.

The clearance letter was difficult to forge and submit, as the clearance came directly from the Divisional Police Officer's office; it was signed by him and delivered by his personal assistant. I now had full confidence in the chief priest's ritual and was planning to visit the police station with a member of the student representative, when the hurricane hit.

My name, which had previously disappeared from the Registrar's list, reappeared on the Vice Chancellor's board as a student wanted by the police; this meant that only the VC could sign me back into the university. My name and picture graced the university bulletin board, and the police were intensifying their efforts, as they were upset that I had eluded them for this long; it was just a matter of time before things fell apart.

The university was becoming very unsafe for me, as students had begun vacating both campus and the town after the end of the semester examinations. Hammer and my Executive Council members could not dare to leave town, as I was still there.

I had no other option but to go home to seek a resolution to this whole madness. I asked Hammer and my Seer to create a safe passage for me to the next town through the back roads, and from there I would navigate my way to Asaba.

Chapter 27

I had been at home in Asaba for two days, and was still drawing a blank. There was no hope of defending my dissertation without the VC's consent and clearance. Out of desperation and frustration, I went to see my eldest brother, a practising lawyer who lived in the nearby town.

There was no love lost between lawyers and the police in Nigeria. Lawyers saw the Police as very corrupt and quick to misinterpret the law in order to extort money from the public, while the police saw lawyers as pompous, arrogant and over-read know-it-alls.

I painted a different picture to my brother; I told him that I was wanted by the police for something in which I had not been involved. I stressed that it was a case of mistaken identity because I had been in the wrong place at the wrong time, and the police had now roped me in.

My brother was livid. "Typical Nigerian police," he murmured under his breath, "they would not investigate anything properly. I will go to that police station on

Tuesday after my court session and give them hell," he concluded. I slept peacefully for the first time in the last two weeks, and I even had the luxury of dreaming about Tima.

My brother set out on Tuesday afternoon for his proposed visit to the police station. The plan was that I would meet him at his place the next day for an update.

My heart leapt into my mouth as I saw my brother's car pull up to the family house that evening at about 7 pm. As I stood in the balcony upstairs, I knew that it was going to be a very long and unpleasant night.

He looked up at me, shook his head and stomped into the house. I quickly came down and met him in the living room. I had never seen him this angry before; he was looking very pale and drained of colour. "Do you know the implications of what you have done?" he asked. I stood there not knowing if this was a rhetorical question. "You have just ruined your life, my friend. You may even go to jail and that would be the end of you, kai," he exclaimed.

"Buuut ... I have done nothing wrong, I am innocent, it was not me, it is a case of mistaken identity," I said, fervently maintaining my innocence.

"Tell that to the Marines: attempted murder, possession of illegal firearms, secret cultism, Chineke ... in fact, I don't know you ooo, because no brother of mine would be involved in such nefarious activities." Shaking his head, he continued, "What will your parents say, kai, you have just sullied the family name."

"I am innocent and I don't belong to a secret cult, I am only a member of the Rotary Club," I maintained. "So why you of all people in the entire university?" he asked. "The police said that they have a witness in their custody who would testify that you are the Don of the secret cult," he continued.

"Meeee, Don of what, of whom, not me," I said tearfully. "Well, I'll have to tell our parents when they get back from evening mass," my brother said curtly as he stormed out of the room.

I cut a forlorn figure as I sat there with my head in my hands, for what seemed to be an eternity. I eventually looked up when I heard the sound of my parents' car pull up the driveway and stop in front of the entrance.

My brother met my parents outside the house and I could hear him telling them about the situation at hand. After a couple of minutes, my father came storming into the sitting room. I braced myself and stood before my biological maker, exactly as I had done so often when I was younger.

"You see your life," my father began, "I sent you to school to become useful to yourself, and you went and joined a secret cult," he began, mildly enough.

"Daddy, I am not a member of a secret cult, it is a false accusation by the Police. I just have friends and course mates who may be members but I am not a member," I maintained my innocence.

"Why you of all people? Are you the only student in the whole university, that the police would decide to rope you in?" my father enquired. "They said that you are the kingpin. No son of mine will tarnish my good name. I always knew that you would be the one to disgrace this family," he concluded.

My mother sat quietly on the couch across the room from my Dad, with her head bowed. She was listening and would shake her head occasionally. I looked in her direction, trying to glean what was going through her mind, but I could not; the expression on her face was unreadable.

I stood there being berated by my father and after a couple of minutes, my mother raised her head and I could see the look of total disappointment in her eyes; it was a look that haunts me until today.

"What do we do to resolve the situation that this stupid boy has brought on himself; what does the ASP want us to do?" my mother asked the two legal minds in the room.

My father looked at her with a frown on his face, as he slowly got to his feet. As he made his way out of the room, he turned and pointed to me saying, "No son of mine will ruin my name. You are no longer my son; I disown you as of today. And make sure you leave this house immediately," he said as he walked out of the living room.

There was a grave-like silence in the room following my father's exit. I stood there nonplussed, wishing that the floor would open up and swallow me. In a matter of seconds, I could see my life rewinding in front of me. I saw my early years of truancy, from primary through to secondary school; I saw the day I was initiated into the BNM at university.

As I stood there engulfed in my own world, thinking of what the future held, I did not realise that my mum had left the living room and had made her way upstairs to speak to my father.

Sleep was very far from me that night. The only person who could get me out of this whole mess was my father. Without him, I could not see any solution to my predicament; there was no hope or light at the end of the tunnel.

My inner demons gave me no rest. I lay on my bed in a foetal position contemplating the various ways of ending my miserable life. The room was noticeably darker than on the previous night, and as I battled all night long with my thoughts and my conscience, I became convinced that death was the only way out.

The next morning brought the stark realisation that my problem had not somehow disappeared overnight. I stayed in my room for the next two days, feeling miserable and sorry for myself. I neither ate nor had a bath, and would not even open the door of my room.

I kept drifting in and out of my troubled sleep and the nightmares grew graphic and disturbing. I dreamt that I was being engulfed by a quagmire and the more I struggled to get out, the faster I was sinking. In desperation, I called out the name of Jesus.

I awoke from my troubled sleep sweating and feeling feverish, and as I lay there gasping for breath, I did not realise it when I yelled out at the top of my weak voice, "**Father God help me**."

"Remy, Remy, Remy," I heard my name being called persistently. The banging on the door was becoming frantic, loud and annoying. I tried to ignore the knocking but it grew louder and louder and was now beginning to drill into my head.

I crawled out of my bed on all fours towards the door, and asked in a weak voice, "Who is that? Who is there?"

"Na me, Marcus." Marcus was my cousin on my father's side and he was the most righteous person I had ever known. He had lived with us right from the beginning of his university days, and was currently working in one of the state ministries.

Marcus and I had grown very close over the years and he was one person in whom I could confide without being judged or criticised. In all the years that I had known him, I had never seen him get angry or utter a bad word about anybody.

I had not seen daylight for the past two days, and the rays of the sun spread slowly across the room as I opened the door to the figure of Marcus standing in the doorway.

"You look and smell like hell," Marcus said with a worried look on his face. "Yes, and I also feel like hell," I responded in a weak husky voice as I went back into the room to sit on my bed. "Mum told me about the wahala that you are having at university," my cousin said. "This is worse than wahala, I am seeing my future go up in smoke in front of me," I said sorrowfully.

"Well, you know that I have not come here to judge but to encourage you, and see what I can do to help," Marcus said as he sat down next to me.

"I have tried all I can to find a solution to this whole mess but nothing seems to be working. My mates will be going for their youth service in four weeks' time and I have not even defended my dissertation yet. Show me where the light is, my brother," I said to him in complete capitulation.

"My brother, I don't have the solution myself, but I know someone who does; all you need to do is to sincerely ask for his help and it is yours," he said with great conviction.

"Really," I said as I jumped off the bed to face him, "Who is the person, let's start going now now now," I added excitedly. "I will take you to have an encounter with him this evening, but you must be ready to let him help you," my cousin concluded as he got up and made for the exit.

I sat in bed after my cousin had left the room, feeling slightly perked up but apprehensive. I could not fathom where any help could come from, other than from my father; maybe Marcus knew somebody at his workplace with serious clout and connections who could push some buttons.

I was ready and pacing around my cousin's car that evening, waiting for him to appear. I was not keen to enter the main house and risk any encounter with my parents, especially my father.

My cousin joined me in about five minutes and we got into his car and drove out of the compound. Our conversation during the fifteen-minute drive was patchy at best, as my thoughts kept filtering in and out. I was hopeful, yet sceptical of finding some kind of resolution.

The surprise and disappointment must have been apparent on my face as we drove into the compound that housed one of the parishes of a well-known church of God; but my cousin put his reassuring hand on my shoulder and said, "You will find your solution here, just keep an open mind."

I got out of the car like a zombie. This was not what I was expecting. *"Maybe the important man with serious connections goes to this church,"* I thought to myself. *"Maybe my cousin has set up a meeting with him after church,"* I concluded in my mind. If I had to sit through these religious shenanigans in order to have an audience with this powerful individual, then that was what I would have to endure.

My cousin's church was a fast-growing Pentecostal gathering. I had attended a few similar gatherings at my university because that was where most of the pretty babes worshiped. Most predators at university would turn up there to try to get closer to their mark.

My cousin's Pastor was a young and charismatic chap. He was well-dressed and the sermon was on the Love of God. He took his Bible texts from Isaiah 1:18, John 3:16 and Roman 5:8; he talked about God's love knowing no bounds, and how sins could be permanently forgiven.

I sat in my seat feeling slightly bemused and thinking that this chap did not know what he was talking about. I wished he knew my story and the terrible things that I had done. *"If he knew that I had sold my soul to the devil, I don't think there would be any come back for me,"* I concluded.

As if he was reading my thoughts, the Pastor said, "There might be somebody under the sound of my voice who has given up hope, feeling that there is no solution; well, I have got good news for you. The living God has asked me to tell you that it is finished," he concluded emphatically.

He rounded off the sermon by touching on the parable of the prodigal son and the lost sheep; God has your name specifically engraved in the palm of his hand, and would never forsake you nor deny you as long as you accept him as your Saviour.

I knew the Bible relatively well; after all, I had achieved a distinction in my secondary school examination. But nobody had made it come alive like the Pastor did in front of me. All through the sermon, I felt as if he was talking to me specifically, and his words became a poignant reminder of how far I had drifted to the other side of the track.

After a few minutes of hesitation, I found myself gravitating towards the pulpit during an altar call by the young Pastor. As I stood in front of the pulpit struggling to pray and being prayed for by the Pastor, I felt a sudden feeling of calm and reassurance in my spirit.

After the service had ended, my cousin introduced me to the Pastor, who coincidentally had graduated from my university some years back. He showed a lot of empathy for my plight, and prayed with me again and promised to keep me in his prayers. He gave me some Bible verses to read. He concluded our meeting by saying, "Watch God do what he does best."

I left the church with the Pastor's words still echoing in my ears, but unsure about what had transpired within the last few hours. I still did not see how this was going to work out for me and resolve my plight, but I was desperate to hold on to some glimmer of hope.

My cousin and I spent the next seven days praying and fasting together and asking for God's mercy. We attended the mid-week service at his church and his Pastor continued to encourage me to stay strong and completely rely on the almighty God.

Some part of me could not help but try to second-guess how God was going to perform this miracle; what if God failed to come through for me? What if God felt that I was receiving the right comeuppance for my sins and reckless actions; or what if my problem was just too great for him to handle?

I was continuously buffeted by the what's and the if's over the next five days, but I was determined to hold on to whatever hope I could hold on to.

My university was due to reopen in seven days' time and those students who had met the graduating criteria would be finalising their plans and collecting their convocation invites. The issuance of convocation invites was a prerequisite for receiving a call to join the mandatory National Youth Service.

I still had not defended my dissertation, and there seemed to be no hope of doing so before the convocation. The implication was that I was going to miss going for the National Youth Service that year. I would have to come back the next year to defend my dissertation, after I had sorted out my issues with the law.

Life was becoming one big conspiracy to me; but I had no one to blame but myself. I realized how helpless and hapless I was, and I had no choice but to rely on the mercy of the Big Man above.

I awoke suddenly in the middle of the night with my heart beating and my pulse racing. At first, I thought that it was a bad dream, but I could not shake off the strong feeling that I was having an epiphany, showing me the solution to my problem.

There was this unexplainable urge for me to sit down with my biological father, express my remorse for the whole debacle, and start showing a positive attitude towards my parents. I had not seen my father since that evening in the living room; I had taken great care to avoid him.

I had my bath early and prepared to meet him before he set out for work. I headed for the main house, and as I entered through the kitchen door I bumped into Okon the cook, who informed me that he had been sent to call me by "Oga," my father. I struggled to hide my surprise. Keeping a brave face, I approached my father's bedroom.

I knocked and waited for an invitation to come in. My father was a relatively tall man with the posture and carriage of a Hollywood movie star. He was standing in front of the mirror knotting his tie. He did not turn around to acknowledge me as I walked in and stood close to the door, cutting a subdued and forlorn figure.

The few seconds of silence in the room were very uncomfortable. I stood there waiting for my father to speak. When he had finished knotting his tie, he turned around to face me, with a frown playing across his eyebrows.

"I have spoken to both the DPO in charge of the Police force in your university town and the Vice Chancellor of your university," my father said. "You will travel this morning with your brother and present yourself to the station's ASP. Do not admit to any of the charges, maintain your innocence and let your brother do the rest," he concluded.

"Your brother will help collect your clearance letter from the Police and you can present that to the VC of your university on Thursday afternoon," he added as he pointed his finger at me.

"Thank you, sir," I murmured as I struggled to come out of my shock. "Don't thank me, thank your mother, but thank God the most; because for the last five days I have been restless after reading Mathew 18:12 and 22. You are the lost sheep and the cross that I have to carry in life, so I will carry it graciously, but I will not be so

357

accommodating next time," he said. "We did not send you to school just to read but also to get wisdom; so get the wisdom, as it is useful in directing you at all times," he concluded and waved me away.

I left his bedroom feeling immensely relieved and grateful to God, because only He could be orchestrating events on my behalf. I was determined to get that all-important wisdom, going forward. I let Marcus know what was happening and he was not in the least surprised as he declared, "We serve a living God."

The journey back to the university town took about an hour and thirty minutes. My brother was busy going through his briefs and some law articles during the journey. We reached the town at about 11 am and drove towards the police station. As we drove along the high street, memories came flooding back – especially when we reached the spot where I had fallen to my knees in front of Hammer and other Marauders on that eventful day.

I stepped into a police station for the first time in my life with my eldest brother ahead of me as my representative, wearing his lawyer's robe. I was asked to wait in the foyer while my brother was ushered into the ASP's office for his appointment.

After about twenty minutes, I was becoming slightly impatient, but as I was about to take a short walk around the compound, my brother came out of the ASP's office with another man behind him.

The ASP was a short pot-bellied man and from his appearance, he was someone who needed plenty of exercise. I did not need to search him to know that he had his service pistol tucked into the left-hand side of his waistband, indicating that he was right-handed.

He approached me as I stood there, not knowing how to react. "So you are the Remyleon that we have been looking for," he enquired with a devilish grin on his face. "So it is the innocent and angelic looking ones who are the kingpins of secret cultism in this town." He paused and then continued, "Well thank your lucky stars that we did not catch you beforehand, because *if say we catch you eeem, your eye for see pepper,*" he concluded.

The ASP did not wait for any reply from me before turning around and beckoning to one of his men behind the counter. He said, "Sergeant Oko, take this boy's statement," shook my brother's hand and stormed back into his office.

Sergeant Oko took me into an inner room with just a table and two chairs; he sat opposite me while I wrote a statement of half a page maintaining my innocence. He took the statement from me, read it, and burst out laughing. "So na this rubbish you wan give me," he said, "We get all the intelligence about you and your other lieutenants for our hand, *abeg you think say we no get our own insiders for your cult?*" he asked with a smirk on his face.

"Well my Oga at the top, don give order make I collect this rubbish but you go settle me my own for here now now," he said expectantly. I quickly and easily parted with all the Naira notes in my pocket, which the Sergeant promptly pocketed without counting.

"Wait for here make I go get your police clearance," he said as he left the room leaving the door wide open. I sat there staring into space until I heard voices coming from the open doorway. I looked towards the open door and saw two female police constables standing there, whispering and pointing their fingers at me.

As Sergeant Oko came back into the room with my clearance in his right hand, one of the women asked, *"Na the Remyleon be this?"* pointing at me. *"Yes ooo na this bandit be Remyleon,"* replied the Sergeant. One of the two female officers gave me a stern look before saying, "Kai, *I be think say na only ugly and yeye people dey join all this secret cult, I no know say fine pickin like this fit be Oga patapata for the thing.* O boy, change your way ooo," she said as I was ushered out of the room to re-join my brother in the foyer.

I left the police station with my emancipation in my right hand. As I got into the car and the police station started to recede behind me, I could not help but be grateful that I had an influential biological father, but more grateful that I had the almighty God on my side.

Chapter 28

Two days after the university formally reopened, I stood in front of my Vice Chancellor with my Police clearance in my right hand.

The VC was a very distinguished-looking man, with a grey goatee and spots of grey hair on his head. I made him out to be about my father's age. He had studied and taught in the UK for a very long time before returning to Nigeria to take up his current appointment.

As I stood there, my hands crossed behind my back as a mark of respect and submission, I saw him peer at me over the top of his glasses. After a few seconds of my waiting in anticipation, he finally spoke, "So you are the wanted fugitive called Remyleon. I heard that you are the Oga Patapata of the Marauders?" he enquired.

"No, sir," I replied, as I was determined to keep all my replies short and direct. "Well, that is not the information that I have gathered," he continued, "I have been told that you are the first Vice Chancellor of this University and you can even make me disappear if you wanted to," he continued to enquire from me.

"No, sir, there is only one VC and that is you, sir," I responded. The VC paused, took one look at me, and continued, "I know your father quite well; in fact we were students in the UK at the same time and he was and is still a decent and likeable gentleman." I held my breath anticipating what was going to come next.

There was a saying in Pidgin English that said, *"When person wan curse you, e go first praise your Papa,"* so I was waiting for the tirade and invective to proceed from the mouth of the VC; but I was very wrong, because what he then said was more of a reality check than a tirade.

"So what happened to you?" he asked. "It beats my imagination why someone from such a decent background, with a family name such as yours, would want to dilute and mess it up in the name of juvenile delinquency." He looked at me, baffled.

I was not sure if the question was a rhetorical one or needed a response, so I kept quiet and maintained my meek demeanour.

"I have never done this for any student, but on this occasion, I will do it for you because of your father. Go to your department tomorrow and clear things with your Head of Department." With that, he dismissed me with a wave of the hand.

"Thank you, sir," I said, as I began to walk towards the door of his office. His voice stopped me in my tracks as I reached to open the door. "Young man, there are so many people out there wishing for half the opportunities that you have; please do not disdain what you have, use it wisely," he said, staring straight at me.

As I stood there looking at him, he said something that has stuck with me to this day: "In the multitude of wise counsel, there is safety, and wisdom is always profitable to direct." With that, he dismissed me again with a final wave of the hand.

I defended my dissertation three days after meeting with the VC. The university convocation was set for the 20th of November 1996, less than two weeks before the start of the National Youth Service orientation camp.

I was the first Alfa in a very long time to be graduating without an extra semester, and I was graduating with a second-class upper division, which no Alfa had managed in the history of the BNM.

My intention was to sneak in on the day of my convocation, get it finished, and then sneak out again; but Hammer and the other Marauders were not having it. They were ecstatic and had big plans for my convocation.

During the turbulent past weeks, I had had ample time to put many things into perspective; and I had sworn to walk away from the BNM and be diligent in my pursuit of God. However, deep down I knew that I still had unfinished business with the BNM. I was still the Alfa, as I had not yet handed over the staff of office – crucial business that had to be done immediately.

I travelled back to the university on the day of my convocation with plenty of food and drinks. The university compound was buzzing with activity.

Hundreds of cars were parked on the lawn and thousands of people were milling about.

The various confraternities had their colours and flags flying at different corners of the campus, and they were singing and celebrating with their graduating brothers who had made it through the rough and challenging terrain.

The boring convocation ceremony ended at about 2 pm, shortly after the collection of our scrolls. We all filed out, and that was when the party officially began. The boot of my car was packed full of food and drinks, and people ate to their heart's content. A handful of Marauders were graduating and we were hell bent on making the most of this great achievement.

We partied on campus until 6 pm, after which we moved the gathering to Den's Cook, a local joint in town patronised frequently by Marauders. I discharged Sunny the driver at about 7 pm.

During the party, Hammer pulled me to a corner of the noisy room to enquire about handing over to my successor. I was of two minds; part of me wanted to walk away from the BNM once and for all, while another insisted I must first finish the work that was pending.

I had already made BNM history by becoming the longest-serving Alfa in my university and by holding the position as a graduate; but there was one kind of history that I did not want associated with me and that was having an uncompleted tenure.

"Let us enjoy today, and we go talk tomorrow before I travel," I reassured Hammer as I patted his shoulder and ordered more drinks for all at Den's Cook.

I had given up my flat in town and had to spend the night at Tima's place. She was elated to see me, but still upset that I had not invited her to my graduation celebration on campus and at Den's Cook. I had always taken great care to protect Tima, especially after the whole Victor saga; I did not want her to become a target or the face of the BNM babe, and so I kept her at a distance from all BNM functions and activities.

We stayed up all night and into the early hours of the morning, talking and catching up. She was very intrigued and taken aback at all the things I had been through, but she did not judge me or condemn me in any way. We made passionate love, and later fell asleep in each other's arms at about 4 am.

I woke up at about 1 pm the next day with a terrible headache, to find movement in the room. Tima was getting ready to go to her afternoon lecture, and at the same time preparing lunch in the kitchen. "I thought that you were never going to wake up, sleepy head," she said as she bent down to kiss me. She did not wait for a response before saying, "There is Jollof rice and plantain in the kitchen with fried fish, just the way you like it."

"Thank you, sweet heart, I will see you later," I murmured as she hurriedly left the room. "Please make sure you come back early ooo, because I want to spend every minute with you today," she called back as she left the flat.

I slowly dragged myself out of bed and headed for the bathroom to freshen up, before hungrily devouring my food. I had to see Hammer urgently today, because I was due to leave town for Asaba tomorrow.

It took me about twenty minutes to locate Hammer and as we greeted each other in the usual brotherhood way, I could see the look of sadness in his eyes. I knew that he was going to miss me; but we both knew that people had to move on.

Hammer knew about some of the difficulties that I had faced, and I filled him in on more of my overwhelming challenges and how alone and dejected I had felt. I told him of my intention to move on and leave the BNM to sort itself out, just as I had sorted myself out with no help from the BNM.

Hammer looked at me with a deeper sadness in his eyes. He shook his big head and said, "My Alfa, you are my Alfa for life, you have been the one and only Alfa that united BNM together so tightly. Marauders are always singing your praises; even the region acknowledges and appreciates your leadership. Please, *abeg*, do not let people remember you as the Alfa *wey no hand over. You too bam for that*, you get to finish the good work that you started. If not, Victor and his crew would have won," he concluded.

I sat there caught in a quandary. I knew that the last thing I wanted was for all my tribulations to be in vain. I hated the thought of Victor and his belligerent crew being triumphant; but I had vowed to God during my tribulations to stay on the straight and narrow moral path.

As I sat there deliberating, I knew deep down that I would not be able to resist the lure and enticement of adorning myself in my Alfa regalia one last time and entering into the belly of the forest, to finish what I had started.

The thought of it filled me with great excitement but at the same time, it filled me with dread and trepidation; it was an inexplicable high and I was flying.

We agreed upon a date for the handover ceremony, which had to be ratified by what was left of the council of wise men. We decided to have the ceremony on a Saturday, one day before I left for my National Youth Service orientation camp in Abuja.

This gave Hammer, his deputies, the Voice and the Seer barely eleven days to get all the arrangements in place. There was a lot to be done, from finding and preparing a location for the ceremony to planning the exit routes, from ensuring security throughout the event to arranging my final departure from the town.

I left Hammer in charge with the backing of the Council of wise men, and headed for Asaba the next day to start my preparation for my NYSC in Abuja.

It was now down to the Council to decide who the next Alfa was going to be, and I was no longer interested in who would be chosen – all I wanted was to hand over my responsibilities and set off to new pastures. Sebastian was still in the running as my initial candidate for the Alfa's position.

I did however wish that Hammer was not such a well-known face in the confraternity circle and was not the warlord of the BNM, as he would have made the perfect Alfa – a man of integrity, loyal to the core, with the heart of a lion.

My time back home went by very quickly, as I was involved in many activities at my cousin's church. I attended the mid-week services and house fellowships that were dedicated to searching out and studying the word of God. These meetings always seemed to challenge my lifestyle, but they also had a way of tugging at my conscience for wanting to enter the forest again.

The scriptures in the Bible that most sharply pricked my conscience were the ones that talked about a dog going back to its vomit, and God hating people who were lukewarm. I did not want to see myself as the proverbial dog; but I knew deep down that both texts were chastising me.

I left home on Friday morning with my father's blessing and warning: "Keep away from those your cult people." I bade him and my mum farewell. I could hear that soft voice again in my ear, whispering and asking questions of me: "Why do you want to do this again, what if something goes wrong in the forest, what if you get apprehended by the police?"

I shut my ears to all these doubts and focused on what I had to do, as I set out on the journey to my university instead of going to Abuja for my National Service.

I arrived at the university town in the early afternoon and made my way to Mosco hotel, where a room had been booked for me by Hammer. Nobody knew where I was staying except for Hammer and my suicide squad. I was due to meet the Council of wise men later in the evening, to find out their final decision on the choice of my successor.

I sent a message to Hammer through the bike man who had been stationed at the hotel for me. He was to meet me at the hotel a couple of hours before the meeting with the Council of wise men. I had a quick shower before ordering a bottle of cold beer with some bush meat, and relaxed on the soft mattress watching MTV.

I let Hammer into the room after he knocked and identified himself. We greeted each other warmly and he gave me a very positive situation report. All was now set, and we were ready to roll for tomorrow's ceremony. The Voice and Seer had fulfilled their duties efficiently and we were now waiting for the outcome of the Council's deliberation.

I asked Hammer to carry a message to the Council of wise men regarding a change in the venue and time of the meeting; I did not want to take any chances, based on my disastrous previous experience of meeting with them for the same purpose.

Hammer quickly set off to communicate this change in plan, and was back within forty-five minutes. We arranged that Hammer and the squad would meet me at 7:45 pm at the primary school close to the Mosco hotel, where I would be properly geared up before going to the meeting.

I arrived at the new venue with Hammer and the squad in tow; they were fully armed and stationed themselves around the venue. They were not there to take any prisoners.

All the wise men rose to their feet as I walked into the room. There were loud cheers and greetings around the room. I shook hands with all the Marauders present, and declared the meeting open. Theo was not yet back in the fold, but had cast his vote previously. After about ten minutes, I was handed a piece of paper bearing the name of the new Alfa and his Executives, for my ratification.

I looked expressionlessly at the names on the paper for a few seconds, before handing the paper back to the acting leader of the Council. I thanked them for all their effort and confirmed, as I rose to my feet, that the ceremony would proceed as planned tomorrow.

It became clearer to me at this point that if I was not going into the forest for the handover ceremony, then I did not really need to care who was to become the next Alfa; but if I did go, then who attained the position was critical. This was for two reasons: firstly, I had to protect the future of my loyal troops; but more importantly, I needed an Alfa who would guarantee my safe passage out of the forest after the ceremony.

My authority as Alfa would cease upon my handing over the staff of office to my successor. All clan weapons and artillery would be under the sole control of the new Alfa; Hammer and my squad would no longer have any authority over them.

According to the constitution, the ratification had to be carried out. The list of new Executives, with the exception of the Alfa, was ratified ten minutes before we went into the forest the next day, with a few minor amendments. This was communicated to the wise men in the forest by the Voice. The existing Alfa and the wise men were the only ones who knew the name of the next Alfa, until the appointed time.

I walked into the ceremonial ground in full regalia, and it felt extremely good. I felt that buzz and that high that was so difficult to explain; in my right hand was my loaded service Berretta and I held my staff of office in the left.

The acting Omega was already in the centre of the circle, serenading the clan with sweet melodies from present and past years. The direction of the songs changed to the praise of their wonderful Alfa, the Alfa who had graduated against all odds. I was on cloud nine.

I rounded up all the wise men to a corner of the ground, and we spent about five minutes deliberating on our final decision.

The music ceased instantly as I stepped into the circle, and from the four corners of the ceremonial ground came gunshots to herald my entry. I stood in the middle of the circle like a brave warrior just back from conquering the world beyond; and I could feel a strange force that gave me goose bumps envelope me.

I let off two shots from my Berretta into the dark night, and as I felt the gun bark twice in my hand, I knew that I was going to miss the power and authority associated with being the Alfa of one of the deadliest gangs in one of the deadliest universities in the country.

With my staff of office now in my right hand and a piece of paper in my left, I started to call out the names of the new Executive members of the BNM, to great cheers and applause. They were all marched off to a corner of the ground, and drilled for about ten minutes.

After the drilling, they crawled one after the other into the circle, where I pronounced and confirmed them in their new positions, after they had sworn an oath never to betray the clan as its new leaders.

There were thunderous cheers, followed by a gunshot into the night. The cheering lasted for about five minutes, and died down as soon as I raised my staff of office. It was now time for me to give my valedictory speech, and swear in the new Omega and then the new Alfa.

I gave the most passionate, powerful and moving speech ever heard at a hand-over ceremony. The silence that engulfed the whole area was palpable, and as I called out Hammer as the new Omega, the ceremonial ground went berserk with jubilation.

Hammer could not step into the circle with me until he had received his physical drilling and was wearing his new regalia as the new Omega.

I invited Hammer back into the circle after five minutes. He was looking fearsome in his regalia. I put the staff of office on his head and confirmed him in the position, after he had taken his oath.

Hammer moved over to the edge of the circle, as I prepared to announce the name of the new Alfa to Marauders. I paused and the whole company held their breath ...

"With the power and authority vested in me as the Alfa of the BNM, I now call ... Sebastian into the circle," I bellowed out.

Sebastian began crawling towards the circle and as he crawled, he was flogged and battered; the beating ceased as he got into the circle, and he crawled until he was kneeling in front of me with his eyes as wide and expectant as a Cheshire cat's.

I helped him up to his wobbly feet, as I started to disrobe myself and put the Alfa regalia on Sebastian. Once he was fully robed, I put the staff of office in his right hand and spoke at the top of my voice: "With the power and authority vested in me, I now pronounce you as the new Alfa of the BNM. May you guide and protect all Marauders near and far. But if you were to betray us, the Oracle would squeeze the life out of you," I concluded.

There were riotous cheers followed by seven gunshots into the dark night, to herald a new administration led by Sebastian. I handed over to the new Alfa all the clan's artillery and a purse of five thousand Naira, which was a first in the history of the BNM.

I stepped out of the circle, making way for the new Alfa, and feeling a bit empty but relatively relieved. As I stood there at the perimeter of the circle, I could not help but remember the day I had stepped into that circle as the new Alfa. Looking around at the whole jamboree going on, I shrugged my shoulders and let myself be carried away in the whole atmosphere of celebration.

It was about 5 am and the first signs of light were beginning to break through the dark night when I left by the third exit with two fully armed Marauders in tow as my bodyguards. We walked along the bush path for about twenty minutes until we got to a point where we could see some bike activity begin.

I jumped on the first Okada to stop for me and headed straight to my hotel room. I went past Tima's flat and was tempted to stop at her place; but that would not have been a wise thing to do. I entered my hotel room at about 6:30 am and was expecting to be fast asleep even before I hit the soft bed. But surprisingly, I spent the next couple of hours battling with my conscience, wrestling the various thoughts in my head.

"God cannot be mocked, you know," I heard a clear voice say in my head, as I rolled from side to side, "You cannot serve two masters at the same time. You can love one and hate the other, but you cannot love both," the voice concluded.

I had come to recognise this peculiar voice as the voice of Godly, moral and righteous reasoning in my existence. It was not malign in any way; it was the same voice that had cautioned me before I pulled the trigger on Udoka, and it was the same voice that had comforted me during my darkest hours. It was the voice of what's and if's, and I was currently being buffeted by it.

I tried to drown out the voice by burying my head under the pillow – but that did not help. I found myself letting out a loud, uncontrollable shriek, as I continued to do battle with my conscience for hours.

I awoke to a consistent, loud knocking on my hotel room door. I looked towards the door, expecting it to cave in any minute now from the hammering. I heard the hotel porter call out from behind the door, *"Oga, your room time go soon expire in the next thirty minutes oo."*

I caught a glimpse of the table clock as I jumped out of bed and headed straight for the shower. It was 2:30 pm and I had to catch the last bus to Abuja at 3:15 pm. Missing this last bus meant spending an extra day in this town, and reporting late to my Youth Service camp.

I watched the last bus pull out of the bus garage on its way to Abuja; and I heaved a sigh of relief and settled in my seat, heading towards a new chapter in my life.

Chapter 29

I had been in London for about six months now and was beginning to hang out more often with Clifton than with Ojo and my other friends at university. Clifton was the guy around town, and had just separated from his beautiful French damsel. He had a white Honda Civic that was pimped up with front and back spoilers and tinted windows. He wore the finest designer clothes that money could buy, and had pounds to burn whenever we went grooving.

Clifton lived in Highbury in one of the nicest council flats that I had ever seen. His flat was tastefully furnished, with real wooden floors, a state-of-the-art Bang and Olufsen sound system, a 50-inch Pioneer wide screen television, and an American style fridge-freezer in his kitchen. Clifton was a man of taste and means.

Hanging out with Clifton was never dull – there were always places to go and babes to chill out with. London's night scenes were fast becoming predictable and stale, as we had sampled so many delights ranging from the West Indian to the Chinese community.

We started to travel outside of London to places like Brighton, Birmingham, Coventry and Blackpool. We found ourselves taking the ferry to Amsterdam, to party hard during the weekends. We were living in the fast lane, and babes were flocking around Clifton and around me because of my association with him.

Sex with different babes was like a game of cards to us. We used to bet who would sleep with the most babes in a week, and we started swapping babes too.

Yes, we were having so much fun; but I still could not reconcile Clifton's spendthrift lifestyle with his refugee status and dependence on social benefits. I knew that there was more to Clifton than met the eye, and every time I brought up the discussion of how he made his money, he would smile and tell me that he was into buying and selling.

As the weeks rolled by, I noticed that Clifton also kept close company and strong links with the Jamaican crew. They were notorious for their involvement in the drug business, and I was beginning to suspect that Clifton's work involved more than just buying and selling.

I tried on various occasions to suss Clifton out, but he was very guarded about his affairs. I had a strong suspicion that he was involved in the sale of "Charlie" or "white chalk," the street name for cocaine.

Eventually I lost interest in trying to figure out Clifton and his source of additional income, and tried to focus on my studies. My MBA programme was getting more demanding, filled with coursework, seminars, presentations, focus group studies and projects.

Part of my programme involved a field trip to Greece to study the Greek market, and analyse how the market and environment responded to various economic factors. The trip was both fascinating and educational. It was not only hard work; we also visited some major attractions such as the ancient Acropolis and the site where the first Olympic Games were held.

We saw the changing of the guards done Greek style, with the guards wearing the most ridiculous footwear I had ever seen. The trip eventually ended with a three-course dinner, with belly dancers on hand to entertain us.

We arrived back in the UK to a very wet and gloomy Sunday afternoon, and I headed back home exhausted but exhilarated by the trip and the wonderful photos I had taken.

I had now completed eight months of the programme. My final examination was fast approaching and I had four modules to study and a dissertation to complete. I threw myself into the thick of things and increased my study hours with Ojo and Shola, as we prepared for our first paper.

My first paper was Environment and Response and it was the first 'official' open-book assessment that I had ever written. It was a good paper, and I was confident of making a good grade. I finished all my exams within a week and now had six months to complete my dissertation.

Examination results were not due for another three weeks, and we had plenty of time to kill on clubbing, parties and babes. I continued working as well, to help maintain my cash flow.

I barely had time for church these days; I attended church only on special occasions such as Easter, Christenings and Christmas. I had not opened the Bible in months, as I was having so much fun getting my groove on.

My results came out earlier than expected. I had passed all my modules, and was now just a step away from acquiring my degree. It was an exciting time for me – my dissertation was going well, and my student visa had been extended for a further twelve months.

I had ample time on my hands to complete my dissertation, so I took on more and longer shifts doing care work. When I was not working I was busy partying hard with Clifton, Ojo and the crew.

It was the early hours of a cold wet Sunday morning in October 1999 when Clifton and I dragged ourselves out of the Electric Ballroom at Camden Town, heading for the next club in Wood Green. As we approached the beginning of Holloway road, we hardly noticed that a police vehicle was tailing us.

The flashing blue lights eventually stopped us and I could see the colour drain out of Clifton's face as he sat motionless behind the wheel. I thought that the worst-case scenario would be a caution for drink driving – but I was mistaken.

The police officers identified themselves and asked us to get out of the car; they wanted to know who we were and what we did for a living. They questioned Clifton about his status in the UK, and how he could afford to own such a flashy vehicle.

More police cars were arriving as backup, and they had sniffer dogs; this was beginning to look like a scene out of Hawaii-Five-O. I was expecting the breathalyser to be used on Clifton as the driver; but the officers were more interested in searching us and the car.

I was beginning to get irritated with the cops for this unusual heavy-handedness, and I made my feelings known to them. I went one step further under the influence of alcohol, and told them that we were being treated this way because of our skin colour.

The police officer was polite and refuted my accusation in a professional manner. He informed us that Clifton's car had been on their radar for months, and that the police suspected that the car was being used in the transportation and supply of narcotics.

This information did not totally shock me; but I was dumbfounded when a black carrier bag was retrieved from the inside of the spare wheel, a spot in which the sniffer dogs had shown great interest.

Our rights were read to us, and we were arrested for the possession of an illegal controlled substance with the intention to supply. Clifton was further charged with driving under the influence and driving a car that did not meet road requirements because of the very dark-tinted windows.

I looked at the police officers in total astonishment and I was truly lost for words. *"This can't be happening to me, I must be dreaming and will soon wake up,"* I thought as we were both hauled into separate police cars, in handcuffs.

As I sat in the police car looking dazed and cutting a forlorn figure, I heard that voice of conscience in my head saying, *"You have been treading this steep and slippery road for quite a while and you have quickly forgotten the lessons you learnt earlier; these are probably the repercussions."*

A twenty-minute drive later, I was taken into the police station at Holloway to be processed; my fingerprints were taken and a DNA sample was extracted from my mouth, before I was put in a holding cell the size of a shoebox.

I had lost all sense of time as I sat on the bed which consisted of a single concrete slab, with my head in my hands and my mind completely numb. I must have sat in that position for over an hour, until I heard the small opening in the steel door being unlatched and saw a tray containing a beef burger and a drink being delivered.

The police officer who delivered the food informed me that I would be attending an interview in about thirty minutes' time with PC Bob Rogers, and that a solicitor would be provided for me. Breakfast on the Police was far from my thoughts, as my mind continued to race and my eyes were bloodshot from the lack of sleep. I knew that I urgently needed to get my story and my composure together.

A temporary solicitor attached to the police station called Thomas Dickinson was provided for me. We spent about thirty minutes together analysing my case and looking at the pros and cons, before my formal interview. Thomas advised me to keep my responses to the questions as short and as simple as possible. He also told me to be relaxed, and use the "no comment" response whenever I felt boxed in.

The interview lasted for over fifty minutes, with my legal representative in attendance. PC Rogers read me my rights before asking many questions. He wanted to know how long I had known Clifton, where we got our supplies, where the drop off was. He went on and on and was becoming quite aggressive in his questioning, so that Thomas had to step in occasionally.

I maintained my innocence and stood my ground all the way. I reiterated to PC Rogers that I was a law-abiding MBA student who had just been in the wrong place at the wrong time in the wrong company.

I was exhausted after the interrogation that seemed to last forever. I was granted bail at about 3:45 pm, and was forbidden from travelling out of the country. Two officers drove me home and confiscated my passport.

The next two weeks were among the darkest days of my life, as I had to report to the police station twice a week. I now had another solicitor, whose chambers were closer to where I lived and who had come highly recommended by the legal aid team. My new solicitor, Dylan White, was quite optimistic that I would be let off the hook because there was no concrete evidence against me; he was pleased that my immigration status was fool-proof and I had never been in trouble with the law before.

My solicitor's reassurance gave me a lot of respite and comfort, and I decided not to mention my current predicament to my aunt in the UK or my family back in Nigeria. My solicitor's fee was being paid partly by legal aid and partly from my savings.

I walked into the Holloway police station confident that the case against me would be dropped that day. This was following a consultation with Dylan three days earlier, when he had told me that he had spoken to the police administrator in charge of my case, and the signs were looking good.

I was ushered into an inner room, where I sat waiting for about ten minutes; I felt that they were preparing my discharge letter and retrieving my passport from the hold. I made a mental note to ask that all my fingerprints and DNA be destroyed in my presence and to seek redress by asking for compensation for all the stress I had suffered.

PC Rogers came into the room and sat down opposite me with no expression on his face. I tried to glean something from his body language, but I could not tell either way; in any case, I was very confident that it was going to be good news.

PC Rogers asked me how I was doing and wanted to know if I was fit and healthy. I answered in the affirmative, thinking that I could not wait to see the back of him. The next sentence that proceeded out of his mouth left me stunned and tremendously dazed. I was being charged as an accomplice in the possession of and intention to supply an illegal controlled substance.

My jaw dropped open and all the mental notes that I had made disappeared. I sat there staring at PC Rogers like a zombie, as my whole world came tumbling down. For a brief second, my father's face came flashing in front of me and I could hear his angry voice bellowing out, "Not you again, don't you ever learn, you are such a big disappointment."

I managed to comport myself with dignity as I went through the procedure, which lasted for about twenty minutes. To date, I still do not remember leaving the station, boarding the double-decker bus, getting off the bus, and sitting down on the kerb in front of the Cricklewood bus garage.

As I sat on the kerb that very grey Tuesday evening with my head in my hands, I was oblivious to my surroundings and the finger-pointing pedestrians. My world had collapsed in front of me once again. *"Where do I turn?"* I asked myself.

I must have sat there for a very long time before I heard that ugly and persistently negative voice in my head saying, "Your achieving an MBA degree was a waste of time —you will now have a criminal record, and you'll become the only convict in jail with a degree. What are you waiting for?" the voice continued, "End it, just walk into the front of the next car that drives past, end it – end it now," It encouraged me.

I sat there holding my hands over my ears, trying to drown the voice; but to no avail. I abruptly got up from where I was sitting, and as I was about to step into the middle of the ever-busy Cricklewood Broadway, I heard that soft and benevolent voice saying, "That is not the solution, all you need to do is retrace your steps and come back to God," It encouraged me.

"Forget that side and do this thing sharp sharp and get it over and done with, God will not take you back ooooo, it is too late now," the negative voice persisted. "It is never too late," countered the positive voice, "Trust me as you trusted me many months ago, trust me son, trust me," It concluded and faded away.

I dusted myself off and headed home, more determined than ever to retrace my steps. I had a very restless night as my mind continued to race, and I could not wait for morning to come. I called my solicitor the next morning to gain more information and get some legal advice. He informed me that the situation was now looking a lot more serious than he had anticipated.

He confirmed to me that Clifton had been charged as well, and in his statement, Clifton was claiming that the suspicious package found in his car had been planted there by the police. He claimed that he had never seen that package before in his life.

My solicitor said that Clifton had not owned up to the accusation and was not exonerating me either; therefore, the police had no option but to charge the both of us for possession with the intent to supply. He also confirmed what I already knew – if we were found guilty then it would be a custodial sentence.

This information was yet another blow to my already fragile state of mind; but I quickly remembered my previous day's resolution to push on and remain upbeat.

On the recommendation of a friend's fiancé, I started to attend one of the leading Pentecostal churches in the city of London. The Pastor was a charismatic middle-aged man, and he preached the unadulterated and undiluted word of God with much vigour and passion.

I poured myself into the church and its activities. I was the first one in and last one out of the church. I became relatively close to the Pastor, who counselled me and prayed with me to solve my predicament.

He was not particular about the legal intricacies of my case. Rather, he focused on God's goodness, mercy and grace; he was always quick to refer to Matthew 6:27. This Bible verse was about trusting God and not worrying about things outside our control, as God is always in total control.

The Pastor encouraged me to inform my parents about the challenge I was currently facing, and trust that the Lord would soften my father's heart.

My parents were very disappointed about the whole situation and my father expressed his regret about sending me to the UK; however, he was optimistic that a good solicitor would be able to argue my case robustly, if I was indeed innocent.

Unfortunately, my father's power and influence was not as far-reaching in the UK as it was in Nigeria, and he could only resign himself to giving me some legal advice and talking to my solicitor. "We will be praying for you," he would always say at the end of our conversation.

I took a lot of comfort in my father's and Pastor's encouragement, and as my court appearance loomed nearer, I drew closer to God, and Psalm 23 became my solace. Verse four of this psalm states, "though I walk through the valley of the shadow of death, I will fear no evil: for thou art with me."

I met Dylan at the Haringey Magistrate court at 9 am on a grey Tuesday morning, two hours before I was due to appear in Court Room Twelve. We found a secluded spot in the very busy foyer of the building, and we sat there doing some prep work for about twenty minutes before Dylan left me, as he had another client to defend elsewhere.

Dylan had run my case past the senior partner of his law firm, and they were sure that the Magistrate would throw it out based on insufficient evidence and my clean record.

I had never before stood in front of a Magistrate in a courtroom as the accused; and as I stood there nervously, I could feel my heart palpitating at two hundred beats per minute. I confirmed my name and address and listened to the charges as they were read out.

I put in a plea of "Not guilty" and the Prosecutor began with the case against me. The court session lasted only ten minutes after the submissions by both parties.

After listening to both sides, the Magistrate agreed with the Prosecution that I had a case to answer. The case was adjourned until Friday the following week.

The rest of the day was miserable. I called my Pastor and family back in Nigeria to give them the news. My Pastor continued to encourage me that all would be well; adding that the darkest part of the night was just before the dawn.

I started fasting and continued with my regular prayers, fervently asking for God's mercy upon my life; I prayed on my knees regularly.

It was at the church gathering that Wednesday evening, during the praise and worship session, that the Pastor called out my name and asked me to come to the front. I advanced, not knowing what to expect as I knelt down in front of the pulpit.

The Pastor stood directly before me and said, "The Lord has asked me to tell you that it is finished, He is the God that can turn the hearts of kings in whatever direction he chooses." I knelt there frozen in time as I did not know how to react to his prophesy.

I left church that evening feeling a bit apprehensive, unsure of what to make of what had transpired a few hours ago. Deep down I felt that the pastor had said this just to encourage me, and I would definitely believe him only when I saw the real manifestation of his words.

I lay in bed that night resigned to the fate that awaited me in court in two days' time. Twice I had been told by my legal team that the case would be dismissed, and twice I had been disappointed.

It was about 1:45 pm the next day that I got a call from my solicitor. Initially I thought that he was calling to prep me for the court session; but what he said next blew me away. "Don't bother going to court tomorrow," he said.

"Why?" I asked, surprised.

"The case against you has been dropped by the Prosecution. They have now realised that they don't have enough evidence against you to proceed," he said. I had many questions to ask, but he told me that he had to dash to court to defend another client and that PC Rogers would be in touch with me soon.

I let out a shout of joy and victory as I sank to my knees in relief and thanksgiving to God. This could not have been a coincidence; only God could have done this for me again. As I knelt there thanking Him, I vowed to keep my feet on the straight and narrow path, and never depart from the ordinance of my faith.

I picked up my mobile phone and called my Pastor to break the news to him. He was not surprised at the outcome, and encouraged me to hold on firmly to God and fulfil the destiny that He had mapped out for me. I thanked him for all his support and assured him that my focus would be on God from now on; not on friends or any man.

I received the much-awaited phone call from PC Rogers at about 3 pm, and I gave him some attitude. I demanded that my passport be returned immediately and also that all of my DNA and fingerprint samples be destroyed. I even booked a date to go to the police station to collect my document and witness the destruction of my fingerprints and DNA records.

My father's response to the good news was far from jubilant. It was quite muted, and he used my phone call as an opportunity to give me some very strongly worded advice. Nevertheless, he said something that still resonates with me today: "I do not think that you are a hopeless case or a bad boy; it is the company you keep that lets you down. My son, always learn to put your best foot forward, and that will stand you in good stead for the future. And keep away from the bad eggs – they will drag you down to their level, and then beat you with experience," he warned.

More often than not as a young boy, I had always done the opposite of what my parents demanded. Maybe I was just born a rebel or a foolish recalcitrant looking for a way to get attention. However, with the advent of this particular challenge, it dawned on me that something had to change, drastically and quickly.

I did not need a seer to tell me, because I could see the pattern developing for myself: the older I became, the more serious were my shortcomings. I could tell that my next misdemeanour would be the one that would probably land me in custody or finish me for good.

Deep down, I knew that I had a bag full of potential, which had been either underutilised or misdirected. I knew that I had the gift of an orator. I had always been a people person; this had been evident right from my days in primary school. I knew that I had the ability to influence and motivate people and, as I held the phone in my hand, I felt that this was the time to use these strengths to make a difference in my life and that of others.

Chapter 30

I am just a regular working chap with a wife and three children, struggling with life's challenges. The past seven years that I have been involved in the church, it has not always been easy. In fact, life has become more challenging being a Christian. There are always good and bad days. The trappings and pleasures of the world continuously buffet me, and I have found that I am in constant defence of my faith and belief.

I know that the only way for me to stay on the straight and moral path is to be in the household of God, and to be in the multitude of wise counsel. I have come to realise that in many churches, especially the Pentecostal church, you are first accountable to God, and then to your fellow brethren.

It is with this accountability and wise counsel that I find safety in myself first, and then in the bigger world out there.

Over the past seven years, I have had to examine and renew my mind-set on a daily basis, because a critical part of Christianity is entrenched in love, humility, and the right standing with God. This has been very different from my previous mind-set of being an Alfa, with a control and command mentality.

I am constantly looking for new avenues to be a blessing to people around me; I get involved in Church projects and initiatives geared towards alleviating suffering within and beyond our immediate community.

I feel a strong pull towards mentoring derailing teenagers and young adults, because in them I see a reflection of the young Remy. All the challenges I've been through in my life have only left me better equipped for this particular purpose of reaching out to youths.

I feel the heavy burden of the magnitude of the work ahead, especially at a time such as this. My burden becomes heavier by the day, with the never-ending senseless youth murders and stabbings on the streets in the UK.

"Why did Stephen Lawrence, Damilola Taylor, Kiyan Prince, Michael Dosumu, Jerome Vassell, Annaka Pinto, William Cox, Eugene Attram, Dwaine Douglas and others have to die in such a senseless manner?" I keep asking myself regularly. The statistics show that in the last eight years, one hundred and fifty two young lives have been lost to gang violence and the numbers are still rising rapidly.

These were young people with dreams and aspirations that were taken away from them without their consent; lives cut short in such a brutal manner only because of gangs, gang affiliations, or the colour they represented on the street.

I sometimes wonder what Damilola, Dwaine, Stephen, William and other fallen youths would have been, had they became adults; what career paths they would have chosen. I also wonder if there would have been a Prime Minister, a show-business legend, or a great athlete amongst them; but I guess that we will never know.

I am determined to help in my own little way by serving as a mentor to as many young people as possible, using my experience from the other side of the fence.

I have been given more than two chances in life to make the best of my potential, and I see no reason why the next generation should not have the same opportunity in life. Perhaps I could help save a couple of souls along the way, and that would be worth all the time and effort I could put into it.

I strongly believe that we all owe the next generation the duty of care through mentorship and love; because it takes more than a single dysfunctional family unit to ruin a young life – rather, it takes the nonchalance of a whole community.

I vividly remember, during my early formative years, the efforts that my parents and the entire community put in towards my discipline; although I was headstrong and a rebel, I still knew the difference between good and bad and I still feared the repercussions of bad behaviour.

I look at my three sons, and I sometimes fear for their future growing up in the UK; however, the inevitable question arises: what would their future have looked like growing up in the perilous terrain of Nigeria? My role as a father is to guide them and have them well-equipped to face whatever life presents. My fear is not about the colour of their skin, but more about the extremely negative influences that abound everywhere.

The one most important prayer that I repeat unfailingly for my children is that God should never let me bury them – rather, they should bury me when I am old and spent, just as I buried my own father.